William Francis Brand

Life of William Rollinson Whittingham, Fourth Bishop of Maryland

Vol. 2

William Francis Brand

Life of William Rollinson Whittingham, Fourth Bishop of Maryland
Vol. 2

ISBN/EAN: 9783337414979

Printed in Europe, USA, Canada, Australia, Japan

Cover: Foto ©Raphael Reischuk / pixelio.de

More available books at **www.hansebooks.com**

LIFE

OF

WILLIAM ROLLINSON WHITTINGHAM,

FOURTH BISHOP OF MARYLAND.

Fervent in spirit, serving the Lord.

BY

WILLIAM FRANCIS BRAND.

WITH PORTRAIT AND FAC-SIMILES.

IN TWO VOLUMES.

VOL. II.

NEW YORK:

E. & J. B. YOUNG & CO.,

COOPER UNION, FOURTH AVENUE.

1883.

CONTENTS.

CHAPTER VIII.

CHAPTER IX.

CHAPTER X.

CHAPTER XI.

LIFE OF BISHOP WHITTINGHAM.

CHAPTER I.

DURING THE WAR.

1861–1865.

THE loss spoken of in the close of the last chapter was consequent upon events that filled the whole land with affliction. Suffering in the common lot, Bishop Whittingham suffered also from the withdrawal of the sympathy of many in whom he had trusted. Loving much, and resting much on the love of others, this loss was grievous. But it was not without compensation. It was borne bravely, with the support given to those who are willing to endure the loss of all things in the discharge of duty. The course of conduct which brought it on him gained the admiration of many, and the expression of warm thanks on the part of prominent men of the day who felt his support.* The Bishop of Maryland was honored for his loyalty and for what it cost him.

It is impossible to ignore the change in the relation between the bishop and a large majority in his diocese when antagonism took the place of loving confidence. It is im-

---

* October 13, 1863, Governor Hicks wrote to Secretary Stanton : " We are all under great obligations to Bishop Whittingham for his early and continual personal exertion, and great influence of personal Christian character in behalf of the Government."

possible to treat of this change without reference to the political events that caused so painful a result.

The close of 1860 saw close at hand the irrepressible conflict [*] that was to terminate the sectional strife that had endangered the Union more than once since the adoption of the Constitution, which is its only bond.

It is the misfortune of the South that this strife should have as its seeming origin the extension of negro slavery or its suppression. Unreasoning sympathy will be given to those who profess to labor in the cause of universal freedom. Our justification before the world for throwing off the yoke of the mother country, although written by a slaveholder and signed by the deputies of thirteen slaveholding Colonies, declares it to be a self-evident truth that all men are created equal, and endowed by their Creator with the inalienable right to liberty. Sentiment will not ask the origin or meaning of these utterances, which are as old as the Pandects, or pause to consider the binding force of written pledges of a Constitution that contradicts them.

The party that had triumphed in the Presidential contest in 1860, had reiterated the self-evident truths of the Declaration of Independence, with the special meaning that negro slavery must cease to exist. Their leaders had openly asserted that union with slaveholders was a violation of the object for which the Union was formed, and for which alone it was desirable.

The election of Mr. Lincoln, who was the exponent of this party, was considered in the extreme South to be an avowal of a determination to recognize no longer the obligations of the bond of union. The time had come, it was thought, when, in accordance with the opinion expressed by Daniel

* The phrase irrepressible conflict is of Northern, not of Southern, invention. It was used to express the conviction that arms only could decide the interpretation of a written instrument, the acknowledged result of compromise, concerning the meaning of which men highest on our roll of statesmen have differed, and politicians have always disputed.

Webster, "the South would be no longer bound to keep the compact. A bargain broken on one side is broken on all sides."

The first ordinance of secession was passed in South Carolina, December 20th, and the example was soon followed. In great anxiety citizens of Maryland watched the progress of disintegration, and the efforts of the peace party in Congress to avert disaster. There was no stated session of the General Assembly that winter, and the Governor having refused to call an extra session, no opportunity for State action. A small and border State, Maryland held a difficult position. She was not in full sympathy with either extreme. She had cast her electoral vote for a Southern candidate, Breckenridge, but yet she deprecated what other Southern States considered to be forced upon them. Devoted to the Union, which had been threatened in turn by North and by South, she had devised no remedy for the wrongs which had been borne by her own citizens save that given by the courts empowered by the Constitution. She had always, in some sense, stood between extreme parties. A slave State, as all were when first independent, one of her first acts had been to prohibit, as Virginia also did, the importation of slaves. In the convention which formed the Constitution, her deputies proposed the abolition of the slave-trade, but the effort was vain. The importation of slaves from Africa was continued twenty years by the votes of Northern States joined to those of Georgia and South Carolina.* All the prominent men of Maryland in

---

* Sympathy between those who thus prolonged the American trade in men was not now first shown. The Declaration of Independence, as first reported to Congress, contained a strong passage denouncing the King of England for his cruel war against human nature. In his memoir Mr. Jefferson says: "The clause reprobating the enslaving the inhabitants of Africa was struck out in complaisance to South Carolina and Georgia. . . . Our Northern brethren also, I believe, felt a little tender under those censures; for though their people had very few slaves themselves, yet they had been pretty considerable carriers of them to others."

those days were anti-slavery men, though perhaps none was in favor of immediate and general abolition. The bettering the condition of the blacks, and the bestowal of freedom on the slaves when it could be done with advantage, continuously occupied the thoughts of her citizens, and, at times, of her Legislature. And notwithstanding the general resentment, and the repressive legislation which followed the persistent efforts of Northern philanthropists to breed discontent among slaves, and so to endanger safety, Maryland, ever ready to concede and to insist on constitutional rights, could never be counted as a State ready to sever the Union for the spread or the maintenance of slavery.

If Governor Hicks feared that Maryland would secede if her Legislature were allowed an expression of opinion during the distractions of the winter of 1860–61, such fear was not well founded. In the beginning of these troubles, while they condemned the policy of the dominant party, suppression by force of arms—the great majority of her citizens repelled the idea of secession as a cure for the evils complained of.

It is time to consider how Bishop Whittingham was affected by the discord from which he could not escape. How did he regard the questions which led to it?—" the irrepressible conflict," when only threatened, and when filling all households with sorrow?

While recognizing the obligations of a citizen to the land in which he was born, he—from a sense of clerical propriety—had kept himself free from all bias of party politics.

In 1861 he wrote of himself: "I have never thought, talked, or voted with any of the political parties; while free at all times to express my dissent from what I might disapprove in the tenets or course of any privately. or, if gross infraction of public morals called for it, in the pulpit."

Thus he condemned in private the Kansas movement,

the Sharp's rifle, and Bible emigration; while yet his experience of the effects of slavery made him look with no favor on the extension of its limits.

When speaking of the early years of his episcopate, it was shown how utterly he abhorred that spirit which was cherished as philanthropy and was called abolitionism. Happily his own words will express what were, in most respects, his views with regard to slavery in 1859. In that year, when "the Southern institution" was so much discussed, there was published in Philadelphia a pamphlet written by a slaveholder, who offered to liberate every slave he owned on proof that they would be thereby benefited, and who undertook to prove from the history of three thousand years the utter degradation of the negro; that slavery is his true condition; and that American slavery has done more to elevate the race than all other causes combined. A copy of this pamphlet was received by the bishop, and prompted an answer which was sent to a Philadelphia paper.

EDITOR OF THE P. D.

Sir: I have received a pamphlet bearing the title, "The Heroes of the Nineteenth Century. Philadelphia, 1859." On the inside of the wrapper is printed: "The enclosed pamphlet can be furnished at $16.00 per 1,000. Please to use your influence to obtain orders for general circulation."

I have no doubt of the lawfulness of holding slaves.

But a twenty-years' use of unusually good opportunities for examining the results of slavery has satisfied me that they are highly deleterious to the interests of the community, civil, moral, and religious.

The white population is most injured, and most of all the slaveholding portion.

I am satisfied that no community can permanently thrive, that is, for a course of generations, in which slaveholding prevails.

It is a mode of doing good to the African that is not required of us by the divine precept to love others *as* ourselves. No community is required, out of philanthropy, to subject itself to civil, moral, and religious martyrdom.

For these reasons I regard the circulation of your pamphlet, true in part, and specious, but inconclusive as a whole, as undesirable.

No doubt, the condition of free negroes in our country is worse than that of the slaves. But that gives no man any right to make them slaves.

No doubt, the abolition of slavery in the Southern States is impossible, and its attempt, in any way, by the North, an enormous crime. But that is no reason for encouraging the extension of slavery beyond its present limits. With no prejudice against slavery, and with very strong prejudices against amalgamation of races and colors, and in favor of distinctions in society, I have been slowly brought by my own conscientious study of slavery, as I have lived and moved in it, in all its forms and aspects, for almost a quarter of a century, to acquiesce in its condemnation as a great social evil. And I *know* that it is so regarded by the best and wisest portion of those who have inherited it, maintain it, and have no hope of its being removed from their posterity.

We know that we are right in claiming to be let alone in our position.

We are quite at ease about answering to God for it.

But why should we therefore seek to involve others in its difficulties? Why should we disseminate views of it which are one-sided and incomplete, and therefore false?

I would no more distribute your pamphlet in a slave State, than I would go to a poorhouse to declaim in praise of poverty.

Outside of the slave States, it will be ineffectual and do harm, because it attempts too much.

I cannot, therefore, comply with your request to "use my influence for obtaining orders," because by so doing I believe I should be helping you to do mischief.

The circulators of such a production will hardly expect from one who has expressed himself to them with honest unreserve, more than an assurance that he is in residence, interests, and heart, unchangeably   A SOUTHRON.

The bishop, in this letter, shows that he condemned the aggressive spirit of the Northern Anti-slavery party, and did not share in their convictions touching the sinfulness of holding the negro in bondage, although he had seen the evils connected with slavery.

In 1860, when the foresight of what was coming was

causing greatest anxiety, the prospect of a rupture of the Union was not to him the abhorrent thing which it was afterward. Speaking of the party spirit which refused to look at consequences, he said:

The country will break up, not in two but in three masses, North, South, and West; and in this I see the marks of God's providence, his watching over his Church. This rupture will facilitate the provincial system in the very manner best suited to the Church's present wants.

His views regarding the system of our Government were changed by the arguments of his friend, Judge Chambers.

Writing to a friend, in 1861, he says that he had been compelled to study the question on which the justice of the war hinged; but he does not say when this study was made. He writes:

I regard the case at the time of the rebellion of the Provinces as totally different from anything ever pretended by the authors of the present insurrection, and can look upon the claims of the former, as a precedent by the advocates of the latter, as nothing better than delusive sophistry.

My belief with regard to rebellion and *de facto* government is that of the Church of England, expressed in the twenty-eighth canon of the Convocation Book of 1604.

"If any man," etc., Overall, p. 51, Ox. ed., to "rebel against the same, he doth greatly err."

Born under the thoroughly settled Government of the Constitution of the United States, I have never felt myself concerned with the question of its origin, under the doctrine of the canon just quoted; have never studied that question as I have been compelled to study the question now before us; have consequently formed no deliberate and settled judgment, but have acquiesced with silent deference in the results of counsels and efforts which Chatham and Burke indicated in the councils of the mother country, and Franklin, Washington . . . James Wilson, and William White united in maintaining.

I recognize the majority of people of the thirty-four United States of America as, under God, the true and only sovereign of this country; and to its behests expressed in the Constitution, in constitutionally enacted laws, and constitutionally pronounced and established judgments, and in votes constitutionally given, I hold myself bound to look as the supreme authority of the land. . . .

For this Government I am ready to expend property and life . . . in obedience to its lawful requisitions.

By the Word of God I find myself commanded to render such obedience, and in order to do that, as a reasonable being, I am bound thoroughly to inform myself where it is due. But as a minister of God I am also bound, being so informed, to inculcate like obedience on those who share with me the obligations and privileges of the same allegiance. . . . It seems to me an inconceivable narrowness of mind that should attempt to brand such discharge of duty as "interference in politics." . . .

The question now before this country is no question of mere "politics." It is not honest so to put it. It is the question of the existence of civil government—of the reality of any such bond as allegiance—of the truthfulness of pretended subjection to the authority of God in that of the constituted administrators of popular sovereignty.

The term "politics" has been degraded to express the contest in a State of parties for power. The bishop seems to confine its meaning to this lower sense. But when he set himself to learn with certainty where allegiance in this country is due, he entered on a profound question of politics. In this higher sense it was a question of politics that divided the country. The answer that he had arrived at, through study, was so positive that he could not see room for any other; and therefore the contest which was thought by some to be the result of differing estimates of rights under a certain form of government, he looked upon as for the maintenance or destruction of all government. Under such circumstances his duty, however painful, was all plain. No consideration of expedience ever lessened the vigor of his discharge of duty. As he was fearless in the maintenance of his convictions, so he was not restrained by tenderness in exposing the damning sin of rebellion, which secession was judged to be as the rejection of organic law and resistance to the ordinance of God. As a student, he had reached the conviction that the majority of the people of the thirty-four States are, under God, the only sovereign of this country; and this conviction governed his action as bishop. It went for nothing with him what proportion of the people over whom he was placed as bishop believed that no one question had been decided by or submitted to this majority, not even the choice of President.*

The Governor of Maryland, as has been said, refused to convene the Legislature, fearing that the State might assume a position that might be afterward regretted, and professing to wish to act in concert with the other border States; but at the same time he spoke only of the inexpedience of disunion, and did not fail to express sympathy with the cause of the Southern States. Thus on December 6th, he wrote: "If the Union must be dissolved, let it be done calmly, deliberately, and after full reflection on the part of a united South. . . . I shall be the last one to object to a withdrawal of our State from a confederacy that denies to us the enjoyment of our undoubted rights." And again on the ninth, answering a communication from a Southern commissioner to Maryland, he said, "I am now in correspondence with the governors of the border States." . . . I do not doubt the people of Maryland are ready to go with the people of those States for weal or woe." He had good cause to fear the dismemberment of the Union, since, in such an event, as he said in the letter here quoted from, the border States "will suffer more than all the others combined." This fear increased with the increasing tokens of danger, and—if we are not to discredit his honesty—must have modified his judgment. On January 3d he published an address to the people, justifying to them his refusal to listen to the urgent request of a majority of the Senate praying that he would call an extra session of the Legislature.

* The popular vote given for the electors who chose Mr. Lincoln, the then President, lacked nearly a million of being a majority.

In this address, while the Governor deprecates disunion, and, knowing that the majority think with him, will not incur the expense and meet the risk of an extra session desired by disunionists, he yet condemns secession only on the ground of inexpedience. "When the proper time for action arrives," he says, "then the sister States will be prepared to act together." "Will our courage ooze out by waiting?" he asks.

Bishop Whittingham fully accepted the position now assumed by the Governor, approved of his willingness to wait longer for justice, and his determination not to endanger the peace of Maryland. With a view to express his sympathy, he wrote:

TO HIS EXCELLENCY T. H. HICKS, GOVERNOR OF MARYLAND.

Sir: I am indebted to your courtesy for an official copy of your address to the people of Maryland. I had already read it, though in another form, with intense interest.

In ordinary times I should not feel it to be right to intrude on you an expression of my private opinion. But in the present emergency even the least contribution of support to one in high place, exposed to extraordinary assault upon his firmness and integrity, may be neither inopportune nor unwelcome.

I have been in ten counties of this State since November 1st, in each of them conversant with some among the most influential and respectable men of the county. In all, without any exception, I have found convictions of the present duty and policy of Maryland, in the main agreeing with those expressed by your address, almost exclusively prevalent among those with whom I met. May I be allowed to say that in my own opinion your forcible, frank, manly, and true-hearted statement of your policy, and the grounds on which it has been adopted and will be maintained, cannot but be attended (under the Divine blessing) with the happiest results?

I belong to no party, and have never in any way mingled in political discussions or contests; but it is not possible, in twenty years' incessant and close study of Maryland and its people, not to have formed pretty clear and strong opinions of the prospects and interests of the State. Mine, such as they are, bear out fully everything that you have assumed or asserted concerning those interests and prospects in your address. My humble efforts, therefore, shall not be wanting, in my sphere, to back your noble persistency in keeping Maryland in her only true, right, safe attitude of dignified and quiet expectation of legitimate redress of past wrongs, and provision against contingent dangers in the regular working of the constitutional Government of the United States.

For what you have already done to that effect, and are still doing, be pleased to accept this very sincere expression of the warm admiration and heartiest thanks of your personally obliged and truly grateful friend and servant, W. R. WHITTINGHAM.

BALTIMORE, January 9, 1861.

Governor Hicks immediately returned thanks for "the kind sustaining letter," and asked permission "to publish it, believing that it will greatly assist in quieting the clamor for immediate State action."

The bishop replied:

SIR: Gratified and obliged as I am by your very kind acknowledgment of my letter of the 9th, and earnestly desirous to aid you in the noble work of preserving Maryland from the disturbance of her strong position, I should hesitate about acceding to your proposal to publish what I wrote did I suppose that it would, by any possibility, be understood as an immingling in political discussion. As a minister of Christ, I serve a Master who disclaims interference in secular affairs beyond the line of enforcing individual duty and general peace.

But obedience to constituted civil government, and observance of contract even to one's hurt, are clearly laid down in His word as duties to be enforced on His authority; and to maintain and set forward, as much as shall lie in me, quietness, love, and peace among all men, is an obligation of my office to which I was solemnly sworn on admission to its responsibilities.

The purpose, therefore, "to keep Maryland out of strife" and true to recognized relations and engagements, is one that I am bound to further if I can.

If my testimony as to the opinion of others, observed as I have had opportunity, and expression of my own personal convictions, formed with some advantages as to the knowledge of the State and its people, tend to further such a purpose, I have no right to withhold them.

I firmly believe that in resisting the pressure for immediate State action you represent a large majority of the people of Maryland, and

a still more overwhelming preponderance of its property, intelligence, and manly virtue.

Very respectfully and faithfully,
Your friend and servant,
W. R. WHITTINGHAM.

The publication of these letters produced a marked effect
on the minds of personal friends and of those who were
glad to have the support of a prominent man known not to
be a party man. Thanks were given to the bishop by persons at home, and as well by others without the State.

A letter from Easton, expressing "intense interest" in
the correspondence with the Executive, enclosed a copy of
one sent by the writer to Governor Hicks. In this letter it
is said: "Mr. Lincoln has been elected, and good citizens
should quietly submit to the decision of the ballot box, and
await some overt act on his part after he is installed into
office before they precipitate themselves and their countrymen into a revolution. . . . I am for postponing the
dissolution of the Union until every other remedy of redress
for our grievances is exhausted."

These were precisely the views which Governor Hicks
professed to be his guidance. "The time for action," he
said, "has not yet come." But such was not the principle
for which Bishop Whittingham bore the loss of friends.
"Observance of contract even to one's hurt" is what he had
been taught of Christ. The contract, as he understood it,
could not be annulled. The thought of disunion was in
thought treason.

While there were those who were glad that the bishop
had given his open support to the avowed policy of the
Governor, there were not lacking others, his warm supporters in general, who deprecated what they looked upon as
an interference, as bishop, in party strife. To a prominent
man, who was not a near friend, and who had not tempered
by due respect the expression of his disapproval, the bishop
wrote:

JANUARY 18, 1861.

DEAR SIR:

I am in receipt of your note expressing in rather strong terms your dissatisfaction with a couple of letters which the Governor of the State has thought fit to publish, and your apprehension of the consequences of their publication. For the kind interest you take in my usefulness and reputation I am deeply obliged, and cannot but regret that it should have occasioned you pain on my account. For my own part I have little uneasiness on that score. If loyalty to the constituted authority of the State, in its endeavor legitimately to preserve the State in loyalty to the supreme authority of the country is to be an occasion of loss or damage, I can only cheerfully encounter it. I am set to teach others to be true to their obligations, and must not shrink from doing it by example as well as by precept when there is fitting cause. I am sworn to maintain and set forward quietness and peace among all men to my best ability, and must to that end use, as well as I may, my own discretion. I have no doubt that what I wrote to Governor Hicks, if of any account at all, tends to the discharge of that solemn obligation. The stamp upon your envelope reminds me that I am addressing one who, like myself, is in office under oath. The Constitution and Government, which the —— of the United States —— is sworn to maintain, are what my poor encouragement to the Governor of Maryland was designed to cheer him on in loyally and manfully defending.

Very respectfully your friend and servant,

W. R. WHITTINGHAM.

The bishop insisted that what he had written to the Governor was but "the private expression of testimony and opinion as to matters of fact of a private citizen." But this claim was not conceded by those who complained of the publication of the letters, nor by those who were glad to assert that they had the support of the Bishop of Maryland.*

---

* I can but imperfectly express what I feel in acknowledging the great support and assistance I derived from your known approval of my course at that time. . . . The State of Maryland and the country owe you much. You never wavered or quailed, even in our most trying hours, but gave all the great influence of your high character and position to the cause of the Union.— *Governor Hicks to Bishop Whittingham,* December 28, 1863.

The true policy of Maryland, as set forth by her Governor, was to be neutral and so to hold a position which would enable her to act as intermediary between the contending parties. This neutrality implied a determination, not only not to be forced into the contest, but also not to allow the passage of troops intended for an attack upon a Southern State. As late as April 22d, Governor Hicks made an empty protest against the landing at Annapolis of what General Butler called "United States militia;" and he had repeatedly declared that no forces should be sent from Maryland excepting for the defence of the Capital.

As looked upon from this distance, such a position is seen to be utter folly. Such a neutrality, in time of war, would be considered to be as much a crime against the Union as secession could be; and an armed neutrality can only be assumed when there is the power, which little Maryland had not, to make a protest to be heeded.

This hope of maintaining the dignified position of a mediator was soon seen to be vain. On April 12th Fort Sumter was attacked. Three days later the proclamation of President Lincoln was issued, calling for seventy-five thousand troops for the defence of the Union. On the 19th was the insurrection in Baltimore, caused by the appearance of one or more regiments of Massachusetts militia on their way to Washington.

It belongs to others to tell of this event and of those that followed; of the meeting of the General Assembly in Frederick, and their prompt declaration that they had no constitutional authority to pass "any measure committing this State to secession;" of their protest against the war as "unconstitutional in its origin, purposes, and conduct;" of their protest against the military occupation of the State; of the arrest and imprisonment of certain of their members,*

---

* These gentlemen were confined in Northern forts; the greater number more than a year. They were dismissed, as they had been arrested, by the Government without explanation. While in Fort Warren, a Boston minister kindly

together with other prominent citizens, and of the suppression of the General Assembly, the Secretary of War
having decided that "the passage of any act of secession by
the Legislature of Maryland must be prevented. If necessary all, or any part of the members must be arrested." It
is hard to believe that Mr. Cameron really looked for an
act of secession; but the General Assembly made itself disagreeable; it is probable that an occasion was desired *pour
faire peur;* and General McClellan was of the opinion
that if the arrest "is successfully carried out, it will go far
toward breaking the backbone of the rebellion." At least
the backbone of some of the Marylanders was affected.
Some of the hottest secessionists became ardent Union men,
and were accordingly rewarded.

Above the level of those whose political relations were
changed by personal interests, the Bishop of Maryland
sanctioned all the acts of the Federal power, even those
against near personal friends, as done in defence of the life
of the nation. And when State officials were changed and
a new Constitution was imposed which recognized support
of the Union as the first duty of a citizen, and disfranchised
forever all who had so much as sent a letter across the
Potomac, he thought that every States-rights man should
find his scruples removed by the action of his own State.
The large majority of his diocese were of a wholly different
mind; they thought their State to be, with themselves, under the constraint of force only; and they were thus brought
into collision with their bishop in matters that pertain to
spiritual rule.

offered them a religious service. They accepted his offer on the condition that
they might suggest as the text of his discourse Acts xxv. 27: "For it seemeth
to me unreasonable to send a prisoner, and not withal to signify the crimes laid
against him." From some reason the reverend gentleman did not press his
kindness; and the prisoners had to content themselves with their usual church
service, read by one of their own number. The greater number, if not all, were
churchmen, and in prison prayed: From all sedition, privy conspiracy, and rebellion, good Lord, deliver us.

The bishop was absent on a visitation at the time of the Baltimore riot, and the burning of the bridges by and with the authority of the Executive. He returned during the insane excitement that caused and followed that show of resistance which served only to embitter partisan feeling. He immediately issued two prayers for daily use in his diocese.

PRAYERS FOR THE COUNTRY.

O most powerful and glorious Lord God, the Lord of Hosts that rulest and commandest all things, Thou sittest on the throne judging right, and therefore we make our address to Thy Divine Majesty in this our necessity, that Thou wouldst take the cause into Thine own hands, and judge between those who are engaged in the miserable strife which now distracts our land. Stir up Thy strength, O Lord, and come and help us; for Thou givest not alway the battle to the strong, but canst save by many or by few. Oh, let not our sins now cry against us for vengeance; but hear us, Thy poor servants, begging mercy and imploring Thy help that Thou wouldst be a defence unto us, against the face of every one who would do us wrong. Make it appear that Thou art our Saviour and mighty Deliverer, through Jesus Christ our Lord. *Amen.*

O Almighty God, the Supreme Governor of all things, whose power no creature is able to resist, to whom it belongeth justly to punish sinners, and to be merciful to those who truly repent, save us now, we humbly beseech Thee, and assuage the tumult by which this people is rent and torn; that we being armed with Thy defence may be preserved evermore from all peril to glorify Thee, who art the giver of all victory; through the merits of Thy Son Jesus Christ our Lord. *Amen.*

On the day these forms were published, April 23d, the bishop met the city clergy, held with them a religious service suited to the exigency, and "communicated to them a private and confidential circular about to be issued." This was a copy of a letter written to a clergyman who had asked for instructions, together with a note addressed to each rector in the diocese, giving him permission to regard the letter as written to himself.

BALTIMORE, April 23, 1861.

REV. AND DEAR BROTHER:

In the extreme pressure of this moment, I can only find time to answer your deeply interesting communication by replying that the most careful consideration I have been able to give my duty in these emergencies, results in the conclusion that, under Canon 13 of Title I., I have the authority to provide for the occasion of a secession by prescribing under "the present necessity" the alteration of the prayer "for all in civil authority," so as to read only, "behold and bless Thy servants in civil authority," etc.

If, therefore, the Legislature, at its approaching convention, should decide on an immediate secession of the State, I intend to issue direction for such alteration. We are commanded to "pray for kings and for all that are in authority," but we are also commanded to "live peaceably with all men," and to "give none offence, neither to the Jews nor to the Gentiles, nor to the Church of God," "giving no offence in any thing that the ministry be not blamed," and a great woe is denounced against him who shall offend one of the Master's little ones. Let our prayers, therefore, go up before God in such form that all can join in them with a pure conscience and single heart.

Affectionately and faithfully, etc.,

W. R. W., *Bishop of Maryland.*

This prospective permission to omit the name of the President of the United States from the prayer for those in authority is not to be taken as a sudden conversion from his judgment as to rebellion, or to fear to avow his convictions as a citizen. A short while after this, when it was still safe to show open contempt for the Union, it is said that he saw some sign of disrespect to the flag of the Union shown by a company of Maryland militia, and that he boldly rebuked them. His permission was nothing more than a submission to force, and the providing a form in the use of which all churchmen could join.

Some weeks prior to the outbreak a presbyter, being about to go to Louisiana, asked his bishop for instructions to govern his officiating in the then seceded States, the church authorities of which had not had the wisdom to pray simply for all in authority. The bishop answered:

As regards your visit to our sulky sister, I think the old rule of Ambrose holds—Do at Rome as they of Rome are bound to do. On our side there is no bar to your officiating. What I could not do here in compliance with a usurped authority, I could do without scruple there as one made a foreigner by action with which I had nothing to do, either to give or to withhold consent.

As has been seen, the Legislature promptly declared that they had no power to pass an act of secession. They also declared that it was inexpedient to call a convention which might be enabled to express the will of the people on such a matter. The direction, therefore, of the bishop was never issued. But in some churches, in order to avoid excitement, in others because the clergyman had assumed to decide political questions for his congregation, or with them, the omission was made which had been only contemplated in case Maryland should abandon the Union. In consequence the bishop published a circular for which he received many thanks from persons outside of the diocese.

A CIRCULAR TO THE CLERGY OF THE DIOCESE.

Reverend and Dear Brother:

I have learned with extreme regret that in several instances the "Prayer for the President of the United States and all in civil authority" has been omitted of late in the performance of divine service in this diocese.

Such omission in every case makes the clergyman liable to presentment for the violation of his ordination vow, by the mutilation of the worship of the Church, and I shall hold myself bound to act on any evidence of such offence laid before me after the issue of this circular.

I beseech my brethren to remember that current events have settled any question that might have been started concerning citizenship and allegiance; Maryland is admitted and declared by the Legislature and Governor of the State to be at this time one of the United States of America. As resident in Maryland, the clergy of this diocese are bound to the recognition and discharge of all duties appertaining to that condition. It is clearly such a duty by the express word of God to make supplication and prayer for the Chief

Magistrate of the Union, and for all that are in authority, that we may lead a quiet and peaceable life in all godliness and honesty; and it is as clearly my duty, by the same directions, to put those whom God has committed to my charge in mind, to be subject to principalities and powers, to obey magistrates, to speak evil of no man, to be no brawlers.

To my deep distress and disgust I have too much reason to fear that in at least one instance a minister of Christ may have so far forgot himself, his place, and his duty, as actually to commit the canonical offence known as "brawling in church," while venturing to do what an archangel durst not do, and to defend transgression of the Word of God.

We of the clergy have no right to intrude our private views of the questions which are so terribly dividing those among whom we minister, into the place assigned us that we may speak for God and minister in his worship. Still less claim have we to assume to frame and fashion the devotions of our brethren by our private notions, and to that end mutilate or interpolate the service of the Church. In such times as these we are more strictly than ever bound to adhere to the precise letter of prescribed form, and to deserve the praise of non-interference with others' rights by the closest seclusion within the limits of our own plain duty.

It is not merely my advice, dear brother, but it is the solemn injunction and caution of the Word of God, to be reverenced and regarded accordingly as you believe it to be his. "My Son, fear thou the Lord and the King, and meddle not with them that are given to change, for their calamity shall rise suddenly; and who knoweth of them both? These things belong to the wise."

Your loving friend and brother,
WILLIAM ROLLINSON WHITTINGHAM,
Bishop of Maryland.

BALTIMORE, May 15, 1861.

This circular was thought by some to be not consonant with his late utterances. We have his own defence.

A few days after its issue a clergyman from a Northern diocese preached in Washington, and was, in a newspaper, reported to have said in reference to certain secret traitors against the Government, that "The treason of Judas is white compared with the treason of such men." The bishop at once wrote to the preacher:

While I hope that this sheer blasphemy is falsely attributed to you, I fear that the tenor of the sermon was such as directly to contravene the tenor of an admonition which I have recently found myself constrained to address to the clergy of my diocese. The peculiar situation of my diocese makes it of the utmost concernment to the Church to keep her pulpit free from the strifes which are distracting the community. Of the need of such a course I claim the right as I find it to be my duty to act as judge, and I take it hard that brethren from portions of the Church in less unhappy circumstances should, on coming among us, instead of setting forward quietness, peace, and love, abuse their liberty to blow up the flames of discord already so miserably raging. I enclose a copy of the circular to which I have alluded, taking the liberty of drawing your attention to one of its paragraphs by underscoring.

Your friend and brother,
W. R. W.

The reverend preacher answered in kindness, and sent a copy of his sermon as he had delivered it. He had not used the words attributed to him touching the lesser treason of Judas, but yet he avowed the thought expressed, and justified it; and he also ventured to criticise the circular sent him. The bishop replied:

TO THE REV. C. S. HENRY, D.D.

BALTIMORE, June 6, 1861.

My Dear Doctor:

. . . My individual judgment of the present war, and of the doctrine which is its occasion, accords precisely with that which you express. I construe the Constitution as you do. I see the obligation of allegiance where you find it. Your definition of loyalty is mine to an *iota*.

But while we (you and I) thus agree about the crime of treason, my difficulty is that two-thirds of the most intelligent of the laity of my diocese, and fully one-fifth * of the soundest, most earnest, and

---

* The numeral ⅕ is copied as read in the MS. It is possible that the bishop did not intend to write one-fifth. He had heard from one whose testimony he relied on, under ordinary circumstances, that but one clergyman on the Eastern Shore was in full accord with him, and on the 30th of the following August, after having spoken of the corrupting influence of " subserviency to the South-

devoted, and (strangely enough!) most learned, too, of my clergy, while they agree perfectly with us about the criminality of treason, viz., that it is, as you say, "as fully condemned by the Gospel as any other crime," dispute and deny utterly our (your and my) determination of the crime, and insist that they do true allegiance in contending for "State rights" against treasonable attempts and devices for their subversion. Now I think I understand thoroughly their prejudices and the force of circumstances by which they are kept in error, and I believe myself able to see clearly through the mist of sophistry in which they are lost: but then the whole discussion between them and me turns, not on sacred duties or divine prescriptions, but on human institutions and the origin, history, force, meaning, and intent of merely secular and civil compacts and enactments. These are not themes for the pulpit, nor for episcopal pastoral instructions. Yet on the settlement of the preliminary question the whole force and value of official application of Gospel principle and rule must depend. There is no use in preaching loyalty or denouncing treason to those who agree with every word of your argument, and with all the cool conviction of a resident of Bedlam turn upon you at the close with a crushing "*Bene dixisti: te ipsum condemnasti.*"

In such circumstances my duty is to enforce abstinence from discussions foreign to the duty and place of worship, and confine myself in my endeavors to uphold Government to the maintenance of law in its existing form and bearings. Not without a struggle, I have asserted and vindicated my personal liberty as a citizen; but while doing so have felt myself doubly bound to circumscribe the use of my official influence by the limits of its spiritual character and commission. To your observant perspicacity I need not point out the entire consistency of both the circulars, on which you have done me the honor of remarking, in the observance of this principle. Both alike decline the responsibility of determining for my diocesans the question of allegiance.

Each bases its recommendation on an assumed determination by an authority claiming the power (to say the least) to settle it for them and for me. The rightfulness of that power is neither affirmed nor denied. But then observe, the effect of each is to repress innovation and secure the least change practicable.

---

ern movement," he wrote: "Most unhappily the men (and women) so beguiled are mostly in the Church, and throughout the diocese are among its leading members, both clerical and lay."

When the "private and confidential" circular (it was sent as such, so headed, to clergymen in parochial charge only, and to no living soul besides) of April 23d was issued, the "secession flag" alone flew in Baltimore, and the streets swarmed with an armed mob professing intention to maintain it, with the expectation on all hands (well grounded) that on the third day following, the Legislature and Governor would unite in "act of secession." Two of the largest churches in Baltimore had had no morning prayer (nor, of course, the evening prayer) on the preceding Sunday, because the officiating ministers dared not use the Prayer for the President; and in two other churches of the diocese I was told that prayer for "the President of the Confederated States" would be substituted for it so soon as the act of secession should have been passed. Silence would have left the clergy so disposed to act at their own discretion; which I had then reason to believe, and now know, some of them claimed the right to do.

To hinder them, and render it impossible to foist rebellion into the worship of the Church, I claimed to apply the fourteenth canon to the "special occasion" of a secession, in case of its occurrence, and by prescribing *only* the omission of the words "President of the United States," and afterward "others" to hinder the insertion of any other specification, and leave the prayer to all *loyal* worshippers just what it was before, without affording to disloyal authorities or majorities a pretext for insisting on its omission or further alteration.

The scriptural authorities alleged by me in justification of my action, you will perceive, if you take the trouble to examine them, bear out just such a procedure as I have been describing—no submission to usurped authority, or transfer of allegiance.

On the day when I did this, before I sent the letter to press, I communicated it to some twelve or fifteen of the assembled clergy of Baltimore; . . . and privately informed two or three of the chief among them that it was not my intention, for myself, in any circumstances, to make the omission which I felt myself able to concede to others.

Thus much, to show the consistency of the first circular with the second. In view of a contingency, it provided a limitation of what would otherwise have been larger departure from law of loyalty.

The contingency, thank God, did not occur. After a stormy session, which had brought us to the very brink of rebellion in its worst shape, the pro-secession Legislature, under the joint force of the United States arms and the honest indignation of a majority of the people whom they mis-represented, reluctantly confessed, in a paper put forth immediately before their adjournment, the position of the State to be (what had for months before been hotly contested or indignantly denied by very many of my clergy and laity) *within the Union.*

I seized the opportunity to direct the obligation of my clergy to their duty; and therefore the "reasoning" in the opening paragraphs of my second circular, to which you object, as what you "might not think to be rightly or completely put."

Surely not, as for you, or for me! But they were *argumenta ad homines.* They availed of an occasion given for applying scriptural teaching on grounds incontestable by those who had until then claimed to regard it as inapplicable.

More than that—I was able without any transgression of the bounds set to myself, in official duty, to enunciate distinctly (in the third sentence of the third paragraph) the very root-form of the decision of the whole terrible question before the country. Let men once recognize that "as resident" in any State they are citizens of the United States, and bound to the recognition and discharge of all duties appertaining to that condition, "and the whole baseless fabric of State sovereignty and corresponsive State allegiance crumbles to the ground. . . ."

To heed the warning of the bishop's circular, and to conform to the unchanged service of the Church, seems now a very slight burden on the conscience of either clergy or laity of whatever political sentiments; but one cannot now readily realize the influence of the excitement of the time. Probably in every parish there was, during the war, some sturdy "anti-Yankee," generally a female, who, by change of posture, indicated dissent from the Prayer for the President of the United States; and during the first months of the war there were some of the clergy who thought they could not act counter to their political convictions, and others determinately would not. In dealing with his clergy the bishop made a difference. To some he wrote long and kind letters, reasoning with them; others he presented to the Standing Committee—one, at least, for violation of the rubric, and others for disregard of the days of public service appointed by him. But of the Standing Committee, all of whom had been chosen as bishop's men, the majority differed from him on the subject of loyalty, and ignored the presentations.

In his letter to the Northern D. D. the bishop said that two-thirds of his intelligent laity were "State-rights" men, and that one-fifth, and these the best of his clergy, agreed with them. He overlooked another class who were neither State-rights men—if by this was meant secessionists—nor yet unconditional Unionists; men who desired nothing but the union of the thirty-four States under the Constitution; who believed that the Federal Government could claim support only in so far as it was upheld by the Constitution; who were Southern men in sympathy and held the war to be unconstitutional in its origin and in its continuance, as had been asserted by the General Assembly. Among these were two close and trusted friends of the bishop, utter denyers of the right of secession, and yet ranked among the disloyal—Judge Chambers and F. W. Brune, Esq. To the latter the bishop wrote a letter which is characteristic.

THURSDAY, June 20, 1861.

My Dear Brune:

I cannot allow you to remain in the belief that I admit the reciprocity of your proposal, last evening, never again to talk on the subject then opened. It is all very well for you to make such a resolve for your part, for you are under no responsibility on my account. But for me, I am under a fearful accountability to hold up the weak, heal the sick, bind up the broken in the flock over which I am set; and when I see a loved member of that flock set in the approval and support of that which he is daily praying against because it is under the explicit condemnation of the Word of God, I dare not, for quiet's sake, leave him undisturbed in his most dangerous delusion. There can be no neutrality in a question like that now before the country; whole-hearted loyalty, or "treasonable sedition and privy conspiracy" are the inevitable alternatives. Both as citizens of the United States and as members of the Commonwealth of Maryland, which by popular vote has just declared itself in support of the General Government, we are bound by the express injunction of our Divine Master and of His inspired servants to render honor, obedience, and faithful service to the lawfully inaugurated authority of the country—an obligation utterly inconsistent with the open declarations and efforts and secret machinations unhappily so rife in a certain portion of this community at the present time. Such proceedings partake, according to their degree, of the nature of deadly sin, and as such I am bound, in faithfulness to Him whose commission I bear, to rebuke them whenever they come in my way, and to strive against them to the uttermost. . . .

Your loving friend,
W. R. W.

September 26th was the first of a half dozen or more days which were during the war set apart by the President as days of humiliation or of thanksgiving in times of disaster or of success in arms. The Bishop of Maryland enforced the appointment as a scriptural obligation, and set forth special forms to be used in all churches. In some of these forms is found condemnation in plain terms of existing rebellion, and reference to God's blessing on the means used to suppress it; but in general the bishop sought to prescribe what he supposed could be used by all in his diocese not open or secret rebels. In the pastoral letter accompanying the form of prayer for September 26th, he said:

Remembering the example and injunction of the Apostle of the Gentiles "with the weak" to "become as weak," I have made little change from the form of prayer set forth in December last. The state of the nation has changed since then. The relative position of this State is ascertained. The duties of residents in Maryland as citizens are clear. The authority by which we are now invited to approach the throne of grace is that which God has set over us and which He bids us recognize as His, or resist only at the awful peril of rendering account to Him. . . . In the present circumstances of citizens of the United States in Maryland, there can be no reasonable doubt in what direction our allegiance is solemnly pledged to the Searcher of hearts when we pray to Him to deliver us from sedition, privy conspiracy, and rebellion.

Nevertheless, being painfully sensible how largely even honest and pious men, in the pitiable weakness of human judgment, hoodwinked by natural affection, social relations, and surrounding influences, may be hindered from the perception of the strongest obligations of religious duty; and desiring that in this one common access to the throne of grace may be no stumbling-block at which any may have occasion to take offence, I have taken care to prescribe no petition in which all who believe in the just government of God, and truly desire the accomplishment of his righteous will, may not from the heart consent without mental protest or reservation.

The observance of the day was anything but general throughout the diocese. Many clergy and laity thought that the form, however carefully worded so as not to offend the weak, received its sense from the pastoral and from the recommendation of the President. Simple submission to the just government of God was not intended, nor the asking of the accomplishment of his righteous will. What the President had asked for was that "the united prayer of the nation might ascend and bring down" a special blessing, namely, "that our arms may be blessed and made effectual for re-establishment of law." Many continued daily to use the prayers first set forth by the bishop, asking that God would "take the cause into his own hands and judge between those who were engaged in miserable strife," but they would do no more. At a later period the bishop, recommending the devout observance of a special day of thanksgiving, quoted the words of the canon which authorized him to compose forms for extraordinary occasions and transmit them to the clergy, "whose duty it shall be to use such form." But men whose consciences were at rest under the neglect of daily prayers and of weekly communions and of prescribed offices for saints' days, did not feel the constraining obligation of the canon thus presented to their notice. On the next occasion, with more of urgency, the bishop asserted that compliance with the request of the civil authority

is most distinctly and explicitly enjoined on us in the Word of God, and it is with equal distinctness required of his ministers as a duty of their office to cause it to be rendered. We owe it in accountability to our Master, from whom we bear commission; and we owe it in discharge of trust to our brethren of the laity, the least of whom, if it were but one in a congregation, has the right, before God and man, to demand it of us.

Besides the obligation thus insisted on, the bishop conceived that the incorporation of congregations by the State, and the authority given to ministers of religion "to celebrate the marriage rite," gives to the State the right to exact of minister and congregation an expression of loyalty, such as taking part in the services appointed by the bishop certainly was.

A clergyman who found no difficulty in thanking God for victories over the Southern Confederacy, but lived in a community having a different estimate of right and wrong, desired to avoid wounding "a strong dissentient element," and sought to escape a thanksgiving which could not be a congregational act. He laid before his bishop a statement of his difficulties, and asked: "Can we not render true allegiance to our Government and rightful submission to our rulers without disturbing the peace of the Church in giving any occasion tending to excite the passions of those who may differ from us politically? I hope we may." The answer of the bishop wholly removed the scruples of the clergyman. Returning thanks for the favor done him, he expressed a wish that "the unanswerable argumentation" could be known and read of all. Accordingly the two letters were published in the newspapers. Answers that were sent to the bishop he kindly kept to himself; for never was he moved to wish harm to those who, by their opposition, gave him pain. In the "argumentation" of the bishop is found this passage:

Besides [the Divine rule], as rector of a parish you are the head of a civil corporation from which the Government has the right to expect and exact some corporate symbol and expression of its loyalty, in a way not inconsistent with its true ends, aims, and rights. The ends, aims, and rights of a parish in the Protestant Episcopal Church are observed in any canonical action of its rector. Whenever, therefore, it is canonically in your power, the Government has the right to expect and exact from you the public expression of the loyalty of your corporation to the Government * which gives and maintains its existence and rights as a corporation.

The conviction here expressed enabled the bishop to approve and by his given sanction to promote an act which was very offensive to a number of his clergy.

In February, 1862, a bill was introduced into the House of Delegates, the object of which was to exact of certain classes of citizens, and, among them, of every preacher and minister of the Gospel, "exercising his functions as such," an oath of allegiance binding him to support the Constitution and laws of Maryland, to abstain from giving support or countenance to any plan of separating the State from the Union, and also "to the best of his ability to resist every attempt, by whomsoever made, to effect any such object;" or failing thus to testify his loyalty within a set time, under pain and penalty "he shall cease and desist," the bill declared, "from holding his office." The claim, in the name of the State, to the power to forbid a minister of God the right to exercise his functions as such, was enough to make one anxious: some of the clergy of the diocese conceived that they had an additional grievance. The author of the bill asserted that the clause concerning ministers of the Gospel had been framed in conformity with the advice of the Bishop of Maryland. Having learned from the bishop that this assertion was correct, in so far as that, "after deliberate consideration and conviction, he did advise the insertion of a clause relating to the clergy in the Allegiance Bill," some of the clergy, feeling that they were without the guidance of their head, and needing the support of joint action, met, and determined that they would risk the consequences of

---

* No parish is incorporated by or has received any other right or favor from the Federal Government.

resisting what they deemed an usurpation of the State over the Church. They also ventured on a remonstrance with their father in God, and unfortunately as what he called a "presbytery." They brought upon themselves a castigation such as the bishop in his indignation was so well able to inflict. He threw back on his correspondents the suggestion of mingling in politics. "You, so far as I know, are the very first persons in Maryland who have combined in your character as its [the Church's] members and officers to exert an influence in the strife."

He justified the proposed bill, and his share in framing it, with abundant authority of Cosin and Andrewes. But he failed to change the convictions of men who thought they could see that the Church in America is peculiarly free from all relation to the State. Her members are all citizens, and as such only to be dealt with. What the State gives she can take away; but she cannot, because of erroneous political sentiments, forbid the exercise of God-given functions.

The Legislature adjourned without acting on the Allegiance Bill, and it was forgotten in the multitude of causes for distress; but had it become a law, there would have been excited against the bishop a feeling which, probably, nothing could have allayed.

In May, 1862, the bishop met his Convention after the lapse of two years. In the beginning of his address he said:

Under the first head which the law of the Church assigns for treatment in the address of a bishop to his Convention—the affairs of the diocese since the last Convention—I should have much to say were my unaided private sense of duty to dictate my course.

But I defer to the judgment of respected brethren of both orders when I waive all discussion of the reasons why so long an interval has elapsed since last we were assembled, and forego—together with the exercise of my official privilege of discoursing to my brethren of the clergy in the delivery of a charge touching their duty and mine in our present trials—the gratification of my own earnest longings to set before the people of my diocese views which seem to me of great concernment in relation to our common obligations as Christian men in the conjunctures which have been and still are so seriously pressing on us.

The restraint which the bishop placed upon himself, leaders in Convention felt to be needed in the House. The general desire was to get away as soon as possible. An effort was made to confine the session to one day, but this was impossible.

The business was confined chiefly to matters of routine, and the election of a Standing Committee and of delegates to General Convention ; but these sufficed to bring out painfully an exhibit of the change that had come over the Convention since its last session—the absence of that marked sympathy which had existed in former years between their head and the majority. The bishop was an admirable presiding officer. His ready perception and his prompt judgment prevented the entanglement that is often the result of warmth of feeling in Conventions. The fairness of his rulings could only be doubted by one under excitement ; or, if this must be modified, it is by saying that in cases in which he was specially interested he was sometimes unfair by indulging his opponents. In the chair he was but a chairman, never the bishop, or presenting his opinion as such, until the close of a debate, in accordance with the Diocesan Constitution. But in the Convention of 1862 his indignation overcame him, and, knowing what was implied by the presenting a ticket in opposition to the old Standing Committee, he rose hastily, and with sharp sarcasm introduced to the House the nominator, " who was so young a member that it was impossible that he could be known by any one of those whom he assumed to direct." Immediately an old friend of the bishop, as an old member of Convention, renominated the same ticket, on which was placed the name of no one who could not be trusted as a Southerner, with the exception of that of the venerated Dr. Wyatt, who had been president of this committee during a lifetime. The bishop's sense of duty constrained him to attempt to enforce, by ecclesiastical penalties, obedience to the call of the civil Government for religious services; but this he could not do under ordinary circumstances without the concurrence of the Standing Committee, and therefore the constitution of this committee was a matter of importance to " the recusants," who were the majority.

The election of this safe committee was resented by the bishop as a wrong. But greater indignation on his part was excited by the rejection of Dr. Evans, who had been renominated for the office he had filled with such credit to his diocese—that of deputy to General Convention. " This insult," as the bishop deemed it, " to the most worthy person in the disocese," was deeply felt, and caused the separation of " very friends."

The learned Doctor deserved all the confidence and veneration which his loving episcopal friend claimed for him, and there could have been few in the diocese who did not accord to him high respect; but in the matter of North and South he had spoken words which disqualified him as the representative of the majority in the diocese.

Alas, that this question of North and South was ever forced upon it; it absorbed all others for a time, and changed the tone of the diocese.

The General Convention of 1862 met under circumstances that made it hardly possible that its attention could be confined to those matters that in times of peace—as all would grant—alone pertain to it. Despite the cooler wisdom of some, who could not perceive that danger to the State gave new powers to those legislating for the Church, the patriotic zeal of members in the House of Deputies could not be restrained, and the less because in the House of Bishops a ruling majority was determined to give the support of the Protestant Episcopal Church to the Federal Government, which looked for it and gratefully acknowledged it. The spirit that ruled the House of Bishops was fully manifested in the pastoral letter.

In accordance with the usual custom of the House,* the writing of this letter was the duty of the Bishop of Vermont, who was the presiding officer, the senior bishop, Bishop Brownell, being absent through infirmities of age. But Bishop Hopkins, yielding to no man in loyalty as a citizen and in attachment to the Federal Union of the States, believed that his duty as a citizen was one thing and his duty as a bishop another. He held that as citizens we are bound by the plain precepts of the inspired apostles to bear true allegiance to the powers that be—the earthly government under which Providence has placed us, and that the Church in her various instructions has borne the most positive testimony to the duty of Christian loyalty; but that beyond this they who speak in the name of the Church have no right to go by expressing any judgment on the measures of civil government. He held that under the American Constitution the Church and the State are separate: their respective functions are distinct. Each has its own allotted orbit, and he could not comprehend how any reflecting and intelligent man in our communion should desire that these orbits, in the present condition of mankind, should come together.

A letter written in accordance with these convictions, however worthy of acceptance in other respects, could not be consonant with the tone of those in whose name it was to be addressed to the Church. Through the aid of the Bishop of Maryland it was set aside, and another, prepared by the Bishop of Ohio, was adopted. So often differing and on so many points, Bishop Whittingham and Bishop McIlvaine agreed in their views of loyalty and in their sense of the need of expression of loyalty by the Church.

The letter read and signed by the Bishop of Ohio as

---

* No rule governed the House.

Presiding Bishop *pro tempore* is an able one, judging it from his point of view.

" As official expositors of the Word of God," the bishops, in this their address to the Church, not only clearly set forth the sin of rebellion, but as clearly decide upon the Constitution of the American Government, and declare those who violate this decision to be guilty of sin against God.

The letter was read with unusual circumstance and solemnity. But with one signal mark of disapprobation. The chair of the Presiding Bishop was vacant, in accordance with previous notice that he could not sanction by his presence the act of his brethren. Nor did Dr. Hopkins thus only show his dissent. He read in the House of Bishops a formal protest against what, in his judgment, was a violation of a fundamental principle in our ecclesiastical position. This protest he also gave to the public; and it is the authority for the opinions here attributed to him.

The pastoral was received in Maryland with varying degrees of respect. By some rectors it was read as with full assent. By others it was read in part, or wholly ignored. In one parish, at least, it was given to the congregation in full, but with the comment: " When our fathers in the Church speak to us on matters pertinent to their office, it is our bounden duty to receive their teaching with deference ; but when they take upon themselves to define the government to which we are responsible as to God, who has bid us submit to rulers, then they have as little claim upon your attention as though they should come as a body to settle the disputed boundaries of your farms."

On the last day of the session of the General Convention, Judge Chambers, who with Mr. Carlyle, as lay deputies, represented Maryland, offered a protest against the action of the House in adopting certain resolutions touching the rebellion. He argued that the question was secular, and as such excluded from the consideration of representatives of a spiritual body, the Church. By a vote of the House his paper was not received. The opinions maintained by Bishop Hopkins in the upper, and by Judge Chambers in the lower House, were precisely those held by the great majority of the Diocese of Maryland. There were all shades of political opinion among the members of the diocese, but the greater number, however differing, asserted that their differences, being political, should be kept out of the Church, which has—as they thought—no power to settle them, and out of the parish churches, that the parishioners might with one accord at least worship. There was quietude and a measure of harmony only in those parishes where the services of the Prayer-book were alone given, and all that could be interpreted as political was excluded.

As has been seen, the bishop earnestly forbade political discussions; but his conscience gave such an interpretation to his own rule, which bade him promote peace among all men, that all who did not desire the subjection of the South knew themselves to be condemned as sinners by their bishop, as rebels or fautors of rebellion, and they learned to do without the affection which they had cherished, and some of them barred their hearts against him forever. They could not have done this had they borne in mind that his convictions had been reached in the fear of God—had they but known that when he was forced to condemn, it was with the pain felt by fathers when they chasten their own flesh and blood.

A country clergyman had written to him that he would not offer—and if offered, of the members of his congregation who differed in judgment touching the course of the Southern States, there was not one who would join in—prayers asking God's blessing on arms used against the South.

The bishop answered:

I feel deeply the kindness that breathes in every line of your long letter, and yet feel the whole as one of the many pangs to which I am now daily subjected in the conflict of duty and affection. Your past experience has taught you how little fain I am to shape others' opinions by my own, or prescribe my own convictions as a rule for others' conduct. But there are limits beyond which such a disposition becomes a snare, and its indulgence a wrong-doing. . . . I freely own to you that I do regard you as among the honest and pious men whom natural affections, social relations, and surrounding influences have so hoodwinked as to make them unable to see relations and duties, common to us all, in the clear light which they present themselves to me. Do I love you the less? God knows. I think you do. . . . As to the charge against me [not made by his correspondent] that I seek to exert the influence of my office in favor of a party, I care not for it, for it is simply false. But if any make it a charge against me that I will "let no man despise" me, but "put" all committed to my guidance "in mind to be subject to principalities and powers," even those to whom God in his providence has committed government, whether ordinary or extraordinary, whether constitutional or military, then I say I am not careful to answer in this matter. So God help me, I can do no otherwise.

Your loving but much sorrowing friend and "father."

Another instance must be given showing the faithfulness and tenderness of the man whom many thought to be hard.

A personal friend of the bishop had voted against Dr. Evans in the Convention of 1862. When the bishop was visited the next day by this gainsayer, a sense of faithfulness to the friend dearer than himself, "whom the majority had endeavored to disgrace," led him to speak in such terms that the visiting clergyman ended the interview by kneeling and saying, "It is needless to hear or say more. Give me, sir, your blessing, and let us part." Three years and more passed. The bishop, utterly broken down by long suffering, had gone to Orange, it was said, to die. Then his wronged friend went to him. After the first greetings in surprise, the bishop said: "I am here because I wish to be buried beside my mother, and I preferred coming to being brought, but I fear I am turning back to life." The answer was: "I heard that you thought you were near the time of your release, and therefore I have come to you."

The bishop—his pale face flushing—started from his

couch, and exclaimed: "There was no need for you coming here. I have always known you love me, and I have never for a moment ceased to love you."

Duty enabled Bishop Whittingham to do anything, however painful to himself. Unfortunately vehemence in the discharge of duty sometimes blinded one to the perception of his motive, or roused more determined opposition.

To the many hindrances to visiting country parishes consequent upon the war, there was added the increasing inability of the bishop to travel. Early in 1862 he received a serious bodily injury. Slipping on an ice-covered high stairway, he fell headlong. By violent effort he avoided the striking his head upon a brick pavement, but in so doing he so wrenched his back that he was more or less crippled ever afterward. There were, therefore, few visitations during the war.

Year by year the bishop met the representatives of his diocese. By his own confession he placed a restraint on himself and said nothing of what was always resting on him as a heavy burden. By the Convention nothing was done but what routine made necessary. Former party lines were lost sight of, and elections were made without opposition. If there was felt the lack of the sympathetic response to the enthusiasm of their leader which marked the days before the war, there was no lack of courteous bearing, until an unhappy outbreak of opposition which occurred at the annual meeting in 1865.

The resources of the secessionists were almost exhausted, and that was near at hand which was determined when the North became a unit; and then happened that which, under the circumstances, was the heaviest blow that could have fallen on the broken South. On Good Friday night, 1865, President Lincoln was murdered. His successor, Mr. Johnson, after quietude was somewhat restored, appointed a day of fasting and humiliation for the nation deprived of its head by foul murder. Unadvisedly he designated as this day

the feast of the Ascension. Whereupon the Bishop of
Maryland wrote to him pointing out the fact that very many
Christians could not in conscience make a feast of the Church
give way to a President appointed fast. He also prayed for
the postponement of a single day in consideration of a special
difficulty of his own.

During the whole struggle, said he, against the wicked rebellion
now so near its final suppression, I have steadfastly enforced on the
clergy and laity of my diocese, against much and strenuous opposition, the duty of observing with strictly appropriate services the days
recommended for such observance, whether of humiliation or of
thanksgiving, by the National Government. It would be most mortifying to me to find myself, at the very end of the great struggle,
thrown into association with those who have been hitherto opposing
and resisting the observance of such days. . . .

The President granted the request for a change of day
and postponed the appointed fast to June 1st, which was
that year the second day of the Maryland Diocesan Convention.

The bishop then gave notice by a circular that, because of
this concurrence of the national fast, he would on the meeting of the Convention move an adjournment to September
27th. The result was that many members stayed away.
But on the call of the roll a quorum answered to their names,
and the Convention was constituted. The bishop then
proposed a preamble setting forth the cause, and a resolution for adjournment. To his indignant surprise the motion
was rejected. The majority of those present would make
no distinction between this and other national days for which
forms had been appointed, and which during four years they
had refused to observe. Had they known the terms of their
bishop's letter to the President, they would have been even
more determined in their recusancy.

On the rejection of his proposal the bishop vacated the
chair, announcing his intention of being absent from the
remainder of the convention, and notifying the members

present that they must proceed to the election of their own president.

His departure was followed by a scene of confusion; but, despite the refusal of one member * to recognize the organization of the Convention, order was re-established under the president who had been chosen; and then, better counsels prevailing, nothing was done save to adjourn to the 13th, *not* the 27th of September.

This resistance to the express wishes of the bishop could not but be regretted; among other reasons, because it gave a pretext for the assertion that churchmen in Maryland refused to show an abhorrence of murder, but chiefly because it added a fresh grief and one wholly unlooked for to the many borne by the bishop. It was, however, the outcome of a long war of resistance.

When the Convention met in September no allusion was made to the circumstances attending the adjournment. The bishop made no complaint of any kind; but the iron had entered into his soul, and his address shows that he felt that the bond betwixt himself and his people had been loosened. He intimates a desire to lay down responsibilities, and calmly points out the duties of others, which are not his, because he has done all he could. Very different was the tone of earlier pleadings, when he asked for help.

---

* As an instance of the curious phases of political excitement in Maryland it may be noted that this clerical gentleman, who in the heat of loyalty lectured his brethren for the rebellious tendencies that led them to insult the man whom they called Father, in God, during the wild State-patriotism of April, 1861, helped to organize a company armed to "drive back the Northern invaders;" and being elected captain, accepted the command, although, if the newspapers of the day are to be believed—"with the qualification that while his enlarged military knowledge will be freely given to the cause in which the corps is enlisted, he will decline to bear with him into action any weapon whatever."— *Et nos! Et nos mutamur!*

LETTERS.

TO THE REV. DR. KERFOOT.

CONCERNING HIS LETTER TO THE GOVERNOR OF MARYLAND, ETC.

BALTIMORE, January 25, 1861.

DEAR KERFOOT:

Your very kind letter was doubly welcome, not only as giving me your invaluable support, but also because the first fruits of the step you so cordially approve had been severe censure from some of my dearest personal friends—unhappily linked in with the party whose leaders are desperately striving to cover up their own ruin in that of the country—and coarse abuse in the public prints, *i.e.*, in at least one of them.

I have not for an instant repented of my course, but would do the same again, did the call occur. I regarded the official transmission to me of the Governor's address as a providential indication, through the lawful channel, of duty as a citizen; and endeavored so to do that duty as not to mix up with it my higher official trusts and responsibilities. I neither preached nor taught, but testified in my place when called upon according to my opportunity.

I greatly fear that we are not past the danger which our chief magistrate has so manfully set himself to stave off. A Marlborough gazette, just received, contains a call for a meeting on next Tuesday to elect delegates to a convention of the People, "recommended" (by some self-appointed committee of secret conspirators) to be held on February 14th, "to consider measures for the reconstruction of the Union." That phrase reveals the object—secession. The call is treason to the State, in incipient rebellion taking out of the hands that hold it the exercise of sovereignty entrusted by the Constitution. Secret conspirators call a packed assembly, which will usurp the name of a people that will not be represented by it, and we shall be hurried down the precipice over which at least two of the Southern States have been carried by the reckless wickedness of organized

and boisterous minorities. For myself I am agonized with apprehension as to the bearing of events upon my work and station. O,
may our Great Master vouchsafe us His direction and support!

We are well here, and, so far as I know, quiet—like that before an
August thunderstorm—pervades the Church and its work in the
vicinity.

Your grateful and loving friend,   W. R. W.

TO BISHOP WHITTINGHAM FROM THE BISHOP OF MAINE.

THANKS FOR HIS LOYALTY.

GARDINER, August 27, 1861.

RT. REV. AND DR. BRO.:

I have received your pastoral letter: and small as may be the value
of any testimony of mine, yet I wish to express to you my thanks for
the Christian fidelity with which you have been enabled to meet the
duty of these awful days. That which has been so easy to us who
live amongst an almost united people, you have done with more
courage and openness in the midst of strife and anger. We all owe
you a debt which I trust that in coming times the people of Maryland will pay: when these disorders shall be remembered with calm
sorrow, and our united nation shall know its true champions and
benefactors.

In the meantime, I unite my prayers with yours, that peace, union
and truth may return; and that we may all be humbled in spirit, that
so, in God's good time we may be exalted. Be assured of my deep
respect and sympathy under the trial of feeling which must, in your
circumstances, be unavoidable, and believe me always with sincere
affection,   Your friend and brother,

GEORGE BURGESS.

RT. REV. DR. WHITTINGHAM, Bishop of Maryland.

TO THE REV. DR. KERFOOT.

HIS PASTORAL—POLITICAL MOVEMENTS.

BALTIMORE, September 13, 1861.

MY DEAR KERFOOT:

On every occasion when I have really needed the strength, which
after the grace from above is best afforded by the honest, hearty
approval of a friend whom one entirely trusts and loves, I have
had it promptly and most lovingly given from your true heart
and hand.

I feel now almost as if I must regard you as filling the niche in my heart vacated a year ago, when he whom a third of a century of unbroken love had taught me to know and lean upon as my "next friend," was taken from me.

I expected trials when the occasion came which compelled me to take the ground of my late pastoral, and I have not been disappointed; although I fear I have as yet had only the mere antepast. But even here and now such letters as yours are an ample compensation for all of an opposite character. Some of my brethren in office, too, Bishops Upfold, Williams, and Burgess, have been good enough to write to me very kindly. A few such approvals outweigh any number of censures, of which I perfectly understand the springs and moving causes.

Unhappily, almost every day is adding to the springs of bitterness in this faction-rent city and State. . . .

To-day, too, oil is poured upon the raging flames by the arrest, just announced, of our poor friend—— ——. I wish I did not think the arrest just and wise. Alas! alas! when good men like these can be seduced into measures and plans which make their imprisonment a precaution needful for the public safety! . . .

With heartiest love, yours, as ever,

W. R. W.

TO THE SAME.

BALTIMORE, October 21, 1861.

[After having told how "Man after man of the uninfected portion of her clergy is leaving the poor diocese;" and of the "marvellous delusion of the people here."]

Never before have I felt so prospectless, aimless, hopeless, in my work as now. Thank God, it is most true, though Milton wrote it:

They also serve who *wait!*

TO THE RT. REV. GEORGE UPFOLD, D.D.

HIS PASTORAL AND HIS COURSE OF ACTION DURING THE FIRST MONTHS OF THE WAR.

BALTIMORE, September 5, 1861.

My DEAR BISHOP:

Your kind expression of satisfaction with my recently issued pastoral is very gratifying to me and claims my hearty thanks. In troubling you with it, I had no ridiculous dream of its being of any use to you, but aimed only to forestal the misrepresentations of the document which I had but too much reason for anticipating.

My own peculiar situation made it necessary that I should do one
of four things on the appearance of the President's proclamation :

1. Forego all notice of it ; and keeping silence, leave my diocese
free, and by such silence, tacitly licensed, to disregard it ; in which
case probably not one-fifth of the congregations in Maryland would
have taken any notice of it. This, if I had done, I should have
been self-condemned as disloyal, recreant to my own duty, and participant in the disloyalty and disregard of duty of others.

2. Recommend the observance of the day, and issue for it such a
service as the proclamation called for, and my own judgment and
sense of personal duty prompted ; that is, a form not only of humiliation and supplication for averted judgments, but also of petition
for Divine blessing on the efforts of the nation to maintain its government, restore its own integrity, and suppress and punish "sedition, privy conspiracy, and rebellion."

This, if I had done, I should have satisfied my own judgment of
the abstract fit and right in the premises, and gratified my own
feelings.

But I should have raised throughout my diocese an instant storm
of opposition to my recommendation, my service, and the observance of the day ; and sowed seeds of lasting discord in probably
every congregation in the diocese.

3. Recommend the observance, and issue for it some such service
as I have prepared, without notice or explanation of the discrepance
between the service provided and the call of the civil authority.

By this, I should have no doubt gratified an unhappily too large
proportion both of my clergy and of the laity ; but it would have
been at the cost of my own conscience, 1st, as failing in my own
duty to the government ; and still more, 2d, as leaving my procedure open to the interpretation sure to be put upon it, of conniv-
ance with those to whom such a service would be perceived to be
specially adapted, whether so avowed to be or not.

4. The remaining course was that I have adopted : to regard myself,
in preparing the service, as the mouth-piece of my people, as a
whole, in the expression of devotion in which none could plead
conscientious hindrance of participation ; to invite them all to join,
on common ground, in common appeal to the Just Judge of all, and
to clear my own conscience by explaining in kindly frankness the
ground of my procedure.

I think it must be willing misconception, or perverse ingenuity,
that could put any other construction upon my pastoral than that I
claim for it, as an explanatory statement of the reasons for my not

coming up to the requisitions of the President, in accordance with the dictates of my private personal judgment.

Yet, on the one hand it is sneered at, as a pitiful piece of truckling subserviency to the secessionist proclivities of my aristocratic diocesans ; or, on the other, it is fiercely assailed as a "political pamphlet, wickedly prostituting religion to the service of Abraham Lincoln and his hypocritical crew of Yankee oppressors."

Of this I have no thought of complaining. I fully expected it, and have brought it on myself with my eyes open. I am only desirous to explain to those, like you, whose opinion I value and respect, why the document says so much as it does, and yet goes no further.

It is an endeavor to fulfil, in the least offensive or obtrusive way, St. Paul's injunction to the bishop, to "let no man despise" him, but "put" his people "in mind to be subject to principalities and powers, to obey magistrates," but without attempt at offering instructions which would be at once rejected and made ground of denunciation ; and, while doing this, to take away from them all excuse for exhibiting themselves to God and man as a divided household, by affording such a form for the observance of the recommended solemnity, and such reasons for joining in it, as all could accept, on common grounds, without tergiversation or offence of conscience on the part of any.

Visitation for these months past, and I very much fear for these some months yet to come, is quite out of the question in nine parts out of ten of my seething, foaming, hissing cauldron of a diocese.

Very gratefully and lovingly your friend,

W. R. W.

TO THE REV. DR. SMALLWOOD.

EXPLANATION OF HIS COURSE OF ACTION AT THE BEGINNING OF THE WAR.

BALTIMORE, March 22, 1862.

REV. AND DEAR BROTHER :

My heartiest thanks are due for your very kind and cheering letter. Such expressions of approval are not unneeded, for, although the critical hour of Maryland, thank God, has long since passed by, yet we are far from having arrived at the end of our trying dissensions. On the contrary, feelings which for a time seemed to have somewhat lessened in bitterness, have of late been revived, and in some cases intensified, both by the necessary action of the loyal

State authorities (although that has been even surprisingly moderate and wise), and by the extraordinary run of successes on the part of the Federal Government, and consequent disappointment of the hopes and confusing confutation of the prophecies of the (few) avowed secessionists, and (very many) "sympathizers" with "the South."

The measure for which you now applaud me, was not so general as most of the papers out of Maryland (and some here, intentionally) misrepresented it to be.

It has, from the beginning of our troubles, been no small increase of my difficulties, that the situation of the greater proportion of my diocese, in view of the questions of State rights and secession, is entirely different from that of the "District."

With very many in the State it has been a real question, honestly entertained, in what direction their allegiance, to which they are bound by Divine prescription, truly lay.

Such meet me with the grounded objection to chartism in the premises, that it is no religious question, but one of State matters, which I have neither right nor competence to solve for them. This kept me absolutely inactive, except as, step by step, the State position became determinately settled. At the outset I viewed in the Governor the depositary of the State sovereignty (whatever that may be) in all respects not otherwise determined by written constitution or statute. Then I limited myself to action as a citizen, for the purpose of strengthening him by my testimony, that his loyal course did really represent the mind of a majority of the people of Maryland.

This course once taken, I felt at liberty and under obligation, officially to regard and support him as the representative of the majority of the people of Maryland (on State rights views), and as the exponent of the will of the majority of the citizens of the United States in Maryland, in adhering to the Federal Government on any view consistent with the Declaration of Independence and Constitution of the United States.

The election of the new Legislature settled the position of the State, and made my course thenceforth clear.

But still the minority doggedly insist, that they are not the minority; that the present Governor and Legislature do not truly constitute the State authority ; that we are in condition of military subjection. They insist, too, that this is a civil question, not for me to decide upon by official action.

In any necessary action, of obedience to legitimate requisitions of the authorities, whether of the State, or of the Federal Government, to which, in accordance with my personal convictions, the citizens of the State have declared themselves to be duly subject as citizens— I should have no hesitation about my duty; and accordingly, in August last, promptly fulfilled it, in relation to the day of fasting and humiliation recommended by the President, and recently have had some very trying discussions with regard to a proposed oath of allegiance; which, happily, it has not been deemed needful to require.

But when I have a discretion, I feel bound, for peace' sake, to humor what I consider as the unreasonable perversity of my brethren (unhappily, not, by any means, of the laity only), and do nothing to which they can object as deciding for them questions not belonging to my office as a minister of Christ.

I have not, therefore, as represented, "transmitted to all the clergymen in my charge" the Form of Thanksgiving lately issued.

But in the case of the District of Columbia there can be no such plea of doubtful or divided allegiance made in bar of my official action. There the Federal Government is the one "power," under God, to which he bids my diocesans there resident be dutifully subject.

I had no scruple, therefore, about issuing the special form in question, when my official action to that effect had been formally asked.

I waited to be asked, even there; because I knew the strange and totally inexpressible disloyalty of very many members of the Church there; and knew how much offence was likely to be taken, as accordingly has been the case.

But it was a clear duty, and, let what will come of it, I cannot regret its performance. Such a deliverance from siege and blockade as the City of Washington and "District" have experienced, is no ordinary call for solemn public thanksgiving; and that, rendered honestly and truthfully under the circumstances, must be with acknowledgment of the victories by which the deliverance was brought about.

Whole congregations rebel against it, but that does not move me— they sin in doing so; and for what I have done there was a cause.

In the meanwhile, my dear brother, it is no small support to me, in bearing up against the strife of tongues (for here in Baltimore and elsewhere in Maryland, those who think with the offended in the District take their part as grievously injured by a spiritual oppression), to receive such kind, cordial testimony of approval as that with which you have favored me.

May our Blessed Master only vouchsafe me the grace I need to be in any way worthy of the confidence you are pleased so handsomely to express !

Faithfully, affectionately, and gratefully your friend and brother,

W. R. W.

TO THE REV. DR. KERFOOT.

A MINISTER DRAWN TO THE CHURCH BY THE ECCLESIASTICAL PRINCIPLE SHOWN IN CONVENTION CONTESTS.

BALTIMORE, January 29, 1863.

DEAR KERFOOT :

. . . I have had the gratification for the last three months to assist in his struggles out of heresy and schism a very ingenuous and intelligent man, of apparently true and deeply devout religious character . . . none other than the Unitarian pastor who has just resigned his position to become a candidate for holy orders. He ascribes his first serious intention to seek orders in the Church to the effect produced on him by our last diocesan Convention in its conflict with the elements of disorder, and exhibition of the supremacy in all its members of ecclesiastical principle and rule.

By the by, a pleasant exhibition of that same thing is the fact that Calloway, the only member of the Convention who was treated with asperity, has been on the best terms with me for this long time past, and left me only a few minutes ago after a very cordial and even confidential consultation as to his course involving churchmanship, and (I suspect) loyalty too. It is certainly much to his credit as a Christian and as a clergyman that he is willing so to act. . . .   Your loving   W. R. W.

TO DR. GEORGE SHATTUCK, BOSTON.

REJOICES IN RELEASE FROM SLAVERY.

BALTIMORE, August 14, 1863.

DEAR SHATTUCK :

Your note of July 27th was a great surprise to me, for I had been watching, as I thought, diligently all sources of information about travel from the South, and felt quite sure that you must be still at New Orleans. . . . I am delighted with your testimony as to the result of your observations in your late trip, convincing you that if rightly borne the abolition of slavery will be worth all the suffering. It is my own deepest conviction, and I cannot sufficiently admire the admirable train of providentially governed and over-ruled events by which, without and, as it were, in spite of human planning or execution, the absolute and final release of our young nation from the horrible incubus so long brooding over it, has been brought about. *Soli Deo gloria!*

Ever your affectionate   W. R. W.

TO THE REV. E. MULFORD, SOUTH ORANGE.

HIS EFFORT, DURING THE WAR, TO KEEP HIS DIOCESE UNCOMMITTED.

BALTIMORE, January 15, 1864.

REV. AND DEAR BROTHER:

With the exception of one brief circular, I have issued no public "letters or charges having reference to national subjects." My efforts to maintain scriptural loyalty in my diocese have been confined to intercourse and correspondence of an unpublished kind. In that mode they would fill volumes.

At an early period of our troubles I became but too well assured that, while the majority of the population of Maryland—exclusive of negroes—was certainly loyal, a large majority of the class belonging to the Church, and as a consequence of the clergy, was not so. It then became my duty rather to hinder action, which would commit the diocese in a wrong direction, than to act, which could only result in division of the Church, and open declaration of the covert disloyalty of too many of its members.

Sure from the outset—that is, after May, 1861—of the ultimate result of the great struggle, I saw clearly that I could do more for the Church in Maryland by keeping it uncommitted until the paroxysm of disaffection should be over, than I could hope to effect by any public display of official influence or authority. I now see reason to hope that I have been successful; and that by the sacrifice of the prestige which I might have attained by the publication of pastoral letters and charges inculcating loyalty, and confining myself to private inculcation of duty in conversation and correspondence, I have succeeded in keeping the record of my diocese, as such, free from the stain of disloyalty, and even from the exhibition of division on the subject, while my own official position sufficiently vindicated the character of the Church before the world; and while I have also been not unsuccessful in watching and defeating all endeavors to commit either the diocese as such, or the character of the Church, in an opposite direction.

Very faithfully your friend,

W. R. W.

[It is not known what " endeavors " were happily defeated by the bishop.—W. F. B.]

TO THE REV. C. H. HALL, D.D.

ON LEGISLATION TOUCHING BEARING ARMS BY THE CLERGY. THE PRO-
TESTANT EPISCOPAL CHURCH BOUND BY THE RULE AND PRACTICE
OF THE UNIVERSAL CHURCH.

BALTIMORE, Monday before Easter, 1865.

MY DEAR DOCTOR :

. . . On these grounds I say with utmost confidence that the Protestant Episcopal Church in the United States, as a part of the Universal Church, bound by its rule and practice, binds the conscience of its clergy not to bear arms under pain of deposition or worse ; and that such obligation is part of the canonical law of our Church, retained unabrogated, as it exists in the canons of the Church of England.

In such confidence, I should regard it as unwise to attempt anything like original legislation to that effect, but would have no objection to a declaratory canon, setting forth that such is the position of our clergy.

Indeed, late unhappy cases seem to call for some such action on the part of the Church, and in taking it, of course the provisions of the law of the United States would have to be kept in view, and the language used would be adapted to meet the requisitions of that law.

I may observe, in corroboration both of my own remark above as to the declaratory nature of legislation to be taken, and of your suggestion that it should " not be as the enactment of a new article of faith," that the same precaution was felt to be needful seven hundred years ago ; and that when Archbishop Richard of Canterbury re-enacted a canon then three hundred and thirty years old, he thought it requisite to provide that the punishment of clergymen for bearing arms by degradation should be inflicted on them as " despisers of the canons and of ecclesiastical authority," not as for any newly made offence.

Very faithfully and affectionately,

W. R. W.

CHAPTER II.

1864–1865.

THE venerated senior presbyter had gone to his rest since the bishop's last report: the graceful and deserved tribute now rendered to his merit ought not to be forgotten.

Generations must pass before the diocese can again rejoice in the adornment of its clergy-roll by the name of one so honored and revered in his own parish (the largest in the United States); in the city which, for half a century, had cherished him among its worthiest and most influential public men ; in the State through every corner of which his personal and official reputation, without spot or blemish, had extended ; and among the thousands of the clergy of our Church, at the head of whom he had so long sat while health and strength permitted his acceptance of their presidency in the General Convention, as our late venerable father William Edward Wyatt, whom after long languishing, in humble and loving readiness for his change, it pleased God to withdraw from labor on the feast of the Nativity of St. John the Baptist in 1864.

In the address it is said that bodily infirmity had continued to interfere with ability to travel, and that to the kindness of three brethren in the episcopate was due the fact that long arrears of diocesan visitations had been made up. But the bishop made no reference to the important fact that this inability to travel had been earnestly presented to him as an inducement to consider a proposal that might have led to his resignation of a charge which he could not rightly fulfil. This was that he should resume his regretted office of Teacher of Ecclesiastical History in the General

Seminary. From an early period they who were intimate with the work of the Seminary had seen the great need of a head such as have other theological schools, established since the general institution was founded, which, being diocesan, are under the supervision of a bishop. The deans, until lately, were the resident professors in turn, and the result of this was that there could be no permanent control on any extended system ; and practically, as one of themselves has complained, the government was "presbyterian in our independence. Over the Seminary is the whole body of the episcopate, and this has no personal representation. It is unapproachable, and, excepting in one instance, its control has never been felt." In the beginning, during Bishop Hobart's time, and perhaps for a while after, episcopal influence was felt ; but through unfortunate events this ceased, and while it lasted it was complained of out of the Diocese of New York. What was demanded was permanent control—that of a resident bishop, if possible, representing the authority of the Church. Persuaded of this, in 1856 the Executive Committee, or members of it, informally consulted with Bishop Whittingham, suggesting that possibly he could combine the duties of President with those of his former professorship.

Even when the trials he was called on to meet could not have been foreseen, the picture of his former student life and influence over students came before his mind in very attractive colors. He could not at once put it aside, but considered the possibility of changes in the government of the Seminary and in the canon law of the Church which might, through obedience to the expressed will of the Church, restore him to his earlier and more peaceful life. These changes, pointed out by him as essential, it may be presumed were seen to be impossible ; and nothing further was said. War troubles, which affected everything, in 1864 caused the resignation of the chair of History by Dr. Mahan and his acceptance of the parish of St. Paul's in Baltimore. The

Rev. Dr. A. C. Coxe, a loving pupil and friend, who had also, to the solace of the bishop, been a rector in Baltimore, but who in the second year of the war had felt constrained to quit a diocese to which he was attached as a home, and to leave his friend to encounter their common difficulties without his support, being a trustee of the Seminary, wrote to Bishop Whittingham in August, 1864, asking:

Would anything tempt you back to your old chair at the Seminary? It would be doing a service to the Church at this crisis in the Seminary history second to none that could be done by any of her bishops. . . . You could still remain Bishop of Maryland, residing in the diocese six months of the year, and letting them have their own way and choose an assistant. Could you, deprived by the providence of God of locomotive power, devote yourself to any work so worthy of your remaining years?—which I pray the Lord to make many. If you will not say nay, I ask no more.

Besides the defective organization of the Seminary, it needed large sums to maintain its existing work. Its lack of means, it was said, was in part due to the fact that they who ought to have been its friends had withdrawn their confidence because of an odious popular imputation of disloyalty to the Government. To whatever else this suspicion may have been due, it is true that the master-spirit in the Seminary at this time, one of the ablest men in the Church, was a strong Democrat and States-rights man, and had written a very able work on American slavery, which had been published too late for its intended purpose, and which, without being read, was considered to be a defence of "the Southern institution."

It was thought that in this exigency no man in the Church could be so effective as one "well known as an expert in ecclesiastical history, a bishop of large experience, and a patriot."

Others besides Dr. Coxe very earnestly desired to see the Bishop of Maryland again professor. Among these was

Professor Johnson, whose advocacy of his claims has been more than once published.

In September the bishop, together with seven others, was nominated. A few days later Dr. Seabury wrote to him:

I was present, as Dean of the Seminary, at the meeting of the Board of Trustees when you were nominated to your old professorship. The nomination was received with such favor as to leave little doubt, I think, of your election, if agreeable to yourself. As a resident professor of the institution, I trust it will not seem obtrusive in me to assure you, in case you shall accept the position, of a hearty welcome. I am prepared to greet you not only as a professor but as a bishop. I shall gladly do all in my power to promote your influence and uphold your authority. Indeed, I look forward to your presence not only as a blessing to the students but as a source of comfort to myself personally, and shall avail myself of your advice and direction in any and every way that may help to accomplish the great ends of the institution.

I beg you to present my respects to Mrs. Whittingham and the young ladies, and to say to them that if the change which now seems probable shall occur, Mrs. Seabury and my family will unite with me in doing all in our power to make their new-old home agreeable.

To appreciate the generosity of this letter, one must bear in mind what were the relations of the two men toward each other at the time when Dr. Whittingham resigned his professorship. The acerbity and resentment gendered only by sharp newspaper controversies had passed away; the friendship of early manhood was resumed, and with advancing years long-tried mutual esteem was strengthened. In answer to the doctor's letter the bishop wrote:

I am deeply grateful for your very kind letter of the 30th. It will have much weight on one side in my settlement of the very grave question about to be (for it is not yet in any noticeable way) brought before me. Although when asked the question, "Would anything tempt you back to your old chair at the Seminary?" I had replied that "I was, as all my life I had endeavored to be, entirely in the hands of the Church, for that or any work to which her authorities, by regular action, might assign me," it was very unexpected. . . . All my personal propensities and desires would be gratified, in the highest degree, by return to my much-loved occupations in the Seminary, and the knowledge that such return would associate me in the most intimate relations with friends and brethren so highly and entirely respected and beloved as yourself and Drs. Johnson and Eigenbrodt greatly increases the attractiveness of the proposal. But that very tendency on my part makes me uneasy lest it betray me into a snare and lead me unduly to estimate the weight of reasons for a course novel in itself and perhaps fraught with dangerous consequences. . . .

The bishop then sets forth some of these reasons, such as his physical condition, and

the very peculiar situation of my diocese—such as to afford good ground for questioning whether, on the whole, it might not be advantaged by my resignation were I even in perfect capacity for duty.

But yet he cannot find himself able to take, at the present stage of the question, the momentous step of settling it by accepting the nomination. He then enters upon considerations which are more pointedly stated in a letter which may be found on a subsequent page.

The election took place on October 26th, and the result was the next day announced by Dr. Coxe.

My Very Dear Bishop :

Your election was a matter of course since you did not absolutely "forbid the banns." The meeting last night was a very interesting one. Many of our friends had not thought it worth while to come, supposing there would be no opposition ; but it was interesting to see many who, for a second time, had made a long journey to vote for you. . . . The whole *moral* force of the meeting, which was very large, was on our side. There was no *opposition*—not one word. All agreed you were the best possible person, if you could be had. But some were pledged to their own nominees and personal friends before your nomination had been heard of ; a few felt it would be folly to elect a person who would not and could not come, and a few, I think very honestly, thought it wrong to elect a diocesan bishop. When the vote was declared it seemed to give great satisfaction. Because of the scruples of Dr. M—— and others against electing a diocesan bishop, no effort was made to declare it unanimous, but it was virtually so. . . .

This letter did not state all that was to be considered. There were seventy-five ballots cast, and Bishop Whittingham was elected on a second balloting by a majority of two.

In a private letter to the Secretary of the Board the bishop said :

The difference in the board by no means surprised me. Its result was felt to be a grateful relief from the responsibility of taking on myself the decision between the Seminary and my diocese. . . . I could not, of course, accept a position so hesitatingly offered. . . . In all this I have neither seen nor felt anything personally annoying to me. Grave questions arose totally aside from any consideration of my personal character and qualifications, and on the view taken of those questions I am heartily content that the settlement of the affair should have rested.

Had the election been unanimous the result would have been only a less prompt declining. The bishop had only been recalled to the professorship he had before held. The board did not have before them any of the various questions the settlement of which had to be reached before he could consent to weigh the duty of accepting. Without the action of the General Convention they could not have presented what he would have considered to be the command of the Church.

In 1856 he had fully expressed his views to those who had consulted him about the Seminary, and had plainly said that there was little prospect of their being concurred in. Inasmuch as some of these same persons desired his election in 1864, he had reason to suppose—apart from what he had said to others—that his position was understood. If he had not so thought there would have been but little propriety in his withholding the emphatic Nay! which his friend begged him not to utter. What his views were may be understood from his correspondence with the most excellent Dr. John McVickar, who wrote:

New York, November 7, 1864.

My Dear Bishop :

It is long since I had occasion or justification to address a letter to you, though my thoughts have often rested upon you and your self-denying labors, deepened as they now are by bodily infirmity and the distractions of our unhappy times. I now write you, however, in hopes that the sincere words and wishes of an old friend may help to turn what I now understand to be the doubtful scales of your decision touching your removal to this city through acceptance of your recent election to your old professorship. To my mind it seems like a providential call to a change of duties, favorable alike to your own health and comfort, and to (what you value more) your usefulness to the Church, incapacitated as you now are, and above all to your own Seminary, now anxiously awaiting your decision, and to which your return will give new life and influence. If, as our mutual friend Dr. Coxe supposes, the want of a unanimous vote stands as a bar, permit me to observe that it was through no want of unqualified confidence or estimate of your pre-eminent fitness, but solely from canonical doubts on the part of some few, and others again who felt themselves pledged to those whom they had nominated . . . and thus a divided vote under a united sentiment, saving the few who stood upon canonical objections. And now, my dear bishop, permit me to refer to the conscientious scruple that sometimes arises in sensitive minds on such a vote as a ground of duty ; I mean to look on a unanimous vote as a call of Providence, a mere majority as not. But surely this is making it a worldly instead of a religious question. What Providence ordains is the result. The steps to it are in man's hands ; the result is in God's. For myself, I should feel as much bound, as a Christian, in one case as in the other. I do not dare to urge further upon you considerations which you may deem selfish, but which I hold to be a part of Christian duty—I mean those which relate to health, comfort under suffering, and continuance of useful labor in the only path now open to you. But I have detained you too long, though I know you will pardon it from your old friend, your senior in years, but in all else of duty and self-denying labor your scholar and pupil.

With love and reverence, yours till death,

John McVickar.

In answer to this letter the bishop wrote:

My Dear Doctor:

There is no one living whom I regard with the filial reverence and affection which warm my heart toward you. It is just forty years since you first lighted in my bosom the hope of being useful in my generation. The day, the place, the words, the looks, have never faded from my memory, and have never ceased to call forth emotions of grateful love. If any one, then, could sway my decision in any grave question about duty, it would be you. Your advice will ever command from me the most profound and reverent attention.

On that account I am not sorry that your letter of November 7th came to my hands too late to affect a decision already made and finally declared. It would have added greatly to my difficulties in settling a question of itself almost too hard for me, and might have swayed me in a direction which I now think I might afterward have found occasion to regret.

As the thing is done, let me now lay my own future on one side and write to you in the confidence and "abandon" of private friendship about the past.

I will affect no squeamish modesty, but own that I think that the best thing the trustees could have done would have been to get me back to the Seminary as its Professor of Ecclesiastical History and President.

But it would be mainly in the last capacity, taking its full responsibilities, that, in my judgment, I should have been able, if at all, effectually to serve the institution.

For forty years I have been of the settled and yearly strengthening opinion that the Theological Seminary could never attain to its due degree of usefulness to the Church without a head able to give it character and fixed purpose, with energy enough of mind and will to command the respect and confidence of the Board of Trustees, and be regarded by that body, as well as by the faculty and students, as the administrative and directive power.

For such a place any bishopric in the Church might be exchanged, without doubts about relinquishment of duty or diminution of usefulness.

When, therefore, some years ago some members of the Standing Committee, and then informally in behalf of that committee, Bishop H. Potter sounded me as to my disposition to accept such headship of the Seminary, I distinctly answered that I was at the command of the Church on two conditions: (1) that it should be the command of the Church, by having the full sanction of its highest authority, and (2) that such sanction should be fittingly shown by a change of the law concerning resignation of dioceses, so as to leave the bishop at any time made President of the Seminary, and for that office resigning diocesan charge, in possession of his seat and vote in the House of Bishops.

I freely expressed my doubt whether the Church was ready for such action, and particularly whether it could ever be had either in the board or in the General Convention in behalf of me.

I heard no more of the matter, when a few days before the late nominating meeting of the trustees my very dear friend and " son in the faith," Dr. A. C. Coxe, wrote to me [as above quoted]. I knowing nothing of any recent plans or canvassing among the trustees, and knowing that Dr. Coxe had been for months in close counsel and co-operation with Bishop Potter for the restoration of the fiscal affairs of the Seminary, supposed that he might be making this inquiry in connection with the bishop and on the basis of the former communication between the bishop and me.

Unwilling to do anything that should amount to assistance on my part in the process of unsettling me from Maryland, I made no allusion in my answer to Dr. Coxe to anything that had previously taken place, but merely replied to his inquiry that I was now, as I had always been, entirely at the disposal of the Church ; that I came to Maryland, most unwillingly and against my judgment, on that ground ; and if on that ground called away from Maryland to resume my old position, had many reasons for accepting the behest with thankfulness and pleasure.

The nomination was made, and immediately after I learned, to my no small astonishment, what had taken place concerning it. . . . Thus the trustees, through the chief mover in the matter, were informed of my relation to the movement. . . .

To whatever cause it was owing, no reference appears to have been had in the board to anything more than the supply of the vacant professorship. I regarded it as particularly fortunate that the opinions of the board were so much divided, even in that action, as to relieve me of all difficulty about the determination of the answer to be given. . . . I do not, in the least, insist on the mere want of unanimity in the vote as in itself in any way a Providential indication of duty, but I do, my dear friend and father, feel very strongly convinced that the whole course of this matter has been overruled by a most merciful directing Providence, so as to try me, and yet not suffer me to choose for myself and bring myself into a state of lasting self-reproach or condemnation.

Since my decision, every day reveals to me more and more the danger I was in of leaving duty here to seek my own ease and pleasure under the show of promised usefulness elsewhere. If nothing else, masterly inactivity seems to be the province assigned me for the present. Silence, even from good words, is exacted of me by prudential considerations of the strongest obligation, so long as the condition and temper of my diocese continue what they are. Quiet is enforced on me by physical debility. But I still serve as a stop-gap and a drag—humble uses, but not without their advantage in this case, as I verily believe, both to the Church at large and to the unhappy portion of it in which they are more especially needed. . . .

I have but to ask the continuance of your prayers that I may be blessed with increased measures of those holy influences by which alone, in my present trying and uneasy circumstances, I can hope to be enabled to join the wisdom of the serpent with the innocence of the dove.

Affectionately and gratefully
Your life-long debtor and protégé,
W. R. W.

Dr. McVickar replied:

NEW YORK, November 29, 1864.

MY DEAR, DEAR BISHOP:

How can I adequately thank you for your words of love and kindness? They overwhelm me with a sense of my own unworthiness to be so addressed by one to whom I have always looked as my unattainable model of what the Christian minister should be. Yet from my heart I thank you for them. They bring tears into my eyes *now*, but will henceforward in my hours of trial bring comfort too to think that I have awakened such feelings in one whom I so love and reverence. They deepen, however, the pain of your recent decision, though I both appreciate and honor the grounds on which it rested, as well in declining as in remaining.

An episcopal head to the Seminary, while devoted to it as his charge, still retaining rank and privilege, is undoubtedly the true ideal of the institution, and one that in an earlier day might have been carried out; whether now possible may be questioned. . . .

With scanty room for all love and reverence, and earnest prayers for every blessing, I remain, dear bishop,

Affectionately yours in Christ,
JOHN McVICKAR.

When it was known in Maryland that the bishop had been nominated for the vacant professorship and that there was a possibility of his withdrawal from the diocese, there was not a little anxiety felt. Pleadings, remonstrances, protests were sent to him. He must have been moved by an address written by John Henry Alexander and signed by Samuel J. Donaldson, William Woodward, Robert M. Proud, J. G. Proud, Jr., Hugh Davey Evans, Thomas S. Alexander, Haslett McKim, and William J. Albert, than whom there were no men in the diocese more worthy of personal respect. Having spoken of the tie between a bishop and his diocese which they had supposed he considered to be indissoluble, these gentlemen say:

Against the only excuse possible for episcopal resignation, viz., physical disability, our Church has provided a specific remedy, covering the need of the diocese and leaving to the party himself the Christian resort of faith and patient submission to the will of God. We are well aware that there is nothing more trying, both to our sense of responsibility and to our weakness, than forced inactivity; but we need hardly suggest to you, Right Reverend Sir, that Divine Providence can find as much occasion for human helplessness as for human strength, and that sometimes they are perfectly serving Him who only stand and wait. But serviceable waiting is certainly not going somewhere else. . . . One consequence of our unhappy civil division has been a temporary schism in our Church. The restoration of our political Union is by no means certain to heal this schism immediately: on the contrary, the restoration of the integrity of the Church may take place only by gradual and successive absorption of the schismatic dioceses. In the probable cast of this diocese, were you to withdraw from us now Maryland would at least be exposed to the risk of joining with the existing schism. Such a lamentable and sinful result we cannot allow ourselves to dwell upon.

But even if this did not accrue, the dissensions and trouble which would arise now upon a vacancy in our episcopate are unspeakable. . . . We hold it at least certain that any bishop elected at this time by the Convention of this diocese would be a sympathizer with the rebellion, and we submit to you whether the loyal minority, who have already had much to bear, have not a right to expect you to continue standing between them and such a calamity. [The important matters likely to come before the next General Convention were next referred to.]

We therefore implore you, Right Reverend Sir, by all your obligations to the people among whom long ago you cast your lot, and as both sides supposed for life; by all that is owing to those especially represented by us who have clung to you upon principle and from love through these latter evil days; by all the affection of your flock to be remembered, and by all the alienations to be healed; by all the great good you have done in the diocese and the greater good you can still do; and by your solemn vow at the solemnest moment of your life—not to desert your diocese in its hour of sore need, and especially to refuse the ensnaring step which has been proposed, and against which we mean this as our earnest but respectful protest.

The bishop's friends, when thus writing, knew nothing of the conditions which made the resignation they protested against so improbable. There would have been greater cause for their fears had he been one whose judgment habitually took counsel of his inclinations, for many things concurred to make the change offered him most desirable. The disappointments which had come to him in Maryland and the continuous strife of nearly four years had been very painful. Together with resistance from many in his diocese he had also experienced misapprehension on the part of some whose political sentiments he shared. As has been shown, he maintained the claims and acts of the Federal Government, and no one ever condemned in stronger terms secessionists and sympathizers with what he considered to be sinful resistance to constituted authority, imputing to them alone every drop of blood shed and every suffering endured. But yet his fidelity was shown in the discharge of his personal duties as a citizen and his continuous effort to restrain those under his spiritual jurisdiction from violation of Christian and canonical obedience. With the exception of the letter which he suffered Governor Hicks to publish, he took no open part in any political movement. He would not even hang out a flag when it was expected of him, because the episcopal residence was not his own but belonged to the diocese. Early in the war he gave a line of commendation to a young friend from a Northern State who was seeking an office that required an examination before appointment: he learned that his commendation was taken instead of an examination, and he would never again sign any like paper. President Lincoln is reported to have said, "There is nothing which the Bishop of Maryland will ask which I will not grant." But he never asked anything, not even deserved advancement for his son, who was a surgeon in the United States Army. The nearest approach he made to asking any favor was the calling the attention of a General in command to a wrong done in his—the General's—name and authority, viz., the taking through religious partisan persecution a horse from a country parson, whom the bishop certified to be "a harmless, inoffensive person, totally incapable of any dishonest or disloyal act, whatever his opinion may be." The bishop did not trade on his patriotism. He suffered for, but he received none of the substantial benefits of loyalty bestowed on others. From the first he took care that no one should have an excuse for saying that he made gain by discharge of duty. He was simply the Bishop of Maryland, and for being such in all honesty in trying times he asked for no earthly reward.

But even as some of those who were condemned by him could see nothing to extenuate what they received as a wrong, so on the other hand there were those who unwillingly saw and did not understand loyalty tempered by any consideration for the weakness of others.

During the war the bishop abstained from retaliation, in any shape, however provoked: he was ready to aid those who differed from him in everything not forbidden by conscience. Where it was possible, despite the ebullitions of his temperament, he made no distinction among his clergy and laity because of political difference; and so soon as the return of peace made it impossible for further token of resistance to Government, there was nothing on his part to indicate that there had ever been a severance—save perhaps extra effort at times to hide the fact.

Knowing well the bishop and the people among whom he lived, a former presbyter of Maryland wrote in November, 1864:

I rejoiced to see the announcement of your refusal of the position offered you in New York. . . . Your retirement from your diocese would be to it a great evil and in the end an unhappy thing for yourself. I felt sure you could outlive the alienation and coldness which your faithfulness to God and your country has engendered in the minds of a portion of your people, and it seemed to me to be altogether best for them and for you that you should remain at your post of sore trial and suffering until God should either bring you triumphantly out of them or call you to yield your life a sacrifice to them.

Mr. Buel judged rightly. The abandonment of Maryland would have been a great misfortune to the bishop and to the diocese. And if there was never again generally manifested that enthusiasm which had been shown before the war—for the absence of which more than one reason can be given—there was yet never shown, on account of the war, any "alienation and coldness" to hinder the proper relations of bishop and people. Other troubles awaited him, but they had a different origin.

Bishop Whittingham's demeanor toward Southern churchmen after the war, in the estimation of those who had been separated from him, covered over all acts during the war, which, however resented, were in no respect other than the just results of an honest judgment, the freedom of which could not be impugned by those who had chosen to judge for themselves. A touching incident will show the spirit of the man.

Other differences than political had, to some extent, separated Bishop Whittingham and Bishop Johns, of Virginia.

When, after the war, the latter was first in Baltimore with, perhaps, some doubts as to the manner in which he might be received, he called on his once diocesan. On their meeting, before a word had been said, Bishop Whittingham opened wide his arms and caught to his bosom his recovered brother; and in silence the two wept on each other's shoulder. When, long after, Miss Whittingham related this scene to Bishop Atkinson and added, " You too would have been received in the same manner," he answered, "Margaret, I never understood your father."

All the dioceses within the limits of the Confederate States, having separated their legislative connection with the General Convention, united in forming a new synodical body. Supposing that the secession from the United States was as operative as the renunciation of allegiance to the king of Great Britain, their act could be justified by the principle asserted in the preface to the Book of Common Prayer, which declares: "When these American States became independent with respect to civil government, their ecclesiastical independence was necessarily included." But it is noticeable that by some in the South this doctrine of the dependence of the Church on the relation of civil governments was looked upon as Erastian. Because of the resumed independence of the State it might be expedient—necessary even—to sever former ecclesiastical bonds, but this separation was to be made by the diocese. In like manner re-union could be effected only by the diocese. With a clear assertion of the independence of Church and State may be seen tokens of the working of the States-rights doctrine. The organized diocese is looked upon as the unit, and association with others for the purpose of legislation is considered to be a matter of expedience.* The restoration of the

---

* It seems to be assumed that the relation of the States to the General Government, as practically determined by force of arms, has settled beyond question the relation of the dioceses to the General Convention. This is a view which is entirely Erastian and uncatholic. No ecclesiastical organization of associated

unity in the Church in the United States was brought about through ignoring all Southern theories and acts.

The war was begun and justified on the theory that no State could secede from the Union; that all intended acts of secession were null, and that the power of the Federal Government, as given and limited by the Constitution, of right extended, without possible cessation, over all the territory of the federation. We need not inquire how this theory was carried out.

Bishop Whittingham, in common with churchmen in the North, held the same theory with regard to the ecclesiastical organization. An instance will illustrate his position. Three clergymen in New Orleans who, following their Book of Common Prayer, had not prayed for the President of the United States, were arrested and sent as prisoners to New York. A political event, happy for them, saved them from Fort Lafayette, which was their destination. They were paroled. Two of them came to Maryland and had clerical work offered to them here. One of them remained in charge of a parish until he was free to return home after the lapse of two years, because—although he still refused to take the oath of allegiance to the United States, and was a member of the separated diocese of Louisiana—he so expressed himself that the Bishop of Maryland was not forced to consider him as unwilling to be counted within the fold of which the bishop was pastor. The other frankly maintained his position as a presbyter of the Church in the Confederate States, *i.e.*, as a member of a foreign Church not recognized. As such he was inhibited.

diocesies which bases itself upon geographical and national boundaries can urge any higher claim than that either of agreement between the dioceses or of consideration of high expediency. The Southern dioceses held this view with almost entire unanimity, and have, in the most formal and positive way, recorded their judgment.—Bishop Wilmer's Address, January, 1866.

The nationality of a Church is a matter purely conventional and of human arrangement. . . . There is an essential difference between the unity of branches of the Church and their union in one legislative body.—Pastoral Letter, 1865.

Acting on the theory that as secession was null so all the acts of the dioceses in the seceded States that could not be well examined were to be ignored, when the General Convention met in 1865 Bishop Whittingham and the majority of his fellow-bishops were glad to welcome Bishop Lay, of Arkansas, by his older title as the Missionary Bishop in the Southwest; while in the House of Deputies the Secretary, with admirable boldness, put aside a discussion of the right to seats by beginning his roll-call with "Alabama." There was none to answer, but the desired end was gained.

The result was happy; but one can but note an inconsistency in the procedure. The men who came back into the Church had been openly condemned as grievous sinners, if not severally yet as a class. Without confession of error, professing that they felt no need of repentance, they were treated as though they had not erred.

It is well at times to look away from facts. But there are limits to such wisdom. The restoration of the unity of the Church, which is an abiding claim for thanks to God, could not have been effected as it was had the Bishop of Louisiana been still living.

This bishop, Leonidas Polk, had received a military edution at West Point, and had left the army to become a candidate for orders. When the war broke out he had found it not inconsistent with his vocation as bishop to take an active and conspicuous part in what he had called "the last battle for freedom." Late in the war he fell in command at Pine Mountain, in Georgia. He had been engaged in making a reconnoissance with a body of officers. Having drawn fire, all others left the dangerous ground. He remained, and, as was supposed by those who knew his habits and had been with him the moment before, was praying when he was killed by a cannon-ball fired at him singly. Had he survived the war his brethren could not have abandoned him, for their cause had been common; but with him they could not have approached the House of Bishops.

Even the one among the Northern bishops most lenient would not have condoned the error of one guilty, in his judgment, of such varied transgressions, and who was, in addition to all else, such a scandal. By bearing arms Bishop Polk violated canon law, and it must be supposed that he did so knowingly. He also disregarded the warning given him personally by his Lord, if, in accordance with the interpretation by the House of Bishops in 1862, the Lord spake only to the clergy and to the bishops in particular, when he said, "all they that take the sword shall perish with the sword." Doubtless many believe that this word was fulfilled in his case. God knoweth. Certain it is that his death removed the chief obstacle to a peaceful termination of the separation in the Church consequent upon political strife.

There remained another difficulty, which, however, was not insurmountable. Bishop Cobb, of Alabama, died in 1861. In March, 1862, Dr. R. H. Wilmer was consecrated to his see by the Bishops of Virginia and Georgia and the Assistant Bishop of Virginia, with the consent of the bishops and standing committees of the dioceses in the Confederate States, although not yet definitely associated as the Protestant Episcopal Church in the Confederate States of America. Of course this act was not in accordance with the canons of the Church in the United States. A formal recognition of its validity was necessary to a prompt restoration of the unity which doubtless would have blessed the Church later.

Nearly all the Southern bishops had resolved not to consent to any restoration of ecclesiastical relations which did not provide for the recognition of the jurisdiction of Dr. Wilmer as Bishop of Alabama. It is not probable that they would have accepted his ready offer to resign rather than constitute an obstacle to reunion. Some of them, it is true, believed that principle demanded that the Southern dioceses should at once resume their former relations with the General Convention, but there were others who were governed by considerations of expedience only, and were prepared to resent the demand of certain concessions on their part.

What would have been insisted on was given before it was asked for. "The spirit of charity which prevailed in the proceedings of the General Convention" in 1865 "warmly commended itself to the hearts" of the Southern Council, as resolutions adopted at its last meeting testify. This charity thus gratefully acknowledged was not looked for, and, in sooth, caused almost as much surprise and fully as much joy among Northern churchmen as among those in the South.

Although there no longer existed that political separation to which alone was due the severance of the Church, yet brotherhood would not have been recognized had not churchmen been willing to be silent touching the causes of separation. A generous forbearance was due toward those who had staked all in support of what they deemed rights, and had lost almost all.*

Bishop Whittingham went to the Convention not only persuaded of this truth, but also cherishing sincere kindness of feeling which alone could gain confidence and a return of good-will. It is not meant, of course, that he alone among the prominent men was thus wisely kind, but his position as mediator was marked and his influence as such great. Some years later a younger bishop wrote to him : "You kept my anti-secession and that of others from making the breach wider. I am truly grateful that I was restrained. You

---

* During the summer the senior Bishop Hopkins had proposed to his brother bishops to address a letter to the Southern bishops, asserting that the Church had had no part, direct or indirect, in producing the conflict that had separated them, and assuring them of a cordial welcome at the approaching General Convention. The proposal was not acted on, for reasons which may be readily guessed. Bishop Whittingham could not sign a letter about the phraseology of which he had had no opportunity of conference, but cordially authorized Bishop Hopkins to send the proposed letter "as written by you in my behalf, with my hearty concurrence in its purport and end."

only could have influenced me at that time to have voted as I did, and others were equally indebted to you." Throughout the session in every possible way, by eloquent resistance of what he thought unwise and by pleadings in private, he tried to defend his Southern brethren and to shield them from what was wounding, and, if he could not wholly avert, to lessen the force of what was insisted on as necessary for the good name of the Church, but which was in fact unnecessary condemnation of the conquered. Even toward the close of the session, when it was desired to do what the interest of the Church demanded—to present, with the authority of the whole body, a remonstrance to Government against military interference in ecclesiastical matters—because the wrong which gave occasion for the remonstrance had been done to a Southern bishop and diocese, one who could not forgive rebellion exclaimed, "Who sympathizes with Wilmer?" "I do!" cried out the Bishop of Maryland; "I claim to be as loyal as my brother of ——, but I fully sympathize with Richard Hooker Wilmer!"

Two Southern bishops, Atkinson and Lay, were in Philadelphia at the time of the opening of the Convention. Bishop Whittingham, while in the place of meeting of the bishops before service, was told that the Bishop of North Carolina was outside, on the portico of the church. Immediately he went out and urged him to join the bishops, chiefly on the ground of hindering possible evil results of the opposite course. He could not, however, remove fears of the construction likely to be put on a solitary appearance among the Northern bishops. Persuasions by another were of as little avail. But during the service, after an earnest sermon by the Bishop of Montreal, who preached in the place of and at the request of the Bishop of Maryland, and who pleaded effectually for unity and charity, one or two of the junior bishops left the chancel and were soon seen returning and bringing with them Bishop Atkinson, whose fears had been stilled. A place was found for him among the bishops, and the service at the altar was continued. This gracious urgency was the extension of the right hand of fellowship to all the Southern bishops, and was the pledge of more formal recognition. The next day, in their organized House, Bishop Potter asked informally the judgment of the bishops touching the introduction of the Bishops of North Carolina and of the Southwest Mission. Some difficulties having been made, the Bishop of Maryland offered a resolution to the effect that "the Bishop of New York be requested to ask the brethren, in behalf of whom he had consulted the House, to trust the honor and love of their assembled brethren." He also declared that he considered an acceptance of this resolution to pledge all present to make no objection on account of the past to the assumption of a place in the House by Bishop Wilmer. Probably this action was all informal.

The result was a cordial reception of the two returning Southerners by each bishop severally. Having resumed their seats they remained during the Convention. Once on the plea of the great need of their presence in their dioceses they asked leave of absence, but the request that "they should continue to give the House the benefit of their presence" was urged so kindly that they withdrew their petition. Some things hard to be borne they had to endure from time to time, but they were conscious of the kindness of the body of their brethren, and so expressed themselves.

This "binding up of the breach of God's people," however blessed in itself, and rejoiced * in by all, was yet not without a drawback. It was a hindrance to the relief of the stuffed bosoms of patriots in both Houses. There was a desire for a service of thanksgiving for mercies received by the country, and in the setting forth of these mercies patriotism could not be content without the stating of what was an insult over a fallen foe in the shape of a regained

---

* At a meeting of the Board of Missions, on the announcement by a member that the two Southern bishops had that day taken their place in the House of Bishops, the *Gloria in Excelsis* was sung.

brother.   Bishop Whittingham contended earnestly—it was said with unusual eloquence—against any service rendered unnecessary by the lapse of time since the restoration of peace, and failing in this endeavor, against terms that must be wounding.   The walls of the House of Bishops are supposed to be impenetrable to rumors from within, but yet the Maryland delegation did not fail to express their gratitude to their bishop.   And as this claim for thanks became known to them, so also did they become aware of other matters which do not appear in the printed records.

As has been noted, Bishop Whittingham considered the admission of Bishops Atkinson and Lay to be a pledge for the recognition of Bishop Wilmer.   This claim was not assented to by all.   There were two objections to the Bishop of Alabama—one to the circumstances of his consecration; the other to personal conduct offensive politically.   The former was readily removed by the action of both Houses formally admitting him to the rights of an American bishop on the proper condition of his presenting evidence "of his having been consecrated a bishop of the Church of Christ," and his giving in the presence of three bishops "the promise of conformity comprised in the Office for the Consecration of Bishops."   In order to obtain the unanimous consent of the bishops to this "acceptance" of their Confederate brother, it was absolutely necessary to concede the gratification of a vote of censure upon him for his personal offence.   *Tantæne animis cœlestibus iræ?*   Bishop Whittingham, who moved the recognition of Bishop Wilmer, had hoped to gain his end by a promise to move a vote of censure in Council— that is, to administer, "in fulfilment of our Lord's direction in case of offences, a fraternal remonstrance with a brother who had given offence—alone with him—in the hope and expectation of redress, not punishment."   This kind intention was frustrated.   What represents a formal rebuke may be found in the printed journal as having been offered by Bishop Whittingham, and is in these words.   "*Resolved,*

That we do hereby express to the Bishop of Alabama our fraternal regrets at the issue of his late pastoral letter, and assured confidence that no further occasion for such regrets will occur." This resolution was passed *nem. con.*, and followed the resolution admitting the validity of the consecration of Bishop Wilmer, the vote on which was unanimous. The "fraternal disciplinary remonstrance" of the bishops in no way concerned the House of Deputies; but those who desired censure insisted that the two resolutions should be made known together, the second as qualifying and explaining the first. It was finally agreed that the Secretary should *inform the Secretary* of the House of Deputies of the second vote at the same time that he *communicated* the first.

What was the act of the Bishop of Alabama to which so much importance was attached?

He would have said that he had refused to recognize the right of an army officer to dictate to him with regard to his duties as a minister of religion. In his judgment, when the Confederate Government lapsed the Church in the States which had been confederated was not disorganized; and even at the time when the bishops were discussing his relation to them the Diocese of Alabama was a component part of this Church, to the constitution and canons of which alone he had made declaration of conformity. By the canons of their Church there was imposed on the bishop and his diocese a form of worship. One of the prayers in this form had "ceased of necessity" in June, 1865, when there was no President of the Confederate States, and, in Alabama, no one in civil authority, and when it had become "a grave question whether the State of Alabama was thereafter to be regarded as one of the States, or to be held as a military province under military rule." Under these circumstances the bishop issued a pastoral letter in which he declared that the Prayer for the President, etc., was inapplicable to the present condition of things. At the same time he counselled "clergy and laity to heed the teaching of the Church in regard to the scriptural obedience due to the powers that be; . . . and faithfully to discharge their duties to the State;" . . . and, if it should be required of all citizens, to take the oath of allegiance, for "an oath of fidelity to the Government is only the formal and solemn acknowledgment and expression of an already existing obligation."

No sooner was this pastoral issued than Major-General Woods, in command, interdicted the bishop and all who obeyed him from preaching or performing divine service.

In September Bishop Wilmer again addressed his charge and explained and defended his position. In this letter, which is "the late pastoral," referred to by the bishops in their expression of regrets, he says:

The issue raised is not one of loyalty. I have counselled you . . . to take in good faith the oath of allegiance, and have set you the example by taking it myself. . . . The use of the prayer under the present condition of things involves the point of congruity and fitness, and is, therefore, a question for ecclesiastical discretion. . . . Let it not be said that the Church in Alabama looked to any other than an ecclesiastical authority for guidance in worship, or that she was ever frightened from her propriety by the dictation or menace of any secular power, civil or military. Let the clergy await official notification from the ecclesiastical authority. . . . In the exercise of my episcopal discretion . . . I have decided, etc. On the other hand, the military authorities issue "orders" that the prayer shall be used at once, and that all the churches shall be closed until we accede to the demand. Thus the *real issue* before us is this: Shall the secular or the ecclesiastical power regulate the worship of the Church? . . . Remember, that the communication with God's mercy-seat cannot be obstructed by any created power, and that the compensations of divine goodness will supply all our needs through the riches of his grace in Christ Jesus, our only Lord and Master.

In November the General Council, to which Bishop Wilmer looked for guidance, gave to the bishops permission to make the change of confederate to united. But so long as the military " orders " rested on him Bishop Wilmer refused to exercise his granted power; and during two months longer the churches in Alabama remained closed.

At a special Convention in January, 1866,* the diocese withdrew from her union with the General Council and acceded to the General Convention, after which Bishop Wilmer made the declaration of conformity to the constitution of the Church in the United States, and the breach was formally healed.

When reporting to his diocese, in January, the action of the General Convention in his behalf, unsolicited by him, Bishop Wilmer stated that:

There was coupled with the assent of the House of Bishops a certain expression of "*fraternal regrets.*" There were some, he said, both in and out of the General Convention, who regarded this in the light of a censure upon official conduct. But he rejected this interpretation of the bishops' resolution, because he could not suppose they could have so far departed from propriety as to judge one not amenable to them—or, if considered amenable, without a hearing. Then, in the midst of gravest matters finding room for the exercise of his ever-ready wit, the bishop added: "It would seem, that in restoring old relations, the expression of regrets is in order; and it may not be amiss in me to state that, after a careful review of the various pastorals put forth in the last unhappy years, there are very few in which we, who look at all that has transpired from a different standpoint, have not found occasion for regrets to which we can give no adequate expression. For my part . . . I can recall no word that I have written to you as your bishop which now, in this moment of comparative quiet, I would obliterate from the record."

On the second or third day of the session of the General

---

* The Convention met on the 17th. On January 13th the bishop issued a letter to the clergy in which he said: "The recent revocation of the military orders renders it proper for me now to do what I could not properly have done before such revocation. I do now therefore recommend that the ruling of the General Council in the premises have the force of law in the diocese of Alabama, and the clergy thereof are called upon, henceforth to use the prayer for those in authority as it stands in the Book of Common Prayer."

Convention the senior and two other bishops received a joint letter from Bishop Wilmer, giving them a statement of the condition of things in Alabama, and urging them to assert "the true principle in regard to the interference of the secular power with the worship of the Church. Not," said he, "that I personally solicit your help. By God's grace I trust to maintain my stand. But the time is propitious, and the opportunity offers to affirm and maintain a great principle." He thought the opportunity the more favorable because they could not be supposed to sympathize with him politically.

Some of the bishops were fully in accord with the judgment of Bishop Wilmer, and endeavored to obtain from their House a remonstrance against governmental interference in ecclesiastical matters. All that was done was to place the matter in the hands of the Bishop of Ohio, who had been a governmental agent in England, and who fully approved the military prohibition in Alabama. To obtain relief from " military duress" as a favor granted on the application of Bishop McIlvaine was a subjection of Church rights instead of a proper maintenance of them.

The question of the readmission of all the Southern bishops being happily settled, there remained a matter the treatment of which furnished a possible opportunity to mar what had been done. This was the preparation of the usual triennial address of the House of Bishops to the Church.

Bishops then well known, and yet remembered for their zeal for the Union, shown by an ever-ready condemnation of rebellion, could not be satisfied with a pastoral letter that was not a counterpart of the one issued during the war, and which had elicited the approval of the United States Government.

It was in vain argued that the former pastoral spoke in the name of a section of the Church, and that now a reunited Church must address equally Southern and Northern brethren. In vain was it shown that certain desired declarations would tend but little to the strengthening of the good feeling for which they had thanked God. It mattered not. It was answered that the Church should express her loyal convictions in plain language. These fathers in God were of an opinion like to that of the authorities in Washington, who, desiring a renewal of national feeling, have placed among the naval trophies Confederate cannon bearing in the enduring brass the inscription, " Captured in such a *rebel* fort—in such a *pirate* vessel." A draft of a letter embodying the views of these gentlemen, and approved by the majority of the committee of five senior bishops, was presented to the House. When it was read the Bishop of Maryland took upon himself the unpleasant responsibility of moving that it be not adopted as the synodical letter of the House. The result of all the long and earnest debate which had preceded and which followed this motion was that there was no Pastoral issued in 1865, but instead of the usual letter from the Reverend Fathers a dogmatic thesis addressed to the clergy and to students in theology.

A fact which gave great pleasure to Bishop Whittingham was the concurrence of the two Houses in a resolution declaring " the sympathy and admiration of the Convention for the Bishop of Cape Town and his comprovincial bishops in their defence of the Word of God," which involved the deposition of Dr. Colenso. He himself brought the matter before the House of Bishops. He had feared opposition, and considered his success due in part to a good temper on the subject of foreign relations, the result of a gratifying communication from the Canadian Synod, presented with a pleasing speech by the Bishop of Montreal, together with a similar document from the Synod of Nova Scotia.

During this Convention Dr. Quintard, who had been chaplain to General Polk, was consecrated Bishop of Tennessee. The time for the ceremony was hastened, in order that the Bishop of Montreal might take part in the laying on of hands. Thus his consecration was a token of unity with a foreign Church, and also an evidence that what had claimed to be a foreign Church no longer occupied this position. Bishop Otey, whom Bishop Quintard succeeded, was one of the bishops of the Church in the Confederate States.

As a sign, too, of renewed vigor in the Church may be taken the election, by the Convention, of three missionary bishops for the West, and one for China.

CHAPTER III.

1866–1870.

THE excitement of frequent debates, the hard contest he
had undergone in behalf of the South, exhausted our bishop's
physical powers. On his return to his diocese he was unable to resume visitation. With difficulty he took part, in
January, in the consecration, as first Bishop of Pittsburgh,
of his very near friend, Dr. Kerfoot. In February a little
extra exertion at the Lent ordination broke him down utterly,
and during the remainder of the diocesan year he was wholly
dependent on the kindness of his brethren for the discharge
of episcopal duty. When his Convention met, " with a sore
heart he found himself unable to submit his address otherwise than through the borrowed medium of another's voice,
in his own absence, enforced by bodily weakness." This
weakness was such that his address was perforce brief. He
had reached, he said, the conclusion that he must ask for
the " canonical assistance to a permanently disabled bishop ;
but on seeking the needed professional opinion justifying
his conclusion, his medical advisers thought that he ought
not to consider himself permanently disabled." In reference
to this communication the Convention unanimously expressed
their sympathy and their sincere hope " that the diocese may
soon enjoy again the full benefit of episcopal supervision
which has been so highly prized, and the absence of which
is so deeply felt throughout the community." They also requested " the bishop to take such a vacation from all official

cares, with such entire repose of mind and body as may be recommended by his medical advisers."

This rest was sought on the coast of New Jersey. But in order to secure the benefit of change of scene, together with that of rest, friends in Baltimore urged the bishop to go abroad, and furnished the means without which he could not have done so. South America was thought of, but he concluded to go again to England. After a week or more pleasantly spent in Exeter he took lodgings at Sidmouth, on the coast of Devon, where some time was spent in entire seclusion, restful indeed to body, but very wearisome to spirit.

Home letters that immediately follow this chapter tell all the story of this visit to the land that was in many respects more to him than any other.

The expression of his loneliness so moved Mrs. Whittingham that she determined to go to her husband. On receiving notice of her intention, unwilling to subject her to a sea voyage which she particularly dreaded, the bishop decided that he would shorten his stay in England. The telegram which he sent to announce his speedy return to America, and so prevent Mrs. Whittingham's voyage, happened to be the first private message borne by the cable. Correspondence with Mr. Grafton, then in England, shows that the bishop was also influenced by reports of political riots in Baltimore, exaggerated accounts of the contest against the party placed in power during the war. Before the correction came the bishop had sailed for the home where he thought he ought to be in times of disturbance. To Mr. Grafton was left the charge to meet Mrs. Whittingham should she be already on her way.

The bishop's health was partially restored by sea air and his too brief stay in England ; but the effect was transient. To the Convention of 1867 he wrote :—

Again I am indebted to the kindness of another for help to discharge a duty which, in my own person, I am unable to fulfil.

After spending several months in quiet seclusion, and in travel on

the ocean, with much advantage to my health in most respects, I had
hoped to be able gradually to resume the public functions of my
ministry as the pleasant season of the year advanced. But on the
first attempt, a few weeks ago, my voice proved to be wholly inadequate to the strain, and after only three brief services, I have since
remained without the power to speak above my breath.

My presence with you in such condition could be only an embarrassment and a hindrance, from which I feel bound to deliver you,
even at the cost of the sacrifice of my own advantage and exceeding
joy in partaking together with you of the refreshments of joint worship and fraternal intercourse.

His long-continued disability was felt by the bishop to
impose on him the necessity of seeking permanent relief for
the diocese. In his address he discussed two modes of action,
neither capable of bringing about immediate relief. He
might ask for an assistant. One could be obtained in about
nine months. But many in the diocese would oppose the
election of an assistant bishop under any circumstances.

When the election of an assistant was before the Convention a few years later, debate showed that this opposition
was chiefly confined to the clergy and was, in the main, based
on the estimate of what its bishop is to a diocese, a head—a
father; now there cannot be two fathers in one family, and
a body with two heads is a monster. But an assistant
bishop, whatever his inherent dignity and powers because of
consecration, is in a diocese not even a *locum tenens;* he is
but a helper doing duty assigned to him by his head. Such
was the estimate placed on himself by Bishop Pinkney so
long as he was an assistant. When asked, " Did you sanction
such an act?" his answer was, " No! neither that practice, nor any other. I sanction nothing. If you ask my
opinion, I say I do not approve the practice. But I do not
go beyond the expression of my opinion. In the diocese I
do only what I am told to do."

Without sharing that conviction [that an assistant should not be
chosen under any circumstances] in its rigid strictness, I have myself, said the bishop, grave doubts of the consistency of such action

with the principles of the constitution of the Church in this country, and with the tenor of precedent in ecclesiastical history.

Such weight have those doubts with me, that where a gain of only nine months could be accomplished, . . . I should unhesitatingly prefer to resign my office, rather than, with an uneasy conscience, ask a relief of the lawfulness of which I did not feel a full assurance.

I cannot, therefore, now ask you to provide in that way for the necessities of the diocese, even if I were sure—which is far from being the case—that under the terms of our canon I might lawfully do so.

My resignation, if now offered, could only take effect upon its acceptance by the House of Bishops. . . [Which might be obtained in six or eight months]. It is for you to determine whether it shall be sought. On expression of such a desire from you, I will most cheerfully send in my resignation and join you in petitioning the House of Bishops for its acceptance. . . The remaining alternative is the division of the diocese.

Since the first year of my experience in office, I have been thoroughly satisfied that the Diocese of Maryland would never thrive as it ought and might do, until divided into three or more. . . . History, reflection, observation, and experience have combined in my considerations to create in me a conviction, only weaker than divine faith, that a diocese like this, and this diocese in particular, can never thrive until reduced into at least three dioceses of manageable size, of homogeneous constitution, of natural affinity, and having each its individual idiosyncrasy. . . .

In order to such division, I hereby place at the free disposal of the Convention every right and claim which I have, or which it may be imagined that I have, as bishop of the diocese. I make no reservation of any whatsoever. I desire everything in relation to jurisdiction, income, oversight, control, or use, which may now belong to the Bishop of the Diocese of Maryland as at present constituted, to be wholly and unreservedly at the disposal of the Convention, and I hereby do formally assign and declare it so to be.

Nothing could more gratify me than such action of the Convention as should divide the present jurisdiction and income of the diocese into three, and set off with its equal share of the diocesan fund and its proper proportional allotment of territorial jurisdiction, two new sees, of Washington and Easton.

In hope that your faith may be strengthened and your love increased, to see the way opened to the accomplishment of so great an onward movement, and with humble and earnest prayer that wisdom from on high and heavenly grace may be vouchsafed you in order to that end, I am, dear brethren, your poor, inefficient and unworthy, but truly loving brother and servant in the Lord.

Knowing that they had the full sympathy of the bishop, members of the diocese on the Eastern Shore had long sought a separate organization. Before the war they had twice asked leave of the Convention to separate, and at one time seemed to have attained their wishes; fortunately, as subsequent events proved, the bare majority in their favor was changed by votes cast by permission of the House to a like majority against them. They had again come this year prepared to press their request. As a body the petitioners were the same, for it is the abiding, not the floating, members who have really the interest of a diocese at heart.

The address of the bishop was thankfully received as an unlooked for aid. With this aid success was readily obtained. But all men do not share the bishop's convictions urged by him in so remarkable a spirit of self-forgetting. Even yet are lauded the advantages of large respectable bodies in which the presbytery are rightly influential, in contrast with the evils of small dioceses in which petty episcopal over-rule is felt. In conservative Maryland the thought of change was grievous, especially to some of the native clergy. This was betokened by the respected President, Dr. McKenney, who, overpowered by his feelings, could scarcely announce the vote which gave permission for the setting off the Eastern Shore as a separate diocese. In his response to the official notice of this consent the bishop said:

While the contemplation of separation from my brethren on the Eastern Shore, with whom, without a breach of any kind in the cordiality of our official and personal relations, I have been so long connected, is to me most painful, I am consoled under it by the entire persuasion that it is for the advancement of the glory of God, and the good of his Church on earth.

Perhaps the Bishop of Maryland recognized the difficulties attending small dioceses as clearly as do those who oppose division on the plea that it multiplies autocrats. More than once he has been heard to say that none need oversight more than the overseers, that bishops need canonical restraints. But his cure for the evil has not yet been tried. He desired what he believed to be primitive episcopacy, dioceses of such size that a bishop should be, not simply a presiding officer, but a pastor "having personal knowledge of his people." He wished for country bishops as well as city bishops, associated in provinces, and so securing the advantages attributed to larger dioceses. Some of his brethren who agreed with him in general, differed from him in their estimate of their office, and one avowed that he could not understand what was said by him about having personal knowledge of one's people.

During the Convention of 1868 the House of Clerical and Lay Deputies proposed to change the constitution so as to remove all restrictions on the division of dioceses, excepting that no city should form more than one diocese, and with the proviso that before General Convention could give assent to any division, assurance must be had that a suitable provision had been made for the support of the episcopate in the new diocese.

As chairman of the committee to whom, in the House of Bishops, these amendments were submitted, Bishop Whittingham reported against the proviso regarding the salary of a bishop, and in favor of the removal of all restrictions on division, save that there should be but one bishop in a city. Not denying the force of what was said in favor of large dioceses, he argued that "there was a choice between the human element and the divine; each a true element, each having its place." A substitute for his report, based on what he would have described as the human element, was carried by a majority of twenty-five to eight.

At this General Convention of 1868, consent was given

for the division of Maryland as proposed. In November of the same year the primary Convention met. The Right Reverend Dr. Lay, Missionary Bishop of Arkansas, was chosen first bishop, and in due time he was translated. Thus the Diocese of Easton was fully organized.

In conformity with the recommendation of the bishop, and a resolution of Convention, there was promptly transferred to the new diocese an equitable proportion of the episcopal fund, a sum greater than the amount contributed by the Eastern Shore to the general fund.

Time has shown the wisdom of the separation : in 1881 the number of clergy in the mother diocese was greater than the two could claim at the time of the division, and both dioceses have grown the more, doubtless, because of the more effective episcopal supervision.

It has been seen that in 1867 the bishop advised the division of Maryland into at least three dioceses. The committee to whom was referred this portion of the address, after the setting off of the Eastern Shore for one diocese, reported that they concurred in the plan for the further division, only they were not prepared to recommend the line of division proposed in the address, and suggested instead that a committee be appointed to consider and report at the next Convention the best plan and outlines for the division proposed.

Your committee, they said, is unanimously of the opinion that some plan of division is desirable, and almost necessary, and that it ought to be settled in time for final action by the next general Convention.

In order to facilitate such division of the diocese our respected diocesan finally places at the disposal of this Convention every right and claim which he has, or may be imagined to have, as bishop of the present diocese, making no reservation whatever.

The Convention will doubtless appreciate, as your committee does, the magnanimity of this offer. It is entirely of a piece with the disinterestedness and spirit of self-sacrifice which has distinguished our bishop's administration of his sacred office, and which

in this diocese we do not account rare because we have been taught
by him to regard it as an essential grace and virtue of the episcopate. Of course we cannot accept the offer, or recommend the
Convention to accept it, in any way that would trench upon the mod-
est salary hitherto given to the bishop.

In accordance with the suggestion made a committee was
appointed to report to the next Convention. They failed
to agree; and, after long discussion of various proposed
lines, it was observed that the Convention had no assurance
whatever that any of those whom it was proposed to cut
off desired separation. A report by an investigating committee, in 1869, showed so little agreement that the question
for the further division of Maryland was for the time
abandoned.

In 1867, in view of the fact that the then contemplated
division of Maryland into a number of small sees might
tend to impair the unity and harmony belonging to dioceses
co-terminous with States, and detract at the same time from
"the dignity of the episcopate, and might prove detrimen-
tal to many objects of common interest, or at all events deprive the Church of that prestige which arises from her
appealing to those honorable sentiments which cluster
around the name of each State," in order to guard against
possible losses of this kind a committee was appointed to
mature some plan "by which common counsel and action
and unity in all matters of common interest may be secured
among the sees into which the present Diocese of Maryland
may hereafter be divided, and to report such plan at the
next Diocesan Convention."

In 1868 this committee presented a report "On the Provincial System," written by their chairman, Dr. Mahan,
too long to be copied, yet too able and interesting not to be
referred to. It was printed with the Convention Journal
of that year. After long discussion the resolutions attached
to this report were adopted.

1st. Recommending a council of the dioceses in Maryland, through their representatives, "to consider and adopt measures for a permanent synodical or conventional union.

2d. That this Convention petition the next General Convention for such modifications of the constitution and canons as shall enable dioceses formed within the limits of any diocese to organize among themselves a conciliar union.

3d. That this Convention also petition the next General Convention to take the necessary steps for authorizing the erection of provincial courts of appeal.

In response to the petition of the delegates from Maryland, the General Convention enacted the canon "authorizing the formation of a federate Convention," etc., but took no notice of the prayer respecting courts of appeals, if authority to erect such be not given under the general terms of the canon.

In 1869 representatives of the Diocese of Easton attended the Maryland Convention to express the sense of their convention on the separation now formally completed, their thanks for the generous action of the mother diocese, and also the hope that the two dioceses "may still be united in common counsel and action, . . . in all matters of common interest."

Meeting this courteous advance the Maryland Convention appointed a committee to confer with one acting in the name of Easton, and "to mature a proper plan for the organization of a federate Convention of the two dioceses." The joint committee recognizing that "it is greatly to be desired that the bonds of unity and fraternal love should be preserved unbroken between the two dioceses, and cordial co-operation be secured in all matters touching common welfare," through their secretary recommended to the Convention of Maryland, in 1870, a plan of federation. After long debate the consideration of the subject was "postponed until the next annual Convention," and was not then resumed.

It is to be remarked that a plan, the success of which was

much desired by Bishop Whittingham as the beginning of better diocesan relations, was defeated by the votes of those who held opinions supposed to prevail among Southern churchmen; and yet, as Dr. Mahan remarked in his report on the Provincial System:

When it was first proposed, but a few years since, to the dioceses of our Southern States, at a critical period of their history, it was adopted almost by acclamation. By a slight change, which was less a change than a return to first principles, it was agreed that their general Convention or Council should be made a council of States or Provinces, rather than of dioceses. Each province, in that case might have as many dioceses as it needed, and might hold its own councils of those dioceses, without the least danger or alarm. Each diocese, in like manner, might have, as now, its own conventions or convocations.

When, in 1867, the bishop recommended a division of the diocese, he did not believe that he could lawfully ask for an assistant. Certainly his action during the general Convention the next year did not consist with a supposition of permanent disability. He was in his place in the House of Bishops at every meeting, on every day, and his attendance was continuous. He did his share of committee duty, and engaged in the discussion of every important matter, besides attending meetings of missionary boards, etc. The call of duty on such occasions seemed always to infuse new life and strength. A reaction often followed; but the fear of this never deterred him from attendance on the meetings of his brethren the bishops. After his labors in the General Convention of 1868 he was wholly exhausted; and the May following he was constrained to say to his Convention:

The rendering of this slender account [of diocesan work done during the year] may serve to introduce and justify a communication which it costs me much to make.

After nine and twenty years of endeavor, always weak and imperfect, and often, to my full consciousness miserably futile, but still honest and earnest endeavor to serve this diocese in my office, the experiment of the last three years has proved to me that I must either be content to lie as an incubus upon my people, pressing down their energies and thwarting instead of forwarding their work, or must set before them my hopelessness of fulfilling the measure of official duty which their needs require.

I have my own views of what it were best for me to do in this state of our relations; but I defer to those of others when I adopt the course of informing you that I have no longer room for doubt that my case comes within the purview of Section V. of Canon 13 of the Digest; and that if the Convention should think proper to take action under that canon for the relief of the diocese, it will, in so doing, have my frank and cheerfully accorded concurrence and consent.

The committee to whom was referred this portion of the bishop's address thought it unadvisable to make any provision looking to the election of an assistant bishop. They recommended the adoption of resolutions appropriating a sum of money to enable the bishop to defray the expenses of such aid as he might think proper to obtain in the exercise of his episcopal functions; and also, on the part of the Convention, tendering

to its beloved father and chief pastor its deepest sympathy and regret at the occasion of his present appeal, with their earnest prayer to the great Head of the Church, that with the divine blessing upon the measure of relief thus given, his health may be restored, and that the admirable results of his early ministry may be equalled, if not surpassed, by the riper fruits of the future.

The resolutions were unanimously adopted; but yet, in order to meet possible contingencies, a resolution was passed enabling the Convention, under the provisions of the constitution, to elect an assistant in 1870, should it be then found advisable to do so.

When the bishop met the Convention in 1870 he had again to call on another to read his address; in the last five years he had been able but once to dispense with this help. It was not that loss of voice was permanent, but it was frequent, and failure occurred sometimes without warning.

In this address he spoke of the diocese with more of warmth than he had shown during a long while.

We have now, he said, in this diocese precisely the number of clergymen that were at work in all Maryland in 1855, and I am thoroughly satisfied, from careful inquiry and ample sources of information that the services and attendance of this diocese in the present year are fully double those of the undivided diocese fifteen years ago. This is a great thing to say, because it amounts to an affirmation, that the working efficiency of our clergy has doubled itself in half a generation; but I feel confident of the accuracy of the statement, and deem myself bound to make it in justice to my hard-working—in human computation ill-supported and miserably remunerated, but nobly successful, and of God, after the wishes of their own hearts, gloriously rewarded—brethren. If ever patient continuance in well-doing had its reward, even in the present fruits of labor, church work in Maryland is now recompensing the earnest, indomitable zeal of the unpretending, suffering men who make so large a proportion of those engaged in it. Not always provided adequately even with that "food and raiment" which an apostolic rule recognizes as needful wherewith to be content, the rectors of our rural parishes, and—the more shame for us!—of not a few churches which are not rural—plod on in uncomplaining penury, increasing work with no proportionate increase of worldly gain; but, surely, we may hope! and, God be thanked! we do find ample reason to believe, with compensating reward in that at which they aim, and for which they endure and strive, the winning of perishing souls for Christ. Never among us has so large a proportion of the harder and more worldly sex been brought to an avowal of the influence of ministerial work as now. The number of adult males among the unusually numerous candidates for confirmation in the past year has been far beyond all previous example. The attendance of men at all our services, of all kinds, is daily becoming in increased proportion. And, best of all, a spirit of devotion of themselves to doing good for Christ's sake, and in his name, seems to be at last taking hold of our laity of both sexes, and developing itself in voluntary help rendered to the clergy by guilds of young men and sisterhoods in several of our congregations.

It was well known that an effort would be made this year to elect an assistant bishop. Referring to this purpose the bishop said : " I have nothing to add to my communications already made. The welfare of the diocese is in your hands."

After the opening services the bishop asked the Convention to elect a President, and retired. On the second day, during the afternoon session, which was prolonged into the night, it was resolved to proceed to the election of an assistant bishop. But yet of ninety clergymen twenty-four were still opposed to any election. Four persons were nominated, and eight were voted for. On the first balloting the Rev. Dr. William Pinkney received within one of the required two-thirds majority. On the second there were cast in his favor far more than the number necessary, and the nomination of the clergy being made to the laity it was confirmed by nearly the entire vote. The election was then made unanimous. From his ordination Dr. Pinkney had been associated with the old High Church party. On this account he was not the choice of some, and others did not forget that he had not been " loyal ; " but his nomination was equivalent to election. No man not a Southerner could have been chosen, and at the time there was a persuasion that the laity would accept only a native Marylander. One forcible objection to the office of assistant bishop is the possibility of a bishop's attempting to control the choice of his assistant and successor. Without attributing any improper motive, it is said that a bishop must be more than man not to desire to direct the selection of one to be brought into such close relations with himself. This objection would not be heard if all men had the simple faith given to Bishop Whittingham—his trust in the government of divine providence. Whatever might have been his power to influence, by no word or deed did he seek to exert it. The man chosen by those with whom the right of choice rested he received as sent to him by the Head of the Church, and no token of loving welcome from man to man could have been warmer than was shown to the newly elected assistant when, accompanied by a common personal friend, he first called on his chief. This visit was made immediately after Dr. Pinkney had received the congratulations of the members of the Convention, on which occasion—after presentation to the Convention, and after having heard the pledge of cordial support given in their name by their President—with voice tremulous with emotion he said :

Dear Brethren of the Clergy, and dear Brethren of the Laity :
Overwhelmed as I am by this most unexpected and unmerited token of your confidence and love, I can only say I am profoundly grateful. And yet, when I cast my eyes around me, and see so many presbyters beloved who would have worn this mantle with inexpressible dignity and grace, and brought to the discharge of the high duties of this most fearful office a ripeness of experience, wisdom, learning, eloquence, zeal, and energy to which I can lay no claim whatever, I am as deeply humbled. Should your choice meet the approval of the several Standing Committees and bishops of the Church, and my own mind and heart be brought to the conviction that it is my duty to take up the banner of the Cross, as your leader, wishing and seeking to act, at all times and under all circumstances, in the most cordial and fraternal co-operation with the most eminent and distinguished bishop who has for so many years guided the destinies of this diocese, and whose rare learning and burning eloquence have made him so signally known beyond our borders, I shall have to draw very largely on your forbearance and brotherly sympathy.

Having spent the largest portion of my life in the rural districts, there is no part of the field in which I shall take a livelier interest than that, in which a noble band of presbyters and deacons are now serving the Church in a spirit of the sublimest self-sacrifice, in a beautiful contentment with their lot, and a voluntary poverty endured for God and his holy household. Words are powerless to express the feelings that at this moment move me. Deeds, not words, you have a right to expect; for deeds alone can test the issues of this hour.

You have called me from a field of labor where I was happy, and more than satisfied—from a people who have never tired in the kindest offices of love, and who have ever woven around my heart cords, the severance of which must cost me intensest agony. If I am constrained to turn from them to you, I shall confidently look to the clergy and laity of the Diocese of Maryland for a generous construction of my motives, and a warm-hearted sympathy in my cares and trials, and I know I shall not be disappointed.

I leave you, with these few words, to face the responsibility of this hour; and, if confirmed by the Church at large, solve the great question of duty in the chamber of my own heart.

The humbleness which characterizes this reply of Dr. Pinkney is seen also in his first address as assistant bishop.

All that I can hope to do is to labor prayerfully and in meekness of spirit for the good of the body over which I am called to watch as one who must give account. Such as I have I give unto you. For the poverty of the offering others are responsible; for I sought not you, but you me.

Dr. Pinkney was consecrated to the episcopate on October 6, 1870, in Washington City, in the Church of the Epiphany, from some reason preferred to the Ascension, of which he had been rector. Unhappily the Bishop of Maryland was, at the time, ill in New Jersey.

The third decade of Dr. Whittingham's episcopate closed with the event which, with deepest gratitude to God, he acknowledged to be a happy provision for the supply of defect of service, the consecration of his "most willing and indefatigable assistant."

Every such period in every man's life brings changes to him. These ten years in the bishop's life are marked by strong contrasts. He was at the height of prosperity, more loved as a bishop and having greater influence than ever before, at the time when throughout the land—throughout his diocese, at any rate—men were in perplexity, their hearts failing for looking after what came too surely. When the distress was near at hand perplexity came to the bishop too, through the necessity of deciding as to duty; then, as a consequence of his honest decision, faithfully followed, came a falling away of those in whom he had trusted, and the occasion for censure on his part. Despite the support from conviction of being in the right, and afterward, for a time, of the natural strengthening which comes from condemnation of those opposed to one, the years of the war were a season of weariness of spirit. Apart from sympathy with the suffering, and at times of anxiety for the success of the right, there was painful personal regret. One who saw in acts which had a political bearing his chief claim to be honored, telling of the pitiful social martyrdom which he bore, has said, " I was proud of him when he appeared in the chancel, and the disaffected would turn about and troop out of the church. *I* smiled in their faces, but the big tears would well up in *his* eyes."

When he had strength to go about the diocese, during a stay at home enforced in part because visitations in many cases were not desired, he gave himself to labor in his study. Much of the pains-requiring work he bestowed on hymnology was undergone during this dark season of the war.

He has declared that his main effort for his diocese during the war was to keep it from acts of schism, and that, with this end in view, the abstaining from doing anything was often the prompting of wisdom. The danger of schism was not passed when political seceders were conquered. The bishop knew this. It is not to be supposed that this knowledge prompted his acts in 1865 which have been treated of; but he would have been wise in his endeavors for the ready recognition of Southern brethren had he had no other motive. As has been said, his generosity after the subjection of the Southern States produced a great change in the feeling of many members of his diocese. Among the most open-handed in providing for his extra expenditures were men who had not hesitated to show their opposition during the war. I do not know that the bishop spoke of this change, but there is enough of evidence that the latter half of this decade was by it made much happier. There may be seen in his addresses tokens of a return of the old feeling of sympathy. During 1867 and 1868 he resumed his long-neglected diary; and here, with the record of daily

Hebrew readings and other studies, are seen the proofs of the happiness as a bishop which had returned to him. But while he was thus regaining his true hold on life, despite increasing infirmities of body—painful in themselves as well as trying because hindrances in the discharge of official duties—he suffered severely from the loss of friends by death. About the time of the setting off of the Eastern Shore, which in itself affected the character of the Convention, there were taken away a number of laymen who had been eminent in the diocese. The places have not been filled that were made vacant by the death of J. I. Donaldson, Judge Magruder, Judge Chambers, John Henry Alexander, Mason Campbell, and Hugh Davey Evans. Judge Chambers and Dr. Evans had been especially influential in Convention during long years; the former showing, perhaps, a little too much the management acquired in other deliberative bodies;—the latter not so brilliant, but equally forcible in argument, and more convincing by the assurance which waited on his words that his own convictions were presented to others in full charity. All these men had welcomed the bishop to Maryland, and had from the first, during more than thirty years, been his near friends, his counsellors and supporters. With Dr. Evans the bishop had maintained the closest relations; and no other loss could have been to him, as bishop, so serious as that of this most honored and discreet of friends. His estimate of the man was thus expressed to the Maryland Convention in 1869 :

Of our laity the senior member of this body, who had been returned to it for almost an ordinary lifetime with few and short interruptions, and had again and again represented us in the General Convention—Hugh Davey Evans, of St. Paul's Parish, in this city—fell asleep in Jesus, after only a few hours' serious illness, in last July. This Convention needs no testimony from me to the inestimable value of his Christian character and influence. His name, known and honored in our mother-country almost as in our own, will go down to posterity in association with those of Nelson and Watson, Wilberforce and Alexander Knox, as an illustrious example of those teaching laymen, who from time to time shine forth in adornment of the doctrine of Christ, by vindication in their own persons of the rights and obligations of the universal priesthood in his mystical body, the visible Church on earth.

At the time of his death Dr. Evans was a delegate to General Convention. The refusal to re-elect him as delegate to the Convention of 1862, which so angered his friend the bishop, was a mortification to the doctor. He did not appear again in the Maryland Convention until the year 1866, when his reception by old friends and admirers greatly gratified him.

On May 10th he had written to the bishop, who was then in New Jersey:

Apropos of the Convention I have a piece of news at which I know you will rejoice both on private and public grounds. I am to represent St. Paul's. This seems to involve the idea that the Southern sympathizers have given up the notion of working the Convention as a party machine.

On June 4th he again wrote:

My Dear Bishop:

I must congratulate you on the result of the late Convention. I confess that I went to it in some doubt as to my reception, but I soon felt like Charles II., when he said that everybody was so glad to see him that it must be his own fault that he stayed abroad so long. I gradually slipped into my former relations with the whole body and each of its members. My impression is that the effect of the Convention upon the Church, and upon society at large, has been very good.

LETTERS.

TO HIS DAUGHTER, MRS. WILMER.

Royal Clarence Hotel, Exeter,
Nineteenth Sunday after Trinity, October 7, 1866.

Dear Mary :

The incessant occupation of my mind with the thought of you and yours for the last three days, occasioned by your birthday (recurring now, as it first occurred, in my enforced absence from all that is near and dear to me) makes it a thing of course that this my weekly bulletin should be addressed to you.

I have to report progress, in one respect very good, in another doubtful. I cannot honestly say that I am much improved in health as yet. Almost every day, for a few hours together, I am encouraged to think I am, sometimes in one way, sometimes in another. But in ways just as various I find myself suddenly thrown back out of my fancies into the old cough, or debility, or feebleness of appetite, or sleeplessness, or weakening sweats. So that, on the whole, it seems to me about an even question whether as yet I am at all benefited by travel, or whether I am not, insensibly as it were, slowly but steadily wearing away.

Yet I have been greatly favored in my journey and in carrying out my plans. There has been no cold weather, so that the country yet wears its full and most beautifully pleasing and satisfying summer greenness and richness of vegetation. Nor has there been any storm, although I have seen the sun but for about two hours altogether, as yet, during the whole time that I have been in England. All the time the thermometer has ranged from 50° to 65°—never at night below the first, nor at noonday above the second.

And I have been wonderfully forwarded in the main object of my journey—securement of a quiet sunny nook, on the very edge of the sea, in a south-western exposure, perfectly sheltered from the north, east, and west.

At the hotel where I wrote my last to Maggie (the Queen's, Clifton) I met a companionable English clergyman, of good family (he ought to be, for he is one of *twenty* living sons and daughters, by the same parents, themselves still living), who, when he found out the object of my journey, said that at one of the two places which I named as in my mind—and which he perfectly concurred in thinking the best in England for my purpose—he had two brothers living, whom he was then on his way to see. As I must travel more slowly than he would, he cheerfully agreed to act as my avant-courier, and make inquiries about such lodgings as I would need. Accordingly he did, and through his kind aid I have gotten the coseyest rooms you can conceive, in a cottage under a hill, with the surf murmuring (or booming, as the case may be) under the windows out of which I look, with a shingly beach stretching half a mile in a crescent to the south-west, and a green hill, but steep, rising right up behind, at distance enough to leave the house perfectly dry and airy. O how intensely I wish it were possible that your mother could share with me the enjoyment of the wondrous contrast it presents to our lodgings at our American sea-side. The surroundings are so *utterly*, so inconceivably different. The house *more* retired than the Browns', and yet a noble church within five hundred yards, and all kinds of shops as near, accessible by thoroughly dry and clean paths or streets. Then there are walks extending for ten miles in all directions, dry in all but absolutely stormy weather, and a public promenade half a mile long, terminating in a clambering path and terraces, on the Beacon Hill, one hundred and fifty feet or so high, immediately over the sea. This place I went down to see on Friday, twenty miles by rail, and an exquisitive drive through the loveliest country in the world, over a high hill topped by an extensive "heath," and through two thoroughly English villages. Friday night I spent there, and returned hither yesterday. I had previously been, on Thursday, down to Exmouth (twelve miles by rail, at the mouth of the Exe) to see, before I should go to Sidmouth, whether that possibly might not suit me better. I found I could get excellent lodgings there, but considerably more expensive than I afterward found those of Sidmouth would be, and by no means as much to my fancy. A noble sea-wall, very fine terraces and walks, and excellent roads in all directions; but an air of fashion and affectation of gentility which did not at all suit me marred all the other advantages. The exposure very good, but not quite so thoroughly sheltered as that of Sidmouth. From Bristol, on Tuesday, I had gone to Wells, to see the noble cathedral. Singularly enough, just as it had happened in my former visit to England at St. Asaph's, I stumbled, without knowing it till there, upon the day of the annual meeting of the clergy of the diocese for my visit, so that I had the opportunity of hearing a service in the nave of the cathedral, and a good sermon from one of their best preachers, Canon Cook, and of seeing the venerable Bishop, Lord Auckland, who is dying by inches of softening of the brain, and as unfit for work now as I am. Still more singularly, on the railway platform I got into company with Mr. F. W. Dickenson (Dr. J. H. Alexander's friend, by my introduction), and on getting into the cars, whom should I plump down beside but Archdeacon Denison, one of the leading men in the English Church, with whom I soon got into a most interesting conversation on their and our affairs. Of course I had to make myself known to him, and he professed himself extremely pleased to make my acquaintance. Returning to Bristol the same day, the next Wednesday I got here in time to attend cathedral service that afternoon. So I did the next morning before going to Exmouth, and Friday morning before going to Sidmouth, and yesterday afternoon after returning thence. To-day I have twice had the privilege of service at the cathedral; this morning with the Holy Communion, and a good sermon by the dean. This afternoon the immense building, at a service in the nave (not the choir), was perfectly crowded, and a more reverent service I never witnessed. A faithful sermon was earnestly delivered by one of the canons.

Love to Charles, and your mother and sister.

Your loving father,
W. R. WHITTINGHAM.

TO MISS M. H. WHITTINGHAM.

1 BEACON, SIDMOUTH,
Thursday Evening, October 11, 1866.

DARLING MAGGIE:

By a charming coincidence your letter announcing your receipt of the intelligence of my safe arrival on this side reached me, as it were, on the very threshold, on the eve of my occupation of my new temporary home. I left Exeter yesterday, dined at Honiton, came to a hotel here to tea and to pass the night and the forepart of this day—this afternoon having been named as the time when I could enter on possession of the delightfully cosey second-story room whence I write this, with the roaring sea thundering both in deep bass and in a sharp tenor (the rattle of the gravel of the beach) immediately beneath my window. I had written to Liverpool as soon as I engaged this place, ordering transmission of my letters hither, and the consequence was that yesterday yours, with one from Mr. Grafton, were put into my hand by the landlady as my first greeting. Oh, how pleasant it was to be thus welcomed and installed, as it were, into my new home by the dear ones at the real home where my heart is every hour of the day! (I keep the American time on my watch still, so that I see just how the day goes with you—at this moment it is 28 minutes past 3 on my watch, by the village time 20 minutes to 9. I have learned to tell the English time at once by mine.) But the great pleasure your letter gave me was sadly, *very* sadly, damped by the news about my kind, good, true friend, Captain Wallace.

How wonderful are the dispensations of that Providence which allows me, the poor, good-for-nothing, broken-down invalid to learn and comment on such a seizure of one whom five weeks ago I left seeming worth a hundred of me for all the work and chances of life! Oh, that it may please God speedily to restore him to his loving family. Give him and them my warmest love and assurance of deep and continual sympathy. Apart from that terrible change, the five short weeks that have passed have strangely changed the tenor of life for me! Here I am, *settled down*, my things in my drawers, almost at housekeeping (on the English plan, finding my own articles for consumption, my landlady doing the shopping, marketing, cooking, etc.!).

Tell your mother there is plenty of room for her if she can only just get across the water—and I am, oh! so lonely! But, really, the place seems to be the very ideal of what I wanted—so snug, so sheltered, so dry, so airy, with such a sea-view and such high, dry, never-endingly turning and twisting land-walks between hedges full of birds and flowers, with the sweetest views by land and by sea at every corner. The little bay is about a mile and a half across, with bold headlands more than five hundred feet high (bluffs, shelving sheer down into the sea) at each extremity—dry, smooth, gravel paths leading up to the top along the edge of each. To-day I made out to climb the south-easternmost—that farthest from my present dwelling, but nearest to the hotel where I was this morning —resting half a dozen times on the way. On the whole, I have been to-day, at various times, more than four hours walking in the open air, and shall probably be able to do as much most days. People speak of the weather as totally different here from what it is only a few miles inland—and, indeed, the plants show it—the garden hedges are full of laurustinums, daphnias, laurels, myrtles, etc., in the richest bloom, and the cottage windows of geraniums, cactuses, etc. By the by, there are plenty of real cottages—no sham about them—thatch, lattice, wicket, wicker cage with starling in it, and all the rest—and lots of rosy, apple-faced children toddling in and out and roundabout them (oh, how I wish your mother could hear the roar the sea gave just now! She would think *this* was living on the sea-shore, whether Captain Stockton's villa was or not!). I had not been in my room an hour before the vicar of the parish (Rev. Henry G. I. Clements) called upon me, evidently knowing who I was (so that I fear my friend Mr. Druce—the one-twentieth of his father's family—must have told upon me), and offering attentions, books, seat in the vicarage pew, etc. The church is less than ten minutes' walk from my room, but no daily service— only Wednesday and Friday mornings. I shall miss the cathedral services which I have been so very much enjoying at Exeter, and so delighted with seeing so many others enjoying; 100—never less than 100—and on Sunday afternoon, when the service is in the nave, between 2,000 and 3,000—nearer the last than the first. It is indeed heart-stirring to see how the Church in England is waking to her duty everywhere, and everywhere taking hold of the people in all practicable ways. New churches building everywhere, restoration of old ones going on, as the rule, not the exception; people flocking to them, even the coach-drivers telling with interest of the excellence and diligence of the clergy, as they pass their several places of residence or work. But I must put an end to my tale, or you will think that I have a rose-colored tinge in my visual organs! You may at least know by it that I feel better to-night, and really I conceive that my cough has been decidedly less troublesome last night and to-day than for some time past, and I relished hugely my first meal of nice tea, hot and well drawn, and the sweetest possible cream and bread and butter, in my new establishment. It had a good condiment, too, the perusal of the morning's London paper, containing a full report of the doings of the Church Congress in York yesterday, at which I see American bishops made no small figure. I shall send it to Dr. Dalrymple. To you I mean to send a first number of a new magazine just out, which I think you will like. Heart's love to all.

Your loving father,

W. R. W.

TO MRS. WHITTINGHAM.

SIDMOUTH, October 19, 1866.

DEAREST HANNAH:

Although I have been sorely disappointed in receiving no line from home this week, I will not break my habit of writing at least once a week. Thus far a good deal more. You may say . . . But— I'm disappointed, that's all. To-day begins my second week in my lodgings, and thus far my best expectations are very fairly realized. The weather has changed more than once, affording me opportunity to test the comforts, or otherwise, of the place in storm as well as (what in this part of the world they call) sunshine, and in pretty much all the winds that blow right on the beach, and send the sea in with all the force its power can give it. Two nights ago such a wind blew all the afternoon and night, and it was a grand enjoyment to look down upon the tossing waves, tumbling in as if in mad emulation to outdo each other in their leaps and gambols on the grinding mass of pebbles, which they pushed up and down from thirty to fifty feet on the shelving beach to the very foot of the cliff on which I sit perched in my cozy nest, just high enough to be out of their spray, and far enough below the top to allow the wind ample room for curving up quite above us, with hardly even an eddy to disturb our chimney draughts in our singular seclusion from its sweep. I find the roads and paths, too, of such dry material, and so well drained by constant change in elevation, as to be hardly at all affected by even heavy, soaking rain—of which we had a good deal on Sunday ; and through which, with a " water-proof" and " galoches " on, I was able to make my way to church with absolutely no discomfort to myself, and, I believe, stay there without much or any to others. I walk every day from two to four hours, an hour or so at a time. My cough varies a good deal—I can hardly make any guess why—but is on the whole, I think, lessened since my settlement— at any rate, it is decidely less troublesome to-day, without any very distinctly perceptible reason in the day, which is dull, or in the weather, in which a few faint gleams of sunshine now and then struggle through streaks of fog or spits of drizzling rain. I have been to-day, for the third day running (viz., Wednesday, St. Luke's Day, and Friday), to the week-day service in the parish church—a fine old building, admirably well restored a few years ago. To this the Queen was a large contributor, because her father sought refuge here in the close of his life, and died in a sequestered nook hardly a long stone's throw from the spot where I am now writing. By the by, at this juncture " landlady " comes in and lays the cloth for my solitary dinner, which I take at the (for England) barbarous hour of 2 P.M. However, did I care to do so, all I would have to do, in order to be in rule, would be to call it "lunch " and say nothing about my dining hour, into which it would be nobody's business to inquire. As it is, I am snugly through my dinner and have it cleared away before the hour for " calls." So it proved the other day (Wednesday), when Sir John Coleridge and his nephew, the member for Exeter, came over from St. Mary Ottery (nine miles) to make me a morning call at 5 P.M., inviting me to the hospitalities of " Heath Court " (Sir John's residence), and offering books, personal attentions, etc., in the kindest manner. I suppose they must have heard of my being here from Archdeacon Denison, in consequence of my chance interview with him. How they found out my nest in this thatched cottage—for so it is—I cannot guess. I " tea " at 7 and breakfast at 9. A little beaufet just opposite me holds my stores, tea, sugar—white and brown—wine (I take a glass of port every day, and porter, too). Once a week landlady brings her account for settlement—so many pence for butter, farthings for milk, and coals, candles, etc. It is a queer business, make the best of it ! But oh ! how lonely my solitary breakfasts, dinners, and teas do seem !

Here I broke off, dinner on table ! A mutton chop, mashed potatoes, bread, small bottle of stout (price 3½d.)—eat it, ring for remove, and landlady comes up—" Hope you liked it, sir ; " takes off, and sets on a bit of cheese—the seventh time the same has been on table, and it seems likely to last seven times more !—pat of butter (we buy by the half-quarter pound, price 1s. 5d. per pound), and bottle of wine, of which I take one glass. Ring again, landlady comes up, clears all away, and I sit down, desk on lap, at my window over the surf to wind up. I enclose a photogram of Sidmouth Esplanade, taken *from the east*, in which my house is a conspicuous object, viz., the house in the background, with two seemingly long windows (they are not so, but really distinct in the two stories) to the left. The path-like stripe in the middle, running from the background to the fore, is the sea-wall. Look with a magnifier. N. B.—The fat lady in the foreground is *not* my landlady ! Love to all.

P. S.—While writing I am called on by Sir John Kennaway and his son, who have ridden eight miles to see me—neighbors of Sir J. Coleridge. They bring me a brace of partridges—an important contribution toward housekeeping.

TO THE REV. DR. KERFOOT.

MARRIAGE AND DIVORCE.

BALTIMORE, Good Friday, 1861.

MY DEAR KERFOOT:

In answer to your grave inquiry in relation to poor Margaret, I send you a copy of what I wrote some years ago and have more than once copied for use in like cases. I prefer using the old answer, as it obviates any suspicion of prejudice in the particular case, and, by proving the generality of the rule, relieves its unwelcome bearing from the additional odium of being the imposition of an individual hardship.

Your case is complicated, but all its complications fall aside in direct view of the main question behind them—Is she married to the first husband?

Copy.—My dear ——: The case you submit to me is indeed a hard one, but a very plain one. "Whom God hath joined together let not man put asunder." The State may dissolve the marriage bond when the parties are hopelessly separated, *e.g.*, by imprisonment for life, because the State knows of this life only and of nothing beyond this life. But the Church knows and can know of but one cause of dissolution of the marriage tie besides death. As a member of the Church the injured woman whose husband has been taken from her has no course but that of chaste widowhood. Her wrong knows no means of redress. So much the worse for those who did it. Her part is to humble herself under the mighty hand of God and patiently submit to her privation. The duty of the Church, and therefore of her ministers, to such is to teach them the benefit of affliction and the duty of chastity—not to relax her discipline to enable them to obtain relief by a sinful disregard of bonds sacred as ever, however man may have interfered with them.

The "mercy, not sacrifice" which God would have in such a case cannot, surely, be the prostitution of the blessing of the Church to sanction bigamy, but the treatment of the sin of such, should they in their own ignorance, and through want of instruction and care on the part of those from whom it is due, fall into sin, with greater lenity than could be shown it under other circumstances. A connection formed in such circumstances would be adultery, whether the marriage service were used or not. The question is not, Shall the Church become partner in the crime by blessing it?—but, in case the Church is not successful in hindering it, Shall she treat it with the severity which would be due in other circumstances?

To God, I should say, a case like this must be committed. He knows the ignorance and the weakness which alone can excuse a second marriage under such circumstances. If he sees them to be a sufficient excuse, he will never impute the want of the sanction of the Church as an additional fault. He will never suffer the exclusion from the communion of the Church which must follow an unsanctified marriage to be a spiritual injury to those whom he condemns not for the step which has made it inevitable. But while I would leave open this door of hope for the poor victim of oppression and neglect (oppression placing her under temptation, and neglect disenabling her from enduring it), I cannot understand it as in the least affecting the course of the Church. The Church can only know that the woman might abstain from second marriage, that she ought to do so, and that her weakness, however it may avail as an excuse for her with God, can furnish no justification for a sanction of it by the Church. Faithfully, etc.,

W. R. W.

TO THE REV. J. R. JOHNSON.

CANDIDATES FOR HOLY ORDERS : THEIR RELATION TO THE BISHOP AND HIS FREEDOM IN ORDAINING.

BALTIMORE, February 8, 1862.

My DEAR DOCTOR :

I am heartily glad of any occasion for renewing our too infrequent intercourse, especially if I can in so doing be of any kind of use to you.

On the case stated by you, I regard Mr. Richey's views as entirely and fundamentally wrong ; and he certainly is quite in error as regards the Maryland practice.

It so happens that within the current year an applicant for recommendation to be admitted a candidate for holy orders was refused testimonials by the Standing Committee, because (through a mere oversight) he had failed to hand in the customary written certificate from me that he had given me notice, etc.

Now that certificate I hold myself bound to give only after having consented to the postulant's application for testimonials. I have in repeated instances, in the exercise of my discretion, delayed it or totally withheld it, as circumstances seemed to me to require.

Certainly no candidate would obtain testimonals from the Standing Committee of Maryland, under precedent of past practice, of whom the committee had not received evidence of the bishop's approbation and consent to his application.

Nor, on the other hand, have I ever supposed myself concluded by the reception of testimonials from the Standing Committee, in regard of the admission of a candidate. On any ground arising subsequently to my transmission of the first certificate of notice, etc., to the committee, I hold myself perfectly free, and if the case be such, bound to refuse admission, notwithstanding any testimonials or recommendation.

The whole course of preparation for holy orders is, I take it, and ever has been, unreservedly and unlimitedly within the bishop's negative. Canons can limit the bishop's right to confer orders to almost any conceivable extent; but no canons ever have, and no canons ever can, limit or control the bishop's right to refuse orders; and what he can do at the last stage of preparation he can, *a fortiori*, do at any earlier stage. He is, of course, accountable for the use of this absolute exercise of the ordaining power, under liability to procedure against him for malversation in office, but, as I suppose, in that mode only.

It may serve to confirm this view to point out that, while cases of erasion from the list of candidates, from one cause or another, are not unfrequently occurring, there is no provision on the subject in the canons—it being well understood to be a matter at all times within his exclusive province. A canon might provide that in certain contingencies a bishop should be held to erase a name; but it would be an unheard-of thing in church legislation to inhibit him from doing it at his pleasure. He might be required to use certain formalities which would amount to a restriction—as in our Church is done by binding him to notify all the other bishops of the case whenever it occurs—but while the tendency of all such action would be to make the bishop careful about his grounds and reasons of procedure, it would not in the least affect his absolute indefeasible right of decision. Even the English law-books make no question of that, and while they tie the hands of a bishop of the Establishment in almost every other conceivable matter, they admit no right of questioning his exercise of the ordaining power. His return of "*minus sufficiens*" is held to be a perfect estoppal of a patron's claim to have a presentee ordained in order to induction. The English Church has no proper candidateship, and the "testimonials" there go directly from the parish to the bishop, who judges of the whole case once for all. This seems to me to have led Mr. Richey into error in thinking that because our Church had shifted the duty of trying the return upon the "*siquis*" to the Standing Committee, it had done also what no church in Christendom ever did, and that all the churches in Christendom could not do, transferred the bishop's absolute negative to that body, so far as candidateship is concerned. The Church could, if it so pleased, make a class of persons from among whom only its bishops should be allowed to ordain; but it could not make them its bishops' candidates—they would be whomsoever the bishops themselves should see fit to recognize as such. Our canon recognizes the whole distinction in providing that whom the bishop "may admit" he "shall record." . . .

W. R. W.

TO HIS SON.

ON TITHES AND ECONOMY.

APRIL 5, 1862.

DEAR HARRY:

. . . As you are now a man of fixed income, however small as yet, still, owing to your peculiarly fortunate position, more than adequate to your absolute needs, let me as your loving father earnestly advise you to the practice, by fixed, irrevocable resolve, of two things:

1. Set apart the tenth for religious and charitable uses.

Do it whenever you receive your income, in advance; then you know just what your charity-purse is, and can use it on principle.

Be assured, my son, that the money so laid out will bring you royal interest—be the surest and most productive investment that you can make.

2. So apportion your expenses as to your income as that you shall have a fixed residue every quarter for investment in some way or other. A business man is bound, I think, to aim at some accumulation, and when on salary can only make it that way. Be it ever so little, only be sure that it is what you think it ought to be, and that it is actually made, regularly as the receipts come. . . .

Your loving father,   W. R. W.

THE RT. REV. WILLIAM H. ODENHEIMER, D.D.

TO OVERCOME DIFFICULTIES IN SEEKING ORDERS A GOOD PREPARATION FOR THE MINISTRY.

BALTIMORE, November 20, 1862.

MY DEAR BISHOP:

I have not recently made any inquiry about the doings of the "Society for the Increase of the Ministry," but have hitherto thought it right to hold aloof from it, partly in doubt about the principle of its operations and partly from dissatisfaction with some of its proceedings.

I doubt about the principle of the Society in two regards :

1. As to the expediency of holding out the kind of inducement to candidates for holy orders which it affords.

Since forty years' observation of the results of that procedure has wrought in me a strong conviction that the Church is more hindered than helped by it. The twenty years of my own diocesan administration have furnished a good deal of counter-evidence—in favor of letting the encounter of difficulties in preparing for the ministry be one of the tests of fitness, and at the same time an important element of training. Some of my best men I can distinctly perceive to have been much benefited by what seemed to them at the time the great hardship of being totally without such help as it is the aim and business of the "Society for the Increase etc." to afford.

2. As to the consistency of the operations of such a central voluntary association (administered as it needs must be by a more or less "close corporation " of priests and laymen) with the Catholic principle (hitherto so largely preserved inviolate in our branch of the Church) of episcopal supervision of the preparation of candidates for the ministry, with the distinct diocesan responsibility for its conduct and management. I have suffered from encroachments of *soi-disant* "evangelical" associations of the kind, and once at least was annoyed by an overture of this very Society to provide reading for my candidate.

This last particular brings out the second of my grounds of doubt—dissatisfaction with the *modus operandi*. Hitherto it has seemed to me inclined to the "noisy" and "fussy" line, while the very necessity of the case has driven it to a scheme of organized agency throughout the dioceses which must, if successful, go far to change fundamentally the system of preparation for the ministry throughout the Church, and break up the lines of diocesan influence in almost the last remaining province.

Some of these reasons I have stated, more or less distinctly, in conversation with one or two of the friends of the Society, and some I intimated a few years ago in answer to a letter of inquiry from the Rev. Mr. Childs (I think), acting in behalf of a committee of the Pennsylvania Convention.

Faithfully and affectionately yours,

W. R. W.

TO THE REV. LEIGHTON COLEMAN, BUSTLETON, PA.

THE RUBRIC CONSIDERED WHICH REQUIRES CONFIRMATION TO PRECEDE ADMISSION TO COMMUNION.

BALTIMORE, February 10, 1863.

REV. AND DEAR SIR :

I do not like to leave your questions, of moment in themselves, and honestly and intelligently put, without such answer as I may be able to give; and yet, before affording it, I feel bound to remark that, in my humble judgment, it would have been sought with more propriety from him whom the constitution of the Church makes your ordinary, to solve and direct in all doubtful cases of church administrations and observances. What I have to say can in no sense serve as your direction; answers of your bishop to the same questions would be such, with all sufficiency for your ecclesiastical warrant and for the quiet of your own conscience.

I do not think that the rubric at the end of the Order of Confirmation applies to the case of " chance" or " non-parochial " communicants. That the Church recognizes the distinction between such and communing parishioners, appears from the rubric in the English Prayer-book requiring notice to the officiating priest of persons intending to commune—a rubric with which I have more than once had occasion to comply in England and its dependencies. The omission of that rubric from our Prayer-book sets wide open the door for such " chance" or " non-parochial " communication, leaving to the individual conscience the application of the invitation by way of sanctioning approach, and of the exhortation by way of limiting it, or in the Scotch phrase, "fencing the table."

This omission makes the only term of such occasional communication by " non-parochians " freedom from heresy and schism.

Heresy is provided against by the use of the Nicene Creed, which in theory does, and in practice ought to, follow the Gospel. Its public rehearsal by the whole congregation includes every one present and assisting in its declaration of the one true Holy Catholic and Apostolic faith.

Schism is renounced by the very act of receiving the Holy Communion in the Church from the Church after the mode prescribed and practised by the Church.

A *soi-disant* " Presbyterian " seeking the holy gifts from an Episcopalian priest, and kneeling to receive them with his declaration that in them he gives to the individual receiver the Blessed Body and Blood, is no schismatic in any real ecclesiastical sense—no

denier of the Church's orders, of her administrations, or of her
Divine character and warrant as keeper and conveyer of the Lord's
Holy Mysteries.

Such " Presbyterian " so receiving I regard as the occasional and
non-parochial communicant whom the Church distinguishes from
the parochial communicant who can only become such by being admitted and enrolled.

Nor do I conceive it to be any duty (nor therefore any right) of
the parish priest to inquire even into the fact of the baptized condition of such " occasional or non-parochial" communicant.   That inquiry was given up in the relinquishment of the English requisition
of "notice."

Whatever you and I may think of such laxity of discipline, it is
no part of our responsibility, nor have we the privilege or obligation to endeavor its correction.   Our private judgment is precluded
by the action of the Church.   Terms of communion are not at the
will of the individual officiant.   What the Church (whether wisely or
not) leaves open, it is not for you or me to shut.

The last-made remark is the principle on which those who, like
me, have settled convictions about the invalidity of lay-baptism
are prevented from making episcopal baptism a *sine qua non* of
communion.   The Church has left the validity of non-episcopalian
baptism undecided by keeping the greater question of lay-baptism
in that condition, and because the Church has left it undecided I
must, in the individual application, when the question is fitness for
communion.

The same principle settles your other question.   " Confirmation "
is what the Church requires as a pre-requisite to admission of a parishioner to communion, but she has nowhere limited herself to the
recognition of confirmation episcopally administered, and therefore
whatever you or I may think of the laying on of hands by others
than bishops, or elsewhere than within the pale of the only constituted Church of Christ, we have no right to draw a line, by our own
private determination of fitly right, within that drawn by the generality of the language of the Church.

On this ground you cannot be wrong in admitting a Moravian to
communion on the ground of his confirmation.

I am not sure that the Moravians restrict the administration of confirmation to their bishops.   If I were assured that they do, I should
be of opinion that their admission on the ground of such confirmation was clearly right, inasmuch as the *prima facie* claim of their
episcopacy and apostolicity has been made out to the satisfaction of

such men as Archbishop Potter. Maitland and others, within the last thirty years, have assailed the Moravian episcopacy, as I think, without success.

Very faithfully your friend, etc.,   W. R. W.

<hr>

TO THE RT. REV. A. POTTER, D.D.

SMALL DIOCESES: THEY MEET PRESBYTERIAN OBJECTIONS.

BALTIMORE, June 8, 1863.

MY DEAR BISHOP :

I think the "project" of mine, to which you refer as contemplating the division of a diocese with some remaining afilliation between the parts, must be the notice offered in 1856 of a proposed amendment of Article V. of the Constitution, somewhat to the effect of which you write. It may be found at p. 205 of the *Journal of Gen. Con.* of 1856, and on p. 189 of the *Journal* of 1859 a report upon it by Bishops Elliott, Johns, and Upfold.

I never preferred that plan for myself, nor desired to see it rather than simple division carried out in Maryland. But I proposed it as a plan likely in my judgment to meet the most serious objections urged against small dioceses, and for that reason to obtain more general concurrence than might otherwise be expected. I therefore was ready then, and am still, to accept it myself and render all the assistance I can to its adoption and effective execution.

I am thoroughly satisfied that to live and grow at all in this country our Church must greatly diminish the size, and therefore multiply the number, of her dioceses ; and I as firmly believe that the adoption of the primitive standard of diocesan limits, by which, in ordinary circumstances, a bishop should be placed wherever a county court is held (the centres of ecclesiastical and civil jurisdiction being made the same), would, by depriving Presbyterian episcopacy of its one element of truth, bring back multitudes of the followers of parity and congregationalism into the fold of the Church. We need it as much for the restoration of the true pastoral office (both as exercised by presbyters and overseen by bishops) as we do for the prosecution of the missionary trust. Neither can the Church have any genuine efficacy, until she have her country bishops as well as city bishops ; and the latter only with an average of more than from thirty to fifty congregations.

Such are my very deeply settled convictions, strengthening by every year's experience, as well as the fruit of all my studies.

Faithfully and affectionately yours,
W. R. W.

TO THE REV. R. M. ABERCROMBIE.

ON THE FILIOQUE.

BALTIMORE, October 19, 1863.

REV. AND DEAR SIR:

I beg you to accept my thanks for the kind courtesy to which I have been indebted for the opportunity of perusing your "Apology for the Graeco-Russian Church." . . .

You will perhaps pardon me for reminding you that as a presbyter of the Protestant Episcopal Church in the United States, you are under obligation to teach the procession of the Holy Ghost from the Father and the Son by the terms of the fifth of our articles of religion.

I believe that doctrine to be holden by the Holy Orthodox Church, although resisted as an imposition *de fide ;* and to be in accordance with Catholic verity, as ascertained by the Vincentian rule.

As for the clause "filioque," while, in my private judgment, I could wish that it had never been inserted in the liturgical form of the Creed, yet I know no act or document by which our branch of the Church is committed to the assertion of the necessity of the clause to the integrity of the Creed ; much less to the maintenance of its indispensableness as a term of Catholic communion. But while the clause is received and held by the Church in this country as part of our synactical form of the Creed, I conceive that no member of the Church, of any order, has the right to gainsay its doctrine.

With regard to the continuance of the clause in that position, I doubt the right of the American branch of our communion (the Anglo-Hibernico- Scotico-Americano-Colonial), in good faith, to act alone for its removal ; and have no doubt of the great inexpediency of such solitary action, yet should be very willing to enter into joint action of all the branches for that purpose ; and should it ever fall to my lot to have a voice in such a procedure, would, as at present advised, be disposed to give it in favor of the change.

Very faithfully your obliged friend and brother,

W. R. W.

TO THE RT. REV. H. POTTER, D.D., BISHOP OF NEW YORK.

ON SISTERHOODS.

BALTIMORE, November 3, 1863.

MY DEAR BISHOP :

In my endeavors to foster and mould into useful shape the good will of pious women desirous of having a set share in the work of the Church I have encountered much of the same kind of difficulty which has embarrassed you.

I have not yet attained to results which I can venture to propose for imitation. Although much urged to frame definite rules for permanent obedience, I have not yet believed myself qualified for doing so by adequate experience.

In 1856 I accepted, with a good deal of hesitancy, the immediate oversight of an association which had been gradually shaping itself in the two previous years, and was then working under a constitution and rules of its own formation and adoption.*

I made it a condition of my acceptance that the immediate pastoral oversight and official direction should be vested in a presbyter of my appointing, to act under me, and in my absence for me. . . . I have from time to time participated in the conduct of this association by personal assistance at its meetings, etc., and intervention for settlement of its difficulties, personal disagreements, misunderstandings, etc., of which there have been no few. The last mentioned drawback, though very serious, by no means surprised or disappointed me, and does not at all discourage me.

The vice-rectors under me during the nine years of the work have been five. I have had but one "first sister"—now "chief deaconess"—who still fills that office. It is of all parts of the organization the most difficult to provide, and the most important. Our civil calamities, after threatening total dissolution to this association, as well as to much else, have resulted in the growth of an offset in a body of sisters, dismissed at their own request, and re-associated under a presbyter of their own choice—with my consent—as a parochial institution of the same nature, and for the same work as the diocesan, but with no claim to recognition outside of the parochial limits of its rector.

The foregoing statements I give as answer to your first question, "How far are the sisters under my immediate supervision?"

The second, "What have I done, and what do I think best with regard to a ceremonial" for admission? I answer by submitting to you the office used for that purpose, drawn up and adopted after a good deal of deliberation.

You ask, thirdly, "What effect my experience has had on my opinion of the usefulness of 'sisters' for our Church in its present state?"

I answer—Decidedly to increase my conviction that they are needed and may be made greatly profitable.

---

* The bishop "hesitated about taking the immediate oversight." But his advice had been sought at every step taken in the formation of the association.

The difficulties by which I have been met and beset throughout have largely tended to the growth and settlement of such conviction. I think I have encountered most forms that are to be expected of opposition, hindrance, embarrassment, and entanglement; and I feel sure that all are quite within management by the legitimate authority and means of the Church, without any departure from her principles, or serious innovation in her practice; and equally sure that the results are worth the pains.

Fourthly you ask after printed rules. For the reasons stated in the outset we have none.   .   .   .

Faithfully and affectionately,

W. R. W.

THE REV. J. R. HUBARD, CHESTERTOWN.

A DEACON NOT AUTHORIZED TO BAPTIZE AN ADULT.

MAY 31, 1864.

REV. AND DEAR SIR:

.   .   .   There is no just room for doubt that the Church does not allow the baptism of adults by deacons, sanctioning their administration of the sacrament to infants only in the case of absence of a priest.

This becomes certain by noting three facts: 1. That, down to 1660, the Ordinal ran, "It pertaineth to the office of a deacon to baptize and to preach, if he be admitted thereto by the bishop," making both functions dependent on such admission, and both without other limitation.   2. That during all that time the English Church had no office for the baptism of adults—contemplated no other baptism than that of infants.   During all that time no priest could baptize an adult without previous notification of the bishop. 3. That in 1660 it was found needful to provide for adult baptism, to which end the office for its administration was introduced; and that then the Ordinal was so altered as to run, "in the absence of the priest to baptize infants, and to preach if he be admitted thereto by the bishop"—thus, 1, distinguishing between baptizing and preaching, and making admission by the bishop requisite only to the latter; and 2, limiting the power to baptize, thus freed from reference to the bishop, to the class of infants (alone in contemplation previously, but now known in the practice of the Church as having another class, "adults," joined with it) and to the circumstance of absence of the priest.   .   .   .

Faithfully yours,

W. R. W.

TO THE REV. C. W. RANKIN.

THERE SHOULD BE NO PUBLIC RECONCILIATION OF A ROMAN CATHOLIC LAYMAN.

MADISON AVENUE, December 29, 1864.

REV. AND DEAR BROTHER:

Our Church having made no provision for the reconciliation of persons leaving the Roman or any other schism, I presume that the matter rests where it is ruled to lie in the English Church, with the several bishops, each to regulate his respective diocese in that regard.

I should have no objection (but rather the contrary) to the use of some such form as was prepared under Archbishop Tennison (Cardwell Synodalia, II., No. xl., p. 796) for submission to convocation, in order to its adoption for general use in the Church of England; but then I should insist upon its equitable inclusion (as is the case in the form referred to) of all modes of heresy and schism. In the case of lay reconciliation I think it unfair, if not dishonest, to employ the solemn formalities of a public service to signalize the reception into communion of one coming from an ecclesiastically constituted body in which all the faith is held (however overburdened with corruptions of doctrine and practice), and to set no such note on those who have been participant in unecclesiastical organizations, and trained in modes of belief always sadly defective and often contaminated with the present heresies.

The public reconciliation of a Roman priest is a process of the very reverse character, resulting from the discrimination in his favor of his not being required to be re-ordained, while the dissenting teacher is. Having to discharge the public duties of the ministry it is very fit and right that his acknowledgment as a minister should be publicly signalized; while, if that is done, it is obviously proper that the same publicity should be given to his renunciation of the errors in which his ministry had heretofore been involved.

As there is no prospect at present of success in an effort to introduce the practice of public reconciliation of schismatics generally, I think it much preferable not to attempt anything of the kind in the case of return from the Roman schism.

There would be no objection, of course, to the private use of Archbishop Tennison's form, or an equivalent, by a parish priest, in his discharge of pastoral duty, rather at the house of the person to be reconciled, or in his own study, or even in the church, not in the public service, and not before a public congregation. The public act, as I take it, belongs exclusively to the episcopal office and direction. As charged with that responsibility I do not feel myself at liberty, for the reasons given, to sanction it.

Very faithfully your friend and brother,

W. R. W.,
Bishop of Maryland.

TO THE REV. M. L. OLD.

THE BISHOP'S PROPOSED HYMNAL—WHAT HYMNS OUGHT TO BE.

BALTIMORE, St. Andrew's, 1865.

. . . . I expect to have the pleasure of sending you, in a week or two, a specimen of a hymnal, which, as a member of the committee on the subject, it is my intention to submit to that committee whenever it shall meet for action. It contains a number of translations from the German, more from ancient sources, and a considerable variety of English hymns, all carefully adapted to the great norm of common worship afforded in the Prayer-Book.

The duty of the Church, as I suppose, is to mould the popular heart—not to have its worship moulded by it.

I am afraid it is too generally forgotten with regard to hymns that they are a part of worship—in which both reverence toward God and honest conviction of the heart accompanying the utterance of the lips are equally essential. People may be made hypocrites by being taught to sing what in their mouths are lies—an evil which long opportunity of observation has given me occasion to know to be fearfully prevalent in more than one denomination of the Christian sects by which we are surrounded.

Very faithfully and affectionately,
Your friend and brother,
W. R. W.

TO THE REV. WM. F. B.

COUNSELS OF PERFECTION.

BALTIMORE, January 30, 1867.

MY DEAR BRAND :

. . . As regards the " counsels," the received solution of the difficulty seems to me simple and satisfactory. The law of Christ is principle, not rule. Principle relates to ends ; rule to means. The principle underlying the " counsels " is love in its widest stretch and highest reach ; the love of God in the heart working it-self out in the love of man in the life.

The "counsels" themselves are, as it were, samples of the operation of the principle ; suggestive applications to practice ; advisory specifications of ways and means.

The difficulty about them has arisen from mistaking them for rules.

That mistake grows out of another and deeper, which, I think, also underlies the other difficulty about authority ; it is the very root of what in the Western Church developed into Romanism—I mean the untrustful and undutiful disposition to refuse God's saving mercies on his own wise and loving terms, and decline responsibility commensurate to blessing.

His terms are, the conscious choice of what he offers by the individual will taking counsel with the individual conscience under the prompting, enlightenment, and assistance of the Holy Spirit.

That prompting, enlightenment, and assistance are pledged only to the individual will and conscience so receiving them, and our whole present state is probationary just in so far as the process of such reception and use is carried on. Romanism, in all its branches, is the outgrowth of effort to escape that process of probation—to do a life-work, once for all, in the juggling process of substituting authority for responsibility, by leaping into the pit of infallible direction by human agency ; or to make the work of life a fixed routine, once for all entered and adopted, instead of a continual series of successive questions for determination by the will and conscience. (Note how in the Psalms, especially that wondrous one which the Eastern Church makes the daily lesson of her faithful children, the ἄμωμος (Ps. 119), the adverbials תָּמִיד and עֵקֶב come out as the condition of true inner life in victory ; and how being "kept" in the ever prosecuted "way" is the holy writer's ever-present conception of saintliness of character.)

The continual, never-ceasing, unending training of the will and conscience in their ever newly arising need of application to successive questions of expedience in the ways and means of carrying out principles of duty as modified by individual circumstances (viz., gifts, surroundings, opportunities, emergent claims, natural and social obligations, providential calls), is the divinely ordained mean of training man in the fellowship of God in Christ. Romanism shuffles it aside for man's inventions of authoritative churchly rule and counsels of perfection taken as a higher law.

So of the determination of doctrine—the difficulty arises from the desire for what is never to be obtained from external sources, absolute certainty. Comparative certainty—probability relatively commensurate with opportunity of knowledge and diligence in using it—is the divinely established condition of such knowledge as is the prerequisite of faith. Faith once exercised, the inward witness of peace and joy in believing, through conscious intercommunion with the divine teacher in the heart, supervenes. That witness may be obtained in almost every imaginable degree of enlightenment by outward knowledge, the only essential being true submission of the will to truth in its degree of ascertainment, and honest application of the conscience to the use of opportunity in the degree of its enjoyment. The same responsibility is exercised, with the same accountability for its exercise, in adopting "*Papa ex proprio motu*" for the rule of faith, as in adhering to Vincent's rule, the only difference being that the one choice does it once for all, the other holds it for a life-long operation, to go on under reservation of increased responsibility with increase of knowledge, throughout the whole course of individual development of intellectual power and attainment.

Which is in accordance with the ways of God's government in nature and in providence? Which with the whole tenor of his teaching in his word? Which with the promptings of the heart moved to seek its highest blessedness in the full and true enjoyment of fellowship with him? Most certainly not the condensing scheme—the plan of doing a life's work in the given number of hours needful to bring one's self into a state of spiritual "coma," and acquire the rigid, unfeeling tension of conscience overwrought in a task for which it was never meant, in which alone it is capable of acquiescing in a course so contradictory to its nature, its privilege, its powers as renewed in Christ, and its high career as opened before it in revelation of the new life in Christ, kept, guided, helped, brought onward, elevated ever more and more by ever-increasing measures of the Spirit vouchsafed in reward of ever-continuing struggles to obtain and use them.

On the whole, I think Archer Butler's book on "Development" most likely to meet your requirements as concerning the question of authority, it being a healthy and true book, written out of the fulness of his own convictions by one who was every inch a man.

On the "Evangelical Counsels," Thorndike's treatment of the subject in the last chapter of the third book of his "Epilogue" is about as satisfactory as anything I know. It is an enlargement of Field's in § 13 of the appendix to the third book of his treatise of the Church. Jeremy Taylor also treats of it in his " *Ductor Dubitantium*," Book II., ciii., rule 12, and Book III., civ., § 12. A man of a very different school, Penrose, has some observations in his work on " Christian Sincerity " (p. 116), and his treatise on " Human Motives " (App., p. 374), which, although superficial, are worth comparing with the others.

On the other hand, Mountagu, in his " Appeale to Cæsar," c. xvii.–xix., with a clear Anglican ring in his speech, vindicates the distinction between " counsels of perfection " and works of supererogation, without going into the ground and reasons of it.

I think the clear apprehension of the latter saves much labor in casuistry, and results in a better comprehension of the whole gist and bearing of the inquiry. As such I commend my poor attempt at the presentment of it to your charitable acceptance and quiet reflection.

Lovingly yours,   W. R. W.

TO THE REV. C. M. PARKMAN.

HAS HEARD OF THE VIOLATION OF DIOCESAN USAGE.

BALTIMORE, March 22, 1867.

MY DEAR PARKMAN :

I heard to-day in the course of an informal private conversation that you are using divers colors—red, green, etc.—in articles of your vesture in public worship, the tinkling of a bell in the course of your service, and perhaps other things until now unknown in the usages of worship in this diocese. You have hitherto professed some warmth of private regard for me, and great reverence for the office which I bear.

I rely on these professions for my warrant in this private appeal to you to spare me much pain—probably misery—at a time when I am little able to bear it, by surceasing from the things mentioned above, and from any other practice not now prevalent in this diocese. I verily believe them to be violations of the ordination vow, and am determined, so far as it shall please God to give me ability, to hinder their introduction within that portion of the Church for the conduct of which in his Providence he has made me answerable.

But I loathe the exercise of authority in such a case, and dread as exquisite torment the necessity of an appeal to law. Therefore I have recourse to the stronger power and better law of love, and implore you by your own personal affection for me, and by your filial regard for the fatherly counsels of your bishop, to surrender your own views of right and expedience, and give place to mine, in consideration of the different magnitudes of our responsibilities, and the difference of the weight of obligation in our respective trusts.

Your loving friend and brother,

W. R. W.

TO THE SAME.

PROTESTS AGAINST ALL IRREGULARITIES.

BALTIMORE, April 8, 1867.

DEAR PARKMAN:

Your explanation gladdens my heart, by its fulness, by its frankness, and by its conformity, for the most part, with the views and principles by which I am myself endeavoring to steer a difficult course through the shoals and quicksands of our very difficult times.

Nobody brought me tales of you. I believe nobody dares to bring me tales of any of my clergy. A consequence is that I am very ignorant of what many of them do (for instance, I now hear, for the first time, of those whole-rail-ful deliveries of the Holy Gifts at S. A., which, had I known of at the time, I should most assuredly have interposed to rectify, and not having the faculty of multi-presence, make a proportionately ineffective "overseer" of my work-ground.

I told you that the tale came to my knowledge fortuitously, in the course of a casual conversation. It was mentioned as part of what was being said in a conversation on the topic about which the ill-advised "Declaration" has set all loose-hung tongues a wagging. Nothing could have been more remote from the speaker's intention than that it should have been heard by me as a report by which you were to be affected.

And glad I am that I did hear it, and that I did then, as it is in such cases my rule to do, apply at once to the fountain-head of truth on the subject, for I am relieved from no inconsiderable uneasiness, and set at rest, once and for all, about the work which I never doubted you were doing with an honest and true heart, faithfully, and, as I fully believed, very successfully, but still thought it possible might have peculiarities arising from differing views which my view and my responsibilities might compel me, however much to my regret, to interfere with.

With the single exception of your mention of "a chasuble," I find nothing in your report of your "usages" which seems to me to admit question of its being within the liberty of an American presbyter—although I do not myself admit the correctness of quoting

"Sarum use " here, where "Sarum use " never had show of rule.   But
" a chasuble " is a vestment unknown to the American Church, and
its use is not in conformity with " the worship of THIS Church "—*i.e.*,
not the Church of England—far less the Church of Rome—not even
the Church Catholic—but THIS *branch* of the Church of Christ,
whether it be well-appointed for its work or ill-appointed—well-
governed or ill-governed—clad in the beauty of holiness or in unseemly rags.

Oh, dear brother, that we had more among us of the filial spirit
that can see a mother's face, and love it, even though the hard times
through which she has been brought have stripped her of most of
the seemly adornments of a Bride!   Still she *is* the Bride of Christ,
and her least breathing ought to be our law.

All irregularities I protest against—as much (and much more)
those of eight and twenty bishops as those of a solitary country
priest or deacon—all I loathe as indications of the old rebellion
which the father of lies and mischief began by setting up to be wise
on his own account.   From all, may the love of Him whose meat
and drink it was to do His Father's will deliver us.

Your loving friend and brother,

W. R. WHITTINGHAM.

———

TO THE REV. J. H. DRUMM.

ON MEDIÆVALISTS AND SOME OF THEIR OPPONENTS.

BALTIMORE, February 20, 1867.

REV. AND DEAR SIR :

I am free to say . . . 3, that I have no sympathy with those
who wish to dress up in cast-off mediævalism ; 4, that I hold the
law, both canon and common, of the American Church to be clearly
against any use among us of the English imbroglio of statutes, injunctions, rubrics, and absolescent canons ; but also, 5, that I have
a thorough contempt for those in this country who, themselves in
the open and persistent habit of falling far short of the prescriptions
of the Church with regard to ritual and worship, avail themselves of
the English difficulties to make an outcry against pretended dangers
not threatening us in this country, for the dishonest purpose of
throwing unfounded obloquy upon those who are truer than themselves to the mind and usage of the Church.

I hardly need say that I am well assured how far you are from
joining in such a work.

Faithfully and truly your obliged friend and brother,

W. R. W.

TO A BROTHER BISHOP.

THE AUTHORITY OF THE INSTITUTION OFFICE—THE TABLE OF THE LORD AN ALTAR—THE MEMORIAL A SACRIFICE.

BALTIMORE, April 8, 1867.

RT. REV. AND DEAR SIR :

I am indebted to your courtesy, as I presume, for the receipt of a copy of your recent Pastoral Letter.

Permit me to call your attention to the fact that you have omitted to inform the Church, while you were instructing it as to the value of the Office of Institution of Ministers, that at the same Convention at which that office was considered for the second time, and finally adopted, the amendment of the Constitution by which "other offices of the Church" are placed on a level with the "Book of Common Prayer" "or the Articles of Religion" as regards authority and stability, was introduced, though without mention, then, of the Articles ; so that the origination of the difference which you think so important between the liability of canons, resolutions, etc., to change, and the permanent character of the Prayer-book, etc., had reference to the very "Office" in question, then immediately before the attention of the Convention ; and the subsequent ratification of the amendment necessarily had respect as much to the "Office" of Institution (so named by the Convention that originated the amendment) as to anything else named in the Article.

I was not aware that my junior brethren were "condemning" me, with others, in the paper lately put forth over their names, or I should have thought it needful to take precautions for my own defence against a mode of trial so wholly unprovided for in the written legislation of the Church.

As it is, I must be content to take shelter from the pressure of the authority of the Bishop of ——— behind the venerable names of Andrewes and Beveridge, and Thomas Wilson ; and hold myself still at liberty with them to think and call the $\tau\rho\acute{a}\pi\epsilon\zeta\alpha\ \kappa\nu\rho\acute{\iota}o\nu$ an altar, and that which is "done" there as a "memorial" a sacrifice, until they, with Zauchius of Strasburg, and Bullinger of Zurich, be condemned of heresy, for maintaining the sacrificial character of the Holy Eucharist.

With very great respect your brother and servant,

W. R. W.

TO THE RT. REV. H. POTTER, D.D.

OF THE MEETING OF THE BISHOPS IN LAMBETH: SOME THINGS WORTHY OF THEIR ATTENTION.

BALTIMORE, June 12, 1867.

MY DEAR BISHOP:

. . . I now know that it will not be in my power to go to Europe.

In doubt whether that might not be the case, and in the earnest desire of contributing all in my power toward the interest and authoritative import of the meeting, I took the opportunity of the assemblage of my Diocesan Convention to lay before that body the invitation received from the Archbishop of Canterbury, and ask the expression of the views of the clergy and laity upon the subject. A very gratifying vote, *nemine contradicente*, expressed hearty concurrence in the objects and ends of the proposed meeting, so that this diocese—bishop, clergy, and laity—stands committed to the movement of which the meeting of bishops can only be regarded as the initiative step.

What is to follow I cannot prognosticate, and am not careful, fully believing that it is in the hand of One whose wisdom and love are pledged to overrule even the evil that finds its way into His household for the advancement of His own glory in its general good.

.   .   .   .

Two things seem to me worthy of the attention of the meeting.

1. Some distinct settlement of the degrees of relation between bishops, from the (possible) equivalent of the old chorepis-copus, up through diocesan, provincial, and exarchical (or national) arrangements, to the Primus who, by whatever name, must exercise the convening and presiding authority of the whole communion.

2. Some discriminative arrangement of the formularies of doctrine and discipline, by which those not to be touched, except by the whole communion, shall be agreed upon, whether articles of religion, offices, liturgy, or canons, and those matters in which all shall know themselves free to consult the wants of their several States, nations, or colonies, distinctly recognized.

I wish the result of such conference might sooner or later grow to be the adoption of an unchangeable—*i.e.*, unchangeable by any part of the whole communion; alterable only by action of the whole— liturgy, and baptismal and confirmation offices of obligatory use in all—with great freedom in all other services, and the recognition of those offices, the three creeds, the Catechism, and the Articles, as the equally unchangeable norm of doctrine. The ordinal, and a very few canons, might be agreed on, as the similarly general rule of discipline.

Of course, no action of the proposed meeting can go further than the mere origination of movement in the direction of such results. The tests of the wisdom of the meeting, in my poor judgment, will be, first, its clear recognition of results to be aimed at, and next, not least, its prudent selection of the measures by which movement toward those results is to be originated.

The so-called "ritual" difficulty I regard as a mere summer-cloud —stormy enough while it lasts, but sure to go over soon and leave the sky clear, and the earth refreshed. The latitudinarian tendencies are a far deeper evil—harder to get at, and harder to deal with when unearthed, but absolutely needing strict control and wise previsionary counsels. . . .

I am, faithfully and affectionately,
Your friend and brother,
W. R. W.

THE REV. DR. OLSSEN.

FINE CHURCH MUSIC.

June 8, 1868.

Dear William:

I am at last through both my Convention week and my ordination week, and am beginning to look about me and try to collect my pretty much used-up faculties. The fortnight ended yesterday with a great "splurge" in St. Paul's. Such musical doings, the veracious chroniclers in the newspapers say, as never have been in Baltimore before—a terrible feather out of the cap of the Romanists, who have claimed hitherto the undisputed and indisputable pre-eminence in that line. Think of one hundred and fifty singers! and six trumpets! and the two best violins in Baltimore! and trombones, and bassviols, and what not—all in addition to one of the best organs in the country. I rather wonder that I survive it!! I couldn't help asking the rector, while I was signing the letters of orders in the vestry-room after all was over, whether we had been particularly devout that morning? Certes we had a particularly numerous assemblage of spectators and auditors!

Your loving brother,   W. R. W.

CHAPTER IV.

1871.

In his address to the Convention in 1871 the bishop said:
"My own work, through continual feebleness, has been of
slender amount and mostly confined to the city of Washington."

If, in accordance with his recommendation, the diocese
had been divided into three sees, that of Maryland, of Easton, and of Washington, there is little doubt that the bishop
would have chosen Washington. He would have done so
because in his feebleness he could better meet the requirements of a small and compact diocese; but not simply for
this reason. Some years before the war Mr. Beresford-
Hope by letter pointed out the great benefit likely to result
to the Church from the establishing of a cathedral at the seat
of the Federal Government. Bishop Whittingham had already entertained the opinions expressed by this liberal English churchman, and would have been glad to help to found a
diocese which would be, in some sense, national, and at least
be the means of presenting the Church in the fulness of its
claims before representative men from all parts of the continent. There were in Washington persons of influence
who wished the District to be independent, and who believed
Bishop Whittingham to be peculiarly fitted to be its first
bishop. Among these the rector of S. John's Church, in
Washington, was persuaded that many of the benefits of
an independent organization might be secured without the

separation that could not be then obtained. In 1870 he wrote to a number of bishops asking their opinions respecting a national church, and their judgment as to whether or not it would be lawful and proper for the Bishop of Maryland to give his episcopal services to the churches in the District and to entrust the remainder of the diocese to the care of the assistant bishop. The Bishop of Pittsburgh answered that a bishop cannot resign his jurisdiction, but he may assign to his assistant any special field of duty, and that his doing so is a matter which concerns the diocese only. Other bishops, who did more than express the approval of the establishing a national church, agreed with Bishop Kerfoot that it would be lawful for the Bishop of Maryland to confine his episcopal labor to any part of his diocese. The rector next attempted to obtain, by a general appeal, money to erect within his parish a free church which might at some time be the cathedral of a diocese, and for the present be such in effect—the bishop's church with a corps of clergy.

If the efforts of his zealous friend had not been opposed, the bishop might have seen fulfilled what had been a hope during a short while in the early days of his episcopate. Of course the first step toward the accomplishment of this proposal could not have been taken without the knowledge and assent of the bishop. It seemed to him so likely to be successful that he sent members of his family to Washington to examine a house which had been offered to him for a home, and plans were considered for the erecting a fireproof building for his library. To his great disappointment the scheme came to nothing. Not the scheme for erecting a new church—the parish church would have sufficed for the carrying out his chief wishes—but that which promised the organizing cathedral work. It lacked the approval of others of influence. The assistant bishop saw in it only the expression of a determination to do that to which the Convention had pointedly refused its assent. To what was said respecting the special needs of the District, he answered that the fact that within seven months he had visited nearly every parish and congregation was proof that he was able to do all the duty required by the whole diocese.

In Baltimore also, as was natural, friends objected to the removal of the bishop from their midst. Even Bishop Kerfoot, who could see no legal hindrance to what was proposed, while giving this judgment, felt it to be honest to add: "If you ask my private opinion I must say that, recalling my knowledge of things from 1842 to 1864, I would *not*, if I were still a presbyter of the diocese, heartily concur in the arrangement."

In 1871 the General Convention met in Baltimore. Only once before had its sessions been held here. How great the contrast between the assemblies! In the parsonage of S. Paul's Parish a room over the entrance hall is called the bishop's room, for herein the House of Bishops met in 1808. Its area is not more than ten or twelve feet square, yet there was ample room for the two Rt. Reverend Fathers who here took counsel together in the interest of the Church.* Fifty bishops attended their second meeting in Baltimore.

At the opening services and during a part of the sessions of this Convention there were present the Bishop of Lichfield, the Bishop of Nassau, the Dean of Chester, and five clergymen who accompanied them. Bishop Selwyn was the first bishop of the Church in England who had come to America.†

---

* The two who composed the House of Bishops in the Convention of 1808 were Bishops White, of Pennsylvania, and Claggett, of Maryland. There were then living also Bishops Jarvis, of Connecticut, Madison, of Virginia, Provoost, of New York (who claimed jurisdiction, although he performed no episcopal act), and Moore, who in the list of bishops is called assistant, but who was elected when Provoost was understood to have resigned.

† The first exercising at the time jurisdiction in an English see. The clergy who accompanied him were Ed. J. Edwards, Perp. C. of Trentham and Prebend of Lichfield, R.D.; J. A. Bangham, Vicar of Christ Church, L. and Prebend, R.D.; J. H. Iles, Rec. of S. Peter's, Wolverhampton, Preb. and R.D.; Frederick Willett, Vicar of West Bromwich, and the bishop's son, now himself bishop, J. R. Selwyn, Vicar of S. George's, Wolverhampton.

So remarkable an event as the visit of such and so many English churchmen demanded special recognition. The House of Bishops received their brethren and the dean with proper ceremony, and on the second day these dignitaries, with the accompanying clergy, visited by invitation the House of Deputies.

Each one was introduced to the House by its President with a speech of commendation. The response of the Bishop of Lichfield was one never to be forgotten by those who heard it. He had listened to a recital of the chief acts of his life and of his claims to the loving admiration of those before whom he stood, expressed in terms which possibly might have gratified vanity, which would have overwhelmed with confusion timid modesty, a recital which ended with : "I present to you the first Bishop of New Zealand, the Lord Bishop of Lichfield—the ILLUSTRIOUS SELWYN!" There was a pause which made one feel that the bishop was stilling a struggle ; and then, having returned thanks for the kindness shown him and for the honor intended, he said

that he was forced to appear ungracious ; that if a sense of his own worth could permit him to remain silent, and so seem to accept what had been said of him, yet justice to others would constrain him to say, It is not true. It had been said that as a fruit of his labors the world has seen a Christian nation born in a day. Not so. He had only entered on the labors of others.

[This fact he made clear by a relation of the mission work of Williams and of others, and by a sketch of his first visitation.]

It is not safe, he continued, to exalt men even if God have blessed their efforts in his service ; it is better every way to laud only Him without whose blessing there could be no increase. At any rate now, and as regards myself, I must make use of words first applied, though with a different purport, to one infinitely greater : "*Give God the praise ; we know that this man is a sinner.*"

One of the acts of the assembled bishops during this Convention, but in Council,* was to frame and sign a de-

---

* When the House of Bishops meets in council it is not as a co-ordinate branch of the legislative body, the General Convention.

claration that in their opinion the word regeneration in the Office for the Baptism of Infants "is not there so used as to determine that a moral change in the subject of baptism is wrought in the sacrament." This declaration was made, they say, "in order to the quieting the consciences of sundry members of the Church."

Such as did not believe that a "child being born in original sin, and in the wrath of God, is by the laver of regeneration received into the number of the children of God and heirs of everlasting life,"* must have stood in need of something to quiet their consciences when obliged to use even the modified baptismal services of our Church. Some clergymen boldly refused to say words which, taken in a literal and natural sense, contradict their estimate of the work of faith, and they had been for a time "contemplating action most earnestly to be deprecated."

Therefore, in the autumn of 1869, the leaders of the Evangelical party called a meeting, in New York, of clergymen and laymen from various parts of the country to aid them in deciding what should be done. The result was "the conviction that if alternate phrases or some equivalent modification in the Office for the Ministration of Baptism of Infants were allowed, the pressing necessity would be met, and a measure of relief would be afforded, of great importance to the peace and unity of the Church."

Being so persuaded, nine bishops conjointly addressed their brethren by letter and expressed the hope that there would be found in the next General Convention such largeheartedness as would consent to the relief indicated. Not that they needed relief personally, for, as they said, "We have always been fully persuaded that our formularies of faith and worship in their just interpretation embody the truth of Christ, are warranted by the teaching of Holy Scripture, and are a faithful following in the doctrines pro-

---

* The English office for the private baptism of children.

fessed and defended by our Anglican reformers. The difficulties referred to we ascribe in a great measure to the bold
innovations in doctrine and usage, which at the present
time so unhappily agitate our communion and expose the
Protestant and scriptural character of our Church to dis-
trust and reproach."

It is to be presumed that this appeal for modification of
the Church services was not met as had been hoped.

During the General Convention of 1871, Bishop Whittingham was approached by a brother bishop who had had
intimation given him of what would be received in lieu of
the desired alternate phrases, and at the solicitation of this
friend wrote the first draft of the declaration. It was in
these words :

We, the subscribers, bishops of the Protestant Episcopal Church
in the United States, being asked, for the quieting of the consciences
of sundry members of the Church, to declare our conviction whether
the words "regenerate," "regeneration," and equivalent terms used
in the offices of the Church mean such a moral change or renovation
of the heart as involves the submission of the will of the subject to
the converting influences of the Spirit of God, do declare our conviction that such is not their meaning as so used.

After modification by the bishop for whom it was written,
and several amendments in council, a substitute was offered
by an Evangelical bishop and adopted. Our bishop signed
the declaration, as did every bishop present excepting Dr.
Odenheimer, Bishop of New Jersey ; on his motion it was
entered on the minutes of the House of Bishops, and was
communicated to the House of Delegates as " a matter
deemed to be of much gravity and of great present interest."

It may not be meet to discuss the solemn utterance of the
fathers, but it may be noted that their definition of a Catholic term by a Protestant negation gave occasion to some to
assert that the bishops denied the spiritual efficacy of baptism ; while on the other hand the language of the Church
continued to be a burden to tender consciences, and the ten-

dency to schism was not checked; for even of those who signed the explanatory declaration, in less than two years one was the presiding bishop of the body of Reformed Episcopalians.

One is tempted to express surprise that this effort to quiet distressed consciences could have been supposed likely to serve its end. The mere fact, shown by the journal, that the declaration was made known to the delegates on the motion of Bishop Whittingham, must have been to all Evangelicals a reason for looking with surprise on this effort of the bishops to quiet consciences disturbed by the doctrine of regeneration in baptism. Ever since he had been known as a teacher he had been known as upholding the doctrine that those who are born in sin are born again in baptism— that they who are by nature the children of wrath are in baptism made the children of God; he had always maintained the literal significance of church formularies on the subject; he had republished, and he had had placed on the list of books recommended by the Sunday-School Union, "The Sacrament of Responsibility," a tract counted as a subversion of the Gospel by those whom he styled "a clique in the Church which arrogates to itself the exclusive right to be called evangelical." In 1860 he had a controversy in an evangelical newspaper touching the opinions of the English reformers concerning baptism, from which contest he retired, so his adversaries said, " utterly overwhelmed," but yet so convinced of success that he republished his articles * and his opponents' commentaries, prefaced by a more formal treatise on the same subject.

When at the General Convention in 1850, Bishop Whittingham proposed to his brethren a declaration on the subject of baptism that was positive, not negative. He did not seek their assent as a House or in Council, he asked

------

* Baptismal Regeneration held after Luther and Melanchthon by Cranmer, Ridley, and Latimer. Baltimore: Robinson, 1860.

only their signatures to it as individual witnesses to the truth.
It was in these words:

Whereas the minds of many in our several dioceses have been disturbed with doubts concerning the teaching of the Church, that in
the holy sacrament of baptism we are made members of Christ,
children of God, and inheritors of the kingdom of heaven, in so
much that some have fallen into the denial of the Article of the
Faith that there is "One baptism for the remission of sins:" We,
the subscribers, for ourselves as witnesses to the truth which we
have received, and in discharge of duty as teachers and overseers in
the Church of God, do, in testimony to the faith once delivered to
the saints, and for the establishment of the wavering and doubting,
hereby solemnly declare that it is the doctrine of Christ, as this
Church hath received the same, that every infant offered by the
Church to God in holy baptism is therein regenerated by his
grace, and receives remission of sins through the merits of Christ
our Lord: which doctrine we will, as in duty bound, maintain in-
corrupt and entire, as taught in the Catechism, Offices and Articles of the Protestant Episcopal Church in the United States of
America.

There were present at the Convention twenty-four bishops. Of these, thirteen were ready to give their signatures.
Five consented to the teaching, but were restrained from
signing by considerations of expediency; they were influenced by motives which led our bishop, when older, to
write *ne irritare crabrones*—Do not stir up a wasp's-nest.
Therefore the declaration was withheld, and this trumpet-
note with no uncertain sound was not heard by the Church.

In the early years of his episcopate Bishop Whittingham
was charged with being a Puseyite. This reproach was no
longer cast on any one. The movement had gone on, and
they who were now in the advance and were accused—as
the Puseyites had been—of Romanizing were called Ritualists.

In October, 1867, the bishops who had met to act on missionary matters spent a day in the consideration of the
Ritualistic movement, led to do so, it is said, by the publi-

cation, a few days before, of a small book on Ritualism by their presiding officer. A committee was appointed to draft a declaration of the opinions of such bishops as might sign it with respect to Ritualistic innovations.

In the following January this declaration was published, bearing the names of twenty-four bishops, among which was not that of the Bishop of Maryland.* The chief points in this manifesto are the assertion of the right of " this national Church " to prescribe its own ritual, and the condemnation of unauthorized vestments and usages, and in especial such usages "as indicate or imply that the sacrifice of our Divine Lord and Saviour, once offered, was not a full, perfect, and sufficient sacrifice, oblation, and satisfaction for the sins of the whole world."

Whatever of respect may be due to the opinions of a number of bishops, a paper which had been circulated through the post office for signature could not claim the authority of even the signers as an assembly.

When the House of Bishops next sat as a legislative body —in 1868—it was much occupied with Ritualism, more so than the published records indicate. An ineffectual effort was then made to have "the declaration of the twenty-four" adopted as the action of the House. At the same time the House of Deputies received and acted on memorials asking for the enforcement of uniformity in worship and for the repression of Ritualism. From the Committee on Canons, that considered these memorials, came a majority and a minority report. One clause in the latter is noteworthy: "While there is no absolute directory in the canons or rubrics of the Church specifying all official vestments and practices and all ecclesiastical ornaments which may be fitly used therein, yet there is the indication of great simplicity."

The result of the discussion was the adoption of resolu-

---

* Writing to one of the signers with reference to the declaration, the bishop says that his friend has " made a terrible mistake."

tions that the House of Bishops be requested to set forth for the consideration of the next Convention such additional rubrics as in their judgment may be necessary; and that in the meanwhile in all matters doubtful reference should be made to the ordinary, and that no changes should be made against his counsel.

The communication of these resolutions was gladly received, and on the motion of the Bishop of Maryland, the bishops with one voice answered that, in full trust that reference would be made to the ordinary and his judgment followed, " this House deems it unadvisable to enter upon any alteration of the rubrics . . . but that it will appoint a committee whose duty it shall be to consider whether any additional provision for uniformity by canon or otherwise is practicable and expedient, and to report to the next Convention."

In accordance with this promise a committee of five was appointed by the presiding officer. These bishops gave careful attention to their duty, and when the Convention met in Baltimore, made to their House a full report in which—while recognizing that non-essentials should never be unduly magnified and that substantial uniformity is compatible with very considerable individual liberty—they recommended canonical action on many points, specifying even what should be the canonical length of a cassock. The House of Bishops communicated this report to the deputies, but accompanied by resolutions, which had been offered by the Bishop of Maryland, which in effect recommitted the matters treated of to a joint committee, the episcopal members of which to be chosen by ballot.

By this joint committee, of which Bishop Whittingham was chairman, a canon was reported asserting—

1. That this Church recognizes no other law of ritual than such as it shall have itself accepted or provided. 2. Indicating the provision for ritual in this Church to be the Book of Common Prayer with the offices appended; the canons of the English Church in use in

the provinces before 1789, and not superseded etc., by legislation, general or diocesan; and the canonical or judicial action of the Church, or its decision in Convention, general or diocesan, or by its constituted authorities. 3. Declaring that the decision of all questions arising concerning ritual observances appertain to the office and duty of the ordinary.

And providing that contradictory decisions shall be subject to revision by the House of Bishops.

This proposed canon was drawn up by the chairman. With a limitation of the canons of the English Church to those of 1603, it was adopted by the House of Bishops; in the House of Deputies it was not received with equal favor. The Rev. Dr. Mead—the Nestor of the House—whose name as chairman on the part of the Deputies was affixed to the reported canon, would have amended it by a number of prohibitions, all affecting the service at the altar, yet without asserting, as had done the twenty-four bishops, that any act forbidden could imply that the sacrifice of our Lord once offered was not perfect. His and all other amendments were rejected, and finally the resolution of concurrence with the House of Bishops was lost. After this failure the bishops sent down a canon directed chiefly against acts implying adoration " toward " the elements in the Holy Communion. This, too, was not concurred in. In neither case was the proposed canon rejected by a majority; it was simply not passed by a majority of both orders.

In the considering of these two canons Ritualism was fully discussed. When a limit was fixed to the length of speeches those on this subject were excepted. Among those who opposed the proposed legislation, the Rev. Dr. De Koven was eminent. By his ability, his self-control, and his courteous bearing, he gained the respect of those who most regretted his position.

In themselves, vestments and outward acts, he said, are trifles about which men need not contend, either to maintain or to forbid them. They acquire importance only from truths they are intended to express, and these truths cannot be suppressed by the forbidding certain acts or the prescribing others ; the meaning attached to acts will be changed.　It is intended to prevent, by legislation, the outward expression of the recognition of the adorable presence in the house of God, and especially in the Holy Eucharist.　For himself he avowed firm belief in that presence, and he made his own the formula of Dr. Pusey, which the highest English court had pronounced to be not inconsistent with the doctrine of the Church—"I myself adore, and would teach my people to adore, Christ present in the elements under the form of bread and wine."　He was ready to obey any ordering of the Convention touching ritual, for there could be no canon passed that could prevent the prostration of his soul before his present Lord.

Although the subject treated by him in Convention did not lead him to express all his convictions respecting the Holy Eucharist, of a man so bold in the avowal of what many condemn as the idolatry of the mass, one looked up to as a leader, it may be added that soon after he declared, in a private conversation, that while confessing the habitual practice of what is denounced as eucharistic adoration, he yet did not hold all that is deduced by some from the doctrine of the real presence ; he did not accept that reasoning which has led to the Office of the Benediction of the Blessed Sacrament and to reservation as offering opportunity for the worship of Christ under the form of a consecrated element.*

The only action of this Convention on the matter of Ritualism was the passage of two resolutions which, without specifying any, condemned all observances and practices fitted to express a doctrine foreign to that set forth by the Church, and which declared the paternal counsel of the bishops to be sufficient to suppress all that is irregular and unseemly in public worship:—an impotent conclusion to efforts from which so much had been looked for.

That the Convention did not adopt the canon he had

---

* It must be added that while Dr. De Koven's challenge to be placed on trial for heresy was never accepted, yet his doctrine was received with but little favor in the House of Deputies.　As one of the members who heard him has since said, " His speech killed his prospects of being made bishop."

recommended was a disappointment to Bishop Whittingham. Not doubting that to the bishop belongs the ordering, in his diocese, all matters of ritual not ascertained by
law or fixed custom, and wishing to secure uniformity of action, before the bishops separated he offered in council a
resolution affirming that

The saying of the Lord's Prayer, or any other prayer, or part of a
prayer in the Office for the Holy Communion, in an inaudible tone
of voice;

The use of any posture in the administration of the Holy Communion not commanded or implied in the rubrics of the office;

The saying of the words of institution in the Prayer of Consecration in a low, inaudible tone;

The prostration of the celebrant, or of any assisting minister, in
any part of the public service;

The elevation of either the bread or the cup in any part of the
celebration;

The waving of either element in the delivery in the form of a
cross;

Or the use of bread made in the shape of a wafer or wafers, are
contrary to the law of ritual in this Church, and ought to be suppressed by the ordinary of his own motion.

The resolution was withdrawn: in his note, which is
here copied, the bishop does not say why. It is not hard
to conjecture that some others perceived that what was proposed to the council was legislation. Perhaps memory recalled a scene enacted in a former council, when the Bishop
of Maryland solemnly protested against like action on the
part of the body of bishops.

In 1853 Dr. Muhlenberg and others presented to the
bishops in council a memorial based on "the assumption that
our Church confined to the exercise of her present system is
not adequate to do the work of the Lord in this land and
age; that a wider door must be opened for admission to the
Gospel ministry, and therefore praying some ecclesiastical
system broader and more comprehensive," and especially
greater liberty in worship. This memorial was referred to

a committee, who in 1856 reported to the House of Bishops in General Convention a series of resolutions touching the use of the Prayer-book. These were not all reached in the course of legislation. When the first was passed, Bishop Whittingham, "holding that the House of Bishops has not, under the constitution . . . any power of legislation affecting the worship of the Church, except concurrently with the House of Clerical and Lay Deputies, and by alteration of the constitution, rubrics, or canons of the Church as they now exist, and that the resolution just passed does affect the obligation of ministers of this Church to conform to its worship, as regulated by the rubric and canons," dissented from the action of the House and offered his protest against the action so taken to be entered on the journal of the House.

The protest was received, but simply placed on file—not entered on the journal—and therefore the reason for the bishop's action does not appear in the printed volume. Doubtless the bishop perceived a difference between the concurrence which he asked and that which he opposed. The one was to be an agreement among the bishops as to the manner in which they should exercise inherent rights; the other sought the bestowal of new powers in the conducting worship. But yet if the bishop were right there would seem to have been no need for canons regulating ritual.

The legislative body of the Church has grown too numerous, and every three years sees an addition to the number. This inconvenience furnishes one objection to the multiplying of dioceses by division. The remedy is patent, and must perforce be adopted some day.

In 1871 Bishop Whittingham, whose name had long been associated with the advocacy of the provincial system, submitted to his brethren the consideration of this remedy. He proposed alterations of the constitution providing for the organization of eight provinces, the dioceses of each to meet in synod once in three years; and every tenth year a Provincial Synod to be held composed of representatives of the provinces, as the General Convention is now of representatives of the dioceses. The only immediate result of the bishop's action was the appointing of a committee to "consider and report to the next General Convention, etc."

During this Convention of 1871 Bishop Whittingham was enabled, as on all like occasions, to attend every meeting, and, as has been seen, to do his full share of the labor; [*] and besides this to so discharge his duties as host that the House of Bishops returned "their hearty thanks to their right reverend brother, the venerable Bishop of Maryland, for the large and loving attentions extended by himself and family to every member of the House during the sessions of the General Convention."

The Pastoral Letter of the House of Bishops in 1871 treated, in the main, of those matters connected with worship and doctrine about which the General Convention had been asked to legislate.

Repudiating "the popular idea that our Church is a middle way, elaborately contrived as a compromise between opposing systems, and asserting that as a witness to primitive truth she is subject to opposing lines of assault, and that our conflict on the right hand and on the left is with superstition and lawlessness, irreverence and unbelief," the bishops address their godly counsels to those in the Church to be counted as superstitious and lawless, or irreverent and unbelieving.

They communicate to the Church their declaration that the word regeneration in the Office for the Baptism of Infants does not determine that a moral change is wrought in the sacrament. They "entreat" that those infants whom Christ, through the agency of his Church, has taken into his arms and blessed be regarded "as his

---

[*] As an instance of his readiness to do any work, it may be mentioned that, with so many younger members in his House, he was always depended on to keep the run of the business coming from the House of Delegates, and to see that none of it became law by remaining unacted on more than three days. His methodical habits made this less of a burden to him than to others.

own children by adoption and grace, as heirs of God, to be brought up in the nurture and admonition of the Lord." But remember also, they continue, "that baptism does not supersede the necessity of repentance, of justifying faith in Christ, growth in grace and in that holiness without which no man shall see the Lord."

They do not say who they are in the Church who believe that baptism dispenses with the need of faith and growth in grace and holiness, or that a man who has sinned after baptism is forgiven without repentance.

"We counsel you," the bishops further say, "to bear in mind that while on the one hand we must not suffer ourselves to deny any real good by reason of mere popular outcries against ritual forms, so, on the other hand, we are never to allow professions of self-denying labor and service to blind us to the actual dangers of any movement in the Church. What is known as ' Ritualism ' is mainly a question of taste, temperament, and constitution until it becomes the expression of doctrine. The doctrine which chiefly attempts as yet to express itself by ritual, in questionable and dangerous ways, is connected with the Holy Eucharist. That doctrine is emphatically a novelty in theology. What is known as ' eucharistic adoration ' is undoubtedly inculcated and encouraged by that ritual of posture lately introduced among us, which finds no warrant in our Office for the Administration of the Holy Communion." "To argue that the spiritual presence of our dear Lord in the Holy Communion for the nurture of the faithful is such a presence as allows worship to him, thus and there present, is, to say the very least, to be wise above that which is written in God's Holy Word. . . . It is impossible for the common mind to draw the line between the worship of such an undefined and mysterious presence and the awful error of adoring the elements themselves. Wherefore . . . it is the bounden duty of each one to deny himself the outward expression of what to him may be only reverence, if that expression even seems to inculcate and encourage superstition and idolatry."

The next danger pointed out as "connected with the present movement in the Church" is private confession.

With a longing for a deeper spiritual life and with a keener sense of the exceeding sinfulness of sin, there comes, the bishops affirm, a desire for an authoritative assurance of forgiveness. Frivolous and worldly persons, simply because they desire to rid themselves of any sense of present responsibility or future retribution, seek for the same assurance. Advantage is taken of these different spiritual states to insist upon private confession to a priest as either the absolute duty of all Christians, or as essential to any high attainments in the religious life. Meantime, the fact that pardon is granted to any child of God on his repentance . . . is passed by.

The teaching of the Church in this matter is plain and clear. She permits and offers to her children the opening of their griefs in private to some minister. She does not make this the first resort. . . . She simply offers and commends this privilege to those of her children who cannot quiet their own consciences. . . . To make this seeking of comfort and counsel not exceptional but customary, not free but enforced . . . is to rob Christ's provision of its mercy, and to change it into an engine of oppression and a source of corruption.

A tendency to saint worship is rebuked, and as fostering this, alien devotional and doctrinal works of late years insidiously multiplied in England and America, chiefly borrowed from sources confessedly hostile to our communion, together with publications the whole aim of which is to undermine the legitimate authority of the chief pastors of the Church, inculcate irreverence, and stir up strife. Having been thus faithful in warning against evils connected with the Ritualistic movement, the bishops bear their testimony against those who mutilate or fall below the language of the liturgy and undervalue its doctrinal teaching.

. . . The habits of our people, formed necessarily under the imperfect ministrations of our ecclesiastical nonage, are naturally the reverse of sensitive to omissions and neglects in carrying out the system of the Book of Common Prayer. But . . . if nothing more than what is clearly indicated by our rubrics is to be permitted in one direction, we are bound in the merest justice to condemn any disposition to diminish in any manner from their prescriptions as to order and worship.

One observes that the bishops do not suppose that the practices of the Church's nonage should be considered to govern those of the present day, fixing customs which take the place of law with respect to rituals.

This pastoral excited more attention than is usually given to the triennial letters of the bishops. Among those who were rebuked by its teaching concerning eucharistic adoration there were consultations to weigh the exact force of its language, and if letters found in Bishop Whittingham's correspondence could be safely relied on, there were threats made of abandoning a Church which obscured the Catholic doctrine of regeneration in baptism and denied the adorable presence of the Lord in the sacrament of the altar. Probably here and there some conceived themselves to be driven from the Church by the teaching of its chief pastors, but it is not probable that there was any party move toward secession. The perversion of one who had been by him often commended, and who had been his secretary, brought great trouble to the Bishop of Maryland. It is likely that the leaven already received would have produced the same result, but the end was hastened by the warmth gendered through resistance to the pastoral. To the bishop's pain consequent upon the total rupture of a prized friendship, together with anxiety for others for whom he felt responsible, was added, as on other like occasions, reproach as though this were the natural result of his teachings.

The friend who caused this renewed reproach held that " the Lord is in the eucharist, as truly one with and present under the form of bread and wine as he was of old in the stable one with and present under the form of babyhood; that he, the divine and human Christ, is himself first offered in the holy eucharist for the living and the dead, and then put, according to his whole person, into the very hands of the recipient, to be then and there adored." Holding this, and not being willing to try to accommodate, himself to the pastoral, he felt that honesty demanded that he should resign his cure. He informed both his vestry and his bishop of his intention, but thinking that he could be silent for a while on those points of his belief contradicted by the pastoral, he was induced by various considerations to retain his rectorship until the end of the year. He believed still in the validity of his orders and his mission. After this he went to England, and, bearing letters from his bishop, conferred with several of the learned English clergy, but rather through the desire to gratify others than with the thought that his own judgment could be affected by any argument.

From Birmingham on April 1st he wrote with grief to "My dear Bishop" for the last time, formally renouncing his connection with the Church, and in conclusion to his Rt. Rev. and dear Father he reiterated gratitude, veneration, and affection, adding: "Of me you may think what you deem proper, and say what you consider it your duty to say ; of you I shall never think or speak with other than reverence and thanks."

A knowledge of the bishop prepared him—if he ever saw them—for the terms in which was announced to the Convention of 1872 "the deposition of the Rev. A. A. C., presbyter, from the holy ministry, at his own request, on his surrender of himself as a slave to the Roman usurper of lordship over the heritage of God." To renounce one's baptism and ordination in the Church was in the bishop's estimation a sin almost equivalent to apostacy. He was glad to believe that there are in the Roman communion many holy Christians, and he had no wish to deny that the Church of Rome and other churches submissive to her form parts of the Catholic, but yet his judgment of the Roman Church was very severe, and he always justified it because of long familiarity with her perversions of Catholic teaching and close study of the result of her system in countries under her control undisturbed by the influence of other religious bodies.

On one occasion, when a younger bishop vindicated himself for having called the Church of Rome "infernal," Bishop Whittingham said: "There is one bishop in the house who is not afraid at any time, or anywhere, to profess his belief that the Lord has permitted Satan to have posses-

sion of that branch of his Church of which the Bishop of
Rome is the head."   Such a conviction must have been very
painful.

Among the letters appended may be found an elucida-
tion of the bishops' pastoral given in answer to a letter of
inquiry from one of his clergy.

LETTERS.

TO W. F. B.

LITURGICAL MATTERS DISCUSSED.

BALTIMORE, November 29, 1870.

MY DEAR BRAND:

. . . I snatch my pen, in an hurried interval before going out
to a business meeting, to make you such answer as in such circumstances I can.

Indeed, if you could see through the window in my breast, you
would pity the man who, with such inward unreadiness for the battle,
is called upon to address himself to such strifes with men and things
as are now forced upon me. Small quiet of mind have I for the calm
consideration of such questions as your note sets before me!

. . . 2. As to the consecration, I should have thought it more
familiar to you that for fourteen hundred years there has been a
divarication of the East and West on that point—West holding that
it consists in the words of institution only, East maintaining that it
depends on the invocation of the Holy Spirit principally. One
Syriac liturgy does not even at all rehearse the words of institution.
Le Père Simon, in his "Lettres Choisies," has several curious letters
on the subject of this matter of dispute between the Easterns and
Westerns.

3. As to the passage in the Liturgy of S. James, Trollope, in his
valuable edition of that liturgy, at pages 80–83, has some good notes,
citing parallel passages from other ancient liturgies and abundantly
sustaining the Liturgy of St. James from Irenæus, Origen, Cyril,
Jerome, and other like authorities.

4. As to the origin of our form, it *is* Scotch, Keeling to the contrary notwithstanding. Our use was derived, not from the Laudian
"Scottish" book, but from (I think) the second (perhaps the third)
of the modifications of that book made by the Nonjuring bishops in
the first half of the eighteenth century. In my copy of the St.
Ninian's, Perth, Scotch Prayer-book, sent to me as authentic for the
diocesan library, the "Oblation" and "Invocation," occurring precisely *where* they do in ours, run precisely *as* they do in ours, down

to " gifts and creatures of bread and wine, that," when it goes on, " they may become the body and blood of thy most dearly beloved Son. And we earnestly," etc., etc.

This adopts the Eastern hypothesis of the *Virtus Consecrans* to the rejection of the Latin, and so avoids the liability to inference as to the " creature " ship of the *consecrated* bread which may be drawn from the older liturgies and from ours. Yet it has the same *rubric* as ours ; and from that rubric it seems to me to follow clearly that the *first* section of the great prayer is " the prayer of *consecration*," the *second* " the Oblation," and the *third* " the Invocation," as distinct from each other, having distinct objects and effects.

This matter of the question between consecration by recital of institution and consecration by invocation is discussed by Neale, " History of Eastern Church," introduction, vol. i., pp. 492–501. Freeman also, I think, has a valuable disquisition on the subject.

Yours lovingly,   W. R. WHITTINGHAM.

TO THE REV. A. A. C.

THE PASTORAL DOES NOT FAULT THE DOCTRINE OF THE REAL PRESENCE—CONDEMNS AN INFERENCE.

MADISON AVENUE, November 13, 1871.

MY DEAR C.:

You rightly judged of your letter of Wednesday last, that it would give me pain.

I think I have never received one that gave me more occasion for intense anxiety and regret. . . .

And when, on Friday, I found myself at leisure to give it my whole attention, the communication proved to be even less endurable than had been known by the opening announcement.

It was bad enough that you should be led to think of resigning a work in which there seemed to be so many reasons why you should find content and satisfaction ; but it sadly aggravated the distressing nature of the tidings to be informed that the resignation had been resolved on in a spirit so different from any which I had ever known you to manifest before, and for an array of reason which seemed to me, on your own presentation, so miserably insufficient.

You represent your determination as taken because you are profoundly certain that you are totally unfit to retain the care of souls. But of such total unfitness you neither give nor in any way intimate any other ground of proof than your inability any longer to discharge your work according to the mind of your superiors.

And of that inability the whole evidence consists in the asserted impossibility that you could continue to teach without contradicting, intentionally or unintentionally, what the bishops have propounded in their pastoral letter on a single point of doctrine concerning the holy eucharist. Surely, never did a Christian priest contemplate the abandonment of the exercise of his high office with less apparent urgency of reason !

Had the pastoral taught a doctrine of the eucharist contrary to that which you state to be the ground of your own inner life, and of all your teaching, it would, indeed, have become incumbent on you to do one of two things, *either* cease your work, *or* enter on a serious and thorough investigation of your own views, to see if it might not be *possible* that one presbyter was in error and nearly fifty of his superiors right.

All that ever I have known of you would have led me to expect of you the adoption of the last alternative.

But there is no such fundamental contrariety of doctrine to require it.

Who has faulted the doctrine of the real presence, even stated as you have stated it in the fullest strength of language which it is possible to use without running into unscriptural, uncatholic, and rationalistic presumption in definition ?

Your objection is to a condemnation of a practical inference from that doctrine.

You choose to infer from it that your Master presents Himself in His blessed sacrament to you under the form of bread and wine to be adored ; and having made that inference, you speak of being intensely opposed, down to the very root of your nature, to the authoritative document which takes a different view—not of doctrine, but of resulting privilege and duty.

You declare that you do not even try to receive its statements ! That you do not and will not try to accommodate yourself to it !

My dear brother ! I know you do not so mean it ! but let me tell you plainly, this is the very way of talking of a heretic !

It is now my turn to challenge you to give a word of proof that you have the Master's warrant for your inference !

I know the subterfuges by which over-eager devotion has tried to build up for itself a right without that warrant, and the far more objectionable boldness, bordering on profanity, by which human logic works the claim out of premises gotten by its own inventions in the mode of statement ; but what I demand of you is our Lord's authority for inferring, from his gift of himself to you, that he makes it to be adored in it, and holding that inference against fifty of those whom he has set over you in his name, with such tenacity as rather to offend his little ones by throwing up his commission to work among them for his sake, than give up your own individual convictions, and cease your own individual innovations in the public doctrine and worship of the Church in which you are a minister.

Dear C.! Your letter talks about not daring to undertake or try to do certain things! Let me tell you that it is far, very far worse daring to resolve on such a course without incomparably more reason than I have as yet any ground for thinking that you can show!

Your deeply grieved but most truly loving friend and brother,

W. R. W.

TO THE BISHOP OF MARYLAND.

INTRODUCTORY TO THE LETTER THAT FOLLOWS.

JANUARY 28, 1872.

MY DEAR FATHER:

. . . Since the General Convention I have very much desired your instruction on various matters. I have more than once been to see you, and have come away with my budget unopened because of hindrances. I do not know when I shall see you. May I then talk with you on paper about some of the matters that have occupied my thoughts?

What is the authority of a declaration and of a pastoral when it declares doctrine set forth in the name of the House of Bishops? I know neither has legislative authority—if I contradict them I cannot be *therefore* deposed or suspended. This fact does not give me the satisfaction it does to some. I find some argue at times as if the episcopate were the depositaries of the faith; and then when our entire body of bishops utter one voice, cry out, Oh! their word is not law! This utterance had not the consent of the House of Delegates! But there is little unction to my soul in what soothes such churchmen. I do not care for force, and I do care very much for free, hearty reverence for my superiors. Because I do, I would ask—I was about to write the *force* of the declaration respecting the baptismal service—but I suppose you would say, it has no force. But what is its meaning? One of your brethren asked me during Convention, "What do you think of the declaration?" I answered, I have studied it carefully, and knowing from whom it comes—what some of them at least believe—I can give no meaning whatever to "moral change." But a friend says that it strikes her that some attached a meaning of their own to the words, and the others, knowing that they signify nothing—explain nothing—said to themselves, Well, if that will satisfy you we will sign the paper. The bishop replied : "The instinct of women is wonderful, and I should not wonder if this is the whole truth."

I blushed for the bishop when he said so, and I do hope that you will tell me that the successors of the apostles—even though a Peter could dissemble—do not thus treat matters that touch the faith. I do hope, also, that you will be willing to give me some meaning of your words which I can reconcile with what I mean when I say, "I acknowledge one baptism for the remission of sins." The Bishop of Ohio is jubilant over the unity exhibited by Convention. "All this, too, without any compromise of truth, *on our part* AT LEAST." In no unfilial spirit I venture to say that there was a compromise of truth on the part of others, if they meant to justify or give an excuse for such an interpretation of the efficacy of baptism as is set forth in Bishop McIlvaine's letter published in the English record. My trouble is that I see no escape from this conclusion save in what is suggested by the " instinct of women."

Dear Father, I do think great harm must follow if the bishops allow the assertion to go forth uncontradicted that they attempted in their council to interpret regeneration as not meaning a moral change, and then almost unanimously signed a paper which, giving "the utmost latitude for evangelical views of the efficacy of baptism," asserts that our service does not imply a moral change in baptism. " The doctrine of a service having that word [regeneration] is interpreted negatively."

Again—during the Convention there were many attempts to effect legislative action touching ritual, avowedly because of a desire to prohibit " advanced " teachings respecting the doctrine of the holy eucharist. The House of Bishops, or a majority of them, were urgent in the matter, and sent down for concurrence canons on the subject, but without avail. Nothing was done. Then, nothing having been done by the Convention, the House of Bishops in their sole name declare dogmatically what is a judgment on the whole matter discussed in Convention. I mean the gist of the matter. I would know what is the force of the pastoral setting forth this dogmatic teaching. Is it technically a rescript—a declaration which is the end of controversy ? Do the bishops mean that Pusey, and Keble, and those who think with them, have no place in *this Church ?* Do they mean that those among us who teach respecting the holy eucharist what Keble taught must now cease from what is pronounced to be error, or should renounce their ministry? There are many who treat the pastoral with contempt. C., without being wholly consistent, but meaning to be honest, renounces his charge that brought him pay, and waits to see whether he must renounce the ministry. I think you know that I am not censured, but if I were I should not act as C. has done. I should give you the trouble of deposing me, and until you did so I should continue to teach, believing, as he does, my orders to be indisputable. I am in no respect censured, but I feel for and with others who are. I do feel that when some who reject the plainest teaching of our Church have had such excessive tenderness shown them, it is hard that others who may exceed instead of coming short of our standard should be thundered at. If the consent given to the pastoral was unanimous I look upon the fact as miraculous. I cannot conceive of Bishop —— (who wrote to Mr. Keble to congratulate him on the publication of his book on eucharistic adoration) joining *ex animo* with bishops who deny the sacrifice, express scorn for manipulating priests, and publicly declare that the upholding *the Church* is a hindrance to the Gospel.

TO W. F. B.

THE DECLARATION AND THE PASTORAL.

BALTIMORE, January 30, 1872.

MY DEAR B. :

The somewhat sad, and altogether dubious, tone of your letter is in strange contrast with the representations daily coming to me, from every quarter of the compass, of satisfaction with the doings and results of the late General Convention. Whether it was that men generally expected less than you did, and therefore have been less disappointed, or whether that you have looked at our doings through some tinted medium which has lent them a ghastly look, in some way or other you seem to me hardly to have attained a due appreciation of the work done, the position taken, the difficulties overcome, or the dangers avoided.

You yourself set aside the quibbling in which a few indulge about the difference between a declaration and law—a pastoral and a canon. None, I am sure, are better prepared than you to perceive and admit the difference between an appeal to filial respect and submission, made by fathers in God's household, and an enactment laying down definitions for the measurement of faith and canons for enforcement of conformity, emanating from a man-made legislative body glorying in the attributes of a constitutional assembly with all legislative powers and functions, representative and delegated.

The presbyter who sets aside a pastoral because it is not law, just disowns his father's voice because he does not wear a wig and gown when speaking.

The common sense of mankind knows better, and accepts both the declaration and the pastoral, coming, as both did, from the virtually unanimous body of the bishops of the American Church, as the virtual teaching of that Church, with which he, be he priest, deacon, or layman, who differs does so at the peril and condemnation (be either or both great or little as they may) of setting himself out of harmony. He lacks the ὁμόνοια which the fathers of the first three centuries so continually and strongly recommended. He is, in Ignatius' figure, a string of the heavenly lyre that fails to sound its proper chord.

The declaration was no act, either of legislation or definitive teaching. Its singularly limited and negative form was studiedly contrived to hinder the attribution to it of any claim to be either.

It was simply and merely an act of administrative government, by which the bishops controlled the action of the Convention, to the effect of shutting out discussion of the baptismal offices and deliberation about possible alterations in the Prayer-book.

It was asked for and granted—not proposed and carried.

Its passage was communicated to the House of Deputies as information, not as law or doctrine. Had it never gotten beyond the walls of the Deputies, or met other eyes or ears than theirs, it would have done its full work when the Convention finally closed without having wagged a tongue against "regeneration" or laid a finger on the Prayer-book.

I do not understand the kind of conscience which would blush for such an act (as it seems to me now, in the retrospect, with the light of results thrown on it—*I* did not originate it—*I* did not urge it!) of consummate godly wisdom.

As for the meaning of "moral change," it is well explained and illustrated in an extract from *The* (English) *Church Review*, which appeared a few weeks ago in *The Church Weekly*, and is brought to its point in a sentence of an admirable work all in print before a word of the declaration was thought, and yet not seen in Baltimore till more than a week after the declaration had been published (Adams on "Regeneration"): "How much superior this conception of Christ as being really the life of man—of the actual *reception in our regeneration of an organic spiritual life* received from him and abid-

ing in us—is to those *shallow Socinian ideas of* REGENERATION AS A
MERE MORAL CHANGE, *that are so prevalent in the masses!*"

I can speak only for myself as to the inward views of men joining
in the act—I did so in the sense of Adams' words.   Let me say, too,
that in a three days' frank and full discussion of the doctrine of
baptism, in which no man seemed to keep back or conceal his views
—and there were great varieties of expression and illustration—I
heard no single bishop use a word *contradictory* of that view.   I lay
the more stress on this because, in the course of the discussion,
Bishop Davis, now at rest, made a clear and full statement of his
doctrine of baptismal regeneration, distinctly given, in which my
most intent and critical observation could discover no objectionable
point or illustration, and which was, nevertheless, received with
warmth of praise by those who would perhaps rightfully be ranked
among the lowest churchmen in the House.

You lay stress on Bishop McIlvaine's letter.   Have you seen his
(very material) correction, in a second edition, of the distorted form
in which it first appeared?

But as counter-testimony let me refer you to Bishop Coxe's statement, as it appears in the January number of *The American Church
Review*, pages 44, 45.   I have read it since I wrote the first sheet of
this letter, and I there find Bishop Wilmer, of Alabama, saying substantially what I have said on the bottom of my third page.

As for constructions put upon the act, they will live or die as they
be just or not.   I judge no man, but I have my own opinions of
some men's utterances.

The English reviewer, reputed as of the highest school of churchmen, after owning dislike of the declaration on its first appearance,
after two months gives his "sober second thoughts" that it is "consistent with the most straitest orthodoxy."

In going on to talk about other doings of the Convention, you
write a little loosely.

You say "there were many attempts to effect legislative action
touching ritual."   I know of *but one*—in which, to be sure, there
were many turnings and twistings; and that one a legacy from the
Deputies' action in 1868.   That action the *bishops* then staved off.
Coming up of necessity in 1871, they showed their moderation by
remitting it to the joint *re*-consideration of both Houses.   All that
followed was the mere effort to get it into shape.

You say, "The House of Bishops—or a majority of them—were
urgent in the matter."   That is not true.   *Some* were urgent, but
nothing like "a majority."

You say they "sent down for concurrence canons on the subject."

That is not true. They sent down one project of a canon for joint consideration ; and when that consideration drawled along in dreadful longsomeness, a majority of the bishops got impatient and took a part of the same canon and sent it down for *concurrence.*

You say, "Then, nothing having been done by the Convention" (meaning the Deputies), "the House of Bishops in their sole name declare dogmatically," etc., referring to the pastoral—and meaning that because conventional action failed, and as a consequence of its failure, the bishops did what they could to supply the want.

That is not true. The pastoral was prepared and adopted before the Deputies had concluded their consideration of the proposed canon. The bishops, so far as I know and believe, had a single eye to the discharge of their own duty and responsibility in the preparation of the pastoral.

Do you fault the choice of subject? I should like to know how overseers in the household *could* be more faithful than just in taking hold of the matter in which they found men's minds to be most perplexed, and about which, coming up from their several dioceses, each to the others bore his testimony that he most needed to have his hands strengthened by his brethren !

Whether the pastoral be "technically a rescript" or not, it is the united voice of those whom God's word has taught λαλεῖν καὶ παρακαλεῖν καὶ ἐλεγχεῖν μετὰ πάσης ἐπιταγῆς—adding to whom it concerns the warning, μηδεὶς αὐτῶς περιφρονείτω !

As for what "the bishops do mean" about Pusey and Keble, inasmuch as the names of those priests of another branch of the Church were not so much as mentioned in the House, I will not undertake to say; but for myself, I will freely own that while my soul loves and clings to Keble for his poetry, I never thought his logic worth a finger-snap, nor in any wise looked up to and owned him as a leader; while Dr. Pusey has more than once within these ten years past seemed to me to be drawing perilously near the very verge of heresiarchy.

I have not claimed—nor has any other bishop, so far as I know—any right or power to meddle with men for " thinking with " either or both, nor assumed to say that such " thinking " affects any man's " place," clerical or laical, " in *this Church.*" Can you point to the line or word in the pastoral that implies such right, power, or disposition ?

That document deals with *action.* It forbids *change* in the ritual *with a purpose,* and *teaching* man's notions about will-worship instead of Christ's Gospel.

———, whom you cite, renounces his charge against the remonstrance of his bishop, because he cannot forego exalting his own wisdom over that of all the House of Bishops, and holding for saving doctrine that which they tell him is erroneous inference.

——— was too loyal to do as you say he might have done—hold fast to his own ways of thinking, acting, and teaching in defiance of his bishop.

I know nothing about your anecdote of Bishop P. but what you tell me. That gossip to the contrary notwithstanding, I can assure you the pastoral *was* adopted *nemine contradicente*. No line of it came from my pen, and no one, two, or three members of the House can be fairly held responsible for it as a whole; but during my thirty years of attendance in the House never have I seen anything approaching to the unanimous, cordial consent with which that document was prepared, considered, and adopted.

Nor have I ever known a pastoral as well received by the Church at large as all the intelligence that comes to me from every quarter conspires to satisfy me that this has been.

Whatever you may be disposed to think of it, I am well persuaded that the effect has been greatly to elevate the standard of church doctrine throughout the Church. False teaching in the anti-sacramental direction is incomparably more interfered with by the distinct utterances concerning *both* the sacraments now put forth as the voice of the united episcopate, than are the practices and teachings of those who persist in professing to find condemnation of "adoration in the eucharist" in a discommendation of "adoration of the eucharist," and claim for their own invention of a localized presence in the elements priority of right over the primitive and Anglican doctrine of a real presence in the sacrament, and thus run their own inferences into a substitution of an object for an act of adoration.

.   .   .   .

Ever your faithful and loving friend and brother,

W. R. Whittingham.

———

February 8, 1872.

My Dear Father:

I am very grateful to you for taking so much trouble on my account, and none the less so because you condescend to my low estate.

You have answered my queries fully. "The common sense of mankind accepts both the declaration and the pastoral coming from the unanimous body of the bishops of the American Church as the virtual teaching of that Church." The same must be said of all other utterances of that body past and future, if like unanimity can be predicated of them—and of this none outside of the house can judge. As one who would not jar his string in discord, I must not differ from the teaching of the declaration. But yet I must say to you, as a friend, though I seem a fool for so saying, I cannot yet understand what I am to harmonize with.

Giving back to sponsors at the font a baptized babe, I can say to them, "Even as this child when generated received—no man can tell how—life to be maintained an allotted term of years, or impaired, or lost, as an infinite variety of circumstances may determine, so now in the laver of regeneration it has received—no more mysteriously—a new life, the life of Christ, which as God is true shall be unto eternity if the terms of the covenant implied by the giving and receiving of this beginning of life be complied with ; otherwise the result of our act will be that as a' regenerated as well as redeemed child of God, this child must be judged. A great change has been wrought—through the Spirit a child of wrath has become a child of grace." This I can say, for I believe in the new birth in baptism. But if I should add to my words, "yet understand, this child has experienced no moral change," I really should not know what I was saying, and I think my hearers would be simply perplexed if they could associate morals with anything an eight-days babe is capable of.

With regard to my kink of conscience. The bishop I referred to is one to whom I can speak more familiarly than to yourself, though not so from the heart. In answer to his question I gave one interpretation, which, because we trust in our bishops, I did not believe, and my friend did not believe, but which she had suggested might be given by those who do not share our confidence. To my surprise, the bishop gave the reply I have stated. I am glad that I wrote to you, if for no other reason, because you have stated facts which I might otherwise have never known, which show that my friend could not have understood the purport of my words. I am very glad to know that there was a full exposition of every man's views, and, what strikes me with wonder, that all assented to views touching regeneration in baptism in which your critical acumen could detect no objectionable point. You tell me that the declaration was "an act of administration by which the bishops controlled the action of the Convention," etc.

If discussion of the Prayer-book in the lower House was thereby avoided, I ought to be especially glad. Great danger may have been avoided ; but those who have kinks in mind as well as in conscience cannot perceive them, and I in my crankiness have to confess that I cannot see the consummate wisdom patent to you. I do not see that so much was gained when so many were left perplexed and led to suppose that the bishops hold what you utterly reject, and when Bishop McIlvaine finds occasion to write what he has written, justifying this supposition in the eyes of all who receive his statements.

When I said that in C.'s place I should not have resigned, I meant this : A bishop may err, a church may err, a priest as fully as a bishop is bound to maintain Catholic truth. I do not conceive that loyalty to one's bishop requires that one should cease to teach truth deemed vital, or abandon one's charge. Therefore I said if I had C.'s convictions I should give you the trouble to depose me.

TO A REV. PROFESSOR WHO HAD ASKED HIM TO CRITICIZE AN ESSAY.

THE REAL PRESENCE.

BALTIMORE, February 15, 1872.

MY DEAR PROFESSOR :

. . . I would not for all the world write as the expression of my belief the sentence, "There is no such thing as the real presence of the living Christ in the Holy Communion"—believing, as I do, with the most entire conviction, that the real presence of our blessed Lord in his divine person and inseparable human nature is the great characteristic of the eucharistic feast, from its beginning to the end, and that he, as our One Great Priest, himself gives his people, by the agency of his minister, the ἀνάμνησιν, or מִנְחָה of the One Great Sacrifice forever perfected on the Cross, in which they receive from him, in the broken bread, his slain body, and in the poured-out wine his shed blood, in very deed and reality by him given and by them received, as they were given and received in the Last Supper in Jerusalem.

I would venture to inquire of you whether you have met with a recent American book, published by Lippincott, of Philadelphia, under the title of " The Conservative Reformation," by a Lutheran minister, Dr. Krauth. He enters, at much length, into the discussion of the nature of the presence, and exhibits, more fully than any other English book I know, what I think the sound and irrefragable argumentation on the subject of Martin Chemnitz, the great Lutheran theologian. I do not refer to it as recommending it for adoption, but because I think some such acquaintance with that side of the discussion as may be obtained from it indispensable in order to an accurate notion of the Anglican doctrine of a real presence in the eucharist, and an actual and veritable partaking of the body and blood of the Lord in the bread and wine, without change of substance in the sacramental elements.

Very faithfully and affectionately,

Your friend and brother,

W. R. W.

TO THE SAME.

THE SAME THEME—THE BLESSED TRINITY THE OBJECT OF ADORATION IN THE HOLY EUCHARIST.

BALTIMORE, February 27, 1872.

REV. AND DEAR BROTHER:

The receipt of your interesting reply to my last during Ember-week, with some extra pressure upon me at the time, and my own feeble condition interfering greatly with anything like close or steady application, have been the cause of my tardiness in answering.

I have always found in conferences and discussions about the subject of our correspondence between those who differed, however considerably, in opinion only, without running on either side into heretical misbelief, that it was much more easy to come to an understanding and agreement in affirmations than in negatives. I think, indeed, that it might be advanced as a law in dogmatics, that heresies spring out of over-nicety in the negative side of definition. Thus, as soon as you turn the negation which I (rather strongly) objected to in my last, into the correlative affirmation, I find no difficulty. I cordially agree " in regarding the consecrated bread and wine as made to us the slain body and the outshed blood of our Lord by participation of which we [I would not say exactly '*become* incorporated *into*' (because that seems to me to take place, in a sense and to a degree, in baptism), but rather] receive communication of his glorified (viz., not slain only, but risen, and not risen only, but ascended and triumphantly enthroned) body." This, in my belief, results from our participation of his sacrifice in its צוּרָה, or *ἀναμνήσει*. In that we die with him, and are raised with him, and receive earnest of our session together with him in heaven (Eph. ii. 6). How can all this be a veritable transaction, and not " necessarily involve the real presence of our glorified Lord?" It is utterly inconceivable by me that it should not ; as inconceivable as that it should not equally involve the actual giving and receiving of his slain body and outshed blood. If the latter alone were present, where would be the participation in the victory ? if the former alone, where that in the death and sacrifice ? Our Lord's word used of the participation of the βρῶσις and πόσις, which he supplies in his flesh and blood, is most significant, ὁ τρώγων καὶ πίνων μένει—not either " enters " (becoming incorporated) or receives—but keeps up, confirms, perpetuates his relation with me, into which he has been brought, and in which he is by this act habilitated and secured. In a sense, and to a certain degree, the two sacraments inosculate, and it may be said with truth, equally, that in baptism the believer eats the body and drinks the blood of his sacrificed Redeemer by faith in the fact and virtue of His sacrifice, and that in the eucharist he washes away his sins in the outshed blood of cleansing, and receives the sonship and inheritance of life in the communication of the body of the Son and Lord of Life, whose sonship makes him a son, and in whose life he becomes a living heir.

You make much mention of "incorporation." I would rather, for distinctness' sake, talk of the participation, and reason about it, as our *con*corporation with the Lord through reception from his own person of his incomprehensibly communicated gifts of his own body and blood.

In your rationale of the heavenly side of the mystery (I like that good Greek and biblical word much better than the comparatively modern Latin invention, " sacramentum ") you assume that our offering before the Father is " with " and in " the glorified body " of our Lord exclusively. But is it the glorified body which is offered in the sacrificial sense, which is laid on the heavenly altar as " the Lamb slain ? " And are we offered in the sense in which the one sacrifice by which atonement was once for all effected is offered ? Rather, is not the appearance (παρουσία) of the glorified body for us in heaven, that of the Risen Victor, claiming us as His conquest out of the domains of sin and death, and presenting us as such, by the offering in himself of His own once slain, now risen, body, and once shed blood, now resumed in immortality. The presence and the offering, one in person, one in subjective nature, are yet, in idea and objective intent and use, two distinct acts of distinguishable nature and effect.

So in the earthly side of the mystery. Are not the presence of the Conqueror claiming the spoils won by the victory over sin and death, in the great sacrifice and the gift of the offering by which He conquered, to those whom He thereby makes participant in His atoning work through death, resurrection, and ascension—are they not the presence and the gift, while one in person and subjective being, yet distinct in idea and objective operation?

I cannot for a moment admit of difficulty as arising from the scriptural teaching that our Lord, wholly and completely, is engaged in heaven in working out our salvation, as much so as he was on earth, in the desert, in the garden, and on the cross. Did that hinder his appearing (παρουσίαν) to Stephen, and to Saul, and to Paul, in the temple, and to John? Are we to circumscribe him— God the Word—by the conditions of *our* humanity? Unless we do, there is nothing more in the difficulty than this, that it utterly outpasses our conception. Admitted willingly, and inferred, that therein it proves itself divine, and shows that God has really, truly, and with a verity past any human power of thought and expression, taken human nature into the divine.

As to measuring God's power and effort in working out his own εὐδοκίαν for our salvation, or estimating how much or how little of the same might be more or less requisite for its accomplishment, it is about the last employment in which I should think an archangel might have dreamed of wasting his power of thought before he fell.

I would utterly and indignantly disclaim the notion of withdrawment of the Son from mediatorial work in heaven, because of His real presence in every eucharistic act. Was He not in heaven when He said so to Nicodemus? Was He less so when He met Saul on the way to Damascus than when He appeared to Stephen?

Athanasius rightly terms His whole incarnation, in all its circumstances and work, His παρουσία. We must lift up our thoughts to the conception of it as one mighty whole, and not belittle it by the application of our poor attributes of parts and passions to its limitation, when the καιρὸς κενώσεως is overpast, and the original glory of the Word is made the measure of the man in whom dwells all the fulness of the Godhead bodily.

I think that in our endeavors to investigate, as other parts of the plan of our salvation, so this mystery, we need to exercise a continual and most intent watchfulness not to allow ourselves, in the employment of our limited faculties upon any one of the many sides into which their very feebleness compels us to disport the matter of study, to lose sight of the certain, or even possible, correlatives—in particular, of the corresponding yet infinitely outreaching *divine* phase which there must be of every incident in a transaction devised of God for originating, or keeping up, or carrying out, his communication of himself to man.

In the holy eucharist I apprehend God in Trinity to be the object, from the very first word or gesture to the last, of worship in its highest possible form of intentness and acceptance.

God the Father I understand to be addressed, both in the language of prayer and in the one entire action of the whole mystery, as the loving reconciled One whom in humble return of love we thank, by the presentation in word and in reality, of the wondrous Reconciler and His work.

God the Son I believe to be recognized as our present Reconciler, standing, as it were, in the mystery, to hold open for us the door (and so to be the door) of access to our reconciled Father—presenting himself in the whole mystery as one act to us for recognition by our faith ; to the Father, for us and in us, for recognition by his love ; and, in the gifts of his body and his blood, communicating to us a full, true, real, and effectual participation in his death, resurrection, and ascension, as the one atoning conquest of sin, death, and hell.

God the Holy Spirit I believe to be the life-giving worker in us of the faith which so approaches the Father through the Son in the whole mystery ; and specially of the impartation to our prayers and gifts, of their sacrificial character, as an approach to God ; and of the change of our gifts, so offered and accepted, into gifts from our Lord Jesus Christ, in which he, through the operation of the One Spirit, which is his Spirit and which is in us as his Spirit, makes us one with himself, partakers of his flesh and blood, and in them of his inseparable divine and human natures, present, as with us in this participation, so in a manner ineffable because divine and utterly out of the range of human thought or imagination, at the same indivisible moment in the tabernacle not made with hands, where he ever appeareth to make intercession for us with the Father.

I hope I have not been presumptuous in trying to be concise. I write *currente calamo* and in a condition of very imperfect health.

Faithfully and affectionately your friend and brother,

W. R. WHITTINGHAM.

CHAPTER V.

1872.

DURING the Convention of 1871, the bishops, moved by tidings of recent acts of the reforming party in Germany, recorded in the journal of their House an expression of earnest sympathy with the Alt-Catholics in their struggle for religious liberty, and also unanimously resolved that "It is highly desirable that the Right Reverend the Bishop of Maryland should visit Europe to ascertain the state of the church reformation in Germany and Italy, and that he present the result of his observations to the House of Bishops at his convenience."

Whatever may have been the reasons for not acting on this request, want of interest was not one of them. As early as the summer of 1859, Bishop Whittingham had encouraged the Rev. C. W. Langdon in his proposal to establish an American chaplaincy in Rome, in part as a post of observation from which to study the ecclesiastical bearings of the political revolution on which Italy was then entering, and in the hope of influence on the religious changes that might follow.

Soon after the gathering a congregation in Rome by Mr. Langdon, the Rev. Dr. Lyman accepted the charge of one of a like character in Florence. There was at the time an older organization in Paris.

In 1860 the chaplains of these three congregations simultaneously urged Bishop Whittingham to visit Europe, and especially Italy. Their invitation was enforced by private letters from the Senior Bishop, Dr. Brownell, and his assistant, Bishop Williams, and by a formal commission, issued under a late canon, empowering him to visit episcopally and to establish congregations of Americans in Europe. An object sought, but of which mention was not made in the commission, was "to look after the Italian reformation."

The bishop did not positively decline the appointment. "It may become," he said, "possible for me to go abroad with a clear conscience and a light heart. At present I certainly could not." He expressed a hope that the commission would be given to some one else. But the presiding bishop thought him to be "the only bishop on the bench to whom this work can be safely entrusted." The commission was therefore held under advisement. The rapid course of political events soon ended all consideration of such schemes.

Had it been otherwise—had the bishop been able to act under this commission, what opportunities for good, now lost, might have been improved! Not until 1865 was there an occasion for showing the interest that he had not ceased to feel. As the General Convention of that year drew nigh, he advised Mr. Langdon, who had returned home and had found a parish in Maryland, to prepare a memorial to that body, setting forth the facts which prompted the hope of Catholic reform in the Church of Italy, and praying for some action in reference to that hope. Of this memorial he himself took charge. He presented it to the House of Bishops, and a few days later, as chairman of the committee to which it had been referred, he reported two resolutions, one of formal recognition and sympathy with the movement, and the other directing the appointment of a joint committee to sit during the recess of Convention, with power to collect and diffuse information concerning it. These resolutions were in substance adopted, and the committee constituted.

"American interest in this subject now entered upon a new stage."

" For a while, indeed," says Dr. Langdon, " it seemed impossible to go beyond mere words."

In January, 1866, the bishop wrote :

Our [the committee's] interest is so far ahead of that of the Church at large that we are hardly likely, by any effort within our competence, to bring out a sufficiency of reliable support to enable us to carry out any plan of action which in our judgment would seem to be worth undertaking. A large majority, as I fear, of the clergy and laity of the Church is disposed to regard expenditure of labor and money on the affairs of Italy as uncalled-for waste of needed means. A small but very determined and active minority is warmly opposed to any kind of action which tends to the development of the Catholic relations of the P. E. Church, and particularly hostile to the pro-Italian movement on that account. It can and does avail itself of the easy policy of appealing to the innate love of *dolce far niente* by pooh-poohing our anxieties and efforts as mere Quixotism, and in some cases is disposed to go further and lay in our way the serious obstacle of suspicion of Romanizing tendencies and designs.

Thus did the bishop foresee the antagonism which would obstruct the work in which he was interested, and in the end take it out of his hands. The very qualities that made him seem to Bishop Brownell the only man to be entrusted with " what may be the most important work since the Reformation," furnished reasons to others why they should avoid the complicities in which, if he were her representative abroad, " our Protestant Church " might be involved.

We cannot trace the history of the Italian Commission, nor tell of the proposal of Bishop Whittingham in General Convention to meet the wishes of the clergy on the Continent for episcopal oversight by the appointment of a bishop delegate with defined powers ; which proposal led only to the understanding that under the existing canon the presiding bishop should delegate foreign jurisdiction to one of the diocesan bishops for three years.

It is enough to say that the foreign clergy were plainly told that Bishop Whittingham would not and could not be appointed, but that, if they desired it, the presiding bishop was willing to commission another specified bishop. During the three following years the foreign clergy were without the benefit of the briefest visit of a bishop. During these years occurred the Vatican Council, the fall of the temporal rule of the Pope, the removal of the Italian capital to Rome, and the rise of Old Catholicism in Germany. At this time, if ever, the American Church should have had a bishop as a representative on the Continent.

In August, 1870, Mr. Nevin, then American chaplain in Rome, wrote to Bishop Whittingham:

I do esteem it most desirable that the foreign chapels should be visited by some bishop fully authorized and really interested in the matter, before the session of the next General Convention. And this to the end not only of the settlement of existing troubles . . . If we cannot have such oversight as will lead . . . to the regulation of abuses under our present jurisdiction, then let us have a bishop of our own by all means. These chapels are representatives of our Church to a large and very influential body of dissenters in a way that no home churches are. . . . Should the bishop in charge then be unable to make a visitation so deliberate as would seem to be desirable, I may say freely that there is no one that I would more gladly welcome in this office than yourself. . . . When I saw last spring, particularly during the session of the Vatican Council, how loyally some of the American prelates were standing up for the truth, and how disgusted they were becoming every day with the new revelations of the falsehood and unscrupulousness of the whole papal party, I wished more than once that we had on the ground some one their equal in rank and master in theology, who might have turned the moment to good account in shaping their minds toward the reformation that must almost of necessity grow out of this last and greatest of papal usurpations. The overweening claims put forth for the papacy excited to the highest degree the episcopal spirit of the American bishops until sometimes they expressed themselves almost as if they stood on common ground with us.

It was during this period that Bishop Whittingham's relations with the work carried on in Italy in the Church's name were reduced to their minimum. None the less he maintained his personal relations with the Foreign Secretary of the commission, and kept himself fully informed of all that concerned the reformation movement.

The Convention of 1871—when the Bishop of Maryland was requested to ascertain the condition of the reformatory movements—continued the policy of 1868, and still jealously kept distinct the duty that the bishop was asked to assume from that of supervision of the American congregations.

[No man, writes Dr. Langdon, was more conscientiously thorough than Bishop Whittingham in the discharge of any duty providentially laid upon him and accepted by him. No man, therefore, was more reluctant to accept any such responsibility as providential, under conditions which, in his judgment, precluded such a discharge of it. In this case he was too clearly aware of the serious embarrassments which, so far as Italy was concerned, would almost inevitably follow from the concurrent presence there of two bishops whose official relations with the Church's interests and with her clergy and parishes in that land were distinct only in theory, and who did not agree in their judgment of the issues which had arisen there, and to solve which would be the first duty of either on coming thither. Not all the newly aroused enthusiasm of his brother bishops; not the cordial insistance of the presiding bishop and of the bishop in charge himself; not the urgency of the foreign clergy; not his own intense interest in the remarkable developments which were setting open such a door of influence before the Church, could for a moment conceal from him the false position in which he would be placed were he to go to Europe under such circumstances.

As in 1860, he consented only to hold the request under advisement, and await such possible modifications of the situation as time might bring. Indeed, it was said that the European jurisdiction would be given him after the return of Bishop Stevens from his purposed visitation, and it is not unlikely that he thought it best to await the result of some such intentions.]

If this were so, added inducements prevailed. The Italian Reformation Committee formally urged that he would visit the Continent. Mr. Langdon, who had returned to Europe, communicated the expression of the most earnest desire of English bishops, and others, that Bishop Whittingham would be enabled to conform to the wishes of his brethren at as early a day as possible ; he also reported what occurred during a long conference at Munich with Professors Friedrich and Reinkens of the clergy, and Professor Huber of the laity. He had furnished them with a copy of the minutes of the House of Bishops in reference to the Alt-Catholic movement, which they asked permission to publish.

They once more spoke, Mr. Langdon's letter says, of their earnest desire to have the opportunity of conference with some bishop or accredited theologian of our Church. I informed them of the action of the House of Bishops looking in that direction, and told them that you had that request under consideration. They all most earnestly expressed their gratification, and hope that nothing would prevent your coming.

In June, 1872, the House of Bishops, at a special meeting held for missionary business, renewed their request. And soon after Professor Huber wrote, begging that the bishop would accept an informal invitation to attend a meeting of conference which had been decided on, but the day for which had not been fixed. In due time this was followed by a special and formal invitation.

There remained still a hindrance. No provision for meeting necessary expenses had been made, and the time seemed now too short for this and other preparations.

From the outset—such are the bishop's words—I made no secret of my determination to attach much weight to the indications of the mind of the Church by action or inaction in the matter as a practical governance of my own decision whether or not to overcome my own sore misgivings as to the point of duty.

The failure on the part of those whom he was asked to represent to make evidently necessary provision was taken by him as deliverance from the responsibility of decision.

No sooner was this known than ample pecuniary means were secured, and of this fact he was informed by the Secretary of the House of Bishops. The senior bishop went to Orange to urge that the bishop should at once decide to go. He took with him a memorandum of topics of communication to the conference, a condensed statement of the grounds on which the American Church "has always been ready to unite with Christians of the Greek or Latin Church, if willing, as she is, to concede everything not found in the doctrine and practice of the first four centuries." * These last lines are quoted from the bishop's journal. It continues:

Bishop Smith placed [this paper] in my hands as his instructions to me for my guidance in conference or correspondence with the Old Catholics; with the declaration that, to the best of his knowledge and belief, they express the sense of all the (so-called) Low Church bishops, and would be sure of meeting with their approval, which consequently might be depended on for any action consistently based on them or discreetly directed toward their carrying out.

The result of this interview was my consent to reconsider my course and my promise that—on certain conditions—I would go.

By August 24th these conditions were fully met. One grave objection was not removed, but it existed only in the bishop's mind. He had previously written:

My inmost wishes are for the advancement in every way of the interests of the Old Catholic movement, and nothing could be more in accordance with my desires than to be afforded opportunity in any way of lending aid for the furtherance of those interests. To be instrumental, in that way, by my personal attendance in an official capacity would be esteemed by me a very high privilege, and in accordance with all my view of duty to the Church of our Lord, to

---

* If this sentence do not seem wholly clear, see Bishop Whittingham's words given in the relation of what occurred during the conference at Bonn after the congress.

that branch of it in which I am an unworthy office-bearer, and to the deeply respected and greatly admired men whom the Spirit of God, as I entirely believe, is leading in the way of recovery of the old paths by which men may be brought together in the restored oneness of their Father's household.

My painful sense of unreadiness to meet such men on terms implying mutual enlightenment and support, compelled me from the first to hold aloof from any act or expression that could be understood to convey my own concurrence in the selection of myself to go to Germany.

On another occasion he said to a friend in reference to the greatness of the work and his own unfitness, " Perhaps you do not know, but I ought to tell you that I never had the advantage of a collegiate education." The being sent enabled him to overcome the sense of " weakness and fear."

At a very short notice were secured the services, as chaplain, of the Rev. Dr. Hobart, son of his early friend, and those of the Rev. Julius D. Rosé, who was peculiarly fitted for the duties of secretary, not only by his learning, but by his birth and education in Germany. And notwithstanding his infirm condition the bishop set out on " a journey which only the companionship and assistance of such friends could have made practicable." So he reported to his Convention in 1873.

On September 4th, after a special celebration of the holy communion in St. Mark's Church, Orange, the bishop went on board the steamer China.

The bishop's home letters tell of the voyage, of his journey to Cologne, and in part of occurrences in Germany ; but the relation of what took place at the conference would be far less full without the testimony of Dr. Langdon, whose generous aid is gratefully acknowledged.

WEDNESDAY, September 11, 1872.

This seventh day of our voyage finds us so far advanced in it as to warrant hopes of arrival in Liverpool Saturday morning. We have had an uninterrupted run of good weather—the first three days resembling a summer day's excursion on a river more than a sea-going; the inevitable fog and rain on the Banks lasting an unusually short time, and for the last two days a wind the most favorable possible driving us at the utmost attainable speed.

I do not find walking the deck as easy as it once was, not even as it was in 1866, and therefore I am in some degree cut off from the full enjoyment of and the benefit of the sea air. Perhaps on that account I am not sensible of much if any improvement as regards the condition of my head or my cough; on the contrary, the turmoil and confusion of my brain is no little increased by the multitudinous noises of the ship, the engines, the passengers, and the servants. Nevertheless I have been enabled to do something in the way of rubbing up my German and to prepare some business for my secretary.

Seven meals a day are served to solace the *ennui* of those who have nothing better to occupy their minds and bodies. We have the daily morning and evening prayer of the Church in full at 7 and 5, and a noonday service of our own at 12.

ADELPHI HOTEL, London, September 15th.

We reached the dock gates in Liverpool Saturday, 8.35 A.M., at the very time of high tide at which alone they could be opened for us.

At 1.40 we resumed our travel in a train to cross England, through a route shorter by many miles than had been made when I was last in England, and passing through a much more beautiful section of the land—in fact, the most charming agricultural region I have ever anywhere had the delight to feast my eyes upon. . . . Neither head nor back has been the least improved, that I can yet perceive, by my voyage. To-day I have been able to attend and extremely enjoy two services; in the morning at St. Paul's with a communion by which I was strengthened and refreshed as I hardly remember ever to have been before, and in the afternoon at Westminster Abbey. There could not have been less than two thousand in St. Paul's, and there were certainly more than twice that number in the Abbey. . . .

A week later—that is, after the congress—in Cologne he began a letter, but being interrupted by visitors, had to "break off, and now, at half-past 10, after seventeen hours' incessant occupation, I must absolutely go to bed."

The next morning, Tuesday, 24th, half-past 7, he resumes:

Having no early communion of our own this morning, I get half an hour before breakfast for writing home. Hitherto, since the first day after our arrival, either one of the English bishops or I has celebrated at this hour in the upper room used by the English as their chapel, about a quarter of a mile through round-about streets and lanes from this place, which is in the heart of the city.

On Sunday, with the express permission of the Government, the Old Catholics invited us to hold our communion in the Church of St. Pantaleon, which is theirs. Yesterday I celebrated. On Saturday the arrangement was that I should use the American communion office complete. Yesterday I used only our consecration prayer. . . . It was agreed yesterday that the Anglo-Catholic Society should print editions of translations of it in various languages, for circulation of it among the O. C. The same thing was to be done with our institution and consecration offices.

Now to begin my week's narrative. Oh, what a crowded week of work and excitement it is to look back upon!

Monday's business was to get our money affairs arranged, etc. I began the day by going with Rosé to prayers at St. Paul's. How great was our astonishment, on going out (during which, by the by, I was saluted by a grand peal of music from the organ, recognizing my presence as a bishop), to encounter just outside the door Dr. Muhlenberg. Great was the delight on both sides. The doctor told us that he was especially at St. Paul's that day by way of keeping his seventy-sixth birthday. . . . By the way, I take occasion to remark that the change in London in the seventeen years since I last visited it is perfectly wonderful. The marvellous embankment, the many wide new streets, opening great thoroughfares in every direction, the multitudes of magnificent new buildings—all, taken as a whole, completely surpass expectation, not to say any conception I could have formed. . . . We went to Westminster Abbey for evening prayers, and had the great satisfaction to find a large congregation at an ordinary week-day service, among them many evidently of the common people, even of the very commonest, seemingly deeply interested in the whole service.

Tuesday.—All the way was as smooth as New York Bay in its best moods, and the formidable English Channel as easy to cross as our Chesapeake. By daylight Wednesday morning we arrived at Antwerp. Off again for a land journey of some one hundred and eighty or so miles, at half-past 8 o'clock. Even after travelling in England, the cultivation of the low countries through which we travelled seemed wonderful. It appeared as if everything that man could do to turn every inch to the best account had been performed. For neatness and comfort, the very poorest dwellings visible, and all the ground, seemed to compare favorably with the best parts of our country. So we rode all day to Cologne, the famous dome of which we caught sight of at half-past 4. We found Langdon waiting for us. He told us that the Bishop of Lincoln had arrived the day before, and was then in consultation with some of the leaders of the movement at Bonn, and would be with us in the evening. The bishop has with him, and had during the ten days' tour he made to come here, his family. His eldest son is his chaplain. Lord Charles Harvey [a warm personal friend of Bishop Whittingham] came out with us to be the other, bringing with him the pastoral staff of the Bishop of Lincoln. That same staff, by the by, Bishop Wordsworth insisted on lending to me, and on the occasion of my celebrating our American communion was borne before me by Dr. Hobart.

The letter is here interrupted, in order that may be given, in Dr. Langdon's words,* a relation of what happened earlier and later on the day of the bishop's arrival, together with remarks on the nature of the Old Catholic movement which are a proper introduction to that relation.

[To appreciate the significance of the Congress of Cologne, and especially the pregnancy of Bishop Whittingham's presence there, it is necessary to bear in mind that the Old Catholic movement was not, and is not, by any means a popular religious revolt. It has so far appealed only incidentally *ad populum*. It was rather a forward movement of the vanguard of that school in the Church which has for three centuries resisted the Jesuits and their centralizing policy: it is the advance of a small number of manly, conscientious, scholarly churchmen, who, fully recognizing the character of the crisis to which the Vatican decrees had brought the Church, set themselves to explore and open up a way in which such a revolt, inevitably to come, might follow.

In such a movement the Old Catholic leaders did not

---

* Dr. Langdon's kind contributions to this chapter are marked by brackets.

propose either to seek guidance or to ask counsel from
without, nor was it with any such intent that they had invited to Cologne representative members of other Churches.

Their purpose in issuing these invitations was to take, at
the same time, a tentative step in the direction of Christian
unity, and, in view of this object, they were desirous of
conference with such representative ecclesiastics and theologians concerning the inter-relations, actual and possible, of
their respective Churches, that thus they might learn whether
this hope were or were not premature.

These two objects of the congress, however distinct,
were nevertheless closely combined; for, as was said at the
time, "the more frankly it is decided to separate from
Rome, the more necessary it is to establish definitely the
relations which ought in future to exist between the Old
Catholics and the other more important confessions."

Nevertheless, in the conceptions of the Old Catholics
these their two purposes were entirely distinct; and yet it
was evident *in limine* that, with the exception of the very
few who had already enjoyed some personal intercourse
with them, the foreign guests were coming without a very
clear understanding of the limits of the purpose which had
prompted the invitations addressed to them. Of this misunderstanding certain publications found in circulation
among the members of the approaching congress were illus-
trative.

An open letter by "A Russian Layman" urged on the
Old Catholics that the only consistent course before them
was that of merging themselves in the Holy Orthodox
Eastern Church.

A learned Latin letter by the Bishop of Lincoln, in acceptance of their invitation to the congress, reminded them
of the ties which had existed of old between the Churches
of Germany and of England, frankly criticising the inconsistent position in which the Old Catholic movement was left
by the Munich Congress, and urging the adoption at the

congress now approaching of certain observances which would, in the bishop's judgment, more perfectly express their Catholic purpose.

An open letter to Dr. Von Döllinger, finally, by an American writer, combated the above Russian counsel, and disclaimed the wish to offer parallel Anglo-American advice, urging rather that every branch of the Church of Christ must develop its own ecclesiastical life in accordance with its own ethnological characteristics, and that the hope of a better understanding between different confessions must be based upon the principle of unity in diversity, and must depend upon the willingness of all to meet in the spirit of mutual concession and in the consciousness of common needs.

Bishop Whittingham had undoubtedly shared, to some extent, the supposition that the foreign ecclesiastics were invited not for conference only, but as counsellors, and it was this which largely explained his reluctance to accept so grave a responsibility. As he journeyed he read the American letter referred to, and fully approved its positions.

The bishop arrived at Cologne on Wednesday afternoon, September 18th. A preliminary private conference had been held in Bonn that morning.

At this conference Dr. V. Döllinger, Profs. V. Schulte and Reinkens, and other leading Old Catholics, fifteen in all, were present; the Bishop of Lincoln and suite and the Rev. Mr. Hogg represented the Church of England. It had been arranged that Bishop Whittingham should go up also had he arrived in time; as it was, Mr. Langdon was the only American there. Bishop Wordsworth, unconscious of the wide difference between the customs of English churchmen and German Catholics on such occasions, and scarcely realizing how far were the latter, even yet, from being as ready to unite with Anglicans as are we to join with them, quite startled the Germans by proposing that they should unite in asking the divine blessing upon their meeting there. With some hesitation and confusion they were all, nevertheless, in the very act of kneeling, and the bishop was beginning the Pater Noster, when the door opened, and a maid appeared with a large waiter of beer, pipes, and tobacco. She was checked; the bishop quietly went on with some Latin collects, and afterward entering upon the subject of a joint public service for the formal opening of the congress, he laid before them a German programme prepared by himself, and printed for this purpose. In reply it was urged, with a little feeling, that the relations of the two Churches had scarcely reached, as yet, the point which would warrant such a service; nor, moreover, was this their customary way of opening such a gathering.

The bishop pressed the question whether concurrent separate services might not then be had, or, at least, one of joint thanksgiving at the closing of the congress. Pending this discussion the conference adjourned to the afternoon. It is not to be denied that the effect of these proposals was, for a while, to chill the cordial welcome with which the Old Catholics had been prepared to meet their foreign guests. No American was present in the afternoon, but the message was telegraphed to them in German from the Cologne railway station : "The Bishop of Maryland has just arrived, and sends you greetings in the Lord."

This informal conference is noteworthy. It was the first meeting, face to face, of an Anglo-Catholic bishop with the leaders of the Old Catholic protest against the Vatican decrees. It was noteworthy also as the key to the subsequent relations of the Anglican bishops to the congress, and, indeed, to the Old Catholic movement itself.

If, on the one hand, it did produce a temporary constraint in those relations and modify the welcome which would otherwise have been given to the Bishop of Maryland, who, although officially representing the American episcopate, was not officially received by the congress, it none the less, on the other, placed in his hands as an American bishop a work for which he was so singularly fitted, that of disarming the very beginning of antagonism, and drawing the Churches toward each other by the bands of personal sympathy and affectionate confidence. At the same time it gave to the Old Catholics the better opportunity to appreciate the singleness of purpose and the Catholic loyalty of the Bishop of Lincoln, who spoke first, and always from the promptings of his conscientious sense of duty to his office and to Him of whom he held it, without reference to the reception which his words might meet.

If something was lost at the first to all the Anglican bishops at Cologne from this temporary misunderstanding, who shall say how much was, in God's providence, eventually gained for the cause of their coming in truer mutual understanding, affection, respect, and confidence?]

There is doubtless something ludicrous in the first meeting of the English bishop with the pipe-smoking, beer-drinking reformers; but no one will think of connecting ridicule with Bishop Wordsworth, nor any shade of censure for the results of his very excellence. We are touched by the fact that when first he saw Bishop Whittingham his pious prompting was to suggest that they should together return thanks to God and ask for a continuance of his blessing. It was perfectly natural to suppose that an invitation to a conference implied the asking godly counsels. An Englishman could not enter upon religious consultation without prayer; and, being the only bishop present, it was proper that Bishop Wordsworth should bid to prayer. Equally proper was it that he should propose a joint public service for those who had acknowledged each other as brethren.

To make no reference to the misapprehension of the Bishop of Lincoln would be to omit what alone brings to view the benefit resulting from the attendance of the Bishop of Maryland at the conference.

[After dinner, Bishop Wordsworth having now returned from Bonn, Bishop Whittingham, accompanied by two of his clergy, called on his lordship, finding him in the midst of his family. "The bishop," he writes, "asking after my health and voyage, proposes joint thanksgiving for blessing prospering the journeys of us all to this assemblage. We all kneel down, and he offers several collects and other appropriate prayers (including his own blessing on the congress) with much fervor of devotion. He then went into a detailed statement of the occurrences of the day."

In connection with the design of having a daily early eucharistic service during the congress at the English chapel, the Bishop of Lincoln, continues Bishop Whittingham, "at once offered to me, as the senior bishop, the arrangement and disposition of the service. I promptly declined," adding "that I should feel bound to insist on his retaining the direction for two reasons, either alone sufficient to settle the question for me, viz.: 1, that the chapel and its service belong to the Church of England; and, 2, that on an occasion like the present, where different branches of the Church are brought into temporary relations of mutual courtesy, it behooves the younger branch to signify its filial relations to the elder by recognizing in joint services the antecedency even of the junior bishop of the elder branch before his senior of the junior branch."

But Bishop Whittingham was not content to put his refusal to accept the precedence solely on this ground of ecclesiastical principle. "Our bishop," writes Dr. Hobart, "declined any leadership in words of such utter self-abnegation and depreciation as overwhelmed those who were present. I felt bound soon after, in speaking to the Bishop of Lincoln, to qualify what our bishop had said of himself, but was anticipated by Bishop Wordsworth, who was pronounced in his admiration for Bishop Whittingham's character and learning."

Returned to his room that night, the bishop called Dr. Hobart and Mr. Langdon to a consultation respecting the nature of his relations with the congress, which he thought should be clearly understood among themselves and by others, especially by the Germans, from the start. This was likely to be the more necessary since there seemed some difference of judgment between the Bishop of Lincoln and himself in respect to the course to be pursued at the congress. "It was evidently, at first," writes Dr. Hobart again, " the idea [of all the more important foreign guests, Russian, English, and American alike] that the deputations from England and America, with others, would have an important part" to take in the discussions of the congress. This expectation was now seen to be mistaken; but the Bishop of Lincoln thought it due alike to his office and to his character as an English churchman to give plainly and loyally to the Old Catholics such counsel as his position enabled him to offer, and to urge them to such a course as to him seemed most for their advancement in their work, leaving to them the responsibility of ignoring or accepting it.

The Bishop of Maryland, on the contrary, and his American clergy with him, were rather of the opinion that, as foreigners, they were too little acquainted with the circumstances, or with the habits and prejudices of thought of German Catholics, to be able to counsel wisely in an issue of so much delicacy and difficulty; and that, as guests, they could neither enter into the responsibility of the Old Catholics nor properly offer advice upon those questions which concerned their internal reform; that it was only in respect to the questions of the inter-relations between the Old Catholics and ourselves that we could usefully take part in their discussions.

It was agreed, therefore, that Bishop Whittingham should preserve his own distinctive position and pursue an independent course, and thus maintain the distinctive individuality and responsibility of the American Church before the movement.

So ended the first day at Cologne.]

Thursday at 3—the bishop's letter continues—the ten members of the committee, including the Governor of the city and six or seven professors of different universities, with Herr V. Schulte, the President of the Congress, waited on me at my room—fortunately a noble room, ample enough—to welcome us.

After the first multilingual attempts at conversation, the Bishop of Lincoln came down to my room and we all spent half an hour together. I find my German of no use for conversation, though I understand it, better than I had expected, when others speak it.

The bishop thus speaks with habitual simplicity of what was a memorable interview. For what he could not say even in a letter to wife and children we are indebted to Dr. Langdon.

[Several of the Old Catholic leaders wished to pay their respects to the Bishop of Maryland. Von Döllinger and some others of those who had received the Bishop of Lincoln at Bonn the day before were not of the number. . . . They were presented formally to Bishop Whittingham one by one, and he, apologizing for his lack of German, to some addressed a few words in one language or another, and then more fully to all through Colonel Kiréef, a fine linguist, who courteously placed himself at the bishop's service and translated English into German.

Each had his little speech of welcome, writes the bishop,[*] and I had to do what I could toward understanding and stammering out some blundering kind of answer in bad French or Latin, or worse German as the case might be. One thing was very intelligible— kind faces, with the kindliest of kind looks, made the kind intention of the whole quite unmistakable.

Thus far, however, the interview was rather ceremonious. They took their leave, and were proceeding to call on the Bishop of Lincoln, but meeting him on the stairway near, at his request most of them turned back with him to the room they had just left. Here, after the presentation of those whom he had not already met, Bishop Wordsworth

---

[*] In his journal, which Dr. Langdon frequently quotes.

addressed them in French in reference to the hopes and expectations of English churchmen in coming to Cologne.

Professor Huber, begging permission to reply in German, did so somewhat in the language of remonstrance. Bishop Whittingham's eager manner and countenance, all glowing with excited sympathy, showed that he not only fully understood the other, but, indeed, rather sympathized with him than with the English bishop, and no sooner had the professor stopped than Bishop Whittingham, forgetting his lack of German, broke out in that language with the expression of his feelings on an occasion such as this.

This kindled the Germans into perfect enthusiasm. Prof. Reinkens sprang up and replied in the most hearty, reverential, and grateful German, and taking leave again, grasped the bishop's hand in both his own in such a cordial manner that the latter impulsively embraced and kissed him. Others thanked the bishop with no less warmth, and all went away leaving a most hearty feeling on both sides.]

We resume the bishop's recital:

The meeting over, dinner came on. That through with, we had to go to a public meeting of reception at the Gürzenick Saal. There things looked singular enough. Long tables were arranged with beer mugs and glasses, segars and pipes. At a raised part in the end of the room the President of the Congress received the guests and presented them to the members seated, eating and drinking at the tables, and the necessary speaking was done. The Bishop of Lincoln, I, and the Russian delegates, and last of all " their own bishop," as they called him, the Dutch archbishop, who has been confirming for them, were successively presented to the company, greeted, by the president, and made their replies. I spoke in English, admirably well interpreted, sentence by sentence, in German, by Dr. Rosé—having first in French asked their leave so to communicate with them.* Dr. Rosé also interpreted in German a

---

* Dr. Langdon writes: "The call for the Bishop of Maryland was received with vociferous cheering as he rose. . . . 'I come, a poor infirm old man,' said he, as reported in the London *Daily News*, 'under the pressure of the solicitude of hundreds of my brethren, to represent the earnest anxiety with which they are watching the wonderful origin and growth of this movement, for

part of what Bishop Wordsworth said, the rest being partly in French and partly in Latin. The Dutch archbishop spoke, as I did, in his own language, interpreted by his chaplain. Dr. Rosé, too, had a little to say on his own account on behalf of German Catholics of Newark, who had charged him with their greetings for the congress. We got home about 11 o'clock; but I have reason to believe that the agreeable occupations of the natives were carried on three or four more hours.

At 9 A.M. on Friday the public conference began by the re-election of Von Schulte, the former president; and right well he proved himself to deserve the honor, for of all men whom I have ever seen preside in a large assembly, he displayed unmeasurably the most ability. In every quality desirable in such a position he seemed to excel, as if that particular quality had been his distinguishing characteristic; and throughout the three long, trying days of the hardest kind of work there was not once an indication of the slightest failure. He was supported by two vice-presidents, and beneath the three sat three secretaries, below whom were the shorthand reporters filling a large square table. The guests were on either hand of the secretaries. They were quieted by the president, and the Bishop of Lincoln made a formal Latin speech from an already printed copy. It was a lecture on the duty of the hearers, which they, for their part, by no means conceived themselves to need. It was evident at once that the mistake might lead to mischief. The able president hurried the conference into its work—the reception and discussion of reports already prepared by committees appointed at the previous congress. Then it became evident how little the men here gathered needed help or teaching from their guests, how wonderfully well they had prepared themselves for the delicate and difficult work they had before them. The body numbered some four hundred and thirty members, and I have never looked upon an assembly more distinguished by indications of intellectual ability and temperament fitted for discussion and debate. The more

---

which hundreds and thousands of hearts in the Catholic Church of my country are praying. . . . It was to express this and the sympathy of American churchmen for their brethren in Germany that I was forced to come.' He spoke so clearly and forcibly—wrote one who was present—in his best vein, briefly and wisely, that many understood him, and all could see his face and manner and hear his earnest tones. He made a deep impression; while, as he sat down, the Germans and others ran from all parts of the room to clink their glass mugs of beer against his glass of water. During the evening a large number were presented to the bishop."

perusal of the handful of printed papers brought in, as the material on which the conference had to work, satisfied me that we from abroad had done our work—and a very good, welcome, and sufficient one too—by putting in our appearance, and that any help from us in discussion of the matters with which the conference had now to deal was utterly unnecessary and might do more harm than good. Right glad I was to have the conviction that they were able to take care of themselves.

Fortunately, on the breaking up of the meeting I had an opportunity of conversation with one of the most influential leaders of the movement, Professor Reinkens, of Breslau. I used it at once for removing from his mind any impression that might have been conceived that we Americans had come to them for the purpose of interfering in their concerns, or were disposed to enforce on them the recognition of our distinctive system as a condition of our fellowship. So long as we were satisfied of their determination not to be seduced from adherence to the primitive doctrine and discipline on the one hand, and yet not to be content to retain unreformed the corruptions of the middle ages on the other, I told him, we Americans were content and desirous to leave to themselves the entire responsibility of regulating modes of procedure in their movement, and were with them exclusively for the purpose of encouragement by the manifestation of our interest in their work. . . .

The last public session of the congress was the opportunity for declaration of the intentions of the movement, all the preceding work having been for the preparation of its means. Four of the chief leaders spoke successively at length on all the points of needed reformation, and truly they left nothing to be desired in the way of outspoken exposure of mediæval corruptions of doctrine and discipline, as well as of manly protests against Roman tyranny and deceit. They came out boldly against prevalent abuses wrought into a system of iniquity by Roman arts for human ends, and denounced them with a variety of eloquence which carried me back in imagination to the sixteenth century and the noblest of the labors of its reformers. The excitement of listening to such strains and remembering from whom they came, where they were being uttered —in this headquarters of German Romanism—and with what intent, was overwhelmingly great. I went home almost literally drunk with it.

To this story of incidents at the Cologne Conference, written by the bishop for his family, is added a supplement, in part the testimony of Dr. Langdon, in part quotations made by him from the bishop's journal.

The English-speaking bishops, having alike reached the conclusion that the Germans were well able to take care of themselves, breakfasting together on Saturday, agreed that explanations ought to be made to remove false impressions consequent upon the results of a supposition that having been invited to attend a *conference*, they had been asked to *confer*. The two English bishops urgently pressed their American brother to make such explanations on their joint behalf. [But the Bishop of Lincoln, seizing the midday recess for that purpose, entertained at dinner the Archbishop of Utrecht, with his chaplains, the Bishops of Maryland and Ely, with their attendant clergy, and the President of the Congress and other Old Catholics whom he had on Wednesday met at Bonn. After dinner Bishop Wordsworth formally proposed the health of the good old Dutch archbishop, and then that of President V. Schulte, taking occasion to explain "the position of the Anglican bishops in the congress, and apologizing for any expressions in his speeches or in the conference which might have given umbrage," inviting the German theologians to visit the bank of the Thames and criticise the Church of England as freely as he had criticised their own. To this frank and graceful explanation President V. Schulte responded in the most hearty manner, and "general good feeling appeared to prevail very strongly," when the whole party adjourned to the first public meeting of the congress, set for that afternoon at 4 o'clock.

For this meeting thousands were now assembled in the Great Hall of the Gürzenick. President V. Schulte prefaced its proceedings with a cordial reference to their foreign guests, especially to those from England and America, and offered an opportunity to the Bishop of Ely, in acknowledging the compliment, to speak of the presence of the English bishops at the congress, very much as Bishop

Wordsworth had spoken at the dinner-table just before.
The bishop spoke, however, in English, and his words were,
unfortunately, so poorly translated, almost clause by clause,
that their force was lost upon the audience.

On Sunday morning, September 22d, a step was cautiously
taken in the direction at least of ecclesiastical comity, whose
very moderate character served to set in striking relief the
distance which, after all this personal cordiality, was yet to
be passed between the two communions before the time
would come for such a service as Bishop Wordsworth had
urged for the opening of the congress.

A solemn high mass was to be celebrated and a sermon
preached at the Church of S. Pantaleon, whose use had been
conceded to the Old Catholics by the Prussian Government.
Application had been made, through the Cologne committee,
and permission obtained from the Government, for the use
of the adjoining chapel of this church for this morning by
the Anglo-American bishops for their early service, in order
that the two communions might celebrate their eucharistic
offices, though separately, yet as nearly as might be together
in time and place.

At 7.30, therefore, the English celebration was held in
this chapel, all the bishops being full robed and supported
by their respective chaplains; Bishop Browne consecrating
and "using his pastoral staff."

At 9 the Old Catholic congregation assembled in the
church; most of the English and Americans attended also,
the principal invited guests having seats specially assigned
them in the choir. There was even some talk of inviting
the bishops to be present officially in their robes, but it was
decided to be premature for this. Bishop Whittingham did
not himself attend at all, but his clergy were present.

The great church was literally filled with a congregation
estimated at two thousand—of course not all Old Catholics.]
Pastor Tangermann, of Cologne, preached a most appropriate
sermon, in which reference was made to the presence with

them at the congress and at that service of their foreign guests. Many of these, however, were forced to slip quietly away at the close of the sermon for the morning service at the English chapel, at which Bishop Wordsworth preached. Herr Councillor Wülffing was present as an interested and respectful observer of the services.

The second and closing public meeting of the congress was held that Sunday afternoon.

At the earnest representation and request of all the American clergy here—writes the bishop in his journal—and on repeated suggestions and request of the Bishop of Ely, the Rev. Mr. Hogg, and the Rev. Dr. May, I consent, if asked, to read in German a short address to the congress, which accordingly I prepare in English and get translated by the Rev. Dr. Rosé. I am assured that the President of the Congress has expressed his wish that I should address the congress in its native speech. The wish on the part of all the parties making these requests is to have a formal and distinct manifestation of the independent position of the American Church.

Accordingly at 4 P.M. I go, accompanied by Rosé carrying my credentials, to the last great public meeting of the congress in the Isabella Saal, prepared to speak if called on, and am placed by Professor Friedrich among the principals near the president. . . .

This last meeting was the opportunity for declaration of the *intention* of the movement, all preceding work having been for the preparation of the means. Four—Friedrich, Maasen, Reinkens, and Von Schulte, representing Bavaria, Austria, Prussia, and Bohemia— spoke successively at length on all the points of needed reformation, and truly they left nothing to be desired in the way of outspoken exposure of mediæval corruption of doctrine and discipline. They came out boldly against prevalent abuses wrought into a system of iniquity by Roman arts for human ends, and denounced them with a variety of eloquence which carried us back in imagination to the sixteenth century.

These four great speeches . . . so completely engross the whole interest and allotted time—five hours—of the meeting that it would have been folly to attempt an intrusion.

The bishop was therefore, after all, not called on to speak. He continues:

At 9 P.M. the immense meeting, which completely filled the hall, was broken up, rather than dismissed, with a neat parting word from its very able president. His exercise of his difficult office, in every one of its various duties and relations, has filled us all with admiration. His speech this evening was wonderfully wise and powerful, combining in an extraordinary degree an outspoken declaration and maintenance of principles with the most cautious discretion in the proposition of procedures. More or less, that has been characteristic of all the speeches this evening. We have seemed to ourselves to have been carried back three hundred and fifty years, and to be hearing the men then leading religious reformation alternately thundering against falsehood and tyranny, and persuading men, as babes, with the keenest logic and most seductive arts of flashing wit and sarcasm, to receive the truth. But all the while it was in every way evident that three hundred years' experience and attainment had been added to the armory of the sixteenth century reformers.

One thing was indisputable : reformation—thorough spiritual, scriptural reformation, on the historic basis of revealed truth in an unchanged transmission—was the openly avowed aim and end of the movement. The Dutch archbishop was present to the last.

The excitement of listening to such strains and remembering from *whom* they came, *where* they were being uttered (in the headquarters of German Romanism), and with what intent, was overwhelmingly great.

[So Bishop Whittingham did not reach Cologne in time for the informal conference of Wednesday, the 18th; he made no address to the congress at either the business or the public sessions; he was not even officially presented to the congress, and a large number of those who attended its deliberations may have been wholly ignorant that an American bishop was present among its invited guests.

But it was none the less due to Bishop Whittingham, above all others, that the relations between the Old Catholics and the American Church had been brought to the point at which they were disposed to take the friendly hand held out to them; and if, since that day, the Old Catholics of Germany and Switzerland have been drawn nearer and more near, until intercommunion virtually came at Berne in August, 1879, and was ratified by the presence of Bishop

Herzog at the General Convention of 1880, and by that of Bishops Reinkens and Herzog in English cathedrals in 1881, it was due, above all other human causes and influences, to the fact that Bishop Whittingham was present at the Congress of Cologne.]

The immediate purpose of the Old Catholic gathering—the discussion of measures essential to their own better organization—had been attained. There was still to be considered the subject of actual and possible relations with other Christian confessions. This had been entrusted to a commission of their leaders, under the chairmanship of Dr. V. Döllinger, and it was understood that this commission would meet on Monday, September 23d, for a first tentative conference with the specially invited representatives of other Churches, although the president, from whatever motive, had gone back to Bonn.

The Bishop of Lincoln was obliged to leave Cologne. It was agreed, therefore, among the English churchmen, that it should be left to the Anglo-Continental Society, and especially to its president, the Bishop of Ely, and to its secretary, to take part in the conference on behalf of members of the Church of England.

Almost everything, thus far, had tended to lead the Germans to think of the Churches of England and America as virtually one. It had been supposed that the Bishop of Lincoln, at the preliminary conference on the 18th, spoke for both Churches in one; and during the congress the leaders were less careful to secure to Bishop Whittingham an opportunity of addressing them, because of this impression. It was now necessary to remove it. Bishop Whittingham therefore refused to join the Committee on the Reunion of the Churches when invited to do so by the secretary of the English Society, and required as an American bishop a distinct invitation from the Old Catholic commission. It being evident that there was a double danger of misunderstanding, at the suggestion of Dr. Hobart, Mr. Langdon sought Professor Huber, and explained to him the independent and distinctive position of the American Church, on account of which the Bishop of Maryland could not attend such a conference merely as a member of a society which, for the present purpose, represented the Church of England; nor could the American Church be considered as represented at any such conference by the presence and participation of English churchmen.

About half-past 9—to return to the bishop's journal—Mr. Carmichael and Mr. Hogg came to my room, charged with an invitation from Professor V. Schulte, as [acting] president of the committee. In the meanwhile Professor Huber has called, leaving his card and a verbal message. I accept the message, and set out with Dr. Hobart, as my chaplain, for the Gürzenich. About half way there we met Professor Huber coming after me.

At once he begins apologizing for my not having been called on to speak the night before, and solicits my intended address for publication in the *Deutsche Merkur*. I tell him that in that matter I shall be very much disposed to be guided by his advice—that if he thinks the publication likely to do good *here*, and on this ground will advise it, it will weigh much with me. As to the silence on the preceding evening, it was quite in accordance with my wishes. I had no desire to speak on my own account or that of my Church.

There were present in the meeting about two and-twenty persons, and no better summary can now be given of the proceedings of that conference than a slight verbal development of the condensed record of the bishop's journal.

President V. Schulte states the object of the meeting as—

1. Its primary object : its *end*, the reunion of the Churches.

2. Its secondary object : its *means*, to be now discussed and, so far as can be, settled.

He takes the voices of those present as to the first—

Is it desirable? Is it to be hoped for? Are there grounds for thinking it attainable?

An affirmative response was received from several quarters.

He asks, are we *all* agreed in so thinking?—which was affirmatively answered.

As to the *second* he proposes discussion; suggestions that a subdivision of those present into sub-committees representing each its own Church, and prepared to enter into mutual correspondence with all the other sub-committees in the way—

1. Of laying down distinctly the position of its own Church.

2. Of stating clearly and succinctly the objections to the views and positions of others, as so stated.

3. Of giving information and references illustrating the position of its own Church, to which others may have recourse in order to accurate study.

President V. Schulte further expressed the wish that as a personal medium, through whom more definite correspondence could be hereafter arranged, the name of some one should be agreed on as representing each Church.

Bishop Whittingham consented himself to accept that charge on behalf of the American Church.

Prof. Michaelis then proposes that the present occasion should not be allowed to pass without making some attempt at a practical beginning of our work by laying down principles in which, now and here, we can declare our agreement.

[This short speech was, in some respects, as remarkable as any uttered in Cologne in connection with the gathering of the congress. No report of it probably remains save in the memory of those who heard it—no record save the effect produced.

It scarcely seemed the utterance of a single man. It was the occasion itself—it was the Old Catholic movement with all its yet unspoken hopes and latent possibilities suddenly finding expression in a few strong, solemn words. It held every heart even of those who but imperfectly understood him, especially when he likened the Church of Christ, in its present state, to the great Cathedral of Cologne as he had seen it in his own early days—still unfinished after centuries of building; the choir—the nave—the half-raised towers—each separated from the others, and some portions actually going to ruin ere the glorious design of the architect had been realized, and then described the cathedral as they had all seen it that day, now rapidly and surely approaching completion at last, its majestic proportions revealed to the worshipping throngs who pressed into its courts, even in some measure to those who stood to gaze on it without—a Catholic cathedral, but owing this completion, by God's permission, to a Protestant king and emperor. So, the speaker concluded, "it is with the help of Protestantism that the Church Catholic shall itself be reunited and completed."]

As a tentative effort Prof. Michaelis then proposes—

1. That we all agree in professing our faith in one only true God, and one Lord Jesus Christ, acknowledged by us as truly God and truly man, by whom alone we know the Father and come to Him. All accept and profess this by acclamation.

2. That we all believe that our Lord and Saviour Jesus Christ founded a Church on earth.

Declaring that there he stopped, leaving further development for future discussion. Accepting that declaration, all agreed in the proposition of such belief.

The Russian delegates then proposed that the acceptance of the Seven Councils should be professed.

To this at once objections were started on several grounds. It was generally felt that those here and now assembled had not the requisite authority to commit their several Churches to such a profession.

I [Bishop Whittingham] said that I had no representative authority here, being only the bearer of kindly greetings and inquiries, but that, for my own private and personal part, I was free to declare my individual belief that the American Church as a body would be found unwilling to refuse fellowship with any Christian body which (1) held the three Creeds; (2) had an uninvalidated succession from the apostles, and (3) received the first four General Councils. The Bishop of Ely said that the Anglican communion at the Lambeth conference had declared the Holy Scriptures and the six undisputed General Councils to be its basis of profession and practice.

This led to some discussion as to the signification of the limitation "undisputed," and also as to the determination of the canonical authority of the parts of Holy Scripture.

The Russian delegates insisted on the Seven as to be received without question. They presented a printed list of books from which the position of their Church might be ascertained.

I pointed out that I had not given the three articles stated by me as the positive assertion of the American Church, but as what I conceived to be its negative claim—the limitation of its lowest limit of requisition of other bodies as conditions of fellowship in communion, etc. On this distinction the English members generally seemed disposed to agree. We all accepted the Lambeth declaration as a statement of our own position.

It was then proposed by several members that we should add another article of common agreement, viz.:

3. The principle of Vincent : *Quod semper, ubique et ab omnibus creditum, tenendum est.*

President V. Schulte remarked upon it as a rule to be laid down in our subsequent proceedings rather than as an article of faith ; to which all agreed, and then with cordial acclamation accepted it.

[Thus far the Official Memorandum of this Conference, authenticated by the signature of President V. Schulte, agrees with the somewhat fuller record of the bishop's journal. But in the memorandum there appears still another article of agreement not so distinctly recorded as such by the bishop, who has, however, recorded the discussion which led to it.

"4. The external basis of our reunion is the Holy Scriptures, the ancient Fathers, and the undisputed Ecumenical Councils."

The general statement was also, as shown in that document, formally made :

"III.—We regard ourselves only as individuals, not as authorized representatives of the Churches ; but we hope to prepare the way for final union by means of a Universal Council."]

To return to the bishop's journal :

President V. Schulte then, in a formal manner, congratulated the committee on its auspicious beginning of its work. . . . Thanking the members for their attendance, he took particular leave of the Bishop of Ely and of me with neatly turned expressions of regard and gratification by our participation in their work.

[However slight the importance of this conference in the judgment of the world, and almost forgotten as already is the fact that it took place, Bishop Whittingham then and ever after more truly estimated its significance. Worn as he was by his long journey, from which he had not had a day, scarcely an hour, to rest, and by the excitement of the congress, yet, seemingly unconscious of his weariness, he sat there on the edge of the platform, his eager eye resting on every speaker, almost studying every listener, or rose to speak himself, his whole figure eloquent, his every feature glowing with his realization of the meaning of his being there. He was that day, in the influence he was exerting by the magnetism of his presence and his great single-heartedness, the foremost man among those who were there engaged in preparing for the after-conferences of Bonn.

For a day or two more Bishop Whittingham was kept up by the intensity of his sympathies. . . . On Tuesday, Abbé Michaud, who had had an interview with the bishop the evening before, dined with him and the American clergy. In view of the abbé's after-course, the bishop's record of their conversation is of the greater interest.]

M. Michaud freely explains his position [as a worshipper at the Russian church in Paris] as in no respect committing his ecclesiastical relations. He seeks spiritual help at the hands of men who have joined the Eastern orthodox confession merely for individual spiritual benefit, but in no wise as thereby renouncing or forsaking the Church of his native land, or acceding to any claims of exclusive orthodoxy or of intrusive jurisdiction on the part of the Oriental Church. He remains a true and loyal member of the Western Church, praying and laboring for the reform of that Church on scriptural and Catholic principles, after a primitive pattern. He regards the validity of Anglican orders as indisputable, and, so far as he knows it, finds nothing in the system of English and American doctrine and discipline for which he should be justified in eschewing the communion of our Churches. He was ignorant of the difference between the American communion office and the English [upon which difference it should be remembered that the Old Catholics have all laid great stress], and was much pleased with what I told him of the nature of that difference, as well as of the purport of our offices of institution and of consecration of churches.

He expressed himself as disheartened with regard to the immediate future of the Church of France, although fully possessed with the belief that France, always oscillating from one extreme to the other, and now committed to the Ultramontane extreme, would ultimately utterly reject the false claims she now admits, and break the spiritual bondage in which she now lies miserably bound, hand and foot.

He declared his plans for the future to be quite uncertain—his hopes to be that while Loyson should, as he intended, be struggling by his eloquence to win popular support, he (Michaud) would labor to awaken the attention of his fellow-countrymen and inform their minds by the diligent employment of his pen. . . .

"We all partook," adds the bishop, "in the conversation, and agreed in our understanding of Michaud's position."

And on Wednesday again he writes: "About 10 M. Michaud comes in while Langdon is with me. We talk again of his difficulties and plans. I encourage him to persevere, and not to attach too much importance to the difference between himself and Loyson, but make up his mind to go determinedly on, teaching with his pen and watching the time for a revolution in church matters in France."

[That the abbé has since both stoutly denied the validity of Anglican orders and earnestly labored on behalf of Russian at the expense of English influence, is now well known. The memory of the conversations here cited, and the manner in which the abbé ever afterward spoke of Bishop Whittingham, is ground for saying that he was the one man who, could he have remained abroad, could have saved the Old Catholic cause and reformed the Church of Switzerland from the divisions from which it suffered in consequence of the antagonism of the Abbé Michaud to the Père Hyacinthe and Bishop Herzog.

In the nervous reaction and almost utter exhaustion which soon followed such a continued mental strain, the bishop's first feeling was that he must now return at once to America.

The resolution of the House of Bishops had indeed asked

him to visit Italy as well as Germany, and the first notice of the coming invitation to the congress had been coupled with the opinion that he should come to Europe " free to give the autumn to Germany and France and the winter to Italy." In immediate connection with the provision of means for his mission, Dr. Leeds had also written : " The limits of a conference will allow, of course, of only a very imperfect comparison of views, and a still more restricted influence. A stay with the leaders, and a calm, free, unreserved communication with them in the quiet of every-day life, touching the points in which they are most concerned . . . Your lingering after [the congress] by the headquarters of influence will be far more important for the good of the cause."

But the bishop had said explicitly that his continuance abroad, and his going into the South of Europe, would be conditioned upon his having official charge of the American clergy and chapels there ; and although he had been led to expect it, yet no such commission had, thus far, been received by him. As for the German Old Catholics, in his admiration for those whom he had already met, and in his humble self-appreciation, it did not seem to him that there was or could be anything further for him to do among them.

The bishop now, therefore, looked upon his mission as at an end; but Dr. Hobart and Mr. Langdon, agreeing in the judgment of the very serious loss which would result to all the interests involved, and still hopeful of the coming of the commission, availed themselves of the bishop's real need of rest and quiet to induce him to go for awhile to Bonn for these objects, there to await the course of events.

Accordingly with Drs. Hobart and Rosé he went up to Bonn and remained there from October 1st to October 18th, finding in that quaint and quiet home of scholars the refreshment alike for body and mind of which he stood in need.

These were days of that unstudied personal intercourse

which wins the will through the affections. . . . Bishop Whittingham himself never realized what he accomplished during this rest in Bonn, or so much as suspected the subtle influence which he was there exerting for religious unity, and the feelings of respect and even affection toward the American Church which he was drawing out.]

While in Bonn he received not only warm invitations from Dr. V. Döllinger and other Germans to visit them, but also not a few intimations that it was considered important that he should prolong his stay in Germany and the South of Europe at least during the coming winter.

[But the bishop had decided under what circumstances alone he should feel it his duty to remain in Europe and to go on toward Italy. With him it was simply the question whether he should or should not be clothed with the authority necessary for the fulfilment of his charge; and having waited in Bonn—as he felt—long enough to receive such a commission if there was any purpose to send it, he gave up all thought of further travel, investigations, or personal intercourse with other reformers, and on October 18th turned his steps homeward. After his arrival in Baltimore—November 15th—was received back from England "a letter from Bishop Stevens, on behalf of the presiding bishop and himself, requesting [him] to officiate while abroad in the American churches on the Continent." This request, indeed, fell very far short of vesting him with that official charge of those churches which he had been led to expect; but "had they reached me," he wrote on the last page of his special journal, "before determining on return, it certainly would have decided our counsels for staying abroad." It was now too late.

The bishop accepted this delay as "providential." It is improbable that any of his right reverend brethren who survived him did not live also to regret that any reluctance to trust such a man with the power of rendering such services to the whole Church of Christ, should have cost the

Church the visit that he might have made to Munich and the Swiss Old Catholics, and the winter that he might have passed in Italy.]

Early in August, 1873, Bishop Whittingham received a formal invitation to attend the third Old Catholic Congress, to be held at Constance. A congress markedly different from that of Cologne, for now it was declared that "the great end to which we aspire is Christian union," and therefore the bishop was asked "to come and enlighten our congress with your learning and guide us with your counsels." Again he was personally invited to be present at the fourth congress held at Freiburg in 1874. It was impossible for him to comply with the invitation. But his interest was otherwise, and continuously marked. While he lived, this interest extended to all in Europe who were seeking a return to the old paths—was especially given to the reform movement in Italy, which he always believed ought to be forwarded by our Church.

Encouraged and advised by Bishop Whittingham, Mr. Langdon went to Rome with wider views than the establishment there of the congregation of Americans, which he then formed. His work, interrupted by the war of secession, was resumed soon after the restoration of peace, and now as accredited by the Church. With never-flagging interest, whether abroad or at home, he has watched every step taken toward reformation in Latin Christendom ; he has been brought in contact, in some cases into intimate personal relations, with the leaders in that movement, and with the prominent men in England who sympathize with them ; and during all this time he was in confidential relations with his bishop—Bishop Whittingham—reporting to him all that was learned and done, looking to him for counsel and support.

Being thus familiar with all to be told in this chapter, he was asked to write it. He undertook the pleasing task ; but the abundance of his materials was an embarrassment.

He wrote out his story with a fulness that adds to its interest, but that made his contribution disproportionate.

As there was not room for all he had to say, he generously permitted the writer to make any use of his *manuscript*. With regret, omissions have been made. The passages retained as written by Dr. Langdon are included in brackets.

In the end the Church will not lose anything to be gained from the doctor's acquisitions, for happily he is engaged on a history of the present reformation on the continent, and the connection of the American Church with it.

LETTERS.

TO MRS. WHITTINGHAM.

BONN, October 1, 1872.

As I wrote rather a discouraged and discouraging letter this morning from Cologne I think it is but due to you to write again to-night, as I feel now under the still working influence of the pleasantest day I have passed since leaving America, and in a place which has a more home-like air and influence than any that I have been in since I took leave of Orange Valley.

At Cologne we were lodged in a vast palace—everything superlatively grand—but proportionately formal, and oppressively dull. Here we are in a *house;* overgrown, to be sure, but overgrown by spreading over surface, not by lifting itself up in the palatial grandeur of architectural stairways, and magnificent corridors, and statuary and paintings in lieu of settees and boot-jacks. In the Hotel Ditsch I had a room magnificent in proportions, to be sure, but of a gloomy outlook, and lined with the deepest of dark green paper. An alcove before which deep red moreen curtains could be drawn, contained, and, when need was, concealed, my bed, out of which I could look through my only windows, across a street ten feet broad, into a mediæval Romish church, in which, from a quarter before five in the morning until a quarter before nine at night, six or eight bells, two of them, at least, heavy and powerful, were constantly pealing for one or another of the different services in which the people belonging to the various classes in St. Columba's parish seem to be thoroughly provided with spiritual administrations, during sixteen hours of every day. I will own that neither the continual new study of mediæval architecture, nor the unceasing clanging of peals of bells, nor the deep green light-absorbing walls of my lofty and spacious room, had any exhilarating effect upon my mind. I do not think that longer stay there would have been advantageous to my health.

Fortunately our movement, resolved on five days ago, seemed to have brought with it our customary glorious travelling weather—for, after a week of rough, unpleasant, almost wintry weather, we have had to-day, for our sail of thirty miles up the Rhine, as charming October weather as heart of man would wish. For the first time to-day I have really enjoyed myself in travelling, and have heartily wished that it were possible to have my loved ones with me, if so the enjoyment might be manifoldly increased. A steamboat of sensible dimensions and no pretensions, about one-tenth of the size of a North River steamer, far—incomparably—better fitted for enjoyment of everything around us—brought us swiftly and quietly up through scenery, every minute changing—towns, villages, hamlets, churches, chateaux, factories, and manors, and farms, every minute presenting something new, and almost invariably something pleasant to the eye and suggestive to the mind. Then, on board and on shore alike, everything seemed to wear such an air of ease and comfort! The very helmsman *sat* at his ease, and turned to and fro before him a horizontal wheel! No cries! no hurry! no scuffling, pushing, and running to and fro! Every one seemed to have plenty of time, and everybody seemed to be disposed to take it, and to let others take theirs too. A quiet waiter was stealing about from little groups to little groups, and at the crook of your finger would come, to bring to your seat, if you wished it, a cup of coffee, or a glass of Rhenish wine, or a mug of lager beer, or a slice of bread and sausage, or a bit of cheese, or a plate of little red radishes clustered round a little hill of salt—it seemed to make no difference which, for with equal quietness and celerity we saw all these things distributed on demand, here to bonnetless, knitting, and chattering women, there to pipe-furnished paper or book-reading men, elsewhere to laughing, romping, rollicking children. I never anticipated so much pleasure from journeying on the Rhine as this day's experience has afforded me. The glorious old river is worth all the Germans have been doing for it! long may they rejoice in its possession! Not that the natural features of the scenery so far surpass anything that our country can furnish! on the contrary, we have in many respects the advantage. But here all that man can do has been doing for a thousand years! and man can do a great deal to totally change the face of nature, and make it utterly another thing from what it is when unassisted and unadorned!

The strangely *home-like* air of everything in the very pleasant inn

where I am now writing, has quite set me up again to-night with
hopes that here I may really find rest and recruit.   I write in a cozy
room, about sixteen feet square and ten high, which serves as a sitting room, out of which my bedroom opens on one side, and Hobart's on the other, each about ten by sixteen feet.   On the other
side of the hall is Dr. Rose's room.   Each room has two windows
looking into a snug, quiet garden spot, and in each window are three
pots with choice geraniums in magnificent blossom.   All around is
neat as a new pin, clean as the driven snow, and a hundred times
more quiet than the quietest place in Orange, to say nothing of Baltimore.   Hobart sits at the table opposite to me writing to his wife,
and Dr. Rose has gone out on an exploring expedition to find out
where some of the professors live whom I shall have to call upon
or write to.   I must bid you good night now, as I have filled the
measure of my paper and tea will be coming in in a few minutes—
the bells are chiming for 8 P.M.   God bless you all !

Your ever loving

WILLIAM.

HOME LETTER.

NOTHING TO BE GAINED BY A FURTHER ABSENCE.

BONN, October 14, 1872.

A few days' stay here under circumstances of the most favorable
nature gave me but too complete an assurance that I was to look for
no advantage from travel, but had to make up my mind to give up
all attempts at much moving about and all hopes of fitness for
either enjoying or partaking in free and mixed intercourse with
strangers.   The affection of my head rather grows on me than otherwise, and a very few minutes of noisy conversation or of walking fa-
tigues me to the verge of serious illness.   Such being my condition,
it would be ridiculous to undertake the kind of circulating exchange
of civilities and kind attentions in which alone the fulfilment of my
mission could be carried out, and it would be simply dishonest to
remain in the costly form which has thus far been well justified, with
no further adequate aims in view.   I am thoroughly satisfied with
our work, notwithstanding its early close.   The end aimed at in
sending us is accomplished, though, perhaps, very differently from
the expectations of most of those who joined in urging my expedition.   If we had not come, I have ample reason for believing that
far less cordial relations between the Old Catholics and the Anglican
Churches would have taken place.

Although this is now the thirteenth day of our stay in Bonn, I have seen but little of the place and nothing of the environs except an outlook up and down the Rhine, obtainable from the University garden. My inability either to walk or ride about has kept me prisoner.

Four days later, on his homeward way through England, he wrote from Brussels :

Since I wrote I have received a very gratifying letter of thanks for my visit to the congress, signed by all the leading members. The movement is making wonderful progress. They beg me to come again ! Ah me !

TO THE REV. DR. LEONARD BACON.

ESTIMATE OF OLD CATHOLICS—THE CHURCH POINTED OUT BY HISTORY.

BONN, October 17, 1872.

MY DEAR REV. BROTHER :

Your kind note of the 5th found me still here, and painfully satisfied by my patient trial that home, not a mission of exploration, is the fittest place for me during what remainder of days may be my allotted portion.

I have had pleasant intercourse with several of the leaders of the A. K. movement, and the result of free private communication with them is increased conviction that they thoroughly understand their own position and its needs, and increased hope also that they are qualified to carry on their work to very much larger measures of success than it has yet attained. Nor does the impression of their fervent personal piety weaken upon more intimate acquaintance. I cannot see reason to regard them as inferior, in that respect, to the great leaders of the sixteenth century Reformation—so far as men known only from books can be compared with men of whom one has the advantage of reading the flash of the living eye, the inflection of the voice, the curl of the lip, the curve of the mobile brow, or the flush of excitement or shade of pallor on the tell-tale cheek.

I think that both they and I—whatever may be our relative position on the graduated scale of churchmanship, measured by " height " or " depth "—have the advantage of you as regards *breadth*, if I rightly read and estimate your brief *exposé* of your position.

We agree with you in getting our faith historically through the divinely provided channel of a Church entrusted with the keeping of the Word of truth ; but there we seem to me to part, and larger-hearted than our brother, we, so-called " high " churchmen, are content with proclaiming "salvation *by* the Church " while our con-gregational brother can only find the blessing *in* it.

No doubt he is thereby driven, in the impulse of a loving heart, to resort to other modes of comprehensiveness. If salvation is only in the Church, then the Church itself must be made elastic and ex-pand to the comprehension of as many as one is [led, by any reason-ing, to reckon among those saved by God's mercy].* Only, then comes the difficulty about its recognition as the *historical* Church! The question of organization arises. The system of means and channels has to be looked into. Succession and authorization be-come elements in the problem. *History* is a serious, straightfor-ward business. It deals with "He *did*" or "He *did not;*" not "He *might*" or He *would* or "He *should.*"

Our Lord did, or he did not, bring and leave a message as well as do a work. Many seem to think that the work is its own message, because their inmost conviction is that it ought to be. You and I agree in finding the work only in the message, and basing our faith not on human intuitions, but upon external revelation of Divine truth. Well, if our Lord did bring and leave a message, history goes on, he did leave it in trust with men for dissemination and continuation, or he did *not.* If he *did,* then he left it with all, or with *some only*, and so on.

Begin with a historical promulgation of the "Gospel of the King-dom," and accept our present records of the New Testament as the sufficient evidence in the case, and I am utterly unable to see how the acceptance of a segregated ministry supernaturally authorized to constitute and organize a human society, to be in human succes-sion and extension throughout mundane time and space the witness and keeper of God's provisions for recording and sealing the mes-sage of salvation through the Son by the Spirit, is to be logically avoided. No one question in all history seems to me more clearly settled than the historical title of the Christian ministry, examined and decided on grounds of mere historic probabilities (for history, *quâ* history, can never rise out of probabilities) with determinate avoidance of all theological assumptions *à priori*, and rejection of consequential speculations.

" *Where* the offer and means of grace *have been left for presenta-tion* to the world " is surely an utterly distinct question from one,

---

* The copyist of this letter found it not easy to read the MS. and left here a space to be filled up. The omission was not noticed until the original was out of reach. The words included in brackets suggest one mode of expressing the thought that seems evident.

nevertheless, not very different in outward form—"*How* the offer and means of grace *are communicated* to the elect!" You, I think, have pushed your studies to the attainment of the conviction which certainly long ago became deeply rooted in my mind—that the God of nature, providence, and grace has nowhere restricted himself to the employment of the means to the use of which creatures are limited by the laws of their several relations.

It is the merest truism to say that neither force nor life is restricted by the *limits* of conscious receptivity or agency. Trace it upward into the kingdom of will, the law still holds that in morals good is not limited by conscious will either of agent or patient; and in the spiritual life its communication *is* everywhere and forever overrunning the provisions to which man is limited.

We have to seek the blessing according to the measure of our knowledge of its channels; but nowhere in the revealed Word, nowhere in the practical interpretation of that Word in the living work of the true Church of Christ, nowhere in the witness of the Spirit in the inmost consciousness of my individual experience as a Christian man, do I find any warrant for the limitation of divine grace by the accuracy of human knowledge.

When the fruits of the Spirit manifest His presence, I humbly and gladly own that presence, without presuming to ask why He has overstepped His own provided channels. But I see no call, in the largeness of His grace, to find encouragement myself to overstep the limits which, according to my measure of knowledge, I find assigned by history to the authorized divine provisions.

I am sure you do not expect me to accept your personal convictions, however deep and lively, as warrant for your authority to say to me, in Christ's name, that I am a forgiven sinner. I may perfectly believe the truth of your word in so saying, and the truthfulness of your meaning in so doing, too, and yet have no shadow of conviction of your right to do it. And yet I *do* know, as surely as anything about human rights and duties can be known, that there is a way in which you might *get* and *prove* to me and others the possession of that right. History has taught me where to seek it. In faith I thankfully accept the grace which I may look for *by* that road, without daring to assume that God sends it to none but those who travel *in* it.

Your loving friend,
W. R. WHITTINGHAM.

TO THE REV. DR. LYMAN.

THE GOOD RESULTING FROM HIS ATTENDANCE AT THE COLOGNE CONGRESS.

JANUARY 22, 1873.

DEAR THEODORE:

. . . I never in my life set about anything with quite so much reluctance as I had for that mission to Germany, growing out of the deepest sense of unfitness for it in every respect. Yet, without finding myself at all more competent than expected, I have been brought back heartily thankful that it was my privilege to go. Without knowing any reason for attributing the slightest consequence to any of my own individual doings or sayings, I am thoroughly satisfied that the mere fact of the presence of a senior representative of the episcopate of our Church at the assemblage in Cologne, surrounded by and serving as a nucleus to the half dozen able and active representatives of our clergy, who knew and were known to so many of the convening members, was of great advantage to the congress itself and to the ends it had in view—most of all that high aim, the restoration of Christian union on a churchly basis.

I found much more intelligence, piety, and zeal than I had ventured to hope for. Distinct conceptions of a great reformation to be undertaken as the outcome of the culmination of a thousand years of growing corruption and usurpation were in the minds of all. Many had distinctly formed plans, both as regards end and means. Nor were sufficiently outspoken utterances in the least withheld.

But a very brief intercourse with them sufficed for gathering ample proof that they knew their own position, needs, and resources too well to have any occasion for foreign advice or aid at present. The time, I trust, will come—and everything that I saw and heard there, and that has since transpired, tends to nourish the hope that it will come before very long—when counsel may be needed on their side as on ours, and on ours as on theirs, as to the direction and extent of efforts to be made all the world over for bringing back anti-Nicene simplicity of faith and worship, with Cyprianic order and organization. . . .

Your own loving

W. R. W.

THE REV. DR. LYMAN, *San Francisco.*

CHAPTER VI.

THE CANON ON VAIN AMUSEMENTS—MARYLAND EFFORTS AGAINST RITUALISM.

1873–1874.

In 1873 the Convention of Maryland, acting on the recommendation of a committee to whom had been entrusted the revising of the legislation of the diocese, repealed a canon that had been long on its statute-book, and which was in these words:

Theatrical Exhibitions and other Light and Vain Amusements Forbidden.

Attendance upon theatrical exhibitions, horse-races, and other vain and light amusements being considered inconsistent with the Christian character, it is hereby declared to be the duty of members of this Church carefully to abstain from encouraging them by their presence.

The report of the committee was in general readily received, but their recommendation with respect to this canon excited long and warm debate, and was not accepted without the additional statement: "At the same time the committee would not be understood, in recommending the repeal of the present canon, to give any countenance to vain and light amusements plainly inconsistent with the vows of holy baptism"—a statement that means nothing. The objections made to the canon were of more moment—namely, "that, except attendance on theatres and horse-racing, the vain amusements condemned are not defined; and that, under the name canon, is given a mere expression of opinion, no penalty being attached to its violation; moreover, diocesan should be conformed to general legislation, which has not attempted to specify what are violations of the baptismal vows, and has fixed the punishment for all offences condemned by it."

The morning after the repeal of this canon the bishop sent to the Convention his earnest protest against their action:

To the Convention of the Diocese of Maryland:

The undersigned, physically unable to endure the excitement attending a personal attempt to preside in the Convention, takes this method of putting on record his solemn protest against the action yesterday taken in this body for the repeal of the Canon of Lay Discipline, formerly known as Canon XVIII., forbidding theatrical exhibitions and other light and vain amusements.

1. More than thirty years ago the existence of that canon, recognized as an almost peculiar distinction of the Maryland Diocesan Code, had much weight in swaying the undersigned to undertake the responsibilities of the episcopate.

2. No year has passed in which he has not found in that canon, directly or indirectly employed, support and strength in teaching and administration. Not many weeks have gone by since his last resort to it in fulfilment of pastoral duty.

3. The current of the times and the movement in the population of the country are such as imperatively to require of a faithful branch of the Church of Christ increased stringency, and not timid relaxation, in the announcement and enforcement of the rules of holy living, self-denial, and nonconformity to the world.

4. Declarative legislation for the guidance and strengthening of pastoral teaching and discipline has been in all ages practised in the Church, and found to afford its ministers wholesome aid.

5. No qualifying vote can relieve the repeal affected from the interpretation of evincing a change of position in regard to the matters in question. The world, the flesh, and the devil will so understand it, and have a right so to use it.

6. However circumstances may relieve the action now taken from the nullity which must attach to a change in the discipline of a diocese, made without the advice and consent, or even privity of its bishop, they are not such as to bind the undersigned, who must hold his own right in the canon to be unaffected, and consider it to

be, so far as concerns himself and his official action, of force and validity.

All which is affectionately and respectfully represented.

WILLIAM ROLLINSON WHITTINGHAM,

Bishop of Maryland.

BALTIMORE, May 30, 1873.

Whatever may be thought of the wisdom of supplementing the principles given in Holy Scripture by specific rules of life enforced by canonical penalties, the relation of the difference in judgment on this point between the Bishop of Maryland and the majority of his Convention is calculated to make one ponder another matter, viz., the conformity of all diocesan legislation with that of the Church in early ages. The rectors of parishes and certain other designated clergymen, with the delegates of vestries, imposed on the members of the Church in Maryland a certain rule. If the bishop of that day voted at all it was as one of the clergy; his vote counted no more than that of a deacon who had a seat in Convention. The lay delegates could have checked the will of the clergy, but the bishop, as head of his diocese, had no will, and the Convention of 1873 showed that the majority of his "order" [in Diocesan Convention] do not need his support when legislating. The protest of Bishop Whittingham against action taken by the Convention without his knowledge was listened to politely, and on motion of the member who had presented the report of the committee, "the communication was ordered to be spread upon the journal;" it might then have been rejected. It did not even lead to a reconsideration. This was asked for, and was put aside by the resolution—"That the Convention, after the customary religious exercises, do adjourn *sine die.*"

The opinions expressed or intimated in the protest of the bishop were held by him in early life, as has been shown, and they were never changed. His estimate of worldliness was what it is the fashion to call puritan; he thought it to .be primitive. It was not that he condemned any amusement in itself, although called "vain and light," but as having a tendency to destroy that state of mind which is indicated in the opening of the Psalter, "His delight is in the law of the Lord, and in his law will he exercise himself day and night." He knew this day and night exercise in holy things to be the privilege of the Christian, and therefore he thought it to be the duty of the Christian to deny himself whatever has been found to hinder appreciation of the privilege. He desired that every one having hope in Christ, and not a few "religious" only, should live a spiritual life, above the world ; and therefore he feared all that has a sensuous tendency, even devotion to the fine arts.

The protest disregarded at home seems to have made an impression abroad. The bishop received letters from all parts of the country, from bishops and other clergymen and from laymen as well, thanking him for his faithful words and expressing fears of a growing influence of a worldly spirit in the Church. Perhaps these letters may have encouraged him to present in the House of Bishops—as he did on the first day of the General Convention in 1874—an amendment to the Canon of Parochial Instruction, in these words :

§ II. Bishops, priests, and deacons, in their respective offices and cures, shall be diligent in the inculcation, both publicly and in private pastoral teaching, of Christian holiness of life, by the due maintenance of family worship, the religious training of children in observance of the baptismal vows, and such abstinence from [theatrical exhibitions, horse-racing, gaming, and other vain and light amusements] as is required by the apostolic injunction, Not to be conformed to this world.

The words included in brackets having been changed in committee to "gaming, amusements involving cruelty to the brute creation, theatrical representations, and light and vain amusements tending to draw the affections from spiritual things," the bishop's amendment was passed and sent to the House of Deputies. Here it was reported to the

House with emendations, was placed on the docket and lost sight of or never reached.

The " declarative legislation" of Maryland did, as the bishop claimed, strengthen pastoral teaching. It had influence on some who even doubted the propriety of its stringency, but to others it was a snare, being a rule acknowledged but not heeded. It is probable that "the current of the times," which would soon have swept away a barrier to enjoyments attendant on increased luxury, made itself felt when the canon was repealed.

On the request of the House of Deputies in 1874, a Joint Committee on Godly Discipline was appointed, and they are still in existence, for three years were not long enough to devise a plan to meet the difficulty.*

In the Maryland Convention of 1873 a clerical member presented a preamble and a series of resolutions condemning " certain practices" tending toward Romish doctrines, and reaffirming what is contained in the pastoral letter of 1871 on the subject of Ritualism embracing the subject of private confession. The Rev. Dr. Nelson raised the point of order that this Convention has no jurisdiction. The assistant bishop being in the chair, decided that the point was well taken.

This decision, with a kindred one on the same subject, has saved the diocese from much fruitless discussion, and

---

* On the second day of the General Convention of 1877, the Bishop of Maryland offered as an amendment to Canon 21, Title 1, the following resolution:

§ II. Ministers shall also be continually diligent in the inculcation of Christian holiness of life in such following of the example of our Saviour Christ as shall exhibit to the world in the membership of the Church a peculiar people, called out to be separate from all vain pomps and glories, covetous desires, fraudulent dealings, and corrupting associations and frivolities imperilling spirituality of life; and more specifically, as occasion shall require, shall warn their people against habits of gaming, intemperate indulgencies, attendances at places frequented by evil livers, and sports abused to purposes of licentiousness and fraud; exhorting them to the maintenance of family worship and the due observance of the Lord's Day, and calling upon parents and sponsors to train their children and godchildren, both by precept and example, faithfully to observe their baptismal vows.

possibly doubtful legislation, touching ritual; but it seems to be counter to what is assumed by the canon proposed in 1871 by Bishop Whittingham and adopted by the House of Bishops. This proposed canon spoke of diocesan action as one of the sources of church law on ritual.

If the Convention was not permitted to legislate on the matter, yet resistance to advanced ritual and doctrinal errors supposed to be connected with it has ever since affected the action of the Convention. Not that now first were heard denunciations against those who were "betraying the Church." As we have seen, High Church doctrines had been preached against as having been all rejected by the reformers. An altar prominently placed, a surplice in the pulpit, a cross in the place of a weather-cock, outward signs of reverence for what has been given to God, had been all spoken against as proofs of Roman corruption. The fear of Popery was not now first felt, but now it was entertained by and became a motive of action with some who had themselves given alarm to zealous upholders of the Reformation.

There was in consequence a new adjustment of parties in the diocese. Some of the Evangelicals could not refrain from saying to their High Church brethren : " Why should you complain of the development of your own teaching? Years ago, and all along, we told you that you were cherishing as Catholic verities what are but the germs of Popery!" Nevertheless, High and Low made common cause against the advanced ; while a third class, who look upon law as intended to secure liberty as well as to suppress evil, have been judged as though they wished to protect condemned criminals from just punishment.

In 1874 the Convention met in Washington. Until then its sessions had been held in Baltimore continuously since the election of Bishop Whittingham.

The bishop was not able to attend, and his annual address took the form of a letter to his assistant. In this letter, intended to supply particulars of registration and of official correspondence of the diocese, he says: "Of visitations in the full sense of the term I have no report to make. At no time in the year has my health warranted the making needful canonical notice for continuous services at pre-appointed times." This was true of all his remaining years of suffering, although it was surprising how much of duty he could perform in his prostration. When he ceased from his labors there were many grown men for whom he had continuously labored who had only a child's recollection of their bishop. His jurisdiction he retained, and till death came he was the responsible head of his diocese. While having so little of that personal relation with those cared for that brings refreshment, this headship was the occasion of adding frequent distress of mind to almost ceaseless agony of body.

At this Convention in Washington was given proof that whatever Southern prejudices may have lingered after 1865, all such had been set aside through other considerations. An honored churchman, a Marylander by birth, who, because he was a member of the Legislature in 1861, had borne long imprisonment, and who, since his release, had been a delegate to the General Convention, and who was again nominated to fill this office, was made to give place to one who was a member of Mr. Lincoln's Cabinet at the time when the Baltimore members were sent to prison, but who was now recommended by the fact that he was a pronounced anti-Ritualist. No one was chosen as representative of Maryland in the General Convention of 1874 who had not by his past course or otherwise given assurance that he would further legislation for the suppression of advanced ritual and doctrine. Among those returned to the place of honor was one who, by his single vote in the Convention of 1871, had prevented the adoption of the canon on ritual then recommended by the joint committee. The majority now promised one another the certainty of triumph, and

that the honor of giving peace to the Church should belong
to them.

In accordance with this expectation, early in the session
of 1874 one of their deputies introduced a preamble setting
forth the fact that the warning against eucharistic adoration given by the bishops in their last pastoral letter had
proved inoperative; and a canon—"first, forbidding all
exposition of the elements in holy communion as objects
toward which the adoration of the people is to be directed,
and all acts which could be considered to imply such adoration on the part of the priest, and as well every ceremony
not prescribed in the service book; secondly, declaring that
in everything connected with the ritual of divine service,
including vestments used about which there is no specific
direction, the written judgment of the bishop of a diocese
shall be regarded as binding." A provision which would
have defeated the purpose of an act entitled "Canon of
Ritual Uniformity."

Together with memorials on the subject and other suggestions of legislation, this Maryland canon was considered
by the Committee on Canons.

Feeling "assured that it has been under the guidance of
the Holy Spirit," the committee reported an addition to the
canon on the use of the Book of Common Prayer, which
indicated the mode of proceeding against any presbyter accused of practices during the celebration of the holy communion not ordained or authorized in the Book of Common
Prayer, and setting forth or symbolizing erroneous or doubtful doctrines, and indicating as such symbols: *a.* The use
of incense. *b.* A crucifix in any part of the place of public
worship. *c.* Elevation, etc. *d.* Any act of worship toward
the elements.

As in the previous Convention, full opportunity was given
for discussion, and again the Rev. Dr. De Koven opposed
legislation. Many amendments were offered, but the canon
was passed as recommended.

It came back from the House of Bishops modified, and markedly so by the omission of all examples of symbols supposed to indicate error. The House of Deputies refused to concur in their amended canon, and finally a committee of conference reported the addition to Canon 22 of Title I. as it now stands. It is not therein said that incense or the retaining a crucifix in any part of a church building symbolizes erroneous doctrine, but there is specifically forbidden "the elevation of the elements in the holy communion in such a manner as to expose them to the view of the people as objects toward which adoration is to be made," and any act of adoration of or toward the elements in the holy communion, such as bowings, prostrations, or genuflexions.

As yet there has been no trial of any one for violation of this canon. Yet—while no one called Christian would admit that he could worship the elements—with whatever object, the elements are always elevated and exposed to view by the minister, and cannot but be if he would administer; and every communicant worships toward the elements—he must be in a strange state of mind who, being in the attitude of worship, does not worship when receiving.

The canon does not forbid what must take place in every holy communion. The word "toward" does not then mean *versus*, "turned in the direction of." What is forbidden is something that can be proved, if it exist, only by the admission of one accused.

CHAPTER VII.

MT. CALVARY CHURCH AND CLERGY—PRESENTMENT OF THE BISHOP.

1874–1875.

While the General Convention in 1874 was engaged in the effort to still the minds of those disturbed by the practices and teachings of the Ritualists, there occurred in Baltimore an incident which, in Maryland at least, kindled excitement anew, and which was made the occasion for much trouble and mortification to the bishop.

Mt. Calvary was from the beginning an advanced church. It is now, through contrast, a plain building of brick; but when built it was remarkable as an advance in churchly architecture and in churchlike arrangements, and here first, in this part of the world, was made an attempt to adorn the interior with color. Its foundation-stone—as in his diary the bishop notes with satisfaction—was laid with unusual ceremony in the presence of a larger assembly of surpliced clergymen than had ever before been seen in Maryland. It was begun as an offering to God, not to be a place of worship for the advantage of those who gave their money. It was consecrated as a free church, and from that day its bell called to morning and evening service, and after a time its doors were open all the day of every day. This was when it was sought or shunned as a High church. The teaching of its ministers was what was called High Church doctrine—or the sowing of the germs of Popery.

It was the parish church of the bishop's family. And here

he himself was always to be found at time of service, when not prevented by ill health or by duty that called him elsewhere, until, to his regret, through the growth of ritual, he was constrained to absent himself lest he should be understood to sanction by his presence what he did not approve, but did not feel compelled to forbid or to rebuke.

The display at this time was what would be now looked upon by many as meagre, but the teaching was "advanced." If not the first, as is believed, the rector of Mt. Calvary was among the first in the United States to celebrate at the altar daily. His teaching was in all respects what this practice indicates, with the addition that he dwelt chiefly upon those parts of a whole which others seemed to him to neglect. This rector resigned early in 1872, and, as has been stated, submitted to the Roman Church. He was succeeded by a man of a lovely spirit, holy, self-sacrificing, full of labors; as such he was much loved by the bishop, who, when the fire that was in Joseph Richey burnt out his feeble frame, took care to make known to every bishop what was the worth of the man who had been misjudged by many of them, as well as by many others.* This new rector brought with him the principles of the school which is denounced as anti-reformation. For ritual as a matter of æsthetics he cared nothing, and was perplexed by its rules; but all that he deemed Catholic verity—declared as such by the Church or indicated by the practice of primitive ages—he openly avowed in teaching and in life. He desired to introduce no new observance in the parish, but he thought it right to continue such as he found established. This judgment met with disapproval on the part of the bishop, best expressed in his own words.

---

* He sent to each bishop a copy of a sermon preached in Mt. Calvary in commemoration of Mr. Richey.

TO THE REV. JOSEPH RICHEY.

MARCH 15, 1872.

REV. AND DEAR BROTHER:

Will you allow me to plead my earnest desire to avoid any complications of our new relations at the outset as an apology for calling your attention to § II. of Canon 12 of the Digest? . . .

A letter received from Mr. Curtis, after the gratifying interview I had with you, affords the most distressing evidence that I am under the strongest obligations to insist on strict observance of the law of the Church by the congregation of which he has been the rector, for the last two years holding and teaching, as he in this letter avows himself to have been doing. It would be peculiarly unhappy to have a disregard of canonical provisions characterize the beginning of your new and, I devoutly trust, far happier rectorship.

Your affectionate friend and brother,   W. R. W.

TO THE REV. J. RICHEY.

PRIVATE AND CONFIDENTIAL.

APRIL 8, 1872.

REV. AND DEAR BROTHER:

I have been informed that you freely claim the entire approval of the bishop for the services and teachings at Mt. Calvary. This claim must be based on a misapprehension which I owe it to you and to myself to remove. That misapprehension is the construction of toleration as if it were approval. I feel bound to tolerate in the services and teachings of Mt. Calvary Church, as in those of other churches, many things which by no means meet my approval. For instance—to specify, perhaps, the most important—private confession is practised, perhaps recommended, to an extent which is, in my judgment, contrary to the mind and intent of the Church and fraught with dangerous consequences.

In the ritual, lights upon the altar, wafer bread, elevations of the bread and cup, bowings to the altar, crossings of the person of the ministrant and assistants, and the processional use of the gestatory cross and banners in public worship are contrary to the use of this diocese, and whenever opportunity has been afforded for so doing have been distinctly disclaimed and disapproved by the diocesan authority.

I determinately draw the line between disapproval and prohibition in the exercise of diocesan authority, and must not be understood as interfering in parochial management with the latter when I am only seeking to secure distinct recognition for the former. But my disapproval as diocesan, of course, involves the necessity of personal abstention from the services not approved. I am shut out from Mt. Calvary by practices in which I could not participate without being understood to lend them a sanction which in my judgment would be wrong. In this connection I ought to say that I was misunderstood in our last conversation about services over and above the full provisions of the Church if I was supposed to sanction the issuing and use of printed forms, most especially of such as the Jesuit hymn,* "Anima Christi." I had no thought of such procedure in my mind at the time, but spoke and thought only of adaptations of extracts from the Bible or Prayer-book, with the possible— but reluctantly conceded—use of a collect or collects from some other well-approved source, to be used by the minister alone, and, therefore, not requiring imposition upon the congregation in the shape of a printed form.

I do not approve—cannot sanction—most heartily reprobate—the disturbance of the use of a diocese by the introduction of such congregational usages in private forms of printed services outside of those provided by the Church, and possibly (as in the case of the "Anima Christi" prayer) foreign to that reigning in her worship.

Painful facts, daily coming to my knowledge, in illustration of the evil results of "letting alone" your predecessor in the course so disastrously pursued by him, urge me on to this communication, which otherwise I would most gladly indulge myself in refraining from obtruding on you.

Be assured that no one can rejoice more heartily than I do in the auspicious entrance upon your career which you have effected, and that no one more earnestly desires for you a continuance and great increase of usefulness therein.

Your loving friend and brother,

W. R. W.

TO THE REV. J. RICHEY.

APRIL 17, 1872.

REV. AND DEAR BROTHER:

Your answer to my note of the 8th came to my hand yester-morning, a few hours after receipt of a letter from your predecessor in the rectorship of Mt. Calvary, renouncing his ministry and

---

* Of what is here called the Jesuit hymn the bishop elsewhere says: "Androwes may have gotten it from German sources, for it was quite current among the Lutherans as a fifteenth-century hymn."

declaring his act to have been "some time reserved, well weighed, and at last definite and fixed."

The statement of that fact may serve both to explain to you my delay in acknowledgment of your note, and also to account for my inability to accept as sufficient reason for anything in the teaching or ritual of Mt. Calvary that "it was in use under Mr. Curtis." Much that was so "in use" never came to my knowledge until recently, and therefore could not be "condemned by me at either of our interviews."

Even in my last note my purpose was not to "condemn" anything, nor even actively to interpose my disapproval by way of hindrance, but merely to relieve you of an evident misapprehension of my position, and to explain my personal and official course by presentation of the exact grounds on which I feel myself bound to regulate it.

As to "hardships" in the case, I suppose they may be found on both sides. If it is "hard" for a zealous young presbyter to be "only *tolerated*" in his introduction (or maintenance) of what he thinks to be improvements on the use of a diocese, it is not *easy* for a bishop even to "tolerate" what he knows to be insufficiently grounded and dangerous innovations in the doctrine and worship of his diocese; and it is positively "hard" for him and his family, as parishioners, to find themselves compelled to choose between a course which they have seen ensnaring souls in the Roman net, or the abandonment of their much-loved and cherished parochial worship, with all its holy recollections and associations.

But this I bear without complaining, except as now, by way of offset to charges of narrow-mindedness or hardness.

I disclaim interference in your parochial arrangements in anything not touched by actual law, beyond the mere expression of disapproval; and that I make only to hinder misrepresentation of my own position.

Repeating the assurance of my honest and earnest interest in your work, and hearty desire that it may continue to be as effective and prosperous as it has thus far given every indication of promise of becoming,

I am, lovingly and truly,
Your faithful friend and brother,
W. R. W., *Bishop of Maryland.*

The excitement at the time and the suspicion with which Mt. Calvary was watched more than justified the bishop in protecting himself by warning the clergy that they must not plead the sanction of the bishop for departure from the more common usage of the diocese. From his coming to Baltimore until he found rest eternal, the successor of one who had renounced his orders was the object of ceaseless gossip. It is easy to say that a bishop should not open his ears to gossip, but this often took the form of direct complaint to the guardian of the Church. Thus on one occasion three communicants testified that during a specified service the rector had taught that "a priest has power at that altar to make his Lord and his God." The manuscript fortunately used showed that these zealous defenders of the faith were indebted to their imagination for their fears.

Sometimes, in the course of years, the bishop was fretted to a degree of impatience that betrayed him into acts and words to be regretted; at which they only can be surprised who are not harassed while suffering ceaseless irritating pain.

Could the bishop have made himself a partizan on either side he would have been far less troubled. But he was possessed by the idea that he must be just—that it was his duty as bishop to consider the weak and also to uphold a man in his rights, even when persuaded that those rights ought to be freely waived in consideration of the prejudices of others.

Mr. Richey brought with him to Baltimore a near friend, a deacon, to be his assistant and to take charge of a congregation of "people of color" whose church building is in the immediate neighborhood of Mt. Calvary. This zealous and self-denying man, because of holding the views of the rector, was only able to present to the Bishop of Maryland letters of transfer lacking in some formality, accompanied by a very kind letter from his bishop explaining why they were thus informal. Bishop Whittingham accepted the letters without hesitation, and soon prepared to bestow priest's orders on the deacon. So doing he acted in accordance with a principle of his episcopal life. He was always prompt to insist that penalties should not be inflicted by the withholding rights granted by written law. On one occasion he had a warm contest in behalf of a candidate for orders but little attractive personally, and who had no claim on him save the appeal of the helpless.

On another occasion a bishop refused to accept a letter dimissory given by the Assistant Bishop of Maryland acting in full charge of the diocese, on the ground that the presbyter presenting it "has given aid and countenance to certain parties in [this diocese] who have introduced novelties into it which disturb its peace, and which, it is well known, that the bishop wholly disapproves and condemns." Bishop Whittingham demanded that charges should be presented against the clergyman in such definite form as would enable Maryland authorities to investigate them, or else that he be received. He would not allow the letters of his assistant to be dishonored, nor would he suffer a presbyter to be impugned as a law-breaker because of opinions or acts not forbidden by the Church, although objected to by some bishops of the Church.

On the Sunday after the bishop's burial a well-known clergyman, who in his early life had had difficulties with the authorities of his diocese, and who had found refuge in Maryland and ordination from its bishop, said in his sermon: "Bishop Whittingham will be praised by many from many reasons. You owe him gratitude if you find cause to be thankful for the services of one you have called to be your rector. I am here to-day simply because Bishop Whittingham, as a just man, was always the upholder of the helpless against tyranny."

And yet the bishop, in the early days of his episcopate, had been accused of tyranny because of maintenance of his office.

Because of his insisting on the observance of the spirit and letter of the law of the Church against private judgment concerning Catholic usage, the charge was renewed in his old age by a different class of objectors, at the very time that he was exposing himself by being the upholder of the liberty of the law.

At the ordination in S. Paul's Church, Baltimore, of the assistant at Mt. Calvary, the bishop observed that two clergymen friends of the new-made priest, not members of the diocese, remained in the choir while the clergy knelt at the rail for communion; he went to them and insisted on their receiving.

This scene was the occasion of a newspaper condemnation of "episcopal tyranny and sacrilegious conduct." Because of this attack the bishop was asked:

Did you intend to disregard the scruples of conscience of the brethren who, at your bidding, communicated? to make your will or sense of right override their sense of right? If so, you must have been impelled by a very strong sense of duty. Will you tell me what reasoning so constrained you? Of course, dear father, it is not Presbyter William who is asking these questions of his diocesan. But I do not think it unfilial to wish to understand the motive of acts condemned in terms that I have been forced to resent.

The bishop kindly answered at once:

BALTIMORE, June 14, 1872.

DEAR BRAND:

. . . Now for the tyranny, etc.

The thing came upon me very unexpectedly at the time, but did not present a new question, for it had arisen many months before C.'s sad defection, with him assisting at an ordination at Mt. Calvary. He had told me before service in the vestry-room that he should not partake, having already received. I replied that the latter fact was no reason, a priest being not only at liberty, but if a parish priest in large cure not infrequently, in cases of sick communion, bound to receive not merely more than once, but perhaps even several times, within the νυχθήμερον, against which there was no rule nor tradition claiming his or my respect. Objection to receive after having broken fast was a question merely of lesser obligation, to give way to greater.

The greater was that the ordinal requires the bishop to administer to all the clergy, "priests and deacons," present and assisting. An additional obligation would be my official injunction, which I deemed myself bound to lay on a clergyman present, in discouragement of the mediæval corruption of non-participating assistance at mass.

I gave him the option to absent himself from the service or to receive; he preferred the latter, on my responsibility as in obedience to me.

Now, the gentlemen on Trinity Sunday were robed, in the stalls, and had each taken part in the solemnities. They were conspicuously in the eyes of the congregation. My sufferance of their non-participation on that occasion would be a settlement of the question in the wrong way, and establishment of the evil precedent, if it had been at my option to grant it, which, as I understand the rubric, and believe it to have been designedly constructed so as to mean, *it was not.*

I therefore did my duty—went out of the rail to the stall, and when the person approached said, "I have already received," replied, "Receive again—there is no hindrance"—and they *did* receive, the second one having the courtesy to go out of the stall to the altar-rail to receive the cup.

After the service, all having returned to the vestry-room, I asked the attention of the assembled clergy before disrobing, and all standing around the room, first expressed my extreme regret at having had to treat visiting brethren with apparent rudeness, for which I begged them to accept my hearty apology and assurance that there was no unkind intent, and then went on at some length to explain the grounds of my procedure—that there was no violation of either law or conscience required of them under the circumstances, as to receive on command was full justification in case, such as this, of a question of mere fitness, however high the degree of fitness might be in the individual judgment; that their presence and assistance in the solemnities required of me to fulfil my duty in their regard; that it was established by me as the rule of my diocese; and that in this particular occasion, at this special juncture, I had the strongest pressure on me to be firm in maintenance of my diocesan use, in view of unhappy circumstances of recent notoriety, and of my own perfect knowledge that there was at this time in my diocese as elsewhere a tendency to non-participant presence at eucharistic celebrations, the result of which I saw, both in the clear light of history and in my own diocesan experience, to be the revival of the mischievous abuse of "private masses."

This explanation was received by the priest and deacon concerned with much seeming cordiality, each of them separately coming to me and professing himself entirely satisfied. One of them called at my house the second day after, before leaving. The other had left early on the Monday.

I cannot think that either of them either made or authorized the sputtering squib in *The Weekly* ——, of which I first heard on receiving a letter from one of the leading presbyters of the Diocese of New York and of the whole Church, congratulating me on my "firm simplicity in fulfilment of duty," he knowing my act only from the published censure of it.

Nor can I believe that either Richey or Perry had anything to do with the publication. They know—what possibly you may not even yet know—that I risked a great deal in that same service; that I had holden it in resistance of very heavy pressure; that until long after it had begun I had reason to expect the gravest public and personal scandal in the interposition of a formal written protest, at the "*si quis*," from which I was only delivered by the effective interposition of lay influence with the intending protesters, and that I went through it with the knowledge that it would, as it did, afford the pretext for an attempted revolution in the diocese at the Convention then about to assemble.

I had taken every precaution in all the preliminaries, so as to fully assure myself of my ground, and be entirely prepared to meet whatever might offer of opposition or subsequent vindictive procedure, but it was certainly what I did not expect, to have all this—done in maintenance of what I deemed the just rights of men holding views which I disapprove, and in some things persistently setting at naught my solemnly urged advice and counsel—rewarded by such screams of execration from their congerers.

It makes no difference, however, to me. I am thoroughly satisfied that the evil fruit of such evil speaking is the legitimate growth of an evil root in a false, unscriptural, and uncatholic system of doctrine and practice.

Ever lovingly yours,

W. R. W.

In order to show what manner of man the bishop was— bold through a sense of justice, tender toward those whom he shielded at his own cost—a fact referred to in the foregoing letter must be more clearly presented.

The opposition Mr. Perry met in the diocese in which he

had been candidate for orders followed him to Maryland, and when he sought to be advanced to the priesthood remonstrances were presented to the bishop. These failing, one presbyter at least—the bishop intimates that there were more—determined to make a formal public protest at the time of the proposed ordination. The bishop was aware of this intention, and began the service supposing that it would be carried out. When about to go into the chancel he warned the clergy present of what would occur, having before given to Mr. Perry the first intimation he had had of what was looked for. His ever grateful friend shall tell the story in his own words: "'Perry,' said he to me, drawing me to him, 'I am going through a great deal for you.' I answered, 'I know you have done a great deal for me, bishop, and I feel very grateful for it.' 'I do not mean,' he replied, 'what I have done. There is still more this morning.' Then putting his arm about me: 'All I ask is that you will always be loyal to the Church. There will be an interruption in the service. Act as though nothing had happened. I shall have my own way of dealing with it; it will not cause you any further delay.'"

To estimate aright the courage shown in braving the threatened protest to this ordination, it should be borne in mind that there must have been at the time fresh in memory what took place when Arthur Carey was made deacon, and all the consequent sufferings endured by his ordainer—sufferings which Bishop Whittingham himself had in vain attempted to alleviate.

This generous impulse to meet danger, not from having a common cause with those exposed, not from a regard for the need of praise—"It makes no difference to me!"—but from a simple sense of right which made him lose sight of self-interest, was a marked characteristic of Bishop Whittingham—a noble trait. No one possessed more of that spirit of chivalry which, with purpose or not, Cervantes has helped many in this age to ridicule.

An act of the gentleman whom he ordained despite of threats became the occasion for making the bishop, in the end of life, suffer instead of those whom he had protected.

In October, 1874, an infirm clergyman connected with Mt. Calvary as a volunteer assistant died. In the absence of the rector the "assistant priest" conducted the burial service, and in the church used the Commendatory Prayer for a sick person at the point of departure. The supplementing the burial service would have been complained of by no one, for nothing is more common than this violation of rubric. But this prayer so used was a prayer for one departed, and was, in the judgment of two clergymen who were present,* such a violation of the teaching of the Church that, having been certified that it was used advisedly and with the purpose of commending to God the soul of one who had departed hence in the Lord, they felt constrained to seek the condemnation of this act and the vindication of what they deemed to be the doctrine of the Protestant Episcopal Church. Accordingly at the first meeting of the Standing Committee, of which body one of the clergymen was a member, they presented a written statement of the facts that had occurred at the burial. The committee, anxious to avoid a formal presentment for trial, communicated to the bishop a minute adopted by them which, after a recital of the facts complained of, as his counsel of advice, called "his attention to this use of the prayer of commendation as one not only unauthorized in the Office of the Burial of the Dead, but plainly contrary to the mind of this Church, in deliberately omitting from said office all such petitions once incorporated with it as have for their object the acceptance and purification of the departed spirit."

The facts connected with the burial of the Rev. Mr. Morss, which of course must have been all known before, having been thus formally communicated to the bishop, he

---

* The Rev. Dr. Randolph and the Rev. Mr. Peterkin.

wrote to Mr. Perry, and receiving an answer which seems to have been argumentative, he wrote a second letter, which secured all that he was disposed to exact—all that he supposed was asked for, a promise from the offender that he would not again violate the order of the Church by the public use of any petition in behalf of the dead.

TO THE REV. GALBRAITH B. PERRY.

BALTIMORE, December 11, 1874.

REV. AND DEAR BROTHER :

I have been grieved by receiving from two presbyters of the Church who were present and assisting in the funeral services over the corpse of the late Rev. J. B. Morss, in Mt. Calvary Church, a written complaint that you had on that occasion given ground of just offence, by the public use, as part of the service, of the Commendatory Prayer in the Order for the Visitation of the Sick, with the interpolation of the word "departed" between the words "dear" and "brother" in the second clause of the prayer.

It is alleged, and, in my judgment, truly, that (1) this was a depravation of the Prayer-book by misapplication of the language of one of its prayers to a use for which it was not designed, with the effect of giving to that language a meaning which it had not in the mind of the Church when providing and permitting it; and that (2) such misuse amounted to a disloyal employment of ministerial office, to the end of availing yourself of an opportunity for the inculcation in a most effectual mode, and on an occasion giving the attempt peculiar importance, of a doctrine not allowed to find a place in the norm of doctrine of this Church, and of a practice persistently discountenanced by the Church and discarded from all its formularies.

This being so, it becomes my duty to express to you the regret with which I learn that such offence has been afforded, and to warn you against its repetition by the use of the Commendatory Prayer as a funeral prayer, or by any similar attempt, in public teaching or worship, to inculcate or practise prayer for departed souls.

Whatever may have been the practice of the Church in other times and circumstances, and whatever may be your private conclusions from the silence of Scripture and the absence of ecclesiastical prohibition, it is incontestably apparent that no minister of our branch of the Church has the right to teach as by authority, or to practise as in official duty, public prayers for the departed.

I affectionately charge and entreat you, therefore, as a loyal son of the Church, obedient "even as to the guidance by the eye" of your loving mother, to abstain hereafter from doing what the branch of the Catholic Church in this country, having authority to ordain and approve traditions and ceremonies, ignores and discountenances, and more especially from distorting and perverting her public services or any part of her offices to such use.

    Ever faithfully and devotedly,

        Your loving brother in Christ,

            WILLIAM ROLLINSON WHITTINGHAM,

                Bishop of Maryland.

XMAS EVE, 1874.

MY DEAR PERRY :

The foregoing note was ready to be sent to you on the day of its date, but I deemed it my duty, in sending it to you, to make other communications to others concerned, and my miserable health has made the preparation of them so slow a work that it is only just now brought to an end.

I cannot further delay the execution of my most undesired duty—otherwise I would shrink from sending you such a missive on Christmas Eve.

With it, however, take my assurance of warmest love, and the benediction of the season from your faithful friend and loving brother,   W. R. W.

TO THE REV. GALBRAITH B. PERRY.

MY DEAR BROTHER :

I am glad to receive from you what I was prepared to expect: your denial that in using the prayer from the Office for the Visitation of the Sick, at the burial of the late Rev. Mr. Morss, you made any change whatever in the prayer.

By looking again at my letter of the 24th ult., you will perceive that it is an expression of regret for "offence" "*afforded*," not *committed*, and therefore is in the nature of expostulation and warning, not of censure and disciplinary admonition, which I should not have undertaken to administer otherwise than after full opportunity of defence.

No doubt the use of any prayer not contained in the Order for the Burial of the Dead at a public funeral in a church is technically an offence against the order of worship of the Church, and liable to animadversion as such.

But the license taken for several years past, almost universally, when a corpse is borne to a distance from the church for interment, of closing the services at the church by the use of collects and prayers from other parts of the Prayer-book, has been silently allowed, on account of the change of circumstances in city funerals since the preparation of the order in the Prayer-book.

It exists by sufferance only, and is liable to any restriction or limitation which, in the judgment of the ordinary, may become necessary.

The offence taken, not without apparent reason, at your use of a prayer provided by the Church for the committal of the soul of a dying person to the mercies of God in Christ, on occasion of a funeral, when formally presented to my attention as ordinary, makes it obligatory on me, in the discharge of office, to take away occasion for the recurrence of such a mistake.

I can only do so, as I conceive, by such a prohibition as I have notified to you, declaring that the sufferance of unauthorized additions to the Order for the Burial of the Dead must not be understood to extend to the use of the Commendatory Prayer in the Office of Visitation in particular, nor in general to any prayer which, like that, is susceptible of interpretation as prayer for the dead in a sense discouraged by the Church in which we are ministers.

Whosoever he may be who may have instructed you that the Church was actuated in such discouragement (which you call "weakening in expression only the earlier forms") "in an unhappy spirit of concession to the Puritans," I take leave to assure you that he was either ignorant or bore false witness. The explicit and deliberate testimony of Andrewes, Cosin, L'Estrange, and Sir William Palmer, attests that the suppression of public prayers for the dead at the English Reformation was considerately made within limits cautiously and wisely drawn, on grounds irrefragable and incontestable.

I cannot but note in this part of your letter a sign of looseness of thought in your repeated designation of the matter in question as " doctrine "—whereas no doctrinal point is in discussion, but a rule of practice ; and that not of private personal practice, but of the public, official practice of one exercising a trust under authority.

This confusion on your part has led to the misinterpretation and consequent misapplication of St. Epiphanius's comment on the followers of Aërius. They contemned the maternal rule of the Church of their day and country which sanctioned commemorations and prayers on account of the departed. The saint indicates the right of the Church on grounds seeming to her sufficient to regulate such things, and claims for her θεσμοὶ, as ἄλυτοι, μὴ δυνάμενοι καταλυθῆναι, καὶ καλῶς ἔχοντες, καὶ τῶν πάντων θαυμαστοὶ γινόμενοι, the due obedience. Are you and I not children of the American Church? If we are, may we set aside her θεσμός, because *we* think, forsooth, that οὐκ ἀναγκαίως ἡ Ἐκκλησία τοῦτο ἐπιτελεῖ, when she, for reasons arising out of the change of the times, withdraws her sanction from the παράδοσιν λαβομένην παρὰ πατέρων? Who made *us* judges of the reasons of the Church our Mother? Who set *us* up to test her provisions by the practice of the forerunning ages in a matter on which Scripture has not spoken?

If we were thus let loose to the exercise of private judgment in place of law, I should think it might occur to you that we could hardly be equally so! Τὶ εἶχε πρᾶγμα, ἐπίσκοπον πρεσβυτέρῳ μὴ ἐπιπλήττειν, εἰ μὴ ἦν ὑπὲρ τὸν πρεσβυτέρον, ἐχῶν τὴν ἐξουσίαν; καὶ οὐκ εἶπε τινὶ τῶν πρεσβυτέρων μὴ δίξῃ κατηγυρίαν κατὰ ἐπισκόπου, οὐδὲ ἐγράψε τῶν πρεσβυτέρων τινὶ μὴ ἐπιπλήττειν ἐπισκόπῳ. Καὶ ὁρᾶς ὅτι πάντος τοῦ ἐκ τοῦ διαβόλου παρασαλευομένου ἡ πτῶσις οὐ μικρὰ τις ἔστιν—says good old Epiphanius, just before where you quoted him, to that very point—the necessary subjection, in matters of discipline and worship (in which the public ministry of doctrine is of necessity a part), of the lower order to that burdened with responsibility of government.

Most reluctantly do I take up that burden, at a rightful call to do so, in now claiming of you your promised obedience to my directive office in the exercise of your ministerial functions. I meddle not with your private beliefs or persuasions; but I am bound to oversee and direct your public ministrations according to what I know and can prove to be the norm of the Church in which you minister.

Do not, dear brother, with the heretic Aërius, refuse to listen to the voice of your mother, the Church of God in these United States, because you esteem yourself, and it may be with an assenting crowd, a better judge of Catholic tradition and practice and the reasons for its acceptance or alteration than he whom in the providence of God you have been called to recognize as "over you in the Lord."

Faithfully and truly your loving friend and brother,

WILLIAM R. WHITTINGHAM,
Bishop of Maryland.

FEAST OF THE CIRCUMCISION, 1875.

TO REV. J. RICHEY.

FEAST OF Yᴱ CIRCUMCISION, 1875.

REV. AND DEAR BROTHER:

I heartily and entirely accept your explanation of our interview on Saturday last.

I did attribute to words that fell from you a meaning derogatory to my office, and therefore unworthy of yours, but I was only too sensible of my own infirmity, and conscious that the irritability of diseased old age might only too easily, in such an exciting conversation, both give and take offence wholly foreign to the hearts and minds of both of us.

As to the matter of our conversation, I do not remember anything to be regretted on my part; as to the manner, I cordially extend the oblivion of forgiveness, of which I am very willing to believe I may have equal need.

Very truly your loving friend and brother,   W. R. W.

To this second letter Mr. Perry answered:

Rt. Rev. and Dear Bishop:

I am rejoiced to discover that I entirely misunderstood your first letter. While the use of the prayer under consideration seems to me capable of a perfectly natural, literal, and yet Catholic interpretation, and therefore one in harmony with the doctrines of our Church, yet I can see that there are expressions in the prayer so used which to some minds might seem to encourage grave errors in the actual practise of the Roman purgatorial system which I should, I hope, shrink from committing myself to as much as you yourself would.

. . . Even if I did not myself appreciate the grounds of objection . . . I should certainly submit to your godly judgment upon a question in which I have no responsibility while acting under your authority. I shall therefore henceforth not use the Commendatory Prayer, etc., . . . heartily glad that, as you say, no question of doctrine is in your request involved, and therefore I am not obliged to be brought in opposition to one whom I so love and revere in regard to a doctrine which I cannot but believe and teach that our Church holds and practises in conformity with the primitive Church —that of praying for rest and peace, and an outpouring of grace for the faithful departed.

The bishop sent to the Standing Committee a copy of his first letter to Mr. Perry, which contained an echo of their judgment. This was read to them on January 14th.

They met again on the 3d of the following month, when their attention was called to the offence complained of in a more aggravated form, and to charges brought against the rector as well as his assistant.

When Mr. Richey returned to his parish,* which he did immediately on learning that his assistant had given offence, he took all pains—if not to bring himself under like censure —to set forth his own convictions. He openly taught that it is not " superfluous and vain to pray for the dead," thinking that he had a right to teach what was admitted to be primitive ; he circulated tracts maintaining the propriety of praying for the departed ; and he compiled for the use of his congregation a small manual, an aid to them in what had been long familiar to them as a pious act.

Subsequently he, with his assistant, submitted to the godly counsel of the bishop and promised no longer to circulate his publications and to abstain from the use of prayers for the dead in public services. He notified the congregation of his intention to obey the warning given him, but even when so doing he defined the limits of the obedience exacted of him and maintained their and his privileges—they might not give scandal, but they could not be debarred communion with their departed loved ones.

The Standing Committee considered such submission to the bishop's counsel as no abating of the offence, and proceeded to frame a presentment † against the assistant, and

---

* He had been in New York watching with interest the proceedings of the General Convention then engaged with the matter of ritual. After one of the discussions on this subject, he said : '' The Convention can pass no canon that will not receive my ready obedience."

† In a pamphlet entitled '' Law and Prerogative," a defence of the action of the Standing Committee and of the course of the gentlemen who preferred charges against the bishop, it is said, p. 7 : '' It was soon made evident that the hope of the committee to avoid the necessity of a trial was to be disappointed, and the inefficiency of the episcopal authority to restrain the repetition of the offence in a form even more aggravated, was speedily demonstrated." And also (p. 8) that the presentment of the rector contained ''a specification to the effect that at another funeral service, held after the bishop's letter of warning, the rector of Mt. Calvary had himself, in the presence of his assistant, made a like use of the Commendatory Prayer, a further illustration of the efficacy of episcopal discipline in such cases." The writer of the pamphlet did not perceive that justice to the bishop and to the accused required the statement of what was equally a fact, viz., that this '' like use " occurred before any promise or submission had been given to the bishop, and that no '' discipline " through

on the next day against the rector, charging both alike with violation of their ordination vows in not ministering the doctrine of Christ as this Church hath received the same; and, secondly, with holding and teaching doctrine contrary to the teaching of the article entitled " Of Purgatory."

These presentments were delivered to the bishop, but he returned the packet unopened, saying: " Further reflection satisfied me that I should best consult the dignity of the Standing Committee of the Diocese of Maryland, and that of my own office, by declining to open a communication of which the essentially confidential contents had found publicity through the morning newspapers. . . . I decline to enter on official action under the strain of outside pressure."

Ten days later, an apology and explanation having been made by some members of the committee, which was not in session, he consented to receive the presentments; but when, on March 8th, the Standing Committee sent to inquire what action he intended to take, he answered that he should not send the presentments to the ecclesiastical court; that he had settled the case.

He had received from the accused a promise that the scandal, so far as it existed, should be removed, and that the acts complained of should not be repeated; and he had given them an assurance that their offence was in consequence condoned.

He conceived that all that could be reached through the intervention of a trial had been already attained. The ecclesiastical court could do no more than find the accused guilty of the charges brought against them, and, transmitting a report of the testimony on which their judgment was based, recommend what the punishment should be. The infliction of the penalty would rest with himself alone, the only restriction placed on him being that he should not go

the intervention of an ecclesiastical court could have had more " efficacy " than had the word of these clergymen pledged to their bishop, beyond the punishment which, in the opinion of the court, the offence deserved.

The facts charged were not denied, and the accused had submitted to his godly monition, which was all that he would have exacted had they been tried and found guilty.

In the courts of the United States he who has only the pardoning power may exercise that power at any stage of the proceedings against a criminal. The Supreme Court asserting this of the President, whose powers are derived from the Constitution, has said: "The benign prerogative of mercy reposed in him cannot be fettered by any legislative restrictions."

The bishop believed that "the prerogative of mercy" vested in him not as man given, but because he was successor to an apostle who wrote, "I forgave for your sake in the person of Christ."

But the Standing Committee believed that even as a bishop cannot now, of his free will, in the name of the Lord, deliver one unto Satan for the destruction of the flesh and the salvation of the spirit, so his power to have mercy is to be exercised in Maryland only as permitted by Maryland canons. When charges against the assistant at Mt. Calvary were laid before them, they were convinced that he was liable to trial; but in their clemency they tempered justice, and simply called the attention of the ordinary to acts which they considered to be in violation of the order of the Church. This privilege to be gentle with the erring they thought belonged to them alone. When afterward they made formal presentment for trial they thought that, under the canon, the bishop was a mere instrument to carry out their decision; that he was bound to summon the court for the trial of those whom they had criminated. And so convinced were they of the need to maintain this their opinion, that when it was thought that by the withdrawing their disregarded presentments they could prevent the purposed canonical inquiry into the conduct of their bishop with a view to his trial as a violator of law, they, by a majority of votes, refused to avert what he looked upon as the humiliation of his old age.

Had the object of the presentment been the condemnation of specific acts, it is to be presumed that the cessation of these acts, in accordance with the judgment of the bishop, would have ended the matter, whatever might have been the difference of opinion with regard to the right of the bishop to act independently. But the two presbyters on whose charges the presentment had been made not only held, as did the bishop, the public use of prayers for the dead to be unauthorized, but also believed the commendation of the use of such prayers, under any circumstances, to be evidence of belief in the Romish doctrine of purgatory. Therefore their vow to drive away from the Church all erroneous doctrine constrained them to attempt to force a trial, and to this end to procure the condemnation of the bishop for the disregard of an obligatory canon of Maryland.

It is very possible that they thought that the bishop shared in the dangerous errors of those whom he had shielded; and they might have been unwilling to perceive the distinction between what he would have avowed and Romish error which he rejected.

His fatherly correspondence with his young presbyter, which was only a gentle mode of giving episcopal admonition, has shown clearly his judgment with respect to the provision made in our Church for public worship, and the impropriety of going beyond that provision through pretence of conformity to ancient usage. It ought to be as clearly understood that he did not believe commemoration of the faithful departed at the altar to imply belief in the Romish doctrine of purgatory, because it ought to be known that he knew that before there was any peculiar Romish doctrine on any point, such commemorations were made at every altar. He did not think it right to add to existing excitement by offending prejudice through dwelling on doctrine which we are not commanded to set forth as part of the Gospel, and which our branch of the Church has seen fit to keep in abeyance. This was the extent of his condemnation of the following of Cyprianic and Augustinian custom.

A friend of Mr. Richey at his request preached on "The Communion of Saints" on the eve of All-Saints' following his presentment. In part communion with the faithful at rest was treated, and the usual objections to prayers for such as have ceased from their labors were examined. The vestry asked to be allowed to publish this sermon, and consent was given provided the assent of the bishop were first obtained. This was refused, the bishop saying: " It is very probable that nothing was said that I would be disposed to find fault with. But the presentation of this theme in the way you proposed will be received as a challenge to renewed strife. It can do little good, and cannot but do harm."

To the preacher he immediately wrote:

BALTIMORENSIS, VI. a. cal. December, 1875.
S. Lini P. et M.

CARISSIME :

No irritare crabrones.   Prov. xiii. 3 ; xviii. 1.

G. R. W.

On one occasion he submitted to a series of questions.

The Jews now pray for their dead : Did they not in the days of our Lord ? Is it not reasonable to suppose that he, in synagogue worship, took part in such prayers ?

Jewish Christians, including apostles, long continued Jewish customs: Is it not probable that the apostles in public prayers continued to remember the departed ?

It is certain that at a very early period the liturgies contained provision for the commemoration of the faithful; one of the arguments against saint-worship is that even the Blessed Virgin, together with other saints, was thus remembered when imploring blessing on the living and the dead : Is it not probable that this was a continuance of apostolic usage ?

To all these questions, one after the other, he merely answered, Yes! He was then asked, Is there anything in the teaching of the Lord or in the writings of his apostles contrary to what is the prompting of many hearts now?

"No," he said, "there is nothing. But for all that praying for the dead is nowhere commanded. We have therefore no right to make it part of the Gospel touching which the command given to us is, Go, speak to the people all the words of this life. We have no right to refuse to consider the offence we may give by so doing."

As for the question, What is the use of praying for those who are saved, any more than for those who are lost? it was no check to the prompting of his own heart. Do you think—he once said in earnest conversation on this subject: "Do you think that I have ever ceased to remember in my prayers my daughter, or my father and mother?"

Two days before the meeting of the Convention in 1875, the bishop by chance received information that charges against himself were in the hands of the senior bishop. The consequent excitement probably enabled him to preside and to read his annual address, to which he had added a passage referring to the probable ground of his accusation.

A case has arisen in the exercise of discipline of difference of opinion as to the intent of our first diocesan canon of Title B.

It is claimed that under that canon the bishop has no discretion upon receipt of a presentment from the Standing Committee, but is thereby bound to proceed to trial, whether he deem the matters charged to be liable to trial under Canon 2, Title II., of the Digest, or not, and also whether or not he may himself, as ordinary, have proceeded in the matter to the fulfilment in his judgment of all requisitions of the law of the Church.

As one of those who framed our canon, I never supposed that it was to deprive the bishop of all discretion in the protection of his clergy from liability to unnecessary judicial investigation, nor to constitute a body of presbyters the sole arbiters of the justice of such resort to extreme measures for punishment rather than for correction, leaving the bishop to be the mere unreasoning instrument of their coercive power. . . . I could never consent to such unworthy diminution of my office, and for refusing it, it is now reported (for I have no positive notice to such effect) that I am presented to the presiding bishop as a violator of the canons of my diocese. . . . I ask you to relieve me of that danger, and to make the canon clear and throughout consistent by introducing [a proposed clause of reference]. That explains that to obtain the bishop's instrumentality in its prosecution the presentment received must be one duly alleging grounds, as already recited in the canon, and of the dueness of such allegation the bishop must be the judge, as provided in the outset, and meant to be assumed throughout.

After having read his address the bishop moved the amendment of the canon, which was differently interpreted, and confidently trusting that the Convention would accept without hesitation his testimony as to the meaning of those who framed it, and that they would promptly relieve him from what he looked upon as a disgrace, he asked for a vote without debate.

On the request of a near friend and legal adviser, the motion was withdrawn and the amendment was referred to the Committee on Canons. The committee recommended the repeal of the existing canons and the re-enacting of them with changes, making them to conform clearly with the bishop's interpretation.

A vote was taken by orders on the canons as reported after 10 o'clock on the night of the third day, and the resolution of recommendation was lost by a want of concurrence of orders, more than two to one of the clergy voting in favor of the resolution, but a majority of the laity voting against it.

The Maryland Convention is not famed for placidity, but probably it has never shown more of excitement than when its long-tried bishop was virtually on trial before them. The party siding with the presenters seemed to have triumphed, but when the long contest of the day closed there was rejoicing on the other side.

When the rejection of the amendment was announced, the Rev. Dr. Hodges offered resolutions which, while disclaiming any intention to cast censure on the gentlemen who had made the presentment, declared " that this Convention has learned with deepest pain that proceedings have been instituted looking to the presentment of the bishop for trial on charge of violation of the canon law of this diocese, and that the Convention desires to enter upon its records the expression of its profound regret that such steps should have been taken, and of its earnest hope that no such measures may be persevered in."

Efforts were made to get rid of the resolutions; to temper them by the assertion that no opinion was expressed touching the merits of the question involved; to substitute for them a testimonial of love and affection for the bishop and of the conviction that he was undoubtedly conscientious; but a majority was resolved on accepting the resolutions as they were offered. The discussion was protracted until a late hour of the night, until weariness had exhausted all but those who were too much in earnest to feel it. When the roll was called for a vote by orders, not every call was answered. Some had gone to bed; how many were in the back pews waiting to be roused is not known. One failure to respond served for a momentary diversion of thought. As he sat in the chancel in full view of all members—there were few other spectators—a gentleman long known as an ardent admirer of the bishop showed that interest in one's friend cannot always overcome the claims of one's nature. The secretary, who opposed the resolutions, being only a few yards distant, called his name and waited for the expected Aye! A second time, and in a louder tone, he called, and awakened no response. But as the secretary, after an unusual pause, turned from looking into the face of the silent one, could his expression have been felt, as it was seen by others, it would have brought forth a vote on one side or the other, though one of the seven brothers of Ephesus had slept before him.

The resolutions of Dr. Hodges were adopted by a majority

of both orders. Not counting the unrecorded one, the vote stood—of the clergy, 50 aye, 16 no;* and of the laity, 27 aye and 21 no.

"The Convention then, at 1.15 A.M. of Saturday, adjourned till 10 o'clock of the same day."

The earnest hope that extreme measures would not be persevered in were disappointed. The two clergymen and five laymen who had placed in the hands of the presiding bishop charges against their diocesan, saw in the profound regret of the Convention no reason for abandoning the course they had determined on.

The charge they had preferred was violation of the canons of the Diocese of Maryland. The specification was that, having received from the Standing Committee presentments wherein were duly set forth charges against the rector and the assistant minister of Mt. Calvary Church, and the statement of the opinion that these should be judicially investigated, the bishop took no action, and that in consequence the conduct of the said clergymen "has wholly failed to be judicially investigated, in accordance with the presentments of said Standing Committee and the canon of the Diocese of Maryland in such case made and provided."

The charges were signed by A. M. Randolph, presbyter; Geo. W. Peterkin, presbyter; Philip C. Williams, M.D.; Isaac C. Trimble, of Trinity Church, Long Green; Fendall Marbury, of St. Thomas's Parish; Randolph Barton, and William Woodward.

The canon under which action was taken requires the signatures of only two clergymen and three laymen, if all be of the diocese. It will be seen that in the case of Bishop Whittingham there were two more signatures than were

---

* The journal records the vote 49 aye, 17 no. The Rev. Mr. Warner, than whom there was no warmer friend of the bishop, albeit during the war there was no warmer Southern sympathizer, to his great mortification learned first from the printed journal that he was understood to have voted no, or, as he felt, against his friend.

requisite for the settlement of the interpretation of the canon, touching which the bishop, one of those who framed it, ventured to have an opinion different from that of the majority of the Standing Committee.

It was known to all that to be accused as a law-breaker, and to be presented for trial as such by members of his own diocese, was a grievous affliction to the bishop. To make the presentment was to add humiliation to the burden of years and sickness. One might have supposed that so pain-giving a duty would have been avoided, if possible.

But the presenters were not alone. An attempt to remove the basis of the charges against the bishop by withdrawing the presentment against the presbyters was made by a member of the Standing Committee. His effort failed.

The presiding bishop conceived himself to be forced to summon a board of inquiry to decide whether the charges preferred and the evidence offered in their support were such as to warrant a trial of the bishop before his peers. This conclusion was faulted by some, and the accused himself seems to have judged that the presiding bishop might have rightly refused to entertain the charges. The language of the canon is imperative, but the right to disturb the peace of the Church by accusation must have some limit.

The Bishop of Maryland wrote:

TO THE RT. REV. B. B. SMITH, D.D.

BALTIMORE, June 19, 1875.

MY DEAR BISHOP :

Since writing to you this morning, I have (by getting it from a bookstore where it is gratuitously distributed, as I am told) obtained in a pamphlet purporting to be an open letter to you, the first knowledge * which has been in any way afforded to me of the nature of the charges made against me in order to my subjection to a trial.

---

* A full month later, and after had passed the first day appointed for the convening of the board, the bishop was still in vain asking for authentic information touching the charges, and the names of those who had preferred them. The canon does not make it obligatory on any one to inform an accused bishop that

I humbly submit to you that on the face of that letter it appears evidently that the attempt is to apply the Canon of the Trial of a Bishop to a use for which it was never designed—the interpretation of constitutional law by means of a criminal prosecution.

In order to make a show of intention to violate law of my part, which I never had, and utterly deny and disavow, an unfair statement of what passed between my Standing Committee and me is made, with repeated suppressions of important facts, and with a use of documents of which you will have a specimen by reading the enclosed copy of a letter which is garbled and falsified on page 25 of the pamphlet.

Faithfully and affectionately, your friend and brother,

W. R. W.

It is probable that with nerves excited by racking pain the bishop's equanimity was too easily disturbed. One cannot but think that he over-estimated what was done and said. He was even moved to answer what appeared in newspapers. Thus to contradict an article in *The Church and State* on the Maryland presentment, signed "Presbyter," he wrote :

Messrs. Editors :

The assertion that any one has been presented to me for "undiluted Romanism" is absolutely and shamefully *false.*

It is equally untrue that I "ignored the presentment" so misrepresented. The Standing Committee was respectfully informed of the bishop's action and of its grounds and reasons.

It is furthermore untrue that I "refused to observe the law in the case." I claimed to be observing and carrying out the law, both in its spirit and in the letter.

The one point made against me is that I do not understand a canon which I helped to make. W. R. W.

His sense of humiliation, for which there was little real ground, and his resentment, which was natural enough, are expressed in the following letters :

---

his conduct is about to be officially scrutinized, and therefore the presiding bishop did not communicate a copy of the paper presented to him : but if the sole object of trial was the definition of canonical obligations, one might suppose that courtesy would have required of the presenters what the presiding bishop says he had sent them word to do.

TO THE RT. REV. B. B. SMITH, D.D., PRESIDING BISHOP.

BALTIMORE, June 15, 1875.

MY DEAR BISHOP:

Accept my heartfelt thanks for the kind, consoling words of your private note.

I will not deny that this business is a very heavy—almost crushing—blow to me, likely to send me down to my grave besmirched and crippled.

Both in the matter and in the manner of it I am humbled and baffled.

I thought I had the confidence of my diocese, and I find myself branded as a would-be tyrant, and my testimony blown aside as the idle words of a vain talker.

I am attacked without intimation either who are my accusers or of what they accuse me, except as it comes to me through the public prints, and by private intimation gathered from correspondence of your family.

I cannot think of anything possible to be alleged against me besides the one question, growing out of conflicting interpretation of my diocesan canon, about "presentments."

Surely it will not be considered criminal violation of a canon to hold its meaning to be different from that put upon it by men hardly more than born when I helped to make the canon, and brought up in a system and with views different from those favored and designed to be carried out by the men who, with me, framed it!

Can it be possible that the formidable and cumbersome machinery of our Canon for the Trial of a Bishop is to be invoked for the purpose of affixing a stigma upon the man who on such grounds refused to lend himself to what he deems the unwise and unjust narrowness of oppressive zeal!

If I am charged by any one with anything affecting my moral and religious character, or with holding or teaching publicly or privately any doctrine contrary to that of the Church, let me only know what the charge is, and then let the investigation be made the most complete and thorough possible. But if nothing more than I have yet heard of be alleged against me, it is for you, my dear bishop, to consider whether peace and truth are likely to be advanced by gathering men out of Pennsylvania, Ohio, and Virginia, to decide whether the Bishop of Maryland shall be called upon to hold up his hand as a criminal and receive sentence for presuming to know the meaning of a canon, in the making of which he himself assisted, better than a couple of brethren from the Virginia Theological Seminary!

Heartily praying God that your green old age may be prolonged to us for many years and filled with blessings, I am,

Gratefully and lovingly your faithful friend and brother,

W. R. WHITTINGHAM.

TO THE REV. WILLIAM J. SEABURY, PROFESSOR, ETC.

BALTIMORE, June 16, 1875.

MY DEAR PROFESSOR:

I thank you most heartily for the kind expression of your sympathy for me in what I cannot help feeling to be my very painful position. You are quite right in thinking that the public mention of it in my address was no ordinary trial to me. The attempt to have me impeached has been going on for some time in great quietness, and it was only the day before the meeting of Convention that I learned (through a letter received by a lady in Baltimore and shown to my wife) the fact that a presentment had actually been made. Had I persevered in the silence which until then had been my intention, two evil consequences might have followed. The re-election of one of the signers to the Standing Committee would have been construed into an approval of his course by the Convention, and my silence would have been interpreted as disinclination to avow and maintain my position. I thought it best, therefore, to bring the matter to light, and without introducing personal questions, present the point of disputed interpretation to the Convention.

The total misapprehension and therefore misrepresentation of my procedure in *The Church and State* of the 5th enabled me to put that paper in possession of a correct statement, which appeared in the issue of the 12th. In that you will see how thoroughly correct has been your conception of the matters in dispute, though gathered from such meagre and inaccurate materials. I will own that I have been sorely disappointed and grieved at the failure of the laity of Maryland to stand by their bishop. I asked no change in anything, but presented my testimony to a fact, viz., that the late great laymen of Maryland—Chambers, Evans, and S. J. Donaldson—had agreed with myself in framing the canon out of which occasion has been taken to coerce me into action which I esteemed both unjust and unwise, and had never contemplated the subjection of the episcopate to such coercion. A parcel of Virginians and of young men hardly born when the facts about which I bore testimony took place, altogether numbering only about a quarter of the Convention, contrived, by party drill, to defeat the majority and place me in the attitude of a discredited witness. The effect of the thing will no doubt be the strengthening in Maryland of the principles which you so well enounce, attributing to Christ's ordinance the scope and vigor which he imparted to it, and recognizing in all human action in the way of constitutions, canons, etc., merely regulations and restrictions of the exercise of powers and responsibilities in no wise from them derived, but due to God alone.

My whole course in Maryland has been the unremitting endeavor to carry out my convictions of direct and exclusive responsibility for the episcopate as for a stewardship, to Christ alone, and of obligation to all the laws of truth and honesty to observe, in the discharge of that stewardship, all the directions, limitations, and restrictions deriving binding force from agreement in their recognition of the episcopate either of the whole Catholic Church, or of our own communion, or of the American Church, or of the diocese in which God's providence has placed me for its exercise.

I am glad to have this opportunity for again thanking you for the much-prized gift of your father's discourses. I have read them all with great zest, with the entire agreement as to substance of doctrine which I expected, and with great pleasure in the discovery of remarkable coincidences of expression between the writer's utterances and my own, for which I could hardly have ventured to look.

Your obliged and grateful friend and brother,

W. R. W.

Because of the bishop's estimate of the opinion so kindly expressed, and with permission, the letter to which the foregoing is an answer is given after the close of this chapter; and also, with like permission, one marked with the bishop's grateful sense of its support, received from a son of his fellow-student in the Seminary and ever-after friend, the late Bishop of Illinois.

On July 29th the board of inquiry met in Baltimore, thirteen of the sixteen members appointed being present. The bishop's family had gone to their summer residence in Orange, but he remained in the city. When some members of the board called on him he refused to see them because he would not have it said that he had had an opportunity to prejudice them in his favor.

The charges and the testimony supporting them, most of which was documentary, were produced by one of the clerical presenters. The sessions of the board were interrupted only by an intervening Sunday. On the fourth day, by a vote of nine to four, the dissenting voices being those of all the members from Virginia, it was " *Resolved*, That from the evidence before them the board are of opinion that there are not sufficient grounds to put the Rt. Rev. William R. Whittingham upon his trial in said matters."

Having expressed their judgment on the matter which they were convened to decide, and which alone concerned them as a court of inquiry, they appended to their decision the expression of an opinion which must remain a cause of amazement so long as it and they are remembered:

Resolved, That the president of this board be instructed to accompany the charges and the refusal of the board to make the presentment against the Bishop of Maryland, with the statement of our unanimous and emphatic condemnation of the alleged acts and teaching of the Rev. Messrs. Perry and Richey, of Mt. Calvary Church, set forth and complained of in the presentment made against them by the Standing Committee to their bishop, and for which they have been admonished by him.

If the term admonished was used in the canonical sense, implying one of the " three kinds of punishment " for ecclesiastical offences, this statement is not true. The error of the accused clergymen was pointed out to them; they admitted that they had done wrong through misconception of what was lawful, and promised that their admitted offence should not be repeated; whereupon the bishop assured them that proceedings against them should go no farther. Nor is it true that in any sense the bishop admonished the two presbyters to cease from acts and teaching complained of in the presentment made against them as being in violation of the Article of Religion entitled " Of Purgatory." This presentment was received after the bishop, on submission to his counsel, had condoned the offence which had been formally brought to his knowledge as ordinary.

If not misrepresented, a member of the board, of legal training, who voted for the presentment of the bishop, asserted that by the condemnation contained in their resolution the board had passed a severer sentence on the Mt. Calvary clergy than could have been inflicted by the Bishop of Maryland, for the board represented the whole Church. This must have been said as an advocate; for he knew that no court can condemn a man untried, and that the board were representatives of the Church for the one purpose of deciding whether the Bishop of Maryland should be indicted. The only effect of this extra-judicial opinion was the purging of themselves, by those who uttered it, from all complicity with Ritualism.

It was reported at the time that a prominent Evangelical protested against the effort of his friends as utter folly. " You do not know," he said, " what you are doing in seeking to indict the Bishop of Maryland. Should he be placed on trial and be acquitted, his party will claim a triumph for their views; while if he should be condemned, such a cry of sympathy with the godly Bishop Whittingham will be raised throughout the land that our party will be ruined." As it was, there was rejoicing in a personal triumph, and the feelings of many were expressed by what one wrote to the acquitted bishop: " They intended mischief against thee, and imagined such a device as they were not able to perform. Thank God for the fulfilment of the Word as regarding his servant."

So soon as the decision of the board was known letters of congratulation, in numbers, were sent to the bishop from laymen and clergymen, from old friends and new, and not from one party in the Church only.

To one of these letters he answered:

TO THE RT. REV. B. B. SMITH, PRESIDING BISHOP.

ORANGE, Essex Co., N. Y., August 10, 1875.

MY DEAR BISHOP:

Accept my hearty thanks for your kind and welcome congratulations on my deliverance, at last, from the mortifying annoyance to which I have so long been subjected. I have already assured you of my conviction that throughout this trouble you have befriended me in every way consistent with your sense of justice and duty to the Church, and of my corresponding feeling of grateful obligation. It is a sore pity that even to the last error and obliquity of judgment should have marred the course of justice. Did I regard my own rights as for a moment to be set in the scale against the peace of the Church, I could not be content to allow what has been done to pass without most damaging exposures of falsehood (witting or unwitting), as yet only imperfectly denounced, and of impertinent transgression of the line of duty, on partial and incomplete information, by persons clothed with temporary authority of another kind and for a different purpose. I have had, since the failure of the inquisition against myself, to resist a new demand for resort to ecclesiastical litigation (which I forewarned my presenters must grow out of their failure) by men who see their opportunity for establishing as rights what I am estopping them from as abuse of license.

I trust I shall be successful in holding my present ground unchanged, but if I do it will be with no debt of thanks to the unwise brethren who overstepped the line of duty to pronounce judgment in a case and against persons in no wise legitimately before them, thereby subjecting themselves and me to the base insinuation of having collogued together in a compromise on personal considerations, evading the question of fact alone at issue.

A few days later he wrote:

I am full of trouble at the consequences of the unfortunate departure of the late board of inquiry from the limits of prescribed canonical action. It will be only by my utmost effort (if I *do* succeed) that I hinder the matter from taking the shape either of formal protest or appeal to you, or of published letters faulting the action of the board, or both. I have again refused to proceed to the trial of the presented presbyters—this time on their own call. The very consequences I have all along predicted to Drs. Hoff and Randolph are now developing. They have lent new courage and sinew and a vantage-ground of operations to the troublesome clique which their short-sighted movement was designed to crush.

The language was not of the gentlest in which he refused the request of the Mt. Calvary clergy to be put on trial. He considered the natural prompting of resentment to be an act of unkindness toward himself. Protection of them had brought on him what in his sensitiveness he looked on as humiliation, and he thought that consideration of his desire for the quietude of his diocese should have made them more willing to endure the hardship of what he, as fully as they did, felt to be injustice.

LETTERS.

FROM THE REV. PROFESSOR OF ECCLESIASTICAL POLITY AND LAW IN THE GEN. THEO. SEMINARY.

A BISHOP'S POWERS: WHENCE DERIVED AND HOW LIMITED.

NEW YORK, June 14, 1875.

RIGHT REVEREND AND DEAR SIR :

I trust that I shall not appear intrusive if I venture to express to you something of the feeling with which I have seen the report (contained in last week's *Church Journal*) of the proceedings of the late Convention in Maryland. The idea that there should be any one in the Church who could seriously think of presenting the Bishop of Maryland for trial is one so absolutely revolting to me that I can hardly help thinking that the public mention of such a project must have been deeply painful even to one so far strengthened and elevated by the consciousness of faithfulness to right principle as yourself. Therefore I cannot refrain from presenting my humble sympathy to you.

The account which I have seen is so brief and meagre that I am hardly able to know all that is involved in the position which you thought it right to take, but if I have correctly understood your position it involves principles which I highly prize, and for the assertion of which I, for one, feel deeply thankful to you.

There seems to be an idea prevailing in the Church, and manifesting itself in the expressions and acts of men of very different parties, that a bishop has no power or discretion except such as is given to him by constitution or canon. A bishop in such a view becomes a mere executive officer of a society of human origin. It does seem to me that this is simply to invert the matter, and that the correct view is that the power of government belongs to the bishop except in so far as it may have been limited. The limitations imposed by the divine law and by the judgment of the body of the episcopate result from the very constitution of the apostolic office to which he has been appointed, but the canons of a particular Church I suppose to be in the nature of safeguards against the arbitrary exercise of this divinely given power by fallible men. Certainly it is not to be presumed that any discretion is taken away from a bishop in any duty imposed on him to act under any such canon unless such be the express declaration of the canon. Much more, it seems to me, is this true of *diocesan* canons, which, strictly speaking, must be considered as having had their origin in episcopal concession, and therefore carry with them no presumption against episcopal rights.

If I am wrong in finding in your action some countenance for the view which I have taken, I can only ask pardon for my misunderstanding. Of course, in your presence I speak under correction, and would be very thankful if you thought it worth while to correct me.

Believe me, Right Reverend Sir, with sincere respect and regard, very truly yours, Wm. J. Seabury.

FROM W. F. WHITEHOUSE, ESQ.

AN EXPRESSION OF SYMPATHY.

Chicago, June 15, 1875.

My Dear Bishop Whittingham:

I trust that you will not consider it improper for me, although but briefly informed of the proceedings of your late Convention, to express my sympathy for you in the late trial to which you were exposed, and my admiration of the noble stand which you took for the dignity of your order.

There are some who seem to think that bishops are created by constitutions and derive their power from canons. That canons only *limit* the exercise of the privileges of the office, and that the *rights* are *inherent*, they fail to appreciate.

My own father always contended manfully for the dignity of his office, and, in Illinois, always succeeded in his efforts.

There seems to me more in all this than would appear, and that this defence of the dignity of the episcopate is a defence of the integrity of the Church. Such seemed to me the result of your dignified protest.

I trust you will pardon this expression and permit me to remain, with the highest respect, yours most faithfully,

W. F. Whitehouse.

CHAPTER VIII.

THE CHURCH MOVEMENT IN MEXICO.

1854–1879.

FOR the reform movement on the Continent the American
Church has become responsible, in so much as in various
ways fraternal sympathy has been shown to those who
threw off allegiance to their bishops, all of whom continued
under the Roman obedience, even those who had been
counted as opponents to papal aggressions.

On this side of the Atlantic graver responsibility has been
accepted in assuming the tutelage of and conferring the
apostolic succession on bodies recognized as foreign churches
—*Sine Episcopo.* To Haiti a bishop has been given. To
Mexico a bishop, and before this, orders to those who with
other representatives of laymen elected him to be their
bishop.

Bishop Whittingham was chairman of the commissions
charged with forming and maintaning relations with these
Churches, and also of the one under whose care were the
ministerial services in Cuba, to which he attached great importance as the seed of a future harvest. But the labors of
the self-sacrificing priest in Cuba, and the work of the wise
and efficient Bishop Holly, if they have excited interest,
have caused no controversy, and therefore there is here
offered only the result of an attempt to trace the history of
the Protestant movement in Mexico.

A year or two before the dictator, De Santa Anna, was,
in 1855, finally overthrown, seven curates and four itinerant

vicars, it is said,* met in the City of Mexico to consult how best to uproot fanaticism and teach the people the doctrines of Jesus Christ in their purity. Soon after their first convention nine other ecclesiastics acceded to them. A convocation was organized by the election of a president, and meetings were held weekly. These meetings were continued two years, and their novelty attracted to them a great number of ecclesiastics.

The efforts of this body were not confined to the capital. Members having the most zeal were sent into the country, and those in remote curacies were advised to give, from time to time, an account of their labors to the directory and receive such instructions as would tend to unity of action. One common feeling that associated these men was a desire for a National Church. Whatever their estimate of " the fanaticism and impurity of doctrine " prevailing among their countrymen, they did not wish to introduce schism, which had as yet found no entry. This is shown by the fact that when the bishops, resenting reform of any kind, almost altogether defeated the efforts of the Society, they sent a formal complaint to the Pope signed by seventy-four clergymen. This paper was entrusted to the president, but he being then in the United States, where probably he was in refuge from periodical insurrection, instead of forwarding it as intended, transmitted it to Juarez, who had set up his Government in Vera Cruz. Unhappily the liberal chief took the reformers under his protection so far as could be done under a constitution that had abolished all connection of Church and State. He promised that their individual rights, trampled upon by arbitrary superiors, should be preserved, and he gave them two churches in the City of Mexico. This favor, in the estimate of the Church party, merged them with the Constitutionalists. They were so called, and when a suspension of the payment of all governmental debts

---

* Memorial of the Missionaries of the Mexican Protestant Church. Printed in New Orleans under the auspices of Bishop Wilmer. 1866.

gave to the French, English, and Spanish an opportunity to seize upon the country, the reformers were swept away with their affiliated party. Among them there must have been earnest, religious men whose influence continued after they had disappeared.

Two priests who had been driven out of the country on the fall of Juarez, Martinez and Dominguez, spent nearly two years in the United States, becoming more and more freed from Romanism. They had communications with the Committee on Foreign Missions, and relying, probably through mistake, on support from the board, returned to Matamoras, at the mouth of the Rio Grande, which bounds Mexico; but being there in danger of losing life, they soon established themselves in Brownsville, on the opposite side of the river, where they lived in great indigence. Their mode of labor is not stated, but in a paper dated city of Matamoras, July 31, 1866, and signed by "the faithful of the Mexican Episcopal Church," it is claimed that "a congregation of one hundred and ninety-eight families have covenanted to sustain with their blood the new Christian Church of Mexico, and have nominated the Presbyter Rafael Diaz Martinez as the Bishop of the Mexican Church, and have asked the Episcopal Church of the United States to accord him consecration, thus transmitting the apostolic succession, which event will forever exclude the See of Rome from all intervention in their affairs." In November, 1866, Don Martinez, with his associate, Don Dominguez, met a commission of bishops who had gone to New Orleans to consecrate Dr. Wilmer to the See of Louisiana. He applied to the senior bishop, Hopkins, for episcopal orders, and was much surprised to learn of all the canonical hindrances to what he had confidently looked for.

What was the subsequent action of this seemingly devout licentiate, Martinez, or of the "faithful of the Mexican Episcopal Church" in Matamoras, whom he represented, is not known.

Farther south, and under a different name, associations existed having the same desire for deliverance from papal rule.

The English had not remained long in Mexico, but perhaps an unintended result of their short stay may have been more abiding than that of the six years' intervention of the French, who used their power in behalf of the clerical party —probably had invaded the country with that object in view.

With the English came an agent of a Bible society with a supply of Bibles in Spanish.

After the repeal of the guarantees of religious freedom, the body of religionists, called Constitutionalists, drifted back to their old relations, or were scattered; but Aguilar, a respected priest, who had been one of them, remained firm in his convictions and faced the attendant danger, growing more and more decided in his anti-papal views through the study of the Bible. He became pastor of several congregations, and looked forward to the establishing a National Episcopal Church, hoping for the episcopacy from the United States. Over-exertions and the trials of penury—it is said that he lacked food—broke down his health. He died strong in the faith, clasping a Bible. He was made happy on his death-bed by a promise from Hernandez, a layman, afterward bishop elect, that the work undertaken should not be allowed to fall through. His followers, who were chiefly from the class of manual laborers, met for mutual support without the guidance of any clergyman, resisting efforts which were made to draw them aside from the hopes that Aguilar had taught them to cherish.

At the end of two years a commission was sent by them to the United States to obtain clerical aid from our Church. From whatever cause, they were about to return disappointed, when they met Mr. Riley, a Spanish-speaking clergyman, native of Chili. Without commission other than the approval of his bishop, Mr. Riley consented to go with the Mexicans. During several years he bore the discomforts of a minister to the poorer classes, and met the dangers which in that country and at that time beset a teacher whose influence was feared. He purchased from the Government a church that belonged to a suppressed convent, and thus gave to the humble people whom he served more of the air of worldly respectability. A more notable event was a gain from the dominant religious body. Aguas, a priest of some note, had been directed to expose the errors of the foreign teacher, but the disputant became a Protestant, and was led to side with the man whom he was to oppose, through the study of a tract on "True Liberty," written and published by Mr. Riley. Under their joint labors congregations were formed or strengthened in other parts of the country, and all these were united formally as the synod of a Church. For this "Church of Jesus" a book of offices was set forth, and the Presbyter Aguas was chosen bishop with the expectation of obtaining consecration in the United States. Not long after his election this single presbyter of the Church of Jesus died. He has left a mark of his ability and an expression of his theological opinions in a clever satirical letter to the Bishop of Mexico, written when the greater excommunication was fulminated against him.

After, or a while before, the death of Aguas, Mr. Riley returned to the United States, and "left the Church of Jesus without a head. It was necessary," so writes one of themselves, "that a layman should occupy the place of these two, and a suitable one was soon found." It is not intimated that the administration of the sacraments was intermitted. In October, 1874, a report is made of twenty-seven regular congregations, five being in the capital, ten paid missionaries, and a theological seminary, the pupils of which are already preachers.

In the preceding August a council was held in the City of Mexico and a memorial drawn up in these words:

To the Bishops of the Protestant Episcopal Church in the United States of America:

We, members of the Synod of the Church of Jesus in Mexico—a branch of the Christian Church that desires to preserve in all its purity the primitive faith, and the order and ministry of the Church in all their integrity—solicit the bishops of the Protestant Episcopal Church in the United States of America to take such measures as may lead to the granting to us the episcopate, we being ready to give the necessary guarantees for the maintenance of the faith and the due order in the ministry of our Church.

This memorial was signed by one presbyter elect, nine deacons elect, and one reader.

When presented by Bishop Lee, of Delaware, in October, 1874, it was received by the House of Bishops in council " with deep and affectionate interest," and a commission of seven bishops * was appointed " to institute such examination and prepare such articles of agreement as may be necessary to carry into effect the prayer of the memorial." It was also resolved " that in the conduct of such examination it is recommended to the commission to institute a preliminary provisional visitation by one or more bishops of this Church if possible, or at least by two or more learned and discreet presbyters."

Article X. of the constitution of the Church authorizes the consecration of bishops " for foreign countries on due application therefrom," decision as to the application and the qualification and election of the persons designated for the office being left wholly to the House of Bishops. Under this authority the bishops acted on the petition of " the Church of Jesus."

So far as their memorial shows, the clergy of this Church consisted of one deacon, known as such—if indeed this be evidence of the fact—by his signature as presbyter elect. This evinces the need of the preliminary visitation recom-

---

* The commission consisted of Bishops Whittingham, of Maryland ; Lee, of Delaware ; Bedell, of Ohio ; Stevens, of Pennsylvania ; Coxe, of Western New York ; Kerfoot, of Pittsburg, and Littlejohn, of Long Island.

mended. That information only was sought by the House of Bishops is shown by the fact that the visitation might be conducted by presbyters.

At the request of the commission one of themselves, Bishop Lee, of Delaware, decided to undertake this visitation for examination.

On Saturday night, February 6, 1875, he reached the City of Mexico, accompanied by the Rev. Dr. Dyer, as representative of the American Church Missionary Society, " in whose charge this mission is," as was asserted. The Rev. Dr. Riley had preceded them to make preparation for the due reception of the bishop. This visitation was supposed to be not without danger.

Bishop Lee writes:

It is a happy thing to begin my visit with the Lord's day and in the worship of his house. The scene at church this morning was very interesting. The chapel will hold four or five hundred and was quite crowded. The people were largely of the humble class, and the prevailing type of feature and complexion strongly Indian. The simple liturgy adopted by the Church of Jesus was used, and was joined in heartily. The responses were general, and all seemed to unite in the singing. The sermon was preached by the minister in charge.

This minister in charge, Gonzalez, had been lately a Roman Catholic priest; of him Dr. Riley wrote: " He is a man of great power and learning, who has joined this 'Old Catholic' movement, now preaches to large congregations, and is exerting a great influence."

We are not told that such was the case, but we may suppose that the bishop was able to understand the sermon preached and to join in the use of " the simple liturgy " adopted by this simple-minded people, and so was prepared to communicate directly with those, to examine into whose religious state had brought him to Mexico.

The bishop in his intercourse with them was under the necessity of proceeding with care and consideration of the sensitiveness of a foreign people; for industrious efforts had been made both by Romanists and by Protestant missionaries to excite jealousy respecting his mission, as if the Protestant Episcopal Church intended to absorb the Church in Mexico and to impose its own rites and usages. He therefore took special pains to evidence his recognition of its distinct nationality.

He was much encouraged by what he saw and by what was reported to him, and was deeply impressed with the importance of the work, which in extent and promise was far beyond what he had been led to expect.

There was given him a list of thirty-nine congregations in union with the Church of Jesus, varying in number from fifteen or twenty to three hundred members, and he was assured that there were nearly three thousand attached and reliable members, besides a not smaller number of occasional attendants.

As the representative of his brethren, Bishop Lee was only commissioned to make a provisional examination, as has been observed. Acting on his own inherent powers he gave the grace of confirmation—how could he have refused the request for it?—to one hundred and thirty persons in the city. Lack of time and the fear of personal risk did not permit his extending the blessing to the country congregations. Also, to supply the immediate and urgent needs of the Church, which since its beginning in 1865, though suffering great disadvantage, had patiently waited on God's providence, the bishop admitted seven persons first to deacons' and then to priests' orders. The account of this transaction in his own words will be read with interest.

It was a memorable day, February 24, 1875, when the first ordination in Mexico was held by a Protestant bishop. The full service of our Church, in the Spanish tongue, was used, the sermon being preached by the Rev. Dr. Riley. When the Epistle was read —Acts vii., "Wherefore, brethren, look ye out among you seven

men of honest report, full of the Holy Ghost and wisdom, whom we
may appoint over this business "—the unintentional coincidence of
seven persons being presented for ordination made quite an impression.

After the service the emotion shown was very touching, the
newly ordained throwing themselves into each other's arms and
weeping for joy. As it was so uncertain when another opportunity
would be presented, ordination to the presbyterate followed a few
days after.*

The letters of orders given by Bishop Lee were in these
words:

In nomine Patris et Filii et Sancti Spiritus.   Amen.

Tenore presentium, Nos, Alfredus Lee, S. T. D. miseratione divi-
na, Diocœsis Delawarensis, in Rebuspublicis Americæ Septentriona-
lis, Episcopus, notum facimus, quod die　　　　mensis Februari,
Anno Domini MDCCCLXXV., et nostræ consecrationis XXXIV.,
sacros ordines, Dei omnipotentis præsidio celebrantes in Ecclesia
Sancti Francisci, in urbe Mexi censi, dilectum nobis in Christo

　　　　de vita laudabili ac morum et virtutum donis nobis in hac
parte commendatum, atque in sacrarum literarum scientia et doc-
trina competente eruditum, ac a nobis ipsis prius examinatum et
comprobatum ad sacrum　　　　ordinem, juxta morem et ritum
ecclesiæ Christi, admissimus et promovimus ; eundemque
in debita forma, voluntarie et coram nobis, professum se ex animo
credere Scripturas Sacras canonicas Veteris et Novi Testamenti
verbum Dei esse, et omnia continere quæ ad externam salutem sint
necessaria, et se ex animo credere omnes articulos fidei Christianæ
ut in Symbolo Apostellorum et in Symbolo Nicaee declarantur,

　　　　rite et ac juxta veteres canones, præsentibus tam e clero quam
e populi testibus idoneis, ordinavimus.

In cujus rei testimonium, instrumento huic, chirographa nostro
prius munito, sigillum nostrum Episcopale ponendum mandavimus,
anno, mense, die, locoque prædictis.†

Before leaving home Bishop Lee had contemplated this
act of ordination, and had prepared his letters. It is not
to be said of him that he had any intention to exceed the

---

* Bishop Lee, in Church Review, October, 1875.

† It is possible that the copy here *literally transcribed* is a proof-sheet.

limits of the trust confided to him, and his acts were all accepted by those whose commission he bore; but it is as certain that the history of our Church gives no such exemplification of the maxim, Necessity knows no law, and no such evidence that a bishop in the American Church is more than a bishop in the Protestant Episcopal Church.

The bishop bore back with him to the United States a covenant with the Church of Jesus, modelled after the form of that with Haiti, subject to the approval of those whom he represented. This *pacto* between the House of Bishops and the *Junta Central* of the Church of Jesus in Mexico sets forth that, in view of the fact that nearly all the clergy elect and members of the Church of Jesus are Mexican citizens, the House of Bishops recognizes the said Church to be a foreign Church, but that it shall remain under nursing care until it shall attain to a sufficiency in its episcopate.

The House of Bishops agrees to consecrate one or more persons as bishops, and by a commission of its own members, jointly with said bishop or bishops, to administer the episcopal government of the Church of Jesus until such time as there shall have been three bishops consecrated, being governed in their acts, as far as possible, by the laws of the Church in the United States.

The Church of Jesus certifies—

That it receives the Holy Scriptures, excluding the Apocrypha, as the Word of God, and containing all things necessary to salvation; that it professes the Catholic and Apostolic faith as set forth in the words of the Apostles' and Nicene Creeds; that it receives and observes the two sacraments of baptism and the supper of the Lord ordained by Christ himself and none others; that it holds that from the apostles' time there have been these orders in the ministry, bishops, presbyters, and deacons, and desires to perpetuate them for itself; that it rejects the errors, novelties, and superstitions of the Church of Rome as the same are set forth and rejected by the Protestant Episcopal Church, . . . and further covenants not to receive or establish any doctrines or articles of belief contrary to the doctrines held by the Protestant Episcopal Church and set forth in its formularies.

Before March 22d Bishop Lee was ready and desirous to report the result of his voyage, and to this end he addressed Bishop Whittingham, whom, as his senior, he preferred to look to as head of the commission, although in the *pacto* he is himself described as chairman. The brief report of acts and impressions which had been communicated by letter was transmitted to the other members of the commission, and their answers show great gratification. No one of them seems to have shared the opinion of Bishop Whittingham, who in his acknowledgment of Bishop Lee's communication wrote, in effect, "I did not suppose you had been so fully empowered." Bishop Lee could readily justify acts that exceeded expectation, but our bishop, seeking information outside of the report made, became anxious. His dissatisfaction was expressed in a letter to Bishop Coxe, a copy of which he sent to Bishop Kerfoot, and probably to each member of the commission.

BALTIMORE, St. Philip and St. James, 1875.

MY DEAR BISHOP:

Your "dispatch" relative to the Mexican affair is just in hand. You have "heard nothing" because there has been nothing worth writing to communicate, and while from the first it has been certain there would be no meeting of the commission before June, every day something or other seemed to be turning up lessening the probability of any need of a meeting before October. . . .

But—still more—on conference with Bishop Lee I found his report of the state of things in Mexico so little consonant with action under Article X. of the constitution as, in my judgment, to throw the work quite into the missionary field. He could not name any clergy except those of his own recent ordination, nor a single layman of any eminence either for character, attainments, or influence. I could not see how it could be possible for us to recognize a handful of our own converts and the attendants—however numerous—at their services as a foreign Church in the true meaning and intent of the article of the constitution under which only we could act. A promising and encouraging mission it seemed to be, but then it must be established and carried on under our laws governing missionary operations, not under Article X. . . . Still another [reason for delay of summons of the commission] presented itself to me. . . . I became possessed of a copy of a brochure in 18mo, entitled on the cover " *Oraciones é Himnos,*" with six inner titles, such as printers call bastard titles, having in none of them mention of place, date, or printer. The first interior title runs: " *Libro de Oracion para aquella parte que milita en este mundo de la Iglesia de Jesus, una, Catolica, apostolica, y Cristiana.*" The second : " *Himnos* "—of which there are fifteen. The third : " *Culto para los Baptismos.*" The fourth : " *Culto para la Cena del Señor.*" The fifth : " *Culto para los Matrimonios.*" The sixth : " *Culto para los Entierros.*" In all, a tract of ninety very open and small 18mo pages. In this pigmy travesty of the Book of Common Prayer the Apostles' Creed occurs three times—pp. 17, 45, 61—each time without the article : " He descended into hell." The Lord's Supper is administered by the people, without other consecration than the reading *as a lesson* the history of its institution out of 1 Corinthians, xi. The baldest Zuinglianism is distinctly ruled in the rubrics.

Of this thing not one word of mention had been made by Riley or Dyer at the meeting of the commission last November, so far as I remember, or by Bishop Lee now, until at our interview I inquired about it, when he seemed not to care to say much on the subject except that it could be altered, being merely tentative. He thought it the joint work of Riley and Aguas.

For myself I feel bound to say that, without previous disavowment of such a production, the *Iglesia* calling itself *de Jesus,* however loud in its profession of holiness, catholicity, apostolicity, and *Christianity,* could not obtain my consent to any such covenant of recognition and assistance as is proposed.

I think the members of the commission have a right to ask for some explanation of the history and use of the " *Oraciones é Himnos,*" and if it be not disavowed, send for copies in order to its examination before proceeding on the subject of the proposed agreement.

In my poor judgment the unhappy Mexicans would be better off, less torn away from primitive truth and order, if turned over to the officious charities of the Episcopal Methodists or the Old School Presbyterians, than if furnished with an episcopate to perpetuate such doctrine as the " *Oraciones é Himnos* " would embody for a norm.

Ever faithfully and truly, your friend and brother,

W. R. W.

As late as September 21st he wrote again to Bishop Kerfoot:

I have been grievously disappointed as to evidence of the existence of any Mexican Church, properly speaking, or in the sense of Article X. of our constitution, and amazed and shocked at the looseness and shallowness of the very little I have been able to obtain of evidence of doctrinal holdings and ecclesiastical doings by the conductors of the movement.

A painful sense of this state of things makes me feel it to be a duty to give whoever may have charge of this movement every opportunity for supplementing our defective supply of information, and giving the best representation of their case of which it will admit.

Despite the urgency of Bishop Lee, no meeting of the commission could be obtained before October 22, 1875. At this time the "norm" of the nascent Church and all that concerned it were fully discussed in repeated sessions during two or more days. Of what passed in these meetings we know nothing apart from what has been published. We may suppose that the chairman was led to consider as more than a missionary field the Mexican Church with an American ordained clergy. If the service which had been vouched for as " scriptural " was not, as he had required, denounced, the covenant was made to contain a pledge that it should be exchanged for one approved by the commission, and also guarantees for the maintenance of the faith clearer than those of the *pacto* signed provisionally by Bishop Lee. His objections being thus removed, Bishop Whittingham presented to the council, which met immediately afterward, the unanimous report of the commission, and also moved the resolutions under which the commission was reappointed with authority to represent the bishops in conclusive action in the matters with which they had been concerned ; that is, with authority to sign the covenant, which had been read and approved in council, and to take the necessary steps for the bestowal of episcopacy on the Mexican Church.

To the covenant as agreed to provisionally by Bishop Lee was added an article indicating the form of testimonials of qualification for the episcopate, and a second, which seems to bear the impress of Bishop Whittingham, and which is here given literally :

ARTICLE VI.—And for the preservation of the common faith and of the doctrines of the Lord Jesus the said Mexican Church binds itself to prepare a Service Book for Public Worship and for the Administration of Confirmation and other sacred rites; the Apostles' Creed and the Creed commonly called Nicene being therein included; the said Service Book to conform in its essential features to the formularies of primitive and apostolic Churches and to be approved by the Commission of Bishops in this Covenant established. And the said Church further binds itself to require a profession of faith in the terms of the Creeds aforesaid as a condition for admission to Holy Orders. And the said Mexican Church in her office for the administration of Holy Baptism will preserve such a due scriptural presentation of the authority and intent of that Sacrament, with the use of the matter and form prescribed by our Divine Lord and Master, as shall be satisfactory to the Bishops of the Protestant Episcopal Church, or to the Commission of Bishops by them appointed. And in her Office for the Administration of the Lord's Supper the Mexican Church will preserve such liturgical forms as are essential thereto, that is to say, particularly, a due scriptural presentation of the authority and intent of that Sacrament, with the use of the matter and form prescribed by our Divine Master and Lord, and with such further provisions as shall render said office conformable to the general outline and spirit of the Primitive Liturgies in the judgment of the Bishops aforesaid, or of the Commission of Bishops by them appointed.

A change of style and title was also made. Instead of "The Church of Jesus in Mexico" was adopted the awkward name, "The Mexican Branch of the Catholic Church of our Lord Jesus Christ Militant upon Earth." To this change importance seems to have been attached by some of the bishops. But the formal paper that certifies that the covenant was unanimously adopted calls it El " *Pacto que la Yglesia Protestante, &c., celebra con esta Yglesia de Jesus, nacionál é Yndependiente, establicida en la República Mexi-cana.*" The seal of the Synod bears the legend " *Yglesia de Jesus,*" and by this name the Church is still generally known. It was said that the unanimity with which these resolutions passed was due to the personal influence of the mover.

Among those bishops who, by silence at least, had sanctioned all acts done and had consented to the renewal of the trust, there were some who, while they avowed confidence in the members of the commission, feared lest in forming a Mexican Church out of the existing materials, instead of doing what would tend to the advance of the Catholic faith or the unifying of the Church, they might be giving life to a mere sect in Christendom; and, therefore, they would have preferred to delay the execution of the proposed covenant.

Results seem to justify their fears. Seven years have not sufficed for the preparation of a service book and liturgy in accordance with the terms of the covenant.

But granting that an American episcopate in Haiti could be justified, that is, that Roman Catholic bishoprics are not protected by the ancient canons forbidding intrusion; granting that it is ever right to make a venture of faith, that it is ever right to trust fully a solemn promise—what was there in the action of the House of Bishops, in October, 1875, to cause the distress which it gave to some of its members?

A large body of believers had rejected their Roman Catholic teachers. No one who knows what the Mexican Church has been can blame any religious man for desiring better guidance. These six thousand—or three thousand—Christians, associated, not organized, willing to receive none other than primitive organization, and—with whatever departure from right doctrine and order—professing to hold our faith, besought of our bishops that rule and guidance which alone they were willing to accept. When they asked for episcopacy there was not a presbyter to sign the petition.

We have seen what action was taken by the bishops in reference to the application of 1874. No principle prevented the Bishop of Maryland from acting on the commission then appointed by them, seeing that he was already at the head of the commission under which a bishop had been given to Haiti. What was done by the representative in Mexico has been told. Bishop Lee judged it to be essential to do more than make an examination into the condition of the petitioners. Whether his honest decision be accepted or not, it is clear that his acts modified the matter to be decided by the commission and by the bishops.

A presbytery had been given. This act must be either approved or disavowed. Having now a valid presbytery, the former petitioners, in return for an expected episcopacy, place themselves under the tutelage of the bishops and renew a solemn promise to maintain the faith. What would have been the result of an absolute rejection of the covenant provisionally formed? Certainly the danger of establishing a new sect would not have been avoided. "The Church of Jesus" might have listened to suggestions already made to them, and been content with such orders as they had received. Their departure from the faith might have then widened without check. If the establishment of a Church in opposition to that of the Roman obedience was to be thought of—and this had been in view from the first—then surely that was wisest which was done when the House of Bishops sanctioned the compact with increased safeguards of doctrine and practice, and provision for careful watch over admission to the episcopate.

That Bishop Whittingham so judged, and that his conscientious objections to the covenant were overcome by changes from that which had been conditionally signed, was a matter of gratification to those who had been the most active friends to the Mexicans. Thenceforward he was to be reckoned among these friends. The right to treat with the Mexican Church as a Church in the meaning of our constitution had been recognized. His desire was to bestow the episcopate so soon as it could be done in conformity with the conditions imposed by those in whose name he was to act. One associated with him has written:

Bishop Whittingham's relations to the commission were entirely consistent with the great principles he made the base of his action in this and other cases. He referred to our own wretched proposed book as showing what we were without the gift of the episcopate. He confided in the divine guidance when once the episcopate is given to humble Christians wise enough to desire it. He regarded it as their right under the Redeemer's promise to be with us.

Few among us would controvert the bishop's principles. The only question is whether the commission, acting on these principles, duly awaited the fulfilment of imposed conditions.

Whatever may have been Bishop Whittingham's estimate of Mexico in October, 1875, five months later he could find no justification for giving bishops' orders to one chosen by the *Iglesia* and sent for consecration.

On January 6, 1876, the *pacto* as amended by the bishops was "ratified by the Synod of the Church of Jesus in Mexico," and signed in their name by the president and the secretary. On February 24th it was transmitted to the chairman of the commission, together with the testimonials of the bishops elect, Dr. Riley and Don Hernandez. The member of the commission through whom these acts were received thought that "they conform perfectly to the requirements." Again Bishop Whittingham was forced to offer objections.

Referring to a meeting of the commission, he wrote to the Bishop of Pittsburg:

FEBRUARY 25, 1876.

DEAR KERFOOT:

. . . I can't think that more than an hour will be needed for the kind of settlement by the Commission which alone the business seems to me capable of receiving. . . .

All that you write to me about Riley makes me regret more and more that the Mexican business was not brought before us in 1874 sufficiently early to have had thorough discussion and taken the form of a mission. I could join in ordaining Riley to-morrow on the evidence now before us. For taking him as sent us by a competent independent Church I can, as yet, see no possible justification. The combination of appeals for money help with the effort to obtain independent orders is most untimely. As a mission it would be all in due course intelligible and laudable. As a proposal for a new hierarchy it seems to me as much as possible the reverse.

Ever loving you,   W. R. W.

Probably in answer to this letter, Bishop Kerfoot wrote to Bishop Whittingham expressing a hope that he would attend the meeting:

MARCH 3, 1876.

. . . . If we are only to decide that the papers are not yet complete enough, the reason for your coming would still be that we might hear all about your doubts as to the competency of the movement to become a Church.

In April a majority of the commission met in Philadelphia, without the presence of the chairman, who, after the important session in October, 1875, seems to have been with his associates on one occasion only, October 9, 1876, when, according to Bishop Kerfoot's notes, there was a full and important meeting. What was then done is not intimated.

At this meeting in April the commission seem to have been troubled by the difficulty of so discharging plain duty as not to offend the national sensitiveness of those they had to deal with. The covenant laid before them was recognized as *meant* by the Mexican Synod to be fully authenticated, yet it was resolved to ask for a transcript of the proceedings of the Synod so far as relating to the covenant, with the names of the churches represented and of the delegates voting, and this to be notarially certified. It was also resolved to " counsel the election of bishops in accordance with the provisions of the covenant."

The election of Messrs. Riley and Hernandez must have been ignored, if indeed their testimonials were presented. Dr. Riley was, however, informally recognized as the probable future first bishop. As such he must have been considered from the beginning of the negotiations. Dr. Riley was "requested to be diligent in the preparation of much-needed services, especially of a liturgy and of a baptismal office, and with a view to this to seek conference at once with the Bishop of Maryland."

A few days later he probably took with him to Baltimore the minutes of the meeting for the bishop's approval, and, it may be, with the intention of complying with the request of the commission, but he did not then see Bishop Whittingham. The fact is remembered that on some occasion, it is supposed at this time, Dr. Riley called, but, because of illness, the bishop was not at the time informed of the call. There was one interview, and it is believed but one. Of this the bishop spoke in his family with pleasure, and to this he probably refers in a letter written March 28, 1876, in which he says:

. . . As to the Mexican commission, I do not now see the urgency of a meeting—Riley heartily agreeing in my view that "slow and sure" would be better and wiser than hasty and insufficiently informed and advised action.

He heartily concurred in a plan for preparing all things for an ordination of Hernandez alone, for the country work, in the autumn, himself meanwhile to return and reside in Mexico as "bishop elect," exercising jurisdiction as a quasi vicar-general until such time as he and Hernandez should be prepared to offer some third candidate whom we could accept; and then he and Riley to be ordained together so as to give full constitution to the Mexican Church as an independent entity with complete autonomy.

There is no evidence to lead one to suppose that this scheme was ever thought of beyond the walls of the bishop's library. But the mere statement of it is enough to show how readily the bishop could put obstacles out of sight.

He desired that the *Iglesia*, when prepared, should be constituted an independent Church, but he at this time asserted that Mexico was properly but a missionary field; he did not know that Don Hernandez was such as could be ordained bishop; and he did know that the first step had not been taken to comply with the conditions indispensable in the case of any ordination—conditions which he had himself insisted on.

The demand for more formal proof of the ratification of the covenant made by the commission in April was promptly acceded to, and it is probable that the act, certified with all the formality that could be given, was presented to them at their meeting on the 9th and 10th of October. It is possible, also, that at the same time Dr. Riley offered proof of his election as bishop. If so, there was an insuperable bar to the taking any steps for his consecration. Nothing had been done toward replacing with offices such as the covenant imposed, the Zuinglian services denounced by Bishop Whittingham. Reiterated promises were still fruitless. A year later, Bishop Lee complains that "nothing has been done about liturgies. I have urged," he says, "upon Dr. Riley the importance of preparing, with as little delay as possible, the draft of liturgical offices that may be examined, and have felt disappointed that they are not yet in readiness."

If it were desirable, I cannot trace all the relations between the commission and the representatives of the *Iglesia de Jesus.* This much is certain, during more than two years there was growing dissatisfaction. Some of the warmest admirers of Dr. Riley suffered themselves to form very harsh judgment touching his conduct. But this was regretted when in the spring of 1879 the bishops elect, Dr. Riley and the Rev. T. Valdespino, arrived in the United States, bringing with them from Mexico two offices, one for holy communion, the other for baptism. Satisfactory explanations were given by Dr. Riley, confidence in him was renewed, and zeal for the work in Mexico was rekindled with such increased fervor that it quite melted away the opposition of some who had thought that they could never be moved.

In April, 1879, the Mexican commission met in New York and sat during several days. All the members were present except the chairman and the Bishop of Western New York. A minute of their proceedings was published. It states that

the commission were occupied with the examination of the official documents and with very careful consideration of the offices laid before them. The delegates from the Mexican Church were empowered to make such changes and emendations therein as might be proposed and advised by the commission, and such changes were agreed upon and mutually approved and results arrived at as rendered the said offices satisfactory to both parties.

The bishop elect, Valdespino, was found to lack the canonical age for consecration: Dr. Riley's certificates were approved.

The commission desired that all their actions should have the unanimous consent of the members. Therefore the minutes of the meeting and copies of the approved services were sent to Bishop Whittingham, who consented to them without change. They were then sent to the other absent member of the commission. Confiding as he had always been in the judgment of his former teacher on such matters as were now brought before him, Bishop Coxe could not approve what yet bore the *imprimatur* of Bishop Whittingham. He insisted on important modifications, and even when these were conceded he did not accept the offices until "the whole thing was voted temporary, not ultimate." These modifications were not submitted to Bishop Whittingham. He never knew of the scruples of his pupil.

The transcriptions made necessary by these changes, and, possibly, the translation into Spanish of the two offices which was demanded by some of the commission, caused the postponement of the consecration, which had been appointed for some day in May.

On St. John Baptist's day, 1879, the Rev. Dr. Henry Chauncey Riley was solemnly consecrated, in Pittsburg, as Bishop of the Valley of Mexico. The bishops taking part in the act were all members of the commission, and all the members were present excepting the chairman, who yet " desired to be considered as associated with the commission in its action," and whose name was subscribed to the testimonials at his request.

Apart from the consideration of its serious consequences, this consecration of the first bishop for the Church of Jesus has been very severely criticised. It is said the commission went beyond the limits of their powers.

They were " empowered to receive, examine, and report to the presiding bishop upon the evidence of election and testimonials of qualification of the persons presented by the synodical authority of the Mexican branch, etc., for ordination to the episcopate." And on receipt of such report the presiding bishop was charged " to take order for the consecration," etc. Bishop Smith having received the report in the case of Dr. Riley, took order for his consecration by appointing the day and the place and agents.

It is said that he should have waited for the consent of the majority of the bishops as in the case of home bishops. No second consecration can take place without such consent, for now the episcopal privilege has been insisted on, but it had not, as it might have been, when Dr. Riley was made bishop. His consecrators were fully persuaded that they had been appointed with *full power to act* for their brethren —the italics are found in Bishop Kerfoot's notes.

It is said that Dr. Riley was not a person fit for the office bestowed on him. Perhaps not; but there are those who think the same of some who have been approved by the majority of the dioceses and of their bishops.

It is said the consecration was premature, and that greater

care should have been exercised in the securing compliance with the terms of the covenant touching doctrine and worship.   The present state of the Church in Mexico seems to justify the complaint.

To what extent rests on Bishop Whittingham the responsibility of this act the expedience, even lawfulness, of which is denied?

It could be shown, *prima facie*, by printed and written testimony that he took upon himself the whole responsibilty, that he sanctioned what his brethren had adopted, and made his own their acts.   And yet reliance on this evidence would mislead.

At one time—as well as can be recalled about the time when the priests Martinez and Dominguez were among us— the bishop looked forward to a coming reformation among the Spanish-speaking peoples of America—an Old Catholic movement—when the light of primitive truth, borne aloft by a converted priesthood, should shine amid the palpable darkness of Southern American Romanism.

He often spoke of the gross immorality, unchecked by the Church, in the American Roman Catholic countries, and considered a knowledge of the habits of the people among whom, through many generations, the Church of Rome has been the only teacher, as among the strongest proofs against Roman claims.*   And his abhorrence of a Church which, as he judged, is content with anything so long as its right to rule is not contraverted, made him ready to see tokens that God was about to overthrow it.   But the first authentic information received respecting the Church of Jesus convinced him that his hopes with regard to Mexico had been too eagerly embraced.

---

* In order to bring this proof before as many persons as possible, he bought all the copies his purse would permit of A Journey Across South America, etc., by Paul Marcoy—a costly work by a French Roman Catholic who, without a thought of bringing his religion into disrepute, shows how little restraint that religion imposes on the morals of the faithful in South America—how little sin is rebuked by the guardians of the faith.

By seniority he was the head of the Mexican commission, and he really desired that the work entrusted to them should be done—that the poor Mexicans should be guided to a better knowledge of the truth, and this through the perfection of their organization; but the signs of progress were not cheering and all enthusiasm was confined to other members. His share in their joint work was thus characterized by himself: "I have only been a brake to check too rapid progress."

It has been shown that after the covenant had been signed he was still of the opinion that Mexico could only be looked upon, *properly*, as a promising missionary field into which a bishop should be sent as into any other. About this time he was asked, What is the probability of a Mexican episcopate? His answer was, "The great difficulty is to find a person fit to be made bishop." Of course he did not overlook Dr. Riley, who had been prominent from the first, who was desired by the Mexicans, and who, undoubtedly, had some qualifications for this special field of duty. Of Dr. Riley he said pointedly to a member of the commission: "He is not the man to found a hierarchy." Yet when the bishop elect presented credentials fulfilling—so far as election was concerned—the conditions of the compact between the House of Bishops and the *Iglesia de Jesus*, he accepted them as he had done those of others whom he would not have chosen to fill the office of bishop.

In a letter to Bishop Lee, dated June 17, 1879, suffixed to the testimonials of Dr. Riley, and with them printed in the journal of the General Convention for 1880, Bishop Whittingham says: "I have given attention, too, to the comments that have been made on our relation to the Mexican Church, and have found no occasion to depart from my concurrence in the action of the committee presided over by yourself." This plain statement is a matter of regret with some who have revered him as a leader, and know not how to reconcile his "concurrence" with what they have supposed to be his church principles. A thorough knowledge of the man would at least prevent surprise.

In this letter he calls the act of the commission a work "of obedience." * A charge had been imposed by the Church, and they on whom it had been laid were not to be influenced by comments of those who were not responsible. In order to show his estimate of a good deal of "comment," there is given among his letters one that is very characteristic, written to Bishop Lee with reference to publishing without authority of the bishops the covenant agreed to in their names.

Possibly some of the comments referred to were condemnatory of all invasion of Roman Catholic dioceses in Mexico. Such would not have been regarded by him, in accordance with what has been stated to have been his convictions. He judged all bishops in the Roman obedience to be in formal schism, and to have themselves broken down the pale that once protected their jurisdiction. His indignation against "Ultramontane tyranny and falsehood" would have made him seize on an opportunity to build a cathedral under the shadow of Saint Peter's. In answer to those among us who condemn his position, he would have argued that they who make the consideration of prior occupancy of the soil to o'ertop all others, will need special pleading to justify the having carried our Church into some parts of the present territory of the United States.

Had the covenant under which the episcopate was given been fairly carried out by the *Iglesia de Jesus ;* had Bishop Riley gone to his diocese and introduced everywhere the services that the Mexican commissioners accepted; and had these services commended themselves to the Catholic-minded, irregularities now censured would have been condoned.

Were it believed that our seven bishops did, before con-

---

* "Of Christian charity and obedience," are his words. Not of necessity simply obedience to the Divine law which imposes charity and bids go into all the world.

secration, exact compliance with the terms of the covenant, then, even if there remained cause to regret misplaced confidence, but few could think of blame.

Unfortunately, the history of the Mexican movement is not such as can wholly please any one. Some there are who censure the forming the covenant and every step taken under it, and can find no excuse for the giving the episcopate; but the judgment of the greater number of those who doubt the propriety of the consecration of Dr. Riley rests on the estimate they place on the two services which he presented as in compliance with the covenant, which offices were in part amended and then voted to be open to further amendments.

Perhaps in the peculiar circumstances of the Mexicans may be found excuses for the great imprudence of leaving what should have been fixed dependent on that treacherous reliance—an understanding. But here excuses are not sought for, nor are any offered in relating the facts which govern a just estimate of Bishop Whittingham's accountability.

Whatever may be the two Mexican services that were accepted with the condition that they were to be improved—be they Catholic or heretical—their merit or demerit is not to be attributed to the Bishop of Maryland.

This is said with a knowledge that on April 19, 1879, he signed a certificate dictated by himself and sent to the acting chairman of the Mexican commission, which is in these words:

Having heard throughout and carefully considered the offices for the administration of holy baptism and of the Lord's Supper presented by the delegates, . . . I do hereby signify my cordial assent to the acceptance of said offices as sufficient to fulfil the conditions heretofore agreed upon as requisite to the consecration of an episcopate for said Church.

No testimonial could be clearer, and yet, with a knowledge of the circumstances under which it was given, there is no court in the land that would not reject it.

Supposing that these offices be what, on the testimony of one who copied them, there is good reason to suppose they are: "cordial assent" to them is in contradiction of the life-long teaching of the bishop.

It has been shown that he searched for, and had to seek, the first service book of the Mexicans, which in our public prints had been authoritatively announced to be scriptural, and that having examined the book he plainly denounced it as heretical.

When the covenant with the Church of Jesus, provisionally signed, was presented to the commission, while his estimate of the movement was to some extent modified, he insisted on amendments to the covenant wholly calculated to secure what, it is said, has not been secured.

For the protection of faith and improvement of public worship he carefully watched, as his papers show, every step in the early proceedings of the commission.

So earnest was he in regard to the future divine offices of the Mexican Church that he resumed the study of liturgies, giving special attention to the Mozarabic, and he prepared a baptismal service.

He attended none of the meetings of the commission in 1879, of which there were several. After the adjournment of the decisive meeting in April, held in New York, the two offices, as first amended by the majority, were sent to Baltimore and submitted to his judgment. They were read to him, he approved them, and afterward he formally certified his approval.

I asked to be allowed to examine the services to which Bishop Whittingham gave his sanction, and which were yet amended and then voted to be temporary, not ultimate, but not having seen them I can only say: If the baptismal office do not set forth regeneration in baptism, or if the eucharistic office retain traces of that Zuinglian teaching manifest in the *Oraciones*, then the bishop's approval may justly cause surprise as stultifying all his ministerial life.

We cannot suppose that holding what until that time he had held to be truth, he could consent that a Church should be built on another foundation. He must have changed his judgment with regard to what is Christian doctrine, or else when the offices were read to him he did not take in the sense of what he assented to. Is the latter supposition probable? These are the facts.

The bishop had been very ill, dependent upon his daughter for all intercourse with the outer world, for soothing reading and for such writing as was necessary. The busy man he had always been could not lie listless. He must be read to. But his reader learned that whatever the theme his attention wandered, and often without giving certain perceptible sign. She would go on at times doubtingly, and on some word showing a perceived want of connection, would quietly turn back. When too feeble to feed himself and suffering excruciating pain, he would have been more than man had he been able always, or for any length of time, continuously to control his mind. While roused he seemed to others, and was for a while, in his normal condition; but, as has been said, even the watchful eye accustomed to look for the signs of weakness could not always discern when this state was interrupted. This is the ordinary history of infirm men.

When in this condition, or "much better, but very feeble," as he seemed to the trusted brother whose presence was as a cordial that roused him into something like himself—when he was better but very feeble there were presented to his consideration matters that asked for the close attention of a man with all his faculties.

"Was with Bishop W. from 10 o'clock to 12. He heard read the proposed offices and was fully satisfied. Gave warm approval." Without a doubt such approval was given. And with as little doubt it is to be believed that the upright man who makes this statement, and who read the services, went away with the honest conviction that every word had been heard, understood, and duly weighed. But yet it is equally true that after he had gone away to bear back to the commission the approval of their chairman of all their acts and of the services that had been accepted by them, Bishop Whittingham gave to his secretary a report of the contents of the sacramental offices which she knew to be incorrect, and when she wished to show his error by reference to the manuscript he exclaimed, "No! no! no! I trust to my brothers in the commission *and to the House of Bishops.* I have done with these things forever."

Although this was two months before the consecration, except to approve a demand that the services should be at once rendered into Spanish, and to give the certificate which has made this long statement necessary, the bishop never again occupied himself with the Mexican question, which was purposely kept from him by the attendants on his sick-bed.

As to the bishop's conception of the liturgy that he had sanctioned, he seems to have considered that it was in the main a transcript of what the Rev. Dr. Hale had drawn from the Mozarabic office. When the doctor was first admitted to see the bishop he was surprised by warm congratulations: "If you had done nothing else you have lived, doctor, for a very good purpose, seeing that you have secured for the Mexicans so good a service."

Dr. Hale had reason to know that he was not entitled to the credit given him, but the bishop was in too feeble a state to permit a discussion of the subject.

LETTER.

TO A MEMBER OF THE MEXICAN COMMISSION.

BALTIMORE, May 4, 1877.

MY DEAR BISHOP:

.   .   .   .

It does not occur to me that anything in it either needs concealment or seems likely to afford occasion of mischief.

But I have a very strong repugnance against permitting—still more, sanctioning—the communication to what we call "the public" —the mixed crowd of scoffers and believers, of enemies and friends, of infidels and Jesuits—of any instrument of delegated action otherwise than by express instruction or authorization of the constituent body.

Viewed in one light, such procedure seems to me a breach of trust, committing the superior body to an unknown extent, and to unknowable contingent consequences, both out of view in the delegation of authority.

In another, it presents itself to contemplation (and condemnation) as an unauthorized appeal to a tribunal neither concerned in our business nor recognized by us—the sickly, utterly incompetent public opinion, as it is called.

To a limited impression of the "covenant" for communication only to members of the Protestant Episcopal Church in the United States and of the Mexican Church, or to any others having a mind and right to ask for it, I see no ground of objection.

But to its publication in the newspapers that the world and the devil and their servants may be taken into counsel with the Church, I have individually an insuperable repugnance. I say "individually," because I am unwilling to let the accident of my seniority in the commission give my private opinion any preponderance against what may be the differing judgments of my brethren. "Officially," therefore, I asked to be excused from acting. I cannot consent, but I will not, by refusing, forbid.

Ever most faithfully,   W. R. W.

CHAPTER IX.

1877–1878.

THE relation of the bishop's connection with the reform in
Mexico brought us near to the time of his release. We
must now turn back, but not far. His closing years were
marked by little excepting a more general recognition of
the value to the Church of one whose labors in her behalf
were soon to close, and the continued struggle on his part
of faithful diligence under increasing difficulties through
weakness and pain of body.

As the time for the meeting of the General Convention
in 1877 drew nigh it seemed very doubtful whether the
bishop's state of health would allow his attending, and
letters show how many persons felt an anxiety on this subject. But, as on all other like occasions, he was present,
and judging from the printed journal, during no meeting
of his House was he ever more actively engaged. Journals,
however, give but an imperfect history of what takes place
in a deliberative body ; his feebleness could not have permitted the earnest and long discussions in which in former
years he was used to engage.

Among the important matters that occupied the House
of Bishops in 1877 were the attempt to enforce by canon of
the American Church the law received through the English
Church regulating the marriage of those near of kin, and
the passage of a canon on divorce and marriage.

To restore a healthier tone of judgment with regard to marriage had been, in various ways, an effort on the part of Dr. Whittingham during all his responsibility as a bishop.

Soon after asserting their civil independence, men in this country began to lessen legal restraints of matrimony, once considered to be moral obligations. A single century has seen such a change in public sentiment throughout the larger portion of the United States that the estimate of marriage which our fathers brought with them to the Western world is as much out of vogue as the garments they wore. The civil contract is regulated by the statutes of the several States, which enactments are the reflex of the sentiment of voters, which is not the same throughout the Union. Public opinion has been more conservative in the Southern States than in the Northern. Thus, until the time of the conquest of the seceded States, and perhaps still, in Virginia at least, the inherited table of degrees was enforced, and in South Carolina divorce was unknown; but it is to be expected that in the course of time there will be enforced everywhere, by the law of comity, the lowest standard of decency that may have been adopted in any of the States, and, unless the current of opinion may turn back, everywhere in the United States, as in some States now, any man and woman not connected in a direct line of consanguinity may become man and wife, and may break their contract almost as readily as any other civil partnership. So prevalent now is the habit of divorce in some parts of the land that a New England moralist has contrasted, to the advantage of the Mormon standard, what he calls the consecutive polygamy of his people with the synchronic of Utah.

The tradition of a regard for marriage as a divine ordinance has been continued so far that, perhaps, in all the States a minister of religion may be an officer of State, before whom, equally with a magistrate, the contract may be acknowledged, and in some States, as is the case in Maryland, he is the only officer appointed for that purpose.* But yet the prevailing estimate of lawful marriage is dependent on what civil statutes have declared to be lawful. Even among churchmen this is too frequently the case. This result almost follows from the constitution of the American Church, in which the influence of the laity is so much felt, and whose laity is continually receiving accessions through other causes than full acceptance of the Church's teaching. Every man whose marriage is blessed by a minister of the Church is told that the Word of God governs the lawfulness of marriage, but not many care to inquire what that Word teaches; and it is an unhappy truth that if the inquiry were made, the answer would not be always even positive, for there are clergymen who often recite the warning and yet have no clear judgment of what "God's Word doth allow."

While Maryland was a province, English ecclesiastical law governed marriage. Soon after the formation of the State the table of degrees was re-enacted. In a little time the Christian doctrine of affinity was in so far rejected that in 1785 legal sanction was given to the union of those already related by marriage as uncle and niece, and in 1790 the General Assembly repealed the prohibition of the marriage of those who are brother and sister, if man and wife be "one" in such sense that the kindred of one are akin to the other.

When the State of Maryland made its first departure from the older law regulating marriage, members of the newly formed diocese were aggrieved. But as a body the Convention did not recognize the English canon of 1603 as having any longer binding force on churchmen in Maryland. In 1805 a committee appointed "to consider of and report on the expediency of the English canon law respecting marriages being adopted by this Church," recommended

---

* An exception is made in favor of "the people called Quakers," who marry by Friends' ceremony.

the enforcing by canon the English table, and also the adoption of two resolutions. The first directed "the deputies from this Church" to the next General Convention to report the [recommended] canon to that body, and "to use their endeavors to obtain the insertion of the same in the future editions of our Prayer-books. The second resolution requested the bishop and standing committee "to present, in the name of this Church, a petition to the General Assembly praying for the repeal" of their two enactments legalizing certain marriages forbidden in the table. This report was printed and referred to the next Convention. In 1806, after discussion, the consideration of the canon and resolutions was postponed until 1807, when the deputies to the General Convention were directed "to call their attention to the English canon respecting marriages, and the expediency or inexpediency of adopting the same and ordering it to be inserted in the future editions of the Book of Common Prayer." The General Convention met in May, 1808, when the House of Bishops made their "observation" on English canon law. In June of that year the Maryland deputies reported that they had obeyed injunctions, and that the General Convention "had postponed the expression of their sentiments concerning the English canon," etc.

This report conflicts somewhat with that of proceedings of the General Convention. The journal of the House of Bishops shows that on May 21, 1808, the bishops took into consideration the message sent to them by the House of Deputies relative to the table of degrees, and observed as follows: "Agreeably to the sentiment entertained by them in relation to the whole ecclesiastical system, they consider that table as now obligatory on this Church, and as what will remain so unless there should hereafter appear cause to alter it without departing from the Word of God, or endangering the peace and good order of this Church. They are, however, aware that reasons exist for making an express determination as to the light in which this subject is to be considered." They declined doing so, because but few of their House were present, and because of lack of time.

Since this action of the House of Bishops there has been no legislative action in the Church.

Bishop Whittingham has in private conversations repeatedly asserted that the bishops as a body accepted the statement of their House in 1808, namely, that " they consider that table [of degrees] as now obligatory on this Church, and as what will remain so unless there should hereafter appear cause to alter it without departing from the Word of God ; " but that he himself would not assent to a mere declaration which gave no power to enforce what was already recognized as obligatory.

As has been shown in these pages, there is a class of Episcopalians who assume that no church law rests on them save that to which " this Church " has in terms assented ; they reject the principles taken for granted by the bishops in 1808 ; to give force to the table of degrees it is necessary, in their estimation, that it should be enacted by canon of the Protestant Episcopal Church. If their position be correct, then since the independence of the several States there has not been any church law regulating marriage.

Bishop Whittingham fully assented to " the sentiment entertained by " the bishops in 1808 " in relation to the whole ecclesiastical system " of the Church of England, and as regards " the table " he believed its prohibitions to have been the rule of the primitive Church. He believed that the Christian Church from its beginning followed the Levitical law as the unchanged expression of God's will concerning marriage, and had always recognized the tie of affinity as dependent on the oneness of man and wife declared by our Lord Jesus. To give a definite instance of his convictions, he taught not only that nearness of kin forbids marriage, but also that explicitly by God's Word a man may not marry his brother's widow, and that by inference from that Word he may not take to wife the sister of his deceased wife. He held that the oneness in the married state asserted by our Lord establishes between a man and his wife's sister that nearness of kin which is the ground of the Levitical prohibitions. To those who demanded the letter of the law, he said: " By the letter a man is forbidden to take to wife his brother's widow ; by parity of reasoning a woman may not marry her sister's husband." *

No record has been found in the journals showing that the question of marriage as affected by nearness of kin was entertained in the House of Bishops between 1808 and 1874, but, as has been intimated, the matter has been informally discussed.†

During the General Convention of 1874 a presbyter of Maryland addressed a petition to the bishops praying that they would set forth the laws of the Church governing marriage, and placed his paper in the hands of his diocesan, asking its presentation by him. The bishop seems not to have complied with this request, but he did what was more efficient—he himself moved the adoption of a canon in the following terms :

---

* Many reject the bishop's reasoning, and claim that a man may lawfully take to wife the sister of his dead wife, while they confess that God's Word forbids the marrying a brother's widow. Churchmen who profess to find in the teachings of the early Church a right interpretation of the Word of God have maintained this position. The bishop might have referred such disputants to the version of the Seventy. The Septuagint, although some of its words differing from the Hebrew text are canonical, being quoted in the New Testament, is not to us the Word of God. But yet a large portion of the early Church had no other Holy Scriptures. Surely a text in the Septuagint asserting a law applicable to questions of daily life must be received as showing the doctrine received by those who used no other Scriptures and the rule by which they governed themselves. If rules governing marriage were sought by these Christians in their Holy Scriptures they did not infer, through parity of reasoning, that it is not lawful to take to wife a sister by affinity ; their Word of God was definite. In our version of Deuteronomy xxvii. 23, we read : "Cursed be he that lieth *with his mother-in-law.*" But in the Septuagint it is written, ἐπικατάρατος ὁ κοιμώμενος μετὰ τῆς ἀδελφῆς τῆς γυναικὸς αὐτοῦ—*with the sister of his wife.*

† See a letter to the Rev. J. B. Colhoun, Vol. I., p. 475.

Of Marriage with Relatives.

No minister of this Church shall marry persons related within the degrees of kindred forbidden in the table now obligatory in this Church as declared in the General Convention of 1808, nor shall persons hereafter so married be admitted to confirmation or the holy sacraments, unless, after due penitence, with the direction and consent of the bishop.

The Committee on Canons, to whom the resolution was referred, reported a canon simply prohibiting a clergyman to " marry persons related within the degrees of kindred forbidden in the table now obligatory in this Church." The Bishop of Maryland moved as an amendment his original resolution. On the next day the whole subject was referred to a special committee, to report at the next General Convention.

At that Convention (1877) action originated in the House of Deputies. The Committee on Canons was directed to consider " the expediency of printing in future editions of the Prayer-book the table of forbidden degrees as it exists in the Prayer-book of the English Church." But the resolution ordering this was prefaced by the admission that " there exists no authoritative standard in this Church with regard to the limits of consanguinity," etc. The committee, for reasons stated, were of the opinion that any action on this subject ought to be initiated in the House of Bishops, and did not recommend the printing the table in the Book of Common Prayer.* In the House of Bishops a report was made by a majority of the special committee appointed in 1874, and also a minority report was presented by the Bishop of Maryland. The two reports were referred to the Committee on Canons, who, through their chairman, Bishop Atkinson, reported and moved the adoption of a canon setting forth the English table in its en-

---

* Only one edition of the Prayer-book has been found to contain the table. This was published by T. L. Plowman, Philadelphia, 1805.

tireness, and forbidding all ministers to solemnize matrimony among persons related within the forbidden degrees.

After discussion, and after the rejection of an amendment by the Bishop of Rhode Island, who sought to give the sanction of the Church to marriage with one related by affinity as a sister or niece, a brother or uncle, the resolution as offered by the Bishop of Maryland was adopted by a vote of 24 to 20. Subsequently the vote was reconsidered, and the subject of marriage with relatives was referred to a joint committee, with instructions to report to the next Convention. A majority and a minority report were made in 1880, and again "the whole matter was referred to the next General Convention."

A conclusion with regard to divorce has been more readily reached. In 1868 a canon was adopted forbidding a clergyman to solemnize the marriage of any divorced person, excepting the case of the "innocent party in a divorce for cause of adultery." In 1871, in the House of Deputies, an attempt was made to alter the canon so as "to include in the prohibition the lay members of the Church." But the Committee on Canons asked to be discharged from the consideration of the subject. In 1874 a "Canon on Divorce" was promptly passed in the House of Bishops, having been discussed in council, as may be conjectured from the wording of the journal; but when brought before the House of Deputies, with an amendment, on the last day of the session, "the whole subject was referred to the next Convention." On the second day of the Convention of 1877 the Bishop of Maryland offered, without change, the resolution which had been passed by the bishops in 1874. After the rejection of various proposed amendments the canon was sent to the deputies for concurrence, and was by them returned changed, inasmuch as the bishops peremptorily forbade a minister to present for confirmation or to administer the sacraments to any person married in violation of the canon, while the deputies chose to say that in doubtful cases, before admission to these ordinances reference must be made to the ordinary, and also altered in the mode of expressing an injunction which they meant to accept. After having received from a committee of the House of Deputies a satisfactory explanation of the change in language, and also an assurance that at so late a period there could be little hope of the passage of any other resolution, the bishops assented to the canon as it now stands in the Digest under the more appropriate title, "Marriage and Divorce." The canon in part regulates marriage, referring the inquirer as to who may enter into the contract, to God's Word—that is, to the Levitical law, for nowhere else does God's Word treat of who may marry, with the single exception of the passage in which the shameful taking of a father's wife is condemned.

Bishop Whittingham proposed the passage of the canon as it had been already passed by his House, and this declares that it "shall not be held to apply to the innocent party in a divorce for the cause of adultery." It does not follow that his judgment sanctioned divorce for any cause arising after marriage, and it may be said, with almost positive assurance, that it did not. His estimate of the relation of man and wife, the type of the union of the one Lord with his one Bride, was such that he did not approve digamy under any circumstances. A second marriage he believed to be legalized concubinage, conceded to laymen even as bigamy was to the Jews because of the hardness of their hearts; and he held it to be positively forbidden to the priest. Were the object other than to state his opinion, it might be said that the arguments by which he sometimes maintained his opinion were not wholly logical. He had no power over the decision of the Church, but he conscientiously refused his consent to the consecration to the episcopate of any priest who had been married more than once. On an occasion when the confirmation of an election was discussed he bore the laughter of the House of Bishops, called forth by his open avowal of the conviction which

seemed preposterous to his hearers, and certainly was condemnatory of more than one of them.

"Md. wished to make a new canon," it was said. "No!" he answered, "he made no new canon; he passed no censure on the
Church for having no canon; but having taken pains to inform his
judgment, and finding a written rule of his Master according to
which one in the position of this brother, who had been chosen
bishop, was ineligible, he had no other course to follow but to obey
what to him was his Master's own direction."—*The Bishop's Notes.*

During his stay in Boston the bishop was the guest of
his intimate friend, Dr. Shattuck, with whom, as he wrote
home, he was "in too much clover—in danger of being
smothered by comforts." The judicious as well as kind
care taken of him perhaps alone enabled him to fill his
place daily in the House of Bishops and take his full share
of committee duty. In especial he needed what he received, shielding from a crowd of visitors. He was not
able to bear the confusion resulting from the presence of
many persons or from long conversation with any. This
weakness is spoken of in the following letter to his
daughter:

BOSTON, October 21, 1877.

DEAR MAGGIE:
I am again behindhand with my correspondence, partly out of
full occupation of my time during all the week in those portions of
the day in which I find myself fit for writing, in the business for
which I came here, and partly out of disheartenment and dissatisfaction with the way things are going. There are, to be sure, no
factious quarrellings or bad-tempered disputes, but there are mani-
fold indications (to my view, at least) of the beginnings of a general
breaking up of the Church—which may God forbid and save us
from!—with only the poor and slender comfort that it will not come
in my time, but in that of those who come after me. I have been
able to be in my place in all work of the House of Bishops proper,
but not to take any part in the Board of Missions, its work being
always done at night.
In the House of Bishops I find my power much lessened by

physical inability. though every possible kindness is shown by all the members. Not much will be actually done by this Convention, although a good deal of what I think mischief will have been begun. . . . W. R. W.

Besides the intimation of weakness of body, this letter gives painful token of the despondency of old age. Memoirs of a long life, toward their close, often show how, to the old man, "the clouds return after the rain," and that "fears are in the way."

A friend, writing of Bishop Whittingham, has said:

"What a heap of trouble W. R. W. had with his boys! And how charmingly he dealt with them as such! I don't believe the grand young man was ever old except in body."

But years claimed their tribute of Whittingham as of others, despite his fervor. In a letter written a little earlier than the foregoing he speaks of "the bright golden days," referring to the long past, and yet to a period which his own record of his feelings shows to have been beset by cares and anxieties, forgotten when old age looked back to vigorous manhood. All through his busy life he had had to contend against what he deemed evils in the Church, marring her present peace and threatening her future prosperity, and again and again he had rejoiced in what he considered to be proof of God's watchful care; but now he can see only "the beginnings of a general breaking up." To attempt to point out the dangers which seemed clear to his view would be only to express one's own fears, for he has not stated what were the indications of the evils to come from which he would be taken.

After the Convention in Boston, with the exception of what has been already spoken of, the labors of the bishop in behalf of the general Church were confined to the part he took in overcoming difficulties consequent upon what must have given him great sorrow.

The Bishop of Michigan, the second of the bishops in

seniority, who had long been associated with him in church work, sympathizing with him in church principles, had, on the plea of bodily infirmities, resigned his office and had gone abroad without waiting for release from his obligations. There were doubts touching the validity of the action in the diocese subsequent to his resignation, and also many were of opinion that the honor of the Church demanded that there should be a judicial inquiry into charges which were said to have forced the tender of resignation. There is no need to treat of the painful story. The bishops came together and gave their decision in September, 1878. Their award was, of course, public, but their meetings being in council, their transactions are not known. We can, however, speak of the influence of our bishop on the conclusions reached, and this on the testimony of one whose proposals, earnestly maintained, were set aside, he himself in the end gladly voting against them.

The Bishop of Louisiana, on his way home from the council, visiting a connection of his, a daughter of Bishop Whittingham, told of the part he had himself taken, and said that could a vote have been taken on the first day of the council, the decision would have been in accordance with the views he had advocated, but on that day there was no quorum, and the meeting was informal; that every point advanced by him had been successfully controverted by the Bishop of Maryland, who during the session made long speeches, and with such convincing ability that the opinions of the bishops were changed, and the resolutions offered by him were finally adopted. "Thank your father for me," said Bishop Wilmer, "and tell him that I look upon those resolutions as an inspiration; and that I think that had he never done anything else for the Church, this alone is enough to have lived for."

LETTERS.

TO E. II. H.

THE DISTINCTIVE CHARACTER OF A BISHOP'S OFFICE IS OVERSIGHT—
EXECUTIVE DUTY IN A PARISH BELONGS TO THE RECTOR.

BALTIMORE, September 8, 1869.

MY DEAR SIR:

I hope you will kindly excuse my action in returning the enclosed immediately, and unexamined, when you know my motives.

There is in the Church a very considerable number both of clergy and laity who dread the multiplication of bishops, on the ground that the result would be interference with parochial work and management, and consequent destruction of pastoral responsibility and influence.

I regard the objection as of force, and should earnestly deprecate any measure which must produce such consequences.

But they can only result from inattention on the part of bishops to the distinctive character of their office, which is oversight, not execution. Executive duty, where there are parochial organizations, belongs to them, not to the bishop, and he endangers both their life and efficiency, and the true influence of his own office, when he allows himself to be drawn out of his own sphere into that of his brethren in parochial charge.

I have felt in our previous correspondence that there was some danger of my trenching on the work and duty of my respected and beloved brother your rector, but tried to avoid doing so by giving my answers the tone rather of discussion than of pastoral instruction.

But in the matter now submitted . . . except as your rector may choose at any time to consult me concerning it, or may see fit to direct you to me for counsel, I must decline intermeddling in what is entirely within his parochial duty and responsibility.

Heartily wishing him and you " God-speed " in the enterprise of faith and labor of love in which you are engaged,

I am, dear sir,

Very truly and affectionately,

Your friend and servant,

W. R. W.

FROM THE BISHOP OF WINCHESTER TO THE AMERICAN BISHOPS.

ON THE PROPOSED REVISION OF THE AUTHORIZED VERSION OF HOLY SCRIPTURE.

DECEMBER 27, 1870.

RIGHT REVEREND BRETHREN IN CHRIST, GREETING :

I am instructed by the Convocation of the Province of Canterbury to inform you of the steps taken by the Convocation for the perfecting of that rich inheritance of English-speaking peoples—the authorized version of the Holy Scripture—and to ask your fellowship and aid in their undertaking.

That undertaking is to subject the version to the careful scrutiny of the ripest scholars they can find, with a view to removing any blemishes which may be found in it.

To this they have been moved mainly by these two considerations : 1. That it seems to them a duty to clear this sacred deposit of God's Word written, from any, even the smallest, imperfection in its rendering from the original tongue and MSS.; and that the growth of critical scholarship and the collection of MSS. render such a revision possible. 2. Because they believe that indefinite apprehensions of the existence of errors now float in the minds of men, and lead them to suspect the presence, in the received versions, of errors which may affect doctrines ; whereas we believe that the strictest revision would only establish before all men the essential accuracy of that which they have been hitherto taught to receive as the Word of God.

The rule which the Convocation has laid down is that only inaccuracies which scholarship and a careful scrutiny of manuscripts detect shall be altered ; that there shall be no attempt to remove archaisms, but that, on the contrary, the language familiar to Christian ears shall be as closely maintained as possible.

The instruments which Convocation has resolved to employ in this work are the members of a committee of their own body, selected for their known acquaintance, as scholars, with the original languages of the Old and New Testaments. To the assistance of their body, but not to any fellowship in the committee, Convocation has allowed its members to invite known scholars, as experts, without regard to their religious opinions; but the revision, when accomplished, will be finally reported to Convocation from its committee alone, and if adopted by Convocation, and put forth by it, it will be put forth, as becomes the putting forth of the Word of God, by the Church alone. In this good work we affectionately invite your fellowship and aid.

Distance makes it impossible for us to expect the presence with us, in our work, of the scholars of your communion, but we propose, with your consent, to send you, from time to time, copies of our work as it proceeds, and to ask your criticisms upon it. We trust that by this course we may retain one perfected and accepted version of the Word of God in common use among English-speaking peoples.

I remain, Rt. Rev. Brethren,
Your faithful friend and brother,
S. Winton,
Chairman of the Revision Committee.

ANSWER OF BISHOP WHITTINGHAM.

ON THE PROPOSED REVISION.

To the Right Reverend the Lord Bishop of Winchester, Chairman of the Revision Committee.

Rt. Rev. and Dear Brother:

Your letter of the 27th is just received. I answer in haste, and therefore very briefly, lest my reply should not reach you before the announced meeting of Convocation in February.

I fear that your brotherly appeal to the bishops of the Church in the United States is too late to secure the end designed.

That I assume to be the agreement of all the Churches of our communion, throughout the world, in the adoption of the proposed revised text of the English Bible, for obligatory use in public worship.

Anything short of such an agreement must render the publication of a revision of the authorized version, by whomsoever made, under what local authority soever, an undertaking full of obvious dangers, and therefore of extremely questionable expediency.

The aspect of the times is sufficiently dark and threatening without the addition of an unsettlement of the minds of all English-speaking peoples on the subject of the text and tenor of God's written Word.

Such unsettlement must ensue if rival revisions of what all now receive as the English Bible are to be called into existence, with a conflict of claims to the acceptance and confidence of English readers.

It seems to me incredible that far sighted men can imagine it possible to put forth a revision of the English Bible under authority of a bare majority of a body constituted as the Convocation of Canterbury, without calling forth rival attempts from various quarters, possibly some making plausible pretensions to authority hardly less worthy of respect.

Other considerations are unfortunately notorious, which have already, at the outset, done much to undermine any authority which men might otherwise be disposed to ascribe to the procedures of the Synod of Canterbury in this matter.

I am therefore of opinion that no assent or approval which might at this time be given by individual action of American or other bishops of our communion would suffice to remove the difficulties inherent in the project of revision as now undertaken.

I find none here of any other opinion. Admitting, as all freely do, that a properly undertaken and executed revision of the authorized version is desirable, all with whom I have had opportunity of communication regard the present undertaking with much mistrust and apprehensions of great danger.

No greater mistake could be made, as it seems to us, than an attempt to look outside of the Church itself for aid and authority in this work. We cannot deem it in the least probable that the consociation of a few men of other communions, however eminent, would procure for the work in which they might take part any formal or even general acceptance in the bodies which they might be considered as taken to represent. On the other hand, while the confidence of very many in our own communion would be greatly shaken by such an attempt, it would be sure to afford a ground of resistance to the revision so effected capable of rallying a large, widely diffused, and long-lasting party in the Church.

Let the Churches in England, Scotland, Ireland, the Colonies and Dependencies of Great Britain, and the United States of America agree together, by authoritative action in their several modes, upon some simple plan for carrying out a revision of the authorized version for use in their own public worship, binding themselves reciprocally to each other to receive the product of such undertaking. By such action, quietly and steadily executed, a new English Bible would, in less than a generation, be introduced throughout the world, and, in proportion to its merits, find acceptance with English

readers generally without any such previous disturbance of the public mind and unsettlement of the confidence of the whole English-
speaking community as must inevitably result from the attempted
issue of a new English Bible under authority of the Convocation of
Canterbury only, and, worst of all, under the alleged influence of a
few powerful members only of that Convocation.

From the further prosecution of such a movement, so conducted,
it is not possible, viewing the procedure from our standpoint, to
anticipate any introduction of one perfected and accepted version
of the Word of God into common use among English-speaking
peoples.

For my own part, therefore, I must, with thankful acknowledgment of the courtesy shown in your fraternal communication and
offer, most respectfully decline engagement in any way in the undertaking for the revision of the authorized version as now proposed.

I am, with very great affection and regard,
Your lordship's faithful friend and brother,
W. R. W.,
Bishop of Maryland.

Baltimore, January 17, 1871.

TO THE RT. REV. W. H. ODENHEIMER, D.D.

THE IRISH CHURCH—THE ALTERNATE FORM IN THE ORDINAL.

Baltimore, March 7, 1871.

My Very Dear Friend and Brother :

I return the interesting note from the Primate of Ireland.

I hope that you will take the opportunity for urging on his attention the very great importance of his Church's exercising self-control in the use of its newly acquired liberty, and having largeheartedness enough to refrain from making any serious changes in
the Book of Common Prayer without previous consultation and
agreement of all the branches of the Anglican communion. Such a
course on the part of the Church in Ireland would enormously
strengthen both the imperilled Church of England and the Churches
in the United States and in the British Colonies.

It by no means follows that the Prayer-book should necessarily
remain entirely unchanged in every part for any considerable length
of time. Only let it be first agreed what parts shall remain un-
altered, except by consent of the whole communion, and then let
the far larger remainder of services and offices be subject to adap-
tation to the varying needs and circumstances of the several very

variously situated Churches. By reference to the journal of the House of Bishops in General Convention in 1856 (p. 202 of the journal) it will be seen that as many as fourteen years ago, in foresight of things which have since occurred, I endeavored to secure initiation of measures to the effect of what I now most urgently desire to see the Church in Ireland do.

In reference to his Grace of Armagh's questions respecting the alternative form in the ordinal, I have to say that—

1. I am not accurately informed of "the prevalent practice of American bishops," but believe that of two-thirds of them to be the same as my own. In an episcopate of thirty years I have never used the new form, nor ever had the use of it solicited of me or in any way suggested to me as desirable.

2. What communications I have had with the laity of my diocese on the subject have satisfied me of their unanimity in preference of the old form. I have no doubt that a vote on the question of preference in the General Convention would result in a two-thirds majority in favor of the old form.

3. My own judgment is that no benefit of any kind has accrued to the American Church from the change, but, on the other hand, unmixed mischief.

4. Far from having conciliated adversaries, it has merely furnished them with weapons against the system of the Church and doubly weakened her defence by presenting a show of internal inconsistency, and by countenancing a school of utilitarian churchmanship which is ready to give up any distinctive principle for the sake of gain in numbers, position, or popularity (which it calls winning souls), and is all the while, within my own personal observation, tending steadily and rapidly to the latitudinarian form of infidelity. Of course the nourishment of such a school within the Church would not tend either to her prosperity or to her internal peace.

In conclusion, I desire, with profound conviction of its truth, to subscribe to your expressed opinion that alternatives, where doctrine is concerned, tend to the creation and perpetuation of discord ; and to declare that my half century of experience and observation of the working of the American Church affords ample confirmation of that opinion.

Ever lovingly your faithful friend and brother,

W. R. W.

TO THE REV. WILLIAM A. WHITE.

ON RECEPTION INTO THE CHURCH OF PERSONS NOT BAPTIZED IN THE CHURCH.

BALTIMORE, August 3, 1871.

MY DEAR BROTHER :

I need not to remind you that anything I can say on the matter concerning which you consult me can have no official authority ; for instructions having that character you must look elsewhere, and know where to look.

So much premised, I have no hesitation about expressing my individual opinion that " reception into Christ's Church," as provided for by the order for " the Ministration of Private Baptism in Houses," can only be accorded to those whose private baptism has been within the pale of the Church.

You are well aware that in the question about " Lay Baptism " a distinction of great consequence is drawn between baptism by one claiming to administer it as a (lay) member of the Church and that of one not so claiming.

The administration of public reception to a person coming from a sect would be a solemn recognition of the previous administration as done by a member of the Church, and so would decide the question whether ministrations of the sects are ministrations in the Church affirmatively.

If such persons are entitled to such " reception " then they are entitled to confirmation, and that rite would be the " strong tie binding them to the household of faith " of which you conceive them to be in need ; nor can I see why it should be anticipated and, as it were, superseded by any other.

With hearty thanks for your kind wishes and remembrance, and earnest reciprocation of them, I am, very faithfully your loving friend and brother, W. R. W.

TO MR. H. O. H., STUDENT G. T. S.

UPHOLDS THE DISCIPLINE OF THE FACULTY RESPECTING COMMUNION.

BALTIMORE, April 22, 1872.

MY DEAR H.:

I am very glad that you have taken the praiseworthy course of laying before your bishop your difficulties growing out of the Seminary discipline.

It all the more calls for my approval in that I can see no sufficient reason why those difficulties should exist, and certainly must interpose whatever weight you may allow my judgment to turn the scale for your relief.

In the first place, the resolutions seem to me wise and timely—such as eminently pertain to the duty of the dean and faculty, and are called for by pullulating errors of the day.

If they were not so in my judgment I should still have to admit that they were clearly within the statutory purview of official right and duty, and being so, must be regarded as fully binding on the conscience of any student who had taken the matriculatory oath.

But, on the other side, I find myself unable to enter into your views of grievance.

It is as certain as anything of the kind can be that the matter of fasting participation of the holy eucharist is a point of expedience and not of principle, and that its decision has always been by regulation, local and temporary, not by catholic rule ; so that our own Church, in leaving it absolutely to the conscience of the individual, reduces it to that class of observances in which the individual judgment is bound to conform itself to regulation by due authoritative act.

If due authority prescribes communion at an hour precluding a morning meal, it is for the individual conscience to decide between danger to health and obedience. If health is really endangered, the doubtful must give way to the clear. Fasting communion admits of doubt—duty to God (1) in the due regard for preservation of health, and (2) in obedience to due authority admits of none.

I utterly object to your remaining " not minded to communicate " —knowing no other qualification for such a state of mind than that of wilful sin. I know the cluster of sophistries that has been hung around the practice, and regard the whole as alien from the godly simplicity and sincerity which befit the true-hearted, humble follower of Christ.

For a man in health, I see no great hardship in fasting every day, if needful, till 2 P.M. One wholesome meal a day, eaten with good appetite earned by hearty exercise, and then digested with a good conscience, is more likely to preserve *mens sana in corpore sano* than the most part of our modern habits.

But I do not advise on that point. What I do insist on is that the individual " preference " of fasting communion has no right to set itself up against the regulation of duly authorized ecclesiastical superiors—which relation the dean and faculty hold to the students of the Seminary.

The resolutions do "require something not required by the rubrics." It would be preposterous to suppose them necessary did they not.

But do you, by making that an objection, mean to intimate a doubt of the right of the spiritual authority of a religious house like the Seminary to require anything beyond the rubrics? Surely you cannot have looked at the matter in that light!

Nor can I doubt, for an instant, the right of the head of such an institution to require of the members a strict account of the reasons of their conduct in a matter of so much importance as public conformity with public and general rule governing participation in the highest act of common worship. It is absurd to call such requirement "obligatory confession;" because the account is required, not as a religious act, nor as a term of communion, but as a point of discipline, and as a due compliance with the promise in matriculation.

I have long thought that students in the Seminary were much too little mindful of the fact that they are not in the position either of ordinary members of a Christian household or even of mere matriculated members of a secular college.

Their matriculation makes them members of a religious house, and is, for the term of their connection, the vow of obedience to the authority of that house, knowing no limit in things spiritual but those which apply to such vow in any circumstances, viz.: 1st, the canons of the Church, for all; and 2d, for each one appeal to his own diocesan—which last, in the circumstances of the case, may amount either to petition for relief in case of special grievance, or to request for advice, whether to obey or leave, in case of general regulation.

As your diocesan, I heartily approve the general regulations about which you have appealed to me for advice, and if there be in the Seminary any ramification of that conspiracy in the Church which is aiming at the reintroduction of the abomination of "private masses," I think it high time that all the legitimate authority of the institution should be exercised for the extirpation of such a cancerous ailment.

On the questions connected with the point about which your difficulties rise, I am glad to find myself able, now, to refer you with a good deal of confidence to a copious source of full and accurate information in the "Notitia Eucharistica" of Mr. Scudamore, published a few weeks ago. Its sound learning and wide research furnish timely rebuke and correction to the silly and superficial medievalizing tendencies that have been so rife among us for these few years past. God grant that we may soon be well rid of them ! They are the worst hindrance of the work of the Church that has presented itself within my half century of observation of her struggle.

Ever lovingly and faithfully your true friend and pastor,

W. R. W.

TO THE REV. BENJAMIN B. SMITH, D.D., BISHOP OF KENTUCKY.

INSISTS THAT A PRESBYTER BEARING LETTERS DIMISSORY SHALL BE RECEIVED OR PRESENTED FOR TRIAL.

BALTIMORE, December 14, 1872.

RT. REV. AND DEAR SIR :

I have just received your letter, addressed "To the Ecclesiastical Authority of the Diocese of Maryland," refusing to accept a letter dimissory to the Diocese of Kentucky, given to the Rev. —— ——, presbyter, by the assistant bishop of this diocese, acting in full charge of the diocese in my absence, on the ground that for more than six months he has given aid and countenance to certain parties in the Diocese of Kentucky who have introduced novelties into it which disturb its peace, and which it is well known that the bishop wholly disapproves and condemns.

I find in Canon 12, Title I., Section VII., that it is the duty of the ecclesiastical authority of a diocese to which a clergyman has removed to accept a testimonial presented in due form, unless there be matters affecting the character of the minister concerned which would form a proper ground of canonical inquiry and presentment ; in which case the same shall be communicated to the bishop or ecclesiastical authority of the diocese whence the minister has removed, in order to investigation.

It becomes my duty, therefore, to inquire of you whether you are prepared to present charges against the Rev. —— ——, in such form and with such allegation of time, place, and evidence as may enable the ecclesiastical authority of Maryland to bring the same to judicial investigation, in order either to the conviction of the reverend brother concerned or to his exculpation from the said charges.

Very faithfully, your affectionate friend and brother,

W. R. W.,
Bishop of Maryland.

TO THE REV. DR. J. S. B. HODGES.

SISTERHOODS.

Madison Avenue, February 13, 1873.

My Dear Doctor:

The kind, filial frankness and affectionateness of your letter last night received affords me the greatest comfort and satisfaction.

. . . You were quite right in supposing that your course with regard to the Sisters in charge of the asylum was in accordance with my wishes. I should be only too glad to have a hundred of them (were such a blessing imaginable) at work in my diocese in the same quiet, earnest, most exemplary way.

Certainly I should have no thought of meddling with them any more than I have until now. They have my silent blessing whenever I chance to see them, and my continual cordial prayers.

I have accepted their invaluable services with hearty freedom and much gladness, knowing less than I now know of the true nature of their rule and observances, and for that reason less able than I now am to accord them my unhesitating confidence and very nearly unqualified approval.

I certainly do prefer the rules of the Sisters of the Poor to those of S. John Baptist. The former appear to me to have been drawn up with extraordinary care to remove every possible occasion for misinterpretation or objection, and to have been guarded, in the exercise of eminent wisdom, against possible dangers more or less to be apprehended in the growth of associations of the kind.

But beyond the expression of such approval of the rule of the All Saints' Sisters (which had been submitted to me while I was as yet ignorant of that of Clewer), I have in no wise distinguished their position from that of the ladies at your asylum. I have said nothing in favor of them which I am not ready to say, if opportunity or occasion offer, of the Clewer ladies.

In relation to both orders, my position is the same—they are heartily welcome to occasional or temporary work, if for that only they come. They will be still more welcome to work as foundresses of off-shoots of their home establishments, if they can obtain permission of their superiors to do so upon my terms, stated in the letter to Mr. Stewart. Without and until such permission shall have been obtained, I must withhold my consent from their attempt at any manner of organization of women of my diocese in association with themselves under their respective rules.

Faithfully and affectionately, your friend and brother,

W. R. Whittingham.

EXTRACTS FROM THE LETTER REFERRED TO IN THE FOREGOING.

As a ground of your own special interest, you allege the experience of "five years' work," part of it as "a confessor of women."

Without ever having laid claim to exercise a function for which I know no authority, scriptural or Catholic, I have for more than forty-five years been in habitual communication with persons of both sexes more or less desirous of engagement in association for special work for Christ's sake. One of my first serious conversations with a layman, after my ordination to my present office, was on the subject of the need and practicability of organization for that end. Almost immediately after the same subject was earnestly discussed with more than one of the leading clergymen of my diocese. From that time onward I kept it steadily in view, until—now almost twenty years ago—it pleased God to bless me with the realization of my aim.

It is therefore simply amusing to me to be addressed in an apologetic plea, as though for some new thing or measure, in behalf of sisterhoods in general.

There is probably no man in the Church more ready than I to recognize and encourage sisterhoods organized on sound church principles, under conditions consistent with the divinely originated constitution of the Church.

That constitution I understand to be that, under and for the one head, Christ Jesus, by succession from him through his apostles, the bishops of the Church are, each for the place and people for which he is made and set apart, the organizing principle and governing power. . . . Duty to Christ and desire of the glory of his name, and not jealousy of rival sects or fear of hostile religions, I recognize as the true incentive to the kind of zeal in which sisterhoods and kindred manifestations of living faith have their origination. Antagonism to Rome I am not disposed to cherish or honor as a motive. . . .

I am no stranger to the reflections which are so ably presented in your letter. . . . For instance, I quite agree with you that there is no reason why Christian men and women should not be encouraged to give themselves wholly to work for Christ's sake in "following him." But if they are taught and urged to do this, as an embracement of a higher life within and above the life of the Church—an acceptance of "counsels of perfection," whereby they shall merit, over and above their own deliverance through Christ from eternal death, degrees of glory in higher rooms than the common herd of baptized Christians may be encouraged to hope for—then their opportunity is made their delusion, and the old deceiver, in the garb of an angel of light, leads them away from Christ, under pretext of more close and eminent following.   .   .   .

Your affectionate friend and brother,

W. R. W.

——

TO THE BISHOP OF WESTERN NEW YORK.

THE ATHANASIAN CREED AND THE FILIOQUE.

BALTIMORE, February 20, 1873.

MY DEAR BISHOP:

The incursion of daily business for my diocese, with my inability for much or long-continued work, have hindered until now my attempt to fulfil the promise of attention to the very important and interesting note of the Bishop of Jamaica which you so kindly communicated to me. It has been much in my thoughts, but I have not until to-day had it in my power to brace myself up to the endeavor to put in shape briefly and clearly what little I have to say in remark upon it.

Were I in England I should give my vote, in the first place, against any attempt at change, believing that the Church would be strengthened, rather than otherwise, by any defection that might be the result of defeat of such attempt.

Should it appear, however, that a really large proportion of members of the Church, whether clerical or lay, through ignorance or misinformation, so misunderstood the minatory clauses as to be offended with them, I should be willing to concede to such, as an accommodation to weakness, the addition to the formula of an explanatory rubric, stating in fewest possible words the nature of those clauses. Should a majority insist on the omission of the minatory clauses—while it would be, in my judgment, an injudicious measure likely to lead to further attempts at alteration in the future, or to encourage renewed endeavors to be rid of the formula altogether, still I could acquiesce in the procedure, and should regard it as in no degree essentially affecting the nature of the document. Recognizing that, not as a Catholic creed but as a local confession, I view it as a merely human composition of very high authority on account of its millennial acceptance, but never stamped with the sanction of the Vincentian rules as regards its *use*, and therefore quite within the control of any branch of the Church having sufficient ground of action, in its own circumstances and relations, to justify to itself the alteration or abridgment of the phraseology, without essential change of doctrinal statement.

As a member of the American Church, my personal desire is for the restoration of the formula to a place in the Prayer-book, in which it is my judgment that it might to advantage appear, for prescribed use three or four times in the year, and for permitted use at stated times and places in the service, in the discretion of ministers.

I am ready, at once, to join in an effort to replace it in the eighth article.

Should a movement for its reintroduction into the Prayer-book be made without any general or very numerous organized opposition, I should deem it my duty to support such movement.

In so doing I would prefer action on the part of the American Church, omitting the minatory clauses, and adding a brief rubric stating that it was done solely on account of their liability to misconstruction; but I should not oppose the reintroduction of the formula wholly unchanged, provided it were then made of discretionary use, except on Trinity Sunday.

I should deem it my duty to oppose any attempt on our part to replace the formula in our Prayer-book with any change whatsoever beyond the mere omission of the minatory clauses, believing it far better to leave it as we now do, unacknowledged, but certainly unrejected, than to tamper with its phraseology, to the almost sure corruption of its doctrine.

In all this I say about change I have no reference to amendment of the translation, if that should be deemed needful, of which I have not satisfied myself. It seems to me more easy to fault the present translation than to mend it. As for correction of the text, I have seen no evidence to warrant, much less to require it.

I have preferred, before venturing to speak of the Bishop of Kingston's proposals, briefly to state my own views of the subject as it presents itself to the consideration of an American churchman. It has, of course, of late years occupied a good deal of my thoughts.

I am free to own that the American Church, by rash action in the past, has forfeited any right to a voice in the Anglican counsels on the subject.

But if the Anglican Churches, with any considerable degree of unanimity, should propose to us a reconstruction of the formula on the bishop's plan, I should think it our duty to accept it, rather than either remain in our present worse condition or insist on the retention of the old plan.

I cannot agree to the proposed emendation as regards the "Procession."

1. It would, as I apprehend, amount to a serious change in doctrinal statement.

2. It would, as I take it, be an introduction of a new definition of the most dangerous kind, viz., exclusive.

3. It would attempt a new limitary circumscription of the faith.

The Orientals, in my judgment, would not accept it, and would rather be awakened to new jealousies and oppositions by the attempt, as they would say, to reassert a heresy in a new form.

The Latins would be bound to reject, as assuming to correct their definitions.

I could not, for my ownself, accept it.

While I desire to omit the infoisted clause of the Constantinopolitan Creed (at whatever risk of Latin offence), and entirely agree with the Bishop of Kingston's opinion (as opinion) about the difference between the modes or conditions of being of the Second and Third Divine Persons, I know of no warrant for presuming to set this opinion in a declaration of "the faith" which I understand and maintain this document to profess to be.

The Latin "*a*" and our "from" entirely satisfy me by their fit latitude of significance. It is the attempt to discriminate their shades of meaning in the several applications from which I feel bound to shrink.

Begging that you will kindly ascribe anything obscure, incoherent, or curt in this long letter to the infirmities and not the will of the writer, I am, as ever,

Your loving and true friend and brother,

WILLIAM R. WHITTINGHAM,
Bishop of Maryland.

TO THE RT. REV. W. B. W. HOWE, D.D., BISHOP OF SOUTH CAROLINA.

BISHOPS FOR THE SEVERAL RACES IN THE UNITED STATES.

BALTIMORE, May 30, 1873.

MY DEAR BISHOP:

The plan of an episcopate for our colored population is by no means new to me. Long before the civil war I had been driven to meditate on it, by conviction that the blacks in my own diocese could not be efficiently provided for on our present scheme, and that there did seem to be ground for anticipating good success for work among them well organized and diligently prosecuted on the plan of a "race" or "tongue" episcopate, jurisdiction, ministry, and pastoral supply.

The double, mutually compensatory and completory, kinds of jurisdiction, topical and lingual; or distributed by metes and bounds, for a certain portion of the population, and by race or language (distributed over or scattered through the same metes and bounds, with or without recognition of them) to a certain other portion (or several other portions) of a collimital population, I believe to have been existent, and more or less extensively employed as called for, throughout the Church in all ages.

I see no reason why the Church should not resort to its use in our country, so wonderfully peopled and still peopling by myriads of incomers from many and very diverse races and tongues.

On that plan we might have an episcopate for the Scandinavian tongues, another for the German, another for the Chinese, and above all for the millions of our native blacks.

Of course, in the outset, each of these must, of necessity, have a missionary character; and with the exception of the last—and possibly also of the third—be constituted with distinct recognition of a steady process of evanishment, in proportion as the several races or tongues should become merged in the general mass of the community.

But to institute such a work, I suppose we should have to add new canonical provisions—just as was proposed (and, I think, by mistake, not done) in the last General Convention, for our foreign congregations in Europe or elsewhere. A canon, in a few sections, might provide when and where such work should be done—by whom election, etc., should be effected—and what the relations of the new organizations should be with existing diocesan and missionary schemes.

I, for one, am ready to enter upon endeavors to devise and execute such a plan of Church extension (to which Providence seems to be calling us in more than one direction) whenever my brethren shall have faith and zeal to set about it. Our new Indian Episcopate is a long and noble step toward the enterprise.

Heartily thanking you for the opportunity of exchanging opinion upon the subject, and wishing that you and our brethren of the adjoining dioceses would bestow the study and labor which the due preparation of a well-devised scheme would doubtless require, but would certainly thoroughly deserve,

I am faithfully and truly your loving friend and brother,

W. R. W.,
Bishop of Maryland.

TO REV. JOHN WILEY, RECTOR OF SHERWOOD PARISH, BALTIMORE COUNTY.

VOLUNTARY ACTS AND PRESCRIBED RITUAL.

BALTIMORE, April 17, 1873.

REV. AND DEAR BROTHER :

I am sorry that any of your good people should have been troubled at the chanting of a verse of Scriptures in a part of the service where so doing not only neither interrupts nor sets aside anything prescribed in the rubrics, but certainly seems to be as appropriate and as much a help to devotion as the reading certain other sentences. From earliest boyhood I remember the singing of hymns or anthems during collection of alms and offerings as a practice in the Church, and as such its lawfulness is asserted by Bishop White, in his Memoirs of the Protestant Episcopal Church, vindicating the right of singing from Scripture or the Prayer-book at any time during assemblage for worship, when so doing does not contravene or interfere with the order set down in the Prayer-book.

In this city several congregations have within a few years past added to the singing of the verse from Chronicles simultaneous rising on the part of the people, and the effect is certainly excellent. I conceive that no clergyman has a right to prescribe this to his flock, for by so doing he would be doing what neither priest nor bishop has the right to do in our Church—imposing on them new ritual. But what he has no right to prescribe to them, I cannot see but that they have a perfect right to do, if so pleased; inasmuch as the Prayer-book certainly does not forbid it, nor prescribe anything inconsistent with it—the posture of the congregation during collection and presentation of alms and offerings not being directed to be either sitting or standing.

I mention this to illustrate the noteworthy distinction between voluntary acts and prescribed ritual.

So of your singing. On Bishop White's authority, and by immemorial practice of the Church, it is not in itself wrong. Therefore, as a voluntary act, it is perfectly permissible ; while neither you nor I would have the slightest authority to enjoin or enforce its observance as a part of ritual.

Very faithfully your affectionate friend and brother,

W. R. W.

TO THE RT. REV. DR. BEDELL.

ON RECONCILIATION OF A ROMAN CATHOLIC PRIEST OR DEACON.

BALTIMORE, June 4, 1873.

MY DEAR BISHOP :

The case of a person already in Holy Orders was not in the purview of Canon 2, Title I., according to the intention of the committee which reported that canon in its present form ; and although the words "ministry of this Church " do seem to open a door for wide construction, yet the accompanying phrase, "Candidates *for* Holy Orders," sufficiently indicates that a person already *in* such orders would not be in contemplation. I consider the action of the General Convention of 1871 to have left the case of reconciliation of a priest or deacon coming from the Roman obedience just where it was before, *i.e.*, entirely within the discretion of the bishop.

My own practice has been to regard myself as bound *in foro conscientiæ* not to be content with testimonials and probation less than fully equivalent to those required in the case of a candidate from an unepiscopal ministry, and having been satisfied by such, to admit the reconciled priest by a public act, requiring from him a form of renunciation of the distinctive tenets of Romanism, and the examination (as far as applicable) of the postulant in the ordination office, followed up by the use on my part of the formula, "Take thou authority, etc., word and sacraments, etc., *in this Church*."

Very faithfully your affectionate friend and brother,

W. R. WHITTINGHAM.

TO THE RT. REV. DR. BEDELL.

THE REPEAL OF THE CANON ON AMUSEMENTS — RECONCILIATION OF ROMANISTS.

ORANGE, N. J., July 8, 1873.

MY DEAR BISHOP :

I am glad to have your approval of my attempt to hinder injurious misconstruction of what I think was unadvised action of my Convention, thoughtlessly taken without allowing me opportunity for setting before the members the nature and consequences of what they were about to do.

I am glad, too, to be able to assure you that a large majority of the Convention against whose action I have been compelled to record my protest are in full agreement with you and me on the subject of the incompatibility of Christian character and profession with the worldly customs reprobated in the repealed canon, but did what they did in unwise fastidiousness about the *mode* of expressing the mind of the Church—not seeing, what you and I have but too much occasion to know, that ninety-nine out of every one hundred in the world outside will inevitably construe the withdrawal of canonical censure into a change of disciplinary regulation and a "backing down" of the Church before the pressure of the world, the flesh, and the devil.

Were I in condition to do justice to the subject, I would gladly use the occasion given for the issue of either a pastoral letter or a charge, or both; and even in my broken estate have had serious intentions of so doing, but I am afraid of doing harm by a feeble presentation of a cause too good to be championed by a crippled advocate, and am very sensible of the delicacy and difficulty of vindicating lay discipline without stirring up a hornet's nest against "clerical assumptions," and of putting Christian abnegation on the true ground, midway between mediæval asceticism and "broad church" secularity.

I should not have troubled you with a letter merely for the purpose of saying this. The matter of Roman reconciliations seemed to demand some reply to your remarks.

I do agree with you that it might be wisely done to legislate on that subject before long, the rather because I seem to myself to see in the near future a breaking up of the papal denomination in this country, which may throw many of their best men into our communion, whom it would be well that we should be ready to receive on fixed and uniform terms, made as easy but also as safe as possible. Why do you not make it your business to prepare well-digested action to that effect, for proposition in the next General Convention? It ought to originate in the House of Bishops (being in limitation of our present powers), and would be seen to do so with peculiar propriety at the present juncture. I would very cheerfully render you any aid in my power, in the way of revision, and advice when needed.

On *one* point you seem to overrate our difficulties arising out of existing deficiency of legislation. No bishop, as I apprehend, is obligated to receive a letter dimissory unless the bearer have a previous offer of settlement in his diocese. An elected rector or minister he is canonically bound to receive, except in canonically excepted cases. An elected professor, teacher, etc., I suppose he can refuse to receive, if willing to incur the liability to civil suit for damages, in which the suitor would have to show pecuniary injury

by want of *canonical* residence—a difficult task.   An uncalled bearer
of letters dimissory can make no claim compelling the bishop to
acceptance.

Faithfully and truly your loving friend and brother,

W. R. WHITTINGHAM.

TO THE REV. JAS. A. HARROLD.

CONSECRATION IS A GIFT TO GOD—THE BENEDICTION OF A CHAPEL NOT TO BE ATTEMPTED.

BALTIMORE, November 27, 1874.

REV. AND DEAR BROTHER:

I congratulate you heartily on the success with which your labors
have been crowned in the erection of the temporary chapel, of which
your note of the 25th, just received, informs me.

It is natural that you should desire to signalize the occupation of
the new chapel by special and suitable services.

But it is, in my judgment, entirely unadvisable to make them
such as should in any way assume the form of, or be liable to confusion with, the consecration of a church.

In that holy rite there is a special and real significancy which
does not at all belong to the putting in use of a place destined to
temporary subservience to human needs and to resumption, when
those needs shall have been supplied, for lower uses and human
ownership.

The dedication of such a place would be the exact equivalent of a
similar celebration among Presbyterians, Methodists, etc., of the
opening of a meeting-house, deriving all its consequence from the
consideration of the worshippers, none from that of divine acceptance and occupation.

On the other hand, I have still greater objection to the thoroughly
Romish mediæval invention of a "benediction," the very import of
the word signifying an assumed false principle and asserting a false
pretension—the principle that intrinsic holiness can attach to things,
the pretension that man has any ground or warrant for presuming
to make claim to the power of effecting such attachment.

While, therefore, I would gladly, if it were in my power, assist in
enhancing your enjoyment of the inception of the new stage of your
work attained to in the opening of your chapel, and truly regret that
the state of my health is not such as to warrant my doing so, I must
most distinctly beg you to understand that the Church knows nothing of any "benediction" of a place for temporary use, and that I

should be guilty of falseness to her principle and practice if I undertook such a thing myself, and of still worse abuse of trust if I were to pretend to make any grant of a faculty to you for such performance.

The distinction between our "consecration" and Roman "benedictions" is as clear as any other between true and false, between reality and sham, between authority and vain pretension.

My dear brother! is there never to be any end of our running after mediæval corruptions coming to us in the garb of Tridentine ceremonial and perversion of scriptural phrase and use?

I am sure you do not wish to countenance such folly, and am therefore all the more free to write to you as I think of it.

Your loving and true friend and brother,

W. R. W.

TO HIS DAUGHTER MARGARET.

HOME GOSSIP.

ORANGE, August 14, 1874.

DEAR MAGGIE:

Your pleasant well-filled letter came duly to hand last evening and gladdened our hearts. Aunt Phœbe was here, and of course helped us to enjoy the good news. Only we couldn't help regretting that Charles should have had to take to the outlandish fashion of going to bed on having an increase of family—but if it helped to bring M. about so soon and so thoroughly, why, we must make the best of it.

Tell Willie that to make amends for the new-comer's being "only a girl," he has the great news that his friend Marshal Bazaine, who was to have been shot, has run away and got free from his enemies after all, thanks to his courageous, true-hearted little wife, who, with her own hands, rowed the boat that caught him as he dropped from the rock on which his prison stands hanging over the sea, as I have seen it many a time. So that we see that a girl can be good for something, sometimes, after all.

Tell Phœbe that she can't know how much good her old sun-flat does grandma in her garden occupations. The hoops, and the building-blocks, and the spade, and all the rest of the things are sadly idle in the closet, for want of little hands to turn them to account. As for the "bunnie family" [ground-squirrels which had given amusement to the children the previous summer], they don't think us old folk worth coming to see, and so we haven't set eyes on them. But the rabbit is here, paying attention to the cabbages ; and some of our neighbors' hens with long necks are fond of stretching them up to pick blackberries—of which we have any quantity an inch long ; and the old muskrat comes to pay us a visit now and then ; and one evening, just after dark, we plainly, oh, too plainly, *smell*—a skunk ! about the cellar-door, looking, as we suppose, after the eggs.   .   .   .   You may tell Drs. G. and L. that I go entirely with D'Israeli, and rejoice in the turn things are taking in England.

Your loving father,   W. R. W.

THE REV. T. G. DASHIELL, D.D.

CHURCH STANDARDS TO BE UPHELD—PRIESTHOOD IN CHRIST.

BALTIMORE, March 23, 1874.

REV. AND DEAR BROTHER :

You ask me " Do not I think the next General Convention may be relied upon to *do* something worthy of a Catholic Church ? "

If that means by innovating, in *any* direction, on our standards of doctrine, discipline, and worship, I must say most positively, *No !* Whatever might have been the prospect of changes before the miserable consequences of Bishop Cummins' course, I think that they have utterly altered the state of opinion, and that the great body of the clergy and laity will not hear of any attempt to tinker our articles, Prayer-book, or canons, to please either of the schools of churchmanship. The path broad enough for our fathers is broad enough for us. I trust, and verily believe, that a very great majority of the members of the Church are now, and will cause themselves to be so represented in the General Convention as to show themselves to be, disposed to adhere to the wise counsel given to men of old, " Meddle not with them that are given to change."

But that disposition I think very likely to show itself also in cautionary measures to remedy evils which have given offence to many by checking lawlessness on the right hand (if there be any " right hand " in such a case) and on the left—not in the way of legislative tampering with our standards, but in that of repressing individual tampering with our worship by adding or omitting according to the measure of each man's self-conceit or ignorance, the scriptural, primitive, Catholic provisions for the maintenance of Gospel truth and order being overlaid or laid aside, in utter contempt of mutual obligation to obedience to the general laws of the whole associated body by a multitude of self-constituted infallible parish popes.

You attach more importance to my use of the word " presbyter " in writing to Mr. McGuire than belongs to it. I only meant to concede to him his right to his own interpretation of the Prayer-book word "priest." The last thing I could consent to would be the abnegation of that term. For my part I hold to the literal truth of Scripture, and believe that St. Peter and St. John meant what they say when they claim "priesthood" for all believers. Of course that stops the talk about infringement on our Lord's priesthood when his ambassadors (and therefore representatives) are also called priests—in the true proper sense of the term. Are they *less* than the laity because they are *their* ministers as well as Christ's? If not, then they, as well as the laity, share Christ's priesthood, being one with him ; and when they offer the memorial of his one sacrifice, they with the laity, and the laity with them, offer a spiritual sacrifice as true as their union in membership of his mystic body, with him the heavenly head, and just in proportion as the "doing" this is eminently their act by virtue of their office, just in the same proportion are they among, and for, and with their brethren eminently and truly "priests."

This doctrine, I am assured by the studies of a lifetime, the Prayer-book holds, and was meant to hold and witness. And shall I, after the Church has held it for eighteen hundred years, help to put it out of sight and mind by striking it out, or admitting that an alternative which is *not* its alternative may be substituted?

You see, my dear brother, there are consciences on both sides of this question. With Timothy, I have learned of the Holy Spirit through St. Paul, τὴν παρακαταθήκην φυλάσσειν ; and it has been the lesson of my lifetime that in fulfilment of that duty words are not idle things, to be lightly bandied to and fro, in temporary compromise of passing waves of controversy.

Your faithfully loving friend and brother,

W. R. WHITTINGHAM.

TO REV. T. G. DASHIELL.

RESPECTING THE GENERAL CONVENTION IN 1874—OPPOSES ALL
CHANGE IN THE PRAYER-BOOK.

BALTIMORE, May 18, 1874.

MY DEAR REVEREND BROTHER :

Who am I that I should talk about what "I will do" or "won't do" in laying down lines for others? I utterly decline taking any such ground at all.

But I have a right to form, and I recognize the duty of plainly avowing, when fitly asked, my own opinion as to what ought to be done.

The occurrences of every day for a long time past have gone to strengthen my convictions that the present duty of the Church, in her accountability for the truth of God and the purity of his worship, as we have received them through past generations, is tenaciously to hold fast that which we have, with strenuous resistance of all ill-advised and short-sighted clamors for change by way either of pretended improvement or alleged accommodation.

The spectacle exhibited by the men now gathered together in New York, to add one more to the many sects that make "Christian unity" a term of derision and reproach, is sufficient, of itself, to warn us of the fruitlessness of the folly of seeking "relief" of innovators by change.

How many will remain satisfied with any modicum of concession that it might be possible to agree upon, this year, in a General Convention?

Dr. Andrews—who has done more than most men living to advance the interests and consolidate the action of the extremists whom he is trying to cast out of the bosom of the Church—has shown by his tacit assumption of infallibility in his notes, and his utterly unfair method of argument against all who will not accept his "Ego dixi," that what is really aimed at under the cry of relief is conquest, to the extent of exclusion. Men who, like me, for half a century have found in the Prayer-book as it is the nearest approach to the truth of God in its genuine expression in his revealed Word, interpreted by the best lights of history and science, are to be first branded as sacramentalists and sacerdotalists, and then turned out as Romanizing traitors. "Alternatives" and "concessions for relief" are to do the branding part—then, in sure sequence, as aimed at in avowed determination by existing organizations, is to come the settlement by expurgation.

No! the plain meaning of our American Prayer-book as it is is our understanding of the Bible. Keep it as it is and we ask no more. If it is altered, somebody must go ; either we, whom it is to be altered to cast out, or they who have to alter it to suit their views, and then settle extent of alteration by such edifying discussion as is going on in New York!

Your loving brother,
W. R. W.

THE REV. C. M. P. TO THE BISHOP.

PRAYS THAT THERE MAY BE NO DECLARATION TOUCHING THE DOC-
TRINE OF A PRESENCE IN THE HOLY EUCHARIST.

RED BANK, N. J., October 15, 1874.

RT. REV. AND VERY DEAR FATHER:

I am bold to write to you, although no longer under your jurisdiction, but as one who very dearly loves and honors you, and as one
who never ceases to thank God for the honour of having seen some
service as one of your clergy. But, *imprimis*, I must say that with
the current number, the October number of *The Church and the
World*, I bid a final farewell to all editorial work. I do not write
to-day in any capacity (?) as editor, but as son to father, or as
learner to master and teacher. To my point:

I am neither prepared nor ready to accept any of the new and late
definitions of the Presence in the blessed sacrament of the Holy
Eucharist, nor am I ready to *deny* them. 2. I am certainly not prepared to acknowledge any new ritual observances as expressive of
my faith or *of my opinion*. As regards the last—ritual observances—
I will simply say that I believe, and I have repeatedly stated my
opinion, they are *historically* a mistake, if not something worse.

But I was taught in a school which left undefined all manners of
the presence of our Lord. I have ever understood this to reach to
the whole question between us and the Roman Church. There cannot be, or ought not to be, any question as to the presence. This
"*how*" of our days, however, reaches to facts of God's Incarnation.
It comes to mean not only "how," but also "what."

My object in writing now is to beseech that no declaration against
the doctrine of a presence (undefined as to manner, but strict as to
the "*Res*") shall be made by the bishops in the present Convention. I happen to know how widespread will be the effect should
any declaration or definition be drawn up which will compel the
withdrawal of any, or which will prevent any who do not receive
transubstantiation, but who accept the truth "bating that" from
entering the Church.

The ritual matter is a mere bagatelle—the doctrine is of the utmost
importance.

Bear with me, my dear Rt. Rev. Father, if I beg that when this
question comes before your House you will remember that men will
care nothing for canons or ritual (these they will obey), nothing
about details of lights, etc. *But* if men are refused the right to

worship Christ, "whether in the sacrament or out of the sacrament," the result will be disastrous to thousands.

Ever lovingly your son and servant,   C. M. P.

ANSWER TO THE FOREGOING LETTER.

House of Bishops, October 16, 1874.

My Dear Brother:

I think you may set your mind at ease about any apprehended declaration of this House.

It is in my judgment quite out of the range of probability, if not of possibility, that such a thing should be undertaken.

I see no ground to fear the removal of our landmarks in doctrine by a hair's-breadth in any action of this Convention.

Your loving friend and brother,

W. R. Whittingham.

TO W. F. B.

IN ANSWER TO A LETTER SETTING FORTH A CLERGYMAN'S STRAITS.

Baltimore, October 15, 1873.

Dear Brand:

Your kind letter, though it saddened my heart, brought me a message of comfort.

I had had an opportunity of helping our brother, and through my infirmity lost it. He appealed to me for help now almost a month ago, at a time when I was drained to my last dollar, and saw before me responsibilities for the quarter then next ensuing which I knew not how to meet. I could not bear to make that an answer to him, and deferred writing until I should be able to send him help.

A way was opened for me now about eight days ago, and I have been letting my infirmity keep my brother's need out of my poor crippled mind. Your note was to me as if I heard our Saviour's loving voice reminding me, "You had something to do for me! How *could* you let it go out of mind?" That he should have so gone out of his way, as it were, as to stir you up to be his instrument is a precious mercy, and humbly and thankfully do I accept of it as infinitely more than I deserve.

Had I had the means when S.'s appeal came to me, I should have sent him $75. Now, in recognition of our Lord's great goodness to me, I cannot make it less than the enclosed, and trust and believe that you may take its receipt as a pledge from the Master that He will send you the other two-thirds in some way as little likely as this, and perhaps, too, as full of the threefold mercy: one to the poor receiver, one to the privileged instrument of relief, and one, itself a *double* one, to the signally blessed enjoyer of the opportunity of giving.

I return the "draft." It may be used elsewhere.

Ever lovingly yours,

W. R. WHITTINGHAM.

TO THE REV. C. C. GRAFTON.

THE DISTINCTION OF CLERGY AS REGULAR AND SECULAR.

BALTIMORE, February 27, 1875.

MY DEAR GRAFTON :

I am much obliged by the kindness and frankness of your answer to my questions.

I find that you fall back, as I thought you must, upon what I deem the unauthorized and dangerous mediæval man-invented modification of the divine institution of the ministry by the distinction of "clergy" into "regular" and "secular."

Those who do Christ's work by keeping themselves to his own provisions by the instrumentality of his inspired apostles are, forsooth, secular, as in and of the world; while those whose adoption of human inventions in the ἐθελοθρησκείᾳ καὶ ταπεινοφροσύνῃ καὶ ἀφειδίᾳ σώματος of "rules" of their own framing and enforcing being thereby become "regular," are to be "fathers," as ἐν τιμῇ τινι, although οὐ πρὸς πλησμονὴν τῆς σαρκός.

I do not for a moment consider you, or any like minded with you, as chargeable with this anti-Christian spirit and conduct, but all my studies of church history and meditations on its developments of the ways of God and men have been in vain if I be not right in considering the system and principles of "regular" life in Western Christendom for the last fifteen hundred years as an abnormal, unhealthy, and in tendency destructive, disproportioned development of churchly life.

The instincts governing it have been those of the human element, not the divine in Catholicity.

Growing out of social disorganizations, the anchoritic, cenobitic, monastic, mendicant, and military modes of "regular" life have always led to the comparative contempt, neglect, or perversion of divinely instituted means of grace, and substitution of man's vain imagining for the promises of God in Christ and man's futile efforts to work out his own righteousness and holiness for the might of the Spirit working in the Word and sacraments. *Hærebant in cortice.*

Your account of the growth of this evil among us—exactly, as I suppose, in accordance with fact—affords the reason why I think men who have attained to my convictions in the matter bound to interfere—even at the risk of being thought troublesome intermeddlers—to hinder further progress of the sub-introduction of wrong principles into the modes of speech among us. Only fools think words of small account. Their unauthorized introduction is the means of doing much harm, for disturbance of peace, for corruption of principle, for substitutions of erroneous views and practices in lieu of simpler, older, and truer systems. My point is that there is absolutely no authority in this Church, of which you and I are sons, and wish to be filially obedient ones, for setting at nought the letter of our Lord's injunction, πατέρα μὴ καλέσητε ἐπὶ τῆς γῆς, by the appellation of a certain class "fathers" merely by virtue of their profession of a mode of life.

The one instance of the employment of the appellation in the Prayer-book, by its peculiarity and entire agreement with St. Paul's use of correlative terms, confirms the objection. St. Paul called (not himself the father, but) Timothy, etc., his sons, because in the ministry he had begotten them. So when a bishop is engaged in the work of ordaining, then, and then alone, has the Church thought fit to designate the peculiarity of his work by the peculiar appellation then and therein bestowed on him.

I regard the extension of the use of the appellation beyond the limit to which the Church has restricted herself as an abuse, and, as such, feel bound both to protest against it and, if possible, to keep it out of my own diocese.

I have not been unmindful to the request in your last, and am ever your loving and true friend,

W. R. Whittingham.

THE CRY OF THE CATHOLIC CHURCHMAN.

Oh my mother, whence is this unto thee, that thou hast good things poured upon thee and canst not keep them, and bearest children and darest not own them? Why hast thou not the skill to use their services, nor the heart to rejoice in their love? How is it that whatever is generous in purpose, and tender or deep in devotion, thy flower and thy promise falls from thy bosom and finds no home within thine arms? Who hath put this note upon thee, to have a miscarrying womb and dry breasts, to be a stranger to thine own flesh, and thine eye cruel toward thy little ones? Thine own offspring, the fruit of thy womb, who love thee, and would toil for thee, thou dost gaze upon with fear, as though a portent, or thou dost loathe as an offence; at best thou dost but endure, as if they had no claim but on thy patience, self-possession, and vigilance, to be rid of them as easily as thou mayst. Thou makest them stand all the day idle as the very condition of thy bearing with them; or thou biddest them begone where they will be more welcome; or thou sellest them for naught to the stranger that passeth by. And what wilt thou do in the end thereof!

In 1875 this plaint, reprinted as a leaflet, was sent to the bishop with "Regards of F. C. E." The bishop returned

THE ANSWER OF THE CHURCH CATHOLIC IN THE U. S. A. TO THE COMPLAINT OF HER WAYWARD CHILD.

Oh, my child! it is thee of whom thy long-suffering mother hath reason to complain, for that, having her good things in full measure, thou whinest and whimperest for the cast-off toys of the children of other mothers. Why hast thou not the skill to use the services of thy mother, nor the heart to rejoice in her love? Why longest thou for things forbidden to thee, and because thy mother grants them not, undutifully upbraidest her with lack of skill and tenderness? How is it thou unfilially assumest it to thyself to judge thy mother, and taunt her with dry breasts and a miscarrying womb, with which if God had seen fit to visit her, it would be thy part, humbled in the dust, to cry, Mea culpa! mea culpa! pro peccatis meis matrem visitasti, Deus retributionum! Who gave thee wisdom superior to thy mother's to know, when she is ignorant, what is generous in purpose to merit her encouragement, and tender or deep in devotion to deserve her praise? Came the spirit of prophecy to thee, to teach what is hidden from thy mother, wherein her true flower and promise flourish, what she is to cherish in her bosom, and for whom her arms are to provide a home?

Woe to the undutiful discontent that putteth the note of baseness upon its mother, charging her with strangeness to her flesh, and deemeth the eye cruel toward her little ones, which, with the keen glance of divine discernment, would guard them against the tempter and guide them in the way of safety!

Alas for my household! when the children whom my Lord hath begotten to me cry out against my loving rule, and seek after the ways of strangers, forgetting the law of my mouth and hankering for forbidden sweets and delights not after my heart! Therefore do I gaze with fear upon the mad pranks of my lawless household, and see the portent of wrath from on high in their sportings on the brink of the abyss, and loathe as an offence the self-will which refuseth to bear the yoke and despiseth my quiet ways and gentle guidance. Have I not endured, my son?—yea, and borne, and believed, and hoped? but how have my patience and long-suffering charity been abused! Of whom have I rid myself but of those whom the father of lies had seduced to become children of his adoption, giving themselves up to strong delusion and to believe a lie and forsake the truth? Who stand idle but they who choose not to work by my laws, and refuse to labor at tasks other than of their own desiring? Whom do I bid begone but they who weary my loving ears with their railings and reproaches, and fill my walls with strife? My children have forsaken me and sold themselves for naught to the sons of the stranger, and dost thou cast it in my teeth? The end thereof is ruin. But not for me. My Maker is my husband, and my Redeemer the King forever in His house. Him alone I know and serve; in Him shall my children, the meek and lowly, circumcised of lips and heart, find everlasting peace.

TO THE RT. REV. DR. BEDELL.

THE REAL EVILS OF THE PAPAL SYSTEM.

BALTIMORE, January 13, 1876.

My Dear Bishop:

I have read with interest the article in two parts on the papal assumption of the title *Pontifex Maximus.* Its author is evidently a man of discursive learning and facility of pen. I see the quondam Jesuit through every paragraph—broad, glittering, but shallow.

I wish he had not brought his Presbyterianism with him.

I looked, but in vain, for some notice of the withering sarcasm of Tertullian in applying (perhaps the first suggestion of such application) the titles *Pontifex Maximus* and *Episcopus Episcoporum* (probably to Calixtus) in refutation of his pretensions to issue indulgences to sinners *contra pudicitiam.* . . .

As an exposure of some of the many weak points of the miserable system of shams built up into the Popery of our day, the book might do some good, though I can hardly consider that line of attack as of much avail in serious controversy. It is too external. The real evils of the papal system I suppose to be its setting the letter above and instead of the spirit; authority above and instead of conscience; dogmatic formula above and instead of evangelic faith. Little is to be accomplished, in my opinion, by hacking at the boughs and foliage of the upas tree nourished by those roots. . . .

Very faithfully your affectionate friend and brother,

W. R. WHITTINGHAM.

TO THE REV. J. S. B. HODGES, D.D.

SISTERHOODS IN MARYLAND.

ORANGE, N. J., July 17, 1876.

MY DEAR DOCTOR:

I am glad to learn that the Sisters in charge of your orphanage have concluded to seek permission to organize as a Maryland Diocesan Sisterhood.

I trust that they will find no difficulty in obtaining the desired consent of the parent organization in England.

So soon as that shall have been granted, it will afford me the highest gratification to render their further aims every aid and service in my power.

One thing would largely enhance my joy and comfort in participating in such a work—if it should be found practicable, by conference with other Sisterhoods now working in Maryland, to bring about a consolidation of the whole, as several branches, having more or less separate and independent works and variant (though not inconsistent) rules and regulations, under a common ecclesiastical headship and responsibility.

Earnestly desiring and hoping for such result, but in no wise as imposing it as a condition, I cordially assure your Sisters of my sanction for their intended movement and hearty proffer of "Godspeed!" toward its accomplishment.

Very faithfully your loving friend and brother,

WILLIAM R. WHITTINGHAM,
Bishop of Maryland.

TO W. F. B.

ON THE DIVISION OF THE DECALOGUE—REGARD FOR CANON LAW.

BALTIMORE, July 20, 1876.

MY DEAR BRAND:

Among her many errors, Rome is not chargeable with the alteration of the division of the decalogue, although she has contrived to make a great convenience of it. If anything, Luther is more responsible for the so-called "Roman" form than Rome herself, for by adopting it in his catechisms and reviving catechetical teaching, he set Rome an example in the latter which she was compelled to follow, and in doing so, very naturally availed herself of the advantage which her adversary had given her by his mistake in adopting the Augustinian mode of distributing the decalogue. Calvin was wiser, and by adhering to the older and more general division, occasioned one of the war-cries between the "Reformed" and "Protestant" bodies—many and hot debates arising anent a difference at once so obvious and so capable of constructive colorings.

The division of the decalogue is not a simple question, as it concerns both the distribution into "tables" and that into "precepts," or "words," as the original terms them. Our Lord gives his sanction to the first, over and above its natural deduction from the historic fact.

We thus have his authority in proof of the recognition of such division by the old Jewish Church in his day. Philo is, I think, the only other contemporary witness, followed at no very long interval by Josephus. They both testify to a division into two tables of five laws each. I know of no other evidence as old as our era. The Jewish testimony can never be accepted for worth anything further back than the fifth century of our era.

Irenæus, the one great theologian of the second century, unhesitatingly accepts the Jewish distribution into two tables of five laws each.

Clement of Alexandria, in a confused and perhaps mutilated passage, seems to me on the whole still to have retained the same distribution, and there is a trace of it in one or more of Origen's works.

But after their time Christian teachers began to systematize and shape facts to suit theories. They conceive our Lord's distribution of the decalogue into two commands, to rule the distribution into tables, and transferred the fifth commandment (as we count) to the second table, because our Lord includes it in the love of one's neighbor.

Augustine, I believe, is the first who carried the arrangement further, and, to suit his notions of symbolic fitness, made the first table to consist of three commands (the divine triad) and the second of seven (one human perfection).

In order to do that he availed himself of previously existing differences about the distribution of the clauses of the tables—some accounting the opening clause as the first commandment, others not; some reckoning our first and second commands as one, others (the more part) not; some making our sixth commandment the seventh, and *vice versa*, some dropping the ninth and making two of the tenth.

This last peculiarity had a double origin—(1) the difference in the arrangement between Exodus and Deuteronomy, and (2) the twofold significance of the double term used in Deuteronomy, חמד, signifying "covet," desire to appropriate, as *e.g.*, the right of another; תתאוה, signifying "covet," desire to enjoy, as gratification of one's self; and the latter being held to be, *concupiscentia mala*, the very pith and substance of original sin. The distinction between concupiscence and greed, of course, assumed importance in proportion to the stress laid on the Augustinian views of the philosophy of grace; and so tested the acceptance of Augustine's trine-heptenary division. Still, besides Ambrose and Jerome (who preceded Augustine), the great authorities of Nazienzen and Chrysostom are for the older distribution, and all through the middle ages dissentients from the Augustinian are to be found.

I know no better or more instructive account of this whole matter than is to be found in the great Lutheran system of theology, Jo. Gerhard's "Loci Communes," Loc. XIII. (de Lege), XXXVIII.–LIV. It is tom. V., pages 238-253, in Cotta's edition. Gerhard, as a Lutheran, struggles hard to make the best of the Augustinian mode, but it is very clear that whether as regards the reason of the thing or the authority of the practice, he finds it to be but a bad job.

Nothing in all this, you will observe, affords a word of defence of the Roman mutilation of what they call the first and we the second commandment. That is their own invention, and the whole burden of responsibility for it belongs to them alone.

As to your "obfuscation" about the Board of Missions, "*me quoque eo modo affectum esse agnosco.*" Of course the monition must go for what it is worth.*

The question about canon law is coeval with our existence as the Church in America. Its seeds were brought from England in our first settlement, and produced abundant crops in our congenial soil. Puritanism has always denied the force of canons, and after it Erastianism took up the cudgels. Here the course has been one of steady, rapid gain for the authority of (1) *any* "canon" law; (2) the *Catholic* canon law in particular.

Industrious, honest research alone can bring about a satisfactory settlement. In time, I think it will. In the meanwhile it is a com-

---

* Refers to the following: I have received a series of resolutions addressed to me—and every clergyman—by a special committee of the Board of Missions. What right has the Board of Missions to teach me how I should discharge my duty in the cure of souls? And what right have they to address me at all excepting through you?

fort to know that as a whole the mind of the Church is improving in regard of it. Your loving friend,

W. R. WHITTINGHAM.

TO HIS YOUNGER SON.

PLANS FOR THE EVENING OF LIFE.

BALTIMORE, May 8, 1877.

DEAR HARRY :

You write to Maggie about "the hedge." Is that what I asked for along the front line? If so, did you recollect the trees I also asked for? You will smile—though 'tis no joke for me !—when I tell you that I am in treaty for a valet to shave and wait on me and make my goings to and fro less unsafe than they else must be, and expect to bring hime home with me, if I live to come on, in June.

My slow and incomplete recovery compels me to look in the face resignation of office when no longer fit for work. Removal from this house would, of course, be one consequence of that contingency. For that our present consignment of the carload of furniture, including the ante-room library, is an initiatory step. Poor Maggie has the whole load—your mother and me, and housekeeping needs, provisions, and contrivances—on her one pair of shoulders; and she bears it nobly well.

I can make no resolves or determinations yet; must wait to try the effect of Orange air and mode of life ; but it seems to me every day less and less improbable that for your mother and me this may be a close of our many changes and removals in our checkered half century of wedded life. To both of us the thought of crouching toward our descent into the long home under the protection of our son and daughter at home with us, or we with them, according as you choose to put the case, would be simply delightful.

Is it not within the limit of practicability? I have sometimes thought that you, if you have no plans of your own unknown to me, might not be unwilling to take the headship of our house. Your mother's and my joint incomes (putting mine at the limit of retiring pension) would meet household expenses and our and Maggie's personal requisites. If you could put in as your share the keeping a snug, quiet carriage, it would, I suppose, about amount to what your board and lodging elsewhere might cost. The comfort to your mother would be inexpressible. Please draw on my account for expenses about the house, freight charges, etc. Your personal pains expended in all these things for us will be your gift thankfully appreciated, and to the best of our power gratefully acknowledged in returns of love by your mother and

Your ailing, failing, but ever-loving father,

W. R. W.

TO THE RECTOR OF MT. CALVARY.

FORBIDS THE REPETITION OF A "MONKISH INVASION OF HIS DIOCESE."

1879.

REV. AND DEAR SIR:

. . . You cannot be less aware than I am how much babble, distress of mind, misreport, and misunderstanding have already arisen from the late "mission" at Mt. Calvary. It is but too possible that in the future graver consequences are to be looked for. Surely you will regard these as sufficient reasons for quiet acquiescence in the injunction which, as your bishop, I feel bound to lay on you, and now do enjoin upon you, to find means of hindering the proposed reinvasion of my diocese, if such there be.

Sure of your agreement with me in a just sense of the terrible responsibility under which I must be acting in the course now taken, I look for your sympathy and prayers for your loving friend and bishop.

(Signed)   W. R. WHITTINGHAM,
Bishop of Maryland.

TO AN AFFLICTED MOTHER.

MY OWN POOR TRIED L.:

Night before last a note from M. told me of the beginning of your sorrows. Yesterday, as I lay tormented by one of my headaches, a note from A. came with the sad, sad story of the second dreadful blow. My heart bleeds for you, dearest L. I know very well how poor and worthless anything I can say must be to a mother stricken as you have been. I know that a mother's sorrows must have their course, and that even He whose wisdom and love have seen it best for yours and you that your treasures should be snatched from you and laid up elsewhere, does not demand the quenching of those sorrows. No! let them have their course! Let the natural tears flow for the blessings lent and taken back. But then, when the heart's floods are open, what a consolation there is to know before whom they are poured out, and how He looks on the sorrow which He permits, because it is best for the children of His love! Surely

it is at such a time that we learn the priceless value of faith in
Jesus! His voice claiming the little ones as his own; his seal
marking them as the redeemed of his own precious blood; his
tender uplifting of the veil of things unseen when he tells us
how the angels of such have nearest access to the all-glorious Father, are now worth all the world to you. They warrant faith, not
only to take the bereavement in humble meekness, as a loving chas-
tisement fraught with blessing to the parents left behind, but even
to rejoice in the happy certainty of finished redemption for the dear
lambs whom the Good Shepherd has taken to His bosom before
the enemy had time to mar their new created being. Taken from
evil, from temptation, from snares, from anxieties, perplexities, dis-
tresses, dangers, to bliss unchangeable and ever-growing—oh, who
would wish them back again! Not you, dear L., I am well assured!
Even now you can smile, as you think how much better off your
sweet darlings are than their sorrowing mother! You can exult in
knowing that they are laid up for you in the eternal storehouse
where God's own jewels are reserved, and where none can pluck
them from his hand, or do anything to hinder their growth and
ripening for evermore in holiness and happiness.

I write this fearing that before it reaches you the third pang may
have wrung your heart with the last bitterest contest between the
weakness of the flesh and the strength of faith made perfect in submission. But if that should have been spared you this time, then,
indeed, may the rich blessings of your trial be made fruitful in sanc-
tifying, deepening, quickening the whole stores of your maternal
love in its outgushing toward the dear object still left you for its
concentration—all on that alone. But whether baby be left or taken,
you have two, if not three, in Paradise, gone before, as it were, to prepare a place for you by forever drawing the yearnings of your inmost heart toward them, and, it may be, hymning in your stead the
praises of the goodness which even their infant minds may be ri-
pened to understand, in that fuller presence of their Saviour to
which they have been admitted with keenness of the soul's percep-
tions unblunted by contact with the wickedness of the world, while
our blurred minds find it so hard to conceive how the love of God
can show itself in calling us to pass through such inflictions!

To the comforts of his Holy Spirit, dear L., you are committed, in
humble trust that he will grant you its full experience, by your
loving   WILLIAM.

CHAPTER X.

CHARACTERISTICS.

There are biographies—not of necessity the most profitable, or even the most pleasing—the writing of which is justified by the tangible handiwork left by the subjects of them; they are answers to the natural question, "Who did these things that command our attention?" In the lapse of not a very long time, to tell of the fourth Bishop of Maryland there will remain little tangible save the granite which covers his dust and the noble gift to his diocese—which yet does not bear his name—the Steinecke Library. Alas, that the College of St. James, which gave such hopeful promise of being a worthy monument to the wisdom and self-sacrifice of its founder, should have failed under his own eye through causes that could not have been foreseen, and, if foreseen, could not have been avoided. Friends may well regret that through this failure is lost the means of inseparably connecting his memory with blessings secured by his zeal for the future generations of those for whom he labored so long; but in all truth it can be asserted that this thought added nothing to the mortification that followed repeated pleading in vain for the renewal of the work of Christian education in his diocese interrupted by war.

Perhaps there never lived a man of greater simplicity of motive in the discharge of duty. The consequences to himself seem never to have been weighed. Of course the consideration of harvest is connected with the sowing of seed, but if Whittingham sowed seed it was because to do so was a present duty. If he studied hard in early life it was not to make himself the learned man he became, but because of a craving for knowledge and a sense of obligation to study now. And so it was through life and in all his relations in life. His claim for regard in the future will rest not on his regard for the future, but on his faithful and able efforts to use present influence.

Often has been heard the regret that the world would in his death lose all the benefit of his accumulated learning, that no important literary work would testify what it had been. He had had little leisure for literary composition. And although, during a great part of his life, he wrote much, his writings were not by him cared for beyond their fitness to meet an existing need. Being unaffected by a desire for fame as an author, he gladly made use of what he found fitted for doing the good he wished, and all the larger works with which his name has been connected were simply edited by him. Of the multitude of his lesser writings he himself said that it would be impossible to give a list of them.

The extent of the encyclopedian information now lost * was not known except to those who habitually relied on it.

---

* The ready learning of the bishop, and also other characteristics, are shown by an incident told soon after its occurrence by Professor Bache to the Rev. Dr. Lewin, on whose authority it is here related. In company with Professor Bache the bishop visited the Washington observatory. When admitted they were requested to keep silence, inasmuch as Professor Henry was then engaged in scientific observations. From time to time the result of these observations was reported to a group of savans, foreigners. During a conversation lasting several minutes a statement was made which the bishop thought to be incorrect; forgetting in his interest that silence had been enjoined, and that, moreover, he was unknown, he said aloud, "That is a mistake." Tokens of annoyance recalled him to himself. When the conversation was ended he stepped forward and said to Dr. Henry : "I must ask your pardon for indiscreet interruption, but, if you will allow me, I will state my reasons for dissenting from the opinion expressed." He then gave his reasons, and quite an animated discussion took place. At the first pause Dr. Henry turned to Professor Bache and asked : " Who is this man ?" The bishop was introduced, and—to quote the words of Dr. Lewin—" the interview terminated, as Professor Bache stated, with an evident impression made upon Professor Henry and his friends that the Bishop of Maryland was a most extraordinary man."

More especially toward the close of life interviews with the bishop were not strictly conversations, but rather questions and answers, little lectures on any and every theme presented. The store from which he could draw seemed inexhaustible. The answer given, he would probably wait in silence for some other suggestion. Whether pertinent or not to anything that had gone before, the next subject was taken up as if but a continuation. This habit of mind, while lessening the pleasure of a mere visitor, had its advantages. There were those who had learned to say, " Come, let us go to the seer." They would take to the bishop a catalogue of questions which could be entered on without apology, and which being disposed of, the visit ended. Rarely was there hesitation in answering, but if memory did not give as definite information as was thought proper there was never failure to indicate where such could be found, and it was generally found by the bishop himself on the spot. This readiness has been a surprise to many, and never failed to interest those familiar with it. It seemed as if he could never forget anything that he had ever read, heard, or seen, and everything was, like his numberless letters and papers, labelled and put away where he could find it at a moment's notice.

If it were asked, What great thing has Bishop Whittingham done in the Church? It would be enough to answer, There has been nothing done of any importance during more than half a century which has not been, in some way, helped by him. He carried on the work of his acknowledged master, Hobart. As he was moulded, so has he moulded, or guided and strengthened very many others who have done and are doing the work of the Church, and who, perhaps, in the future, because of visible results may seem to have done more than they on whose labors they have entered. And so has he borne a noble part in effecting that wonderful change which has been witnessed in the Church in this country.

When speaking of his early manhood it was said that his seminary training had fitted him to hail the revival of Catholicity in England which was granted when the Church seemed about to succumb as a mere department of State government. Questions then discussed, the proper answer to which alone gives a reason for the existence of any Church, are treated now as touching principles which it is time to leave. If so, yet gratitude is due to those who have secured the present vantage-ground; and a knowledge of the steps by which it has been reached is profitable. In maintaining these principles our bishop's more active life was spent. When he was first in England a prominent member of Oxford wrote to him: "From the Bishop of Fredericton I have heard of the high place you occupy in the affections of all Western Catholics." He had not heard more than was true.

The crown of Whittingham's life is his influence felt and acknowledged by numbers, felt by increasing numbers who are unconsciously benefited by him. Whatever of apparent success, amid disappointments, may have followed his efforts is so much in addition to his proper reward.

It is not to be wondered at if one who in early life was among the advanced be not found with the foremost in old age.

The young men who received their church principles from Professor Whittingham in the lecture-room and in private intercourse rejected Protestantism and held to the teaching of the primitive Church as positively as do those of the present time whose claim for Catholicity is connected with scorn for the P. E. Church; and they who at the Seminary, or who after he had left it, caught his zeal and spirit of self-denial, were as ready to give up all for Christ as are those who now praise monastic institutions. Nashotah now pleads for endowments, perhaps rightly under a change of circumstances, and her professors are married, but the band of

young men who began associated missionary work in this
country, whether under a community rule or not, began in
the spirit of ascetics. None lived a harder life than they;
they asked only for daily bread, were willing to go anywhere,
and, if not untruly reported, indicated their vocation by a
clerical habit as marked as would be now the frock of a religious. As has been said, each of these men was closely
related to Dr. Whittingham. In 1863 Dr. Breck wrote of
him that his "Catholic teaching influenced the young men
to found Nashotah."

The same Catholic teaching has borne other fruit but
little attributed to it. The Rev. C. C. Grafton studied
under the direction of and was ordained by the Bishop of
Maryland. When he came to offer himself as a candidate
for holy orders, the air and bearing of the society in which
he had lived till then excited fears of inconsiderateness,
and provoked such a presentation of what devotion to God's
service in the ministry demands, that the warning was afterward continually rising up before him, like to the text ever
sounding in the ears of Loyola. The impression made was
deepened by the confidential relation which grew up between
the two men; and to this in no small degree was due the
planting of the seed whence has sprung the Society of St.
John the Evangelist, the outgrowth of the act of self-conse-
cration laid upon the altar at the same time by the Fathers
Benson and Grafton. Mr. Grafton, after consultation, went
from Maryland to England to study the spiritual life and
the mode of establishing an order of Evangelists. Before
going he received the special benediction of his bishop, and
while absent his acts and manner of life were duly reported.

It is better to state, in this connection, that when the
bishop's opinion was asked with respect to perpetual celibacy, he could not give his approval to what he, with habitual
honesty, stated to have the sanction of a general council.

What Bishop Whittingham thought of the power to be

wielded by a celibate clergy is shown by what he said at an early period when pleading for proper ministerial support.

Among the cares that crowd upon my office, none are more perplexing than those arising from this source [frequent parochial changes]. Parishes large, populous, promising a rich harvest to the well qualified and faithful laborer, become vacant because their minister, to shun debt or starvation, accepts some offer holding out the prospect of a maintenance less inadequate to his and his children's wants. The churches close, the congregations scatter, the souls of the people starve. I urge them to have pity on themselves and secure the enjoyment of the means of grace, and am told, in reply, that they will gladly receive a minister if I can recommend them a man of piety, zeal, industry, talents, and experience in the ministry who is not burdened with a family. A young man, a single man, is the man of their choice:—young, although inexperienced, and in many respects, perhaps, as yet incompetent because he is single, and whether young or old only so long as he is single.

Should this state of things continue, the result must be to drive the Church to enforce celibacy on at least a portion of her ministry. Souls must be cared for. The ordinances must be imparted, even if those who need them are so insensible to their value and their own duty as to withhold what it is their bounden obligation to contribute—a competent support for the person charged with their administration. Sooner or later the difficulty will be met, and if a married and paid ministry are not provided for, the mercy of God, the spirit that lives and works in his Church on earth, and the faith and zeal of her true sons, will raise up and send forth a celibate and begging ministry, to carry the Word and ordinances to those who are willing to perish themselves and let their children and servants perish, rather than spare a portion of their gettings to maintain on an equality with themselves one set apart exclusively to minister in the things that pertain unto everlasting life.

It is very evident that wherever ten families are numbered in a parish or congregation there is an ability to do this without going beyond the standard that the Lord himself has set as the fittest measure of our return for his mercies by provision for his worship. No man who gives less than a tenth of his income is free from guilt, even the guilt of the blood of souls, if he and his lack the means of grace. A fearful account of his stewardship shall he have to render unto God. Nevertheless, I repeat it, though checked and baffled for a time, the Church will overcome this obstacle. If a married clergy are not maintained, a single clergy shall be raised up. If all maintenance is withheld, men shall not be wanting to go forth for the love of Christ, houseless and penniless, forsaking all, as at the first, to advance the triumph of his name. But let the laity consider well the alternative, and ask themselves whether they be indeed ready to recall into action the machinery that well nigh ground them into powder for ten centuries before the Reformation. I am no alarmist, but it requires no prophet's eye to see in the state of society in this country at the present time indications that may well make the lover of pure liberty and social order tremble, nor needs a prophet's voice to warn our brethren of the laity that for their property, the sacredness of their domestic hearths, the life-blood of their children, they can, under the gracious protection of the Lord of Hosts, provide no more efficient safeguard, no more adequate security, than a numerous married and settled clergy.

To such a class they may look to uphold the pillars of society when shaken. From it alone they may expect effectual resistance to the swelling tide of lawlessness and crime. Such a class we yet have—the best bower anchor of the good ship, our country. But let the stinted maintenance held out to the parish clergy bring in, as it must and will, a celibate and shifting ministry, and the Church itself is rendered one element, and a most powerful and therefore a most dangerous one, of the mass of fermentation. All the influence she now exerts to strengthen, settle, establish, will become available for subjugation and subversion. Let the revealed divine intention that they who preach the Gospel shall live of the Gospel, and that the teacher of the flock shall be also its example in all social duties, by discharging them in the maintenance and government of a well-ordered family—let this arrangement, which is as surely that of God's own choice as the Word of God is true, be fairly and earnestly carried out, and the Gospel will be found fraught with rich blessings, directly bearing on the outward condition of society.

Let it be frustrated by covetous niggardliness in the execution, or wantonly disobeyed, and it will be found not that the Gospel or Church of Christ is thereby stifled or circumscribed, but that it is made an instrument of vengeance on the system with which it is brought into collision—a stone hewed out without hands to overturn and crush all before it.

As the bishop thus helped on associated labor of clergymen long neglected in the English Church, so under him was founded, what has passed away it is true, the first

"House of Deaconnesses" in this country. As has been said, the rector was aided by the counsels of Dr. Muhlenberg, who at an earlier date established a kindred institution.*

The furthering associations for good works of celibate men or women leading an ascetic life under a rule is not far removed from that approval of the monastic life which would be taken to mark one of the most advanced of the present day. Nothing that Bishop Whittingham ever disapproved of is of necessity connected with such a life. And so of all else that characterizes the most advanced, it will be found to be what those who hold it suppose to be an outcome of what the bishop held: his estimate of the Church and her sacramental system, and of the principle of the English Reformation as being a rejection of the false through a return to the teaching and practice of primitive ages, which ages are limited by the date of the acknowledged general councils.

And yet the bishop, who indeed never consented to any party name, would have resented the being classed with those who have carried on the movement which began in Oxford and which he furthered. When a clergyman spoke of having heard himself reckoned among Low churchmen, he answered: "It has happened to you as it has to me. We have not changed while others have. What was counted High once is Low now."

An aid he was to those who had gone beyond him, inasmuch as, although he desired more definite ritual law and was chairman to the committee that reported the canon of 1871, he yet helped to ward off legislative attacks to an ex-

---

* At a later period, under the direction of the rector of the parish church and of the rector of one of the congregations in Baltimore, work was undertaken by Sisters from Clewer and of All-Saints' community. Although expressly disapproving communities owing foreign allegiance, the bishop gave his " sanction " to their work. When after some years the American Sisters belonging to the community of S. John Baptist decided to form an American order, and asked him to become their head, the bishop readily promised all that was asked of him, "so soon as should be received from the mother house consent to the separation of its members, which he did not doubt would be given."

tent not shown by the journals; but he would not be associated with them, and resented the being claimed as their
upholder.

In what did Bishop Whittingham differ from the Ritualists?

In the popular estimation, Ritualism, using the term as a
party designation, consists in certain striking adjuncts to
worship. Are all these intended to mark a sense of the
divine presence? The bishop most deeply felt that presence. His whole demeanor in every act of worship showed
this, and no one has ever seen him draw nigh to the altar
either for highest worship or to present the offerings of the
people, but has seen that he came to appear before the
Lord. Nor was he reverential during worship only. The
house of God was in his eyes God's house. He felt when
in a consecrated building as the Jew did when he said to
himself, "The Lord is in his holy temple." This kindred
feeling was shown by what many would look on as a superstition. If it could be possibly avoided he would have no
burden borne through a church, not even his robe case after
service. His reverence was as much noted during the
plainest service and in the rudest building as under circumstances most likely to impress the senses religiously. Not
because he was indifferent. He appreciated the beauties of
architecture and had a knowledge of music, and would have
had all that pertains to the worship of God to show that his
servants gave of their best. The complaint, Why this waste?
could never have fallen from his lips. Only he knew that
it is acceptance by God that gives worth to any offering
made to him, he would have had God's house "magnifical,"
and each part to teach by its appropriateness to its end.
To say no more, he found no fault with the desire to show
by costliness faith in the facts which make the altar service
the highest of man's service on earth. "Make your altar,
were it possible, one solid diamond," he once said, "it
would not be worthy of the object for which it is intended.
Only do not bedizen it."

This last expression will serve to indicate, in part, his judgment with regard to some of the observances called Ritualistic. In his own diocese he avoided the giving occasion to say that he sanctioned what he thought to be a needless wounding of prejudices. But being from home he once accompanied a friend, whose guest he was, to a church of the advanced. His dissatisfaction was thus expressed, in no measured terms, in a letter to his daughter:

I am in no very good condition for writing, being somewhat shattered by the long service of this morning, with the (for me) long walk to and from it, and most of all by the highly disagreeable impression made and left by the nature of the service. It was irregular from one end to the other. To my *taste* disgusting; in my judgment very injudiciously sensuous, with unsuccessful effort to attain ornate grandeur; and for my spiritual experience harassing and unsatisfactory. In all my life I have never felt myself so much a stranger in my Father's house, nor so unable to put myself into religious sympathy with my fellow-worshippers. I do not intend again to expose myself to so much suffering.

The judgment of his earlier years is marked by a well-remembered answer made by him to one who objected to what was supposed to be a law of the Church enjoining the surplice and the black gown. "So far as law is concerned," he said, "I could pray in a red coat and preach in shirt sleeves. We have no restraint in such matters but a regard for decency and order." We have seen that, when a young bishop, his regard for decency led him to make the altar the prominent object where he could control the arrangement of a church, and to recommend to his clergy to discard what anti-Ritualists call "the decent black gown" and to use the surplice in the pulpit, to do which was then a mark of the advanced, and was as much a violation of American custom as the use of chasuble and colored stoles. Somewhere in the bishop's diary may be found a note of his first hearing that a surplice had been seen in a pulpit.

In a letter which may be found in these volumes, written to Dr. Kerfoot in 1843, he says:

Do not give into the desire for symbolism.* . . . The least thing is perverted, distorted, magnified, until it becomes to the silly imaginations of the vulgar herd of *soi-disant* Protestants an enormous corruption. . . . You know *my* views on these matters; but we cannot afford to destroy such an undertaking as St. James's for the sake of those garnitures which can be most easily brought in when the school has established itself. . . . They are the very bark of Catholicity. Let us strive for the pith and the sap. The bark will grow of itself afterward.

The figure is not true to nature. All parts of a plant must grow together. There can be no living pith, no sap, without correspondent enclosing bark. But yet the meaning of the bishop is clear. "Our present duty is to teach Catholic truth, and in order to secure its acceptance we must take care to avoid wounding ignorant prejudice. It is only the vulgar herd who see corruption in what is a proper 'garniture' to truth; but we can wait—we shall have it in due time." A readiness to accept all that has been called Catholic ritual is not to be deduced from the bishop's words. Then, as later, he might have rejected what he looked on as simply mediaeval. But he accepted the principle which underlies Ritualism, and he looked forward to the time when the chapel service would give symbolic expression of what was then, and is now, counted popish doctrine. One notes with amusement that "candlestick" and "light" are among the things that "can be brought in later," now offensive to silly imaginations. Later in life, while still admitting that there is no written law, he complained of violation of the custom of his diocese and of invasion of what belonged to him as diocesan; and with a view to putting an end to disputation about what he looked upon as trifles in their own nature indifferent, he wished that the American

---

* In 1839 he wrote to a friend: "I hope churchmen may learn from the Whig campaign the benefit of symbols."

Church would more fully exercise her power to decree rites and regulate the manner of conducting worship and the garments of officiating ministers.

In his closing years he took up, what he seems to have overlooked before, a study of priestly vestments and kindred matters, but it must have been without any real interest, for in his remarks on the subject he makes such confusion as would amaze a youthful "ceremonarius." So weary had he grown of ceaseless complaints against Romanizing tendencies, and of the persistent continuance of those complained of in what he took to be a mere indulgence of a fancy for mediævalism, that he was ready to use his episcopal authority against all that exceeds the grave decency of forty years ago, and to censure by letters of admonition " what is alien to the mind and wont of our branch of the Church, with tendency to the offence of weak consciences," and his reason to himself was his vow "to set forward peace and quietness in his diocese, and faithfully to maintain the discipline and the worship of the Church according to its established order." The letter from which the words quoted are taken is one which was not sent because of the wise intervention of an influential presbyter; it was intended to inhibit a practice concerning which, whether it be Catholic or not, the American Church has said nothing.

It is to be assumed that if the few members of the vanguard had been sufficiently wounded by what is counter to their sense of propriety so as to disturb the quiet of the diocese, then there would have been admonitions addressed to another class of offenders. In another letter, which was sent but which was due to reliance on untrue representations, and which therefore is not copied, the bishop wrote to a young friend to whom he expresses the strongest attachment.

I have, as you know, remonstrated with you in relation to matters of various degrees of importance, stating freely my reasons, and leaving it to your own sense of fitness to attach such weight as our relative age, experience, and official position might seem to you to give to the expostulations and entreaties of one who was at once your parishioner and your bishop.

I have been happy to believe that in some respects these may have been effectual, at least in the way of hindrances of further departures from the usage of the diocese.

In other, perhaps more important, particulars you have claimed and exercised under the name of liberty what, in my judgment, was license to introduce usages and services, teachings and practices, unquestionably innovations in this diocese, on the plea that in so doing you violated no explicit law of the Church while carrying out your own view of the spirit and tone of what you regarded as Catholic tradition, while I had learned to know it as mediæval accommodation of primitive truth to the needs and capacities of sensuous and ignorant times and races.

They who wound weak consciences through observances contrary to the practice of the Diocese of Maryland, and they who, on the plea that their acts are not prohibited, feel at liberty to introduce usages novel and alien to the mind and wont of this branch of the Church, whatever other plea may support them, cannot rest on the authority of the late Bishop of Maryland.

It is right to state that at a time when he himself was deemed by many in his diocese to be an innovator and disturber of consciences, the bishop was of the mind shown by the foregoing extracts from his letters.

In the year 1846 a newly ordained priest of æsthetic tastes, living among old-fashioned church people, had given scandal by tokens of his tendencies. The Standing Committee had brought to the knowledge of the bishop charges laid against him. It was said that he had erected in his own house a private altar, at which he had celebrated and before which he had said vespers [not the evening service]; and that in these private services, to which others besides his family were admitted, he had used incense as a part of religious worship. Other indications of an unsettled state of mind had also been given.

The bishop wrote to the young presbyter a most kind letter, from which the following is taken:

If the charge referring to the private mass were correct, it is matter of canonical discipline, no clergyman having a right so to trifle with the holy [illegible] of the altar as to administer it in a way not only not sanctioned by the Church, but forbidden by her intentional silence. . . . The remaining three allegations appear to me mere indiscretions, errors in matter of judgment, points concerning which I have the right and duty to give, and you the obligation to receive and submit to, that godly judgment and admonition which, at your ordination, you promised with a glad mind and will to follow. And I now do admonish you to give up, as cause of scandal to your brethren, however harmless in themselves, anything and everything out of the common way in your devotional practice, whether private or domestic, and in particular the use of a place for prayer fashioned as an altar, of hymns not sanctioned by the Church, of incense, and of pictures or images. Obedience is better than sacrifice. He who requires you to obey those who have the rule over you is able to compensate for any lack of edification which you may think likely to result from your relinquishment of helps in devotion such as the above, which as they are certainly unsanctioned in the Church in which you minister, so are they by me, your bishop, deemed not suitable for the " times of the present distress," and therefore dangerous, and improper in one bearing the delicate trusts and awful responsibilities of the holy ministry. In your public ministrations I more particularly charge you, in virtue of my office, to be careful to practice nothing not strictly accordant with the letter of the rubric in the Prayer-book or perfectly well established and admitted usage. . . . Let there be no crossing of yourself or any other object except in the administration of holy baptism as provided. Let there be no bowing except at the confession of the name of Jesus in the creed. Let there be in the future, on no occasion, any procession in the Church or abroad, except my express previous sanction shall have been obtained.

In this letter the bishop expresses the opinion that intentional silence is prohibition. This accords with a theory, sometimes expressed by him, that the American Church framed her Prayer-book *de novo ;* that what is not copied from the English services, which were adopted with modifications, is forbidden ; and that, consequently, we have no concern in the Ritualistic controversies that have disturbed the English Church, and that the English decisions decide nothing for us.   But his expressions were not at all times consistent.

He held principles firmly.   He held that with the bishop rests finally the direction of all ritual not plainly regulated by the office books of this Church ; that no other person has the right to bring into the Church, or continue, if objected to, any observance whatever on the plea that it is teaching, or English, or primitive.   He did not always seek to enforce this principle, but, more particularly after he had had some experience as an ordinary, he dreaded disturbance, and believing that he had the official right to control, he seemed disposed to a course which was practically a yielding to the " weaker brother " the ordering of all things not specified in the letter of the law.   Not finding always on the part of the advanced a consideration such as he thought the servant of Christ should be willing to yield to prejudice in matters not of faith, he became more decided in his opposition to " innovations," and to those who would have met with deference the assertion of his inherit rights, he imputed the violation of law when they were not conscious of transgression. That the bishop's objection to acts complained of as Ritualistic was—apart from the fact that they were made a ground of complaint—simply that they were unauthorized, is sufficiently shown by the fact that while the Old Catholics go beyond anything attempted by American Ritualists, he had no wish that they should abandon any observance retained by them.

Besides consideration of the dignity of the worship of a God who is not afar off, the aim of Ritualism is to mark that the Church of England did not at the Reformation reject any of its former teaching connected with the service of God's altar save what is specifically denied ; that the table of the Lord is a proper altar ; that the minister at it is a proper priest who offers before God and communicates to the people the body and blood of the Lord the one only sacrifice; that the Lord is to be adored being thus present under the figure of the consecrated elements. Eucharistic adoration is the term used to express what is claimed for and rendered to the Lord thus present, but which by no means brings before all minds the same thought, as indeed is true of other terms used in this paragraph.

Our object is not to set forth the views of Ritualists, except as an aid to reach those of Bishop Whittingham. His opinions may be gathered from what has been written; but they are restated.

He doubted not that receiving the consecrated elements he received the body and blood of the Lord, and therefore receiving he worshipped the adorable One. This is to say that he believed the doctrine of the real presence. He did not doubt the sacerdotal character of the minister who in the name and power of the one true priest offers to God the ἀνάμνησιν of the one true sacrifice, and, as well, imparts to the faithful the blessed body and blood. Nor did he hesitate to call the holy table where this eucharistic offering and communion is made by the sacrificial term altar—he believed that it is so called by St. Paul. He received the teaching of the New Testament in its literal significance. But he did not attempt to find an interpretation of what God's Word has not explained. He would not ask any question to which that Word does not give an answer.

The rubric directs that "when all shall have communicated the minister shall return to the Lord's table and reverently place upon it what remaineth of the consecrated elements, covering the same with a fair linen cloth."

He taught that this rule exacting reverence for what has not been used in communion shows the mind of the Church, holding that it is not merely what it was before consecration. Imparting these remaining elements, he would have felt assured that the body and blood of the

Lord were given to and received by the faithful. But he did not believe that, apart from the end for which they are consecrated, these elements if reserved would make God the more present in that sense which prompts the service of benediction and is the end of reservation in the Roman Church as distinguished from reservation in the Eastern Churches. Although he would have admitted that the term eucharistic adoration is capable of a permissible interpretation, he would not consent to its use, because leading to what is based simply on deductions from God's Word and is an addition to the teaching of the primitive Church. He never read Mr. Keble's treatise on "Eucharistical Adoration," * but when one consulted with him with regard to the patristic authorities quoted in that book, they together examined the four chief quotations, and he pronounced the inferences from them to be unwarranted, that is, that these

---

* When this treatise first appeared a friend in whose theological knowledge and in whose judgment the bishop had full confidence gave to him an outline of the arguments. Knowing well that he could not be led to Mr. Keble's conclusions he would not examine his book, for he would not disturb his feeling of reverence and love for the poet by a mental controversy with the theologian. At the end of the preface to "Sermons Academical and Occasional," by Keble, is to be found this note : "Having read the foregoing essay for the first time to-day, I bless God that, finding its doctrine (with the exception of minor points—not more than three) such as I can heartily accept, I recognize in its principles those by which, now for forty years, I have been more or less consciously restrained and actuated in my individual spiritual life and official course of duty."—W. R. W. Within three pages of this note occurs this passage, quoted because of the many hard speeches of the bishop respecting Roman Catholics, which, however sincere, do not give the full expression of his opinions : " . . . those from whom we are separated are yet in the Church, since we inherit, as it were, from them. If so they are nearer to us, every one of them, than any human relation can make them. We have a special duty of brotherly love toward them, over and above the general tribute, due to all men, of lenient and charitable judgment. If called on by sufficient authority to concur in words which sound harsh toward them, the nature of the case binds us to take those words in the lowest sense which honest interpretation will allow, and to make the most of all remaining sympathies and agreements, except where some special reason is shown to the contrary. If such consideration be due as all will allow, to those yet in communion with us (alas, how many !) who deny and disavow the Catholic meaning of our formularies, it is due no less to those whose creed is substantially the same with our own, though we may not worship together."

fathers did not mean what Mr. Keble drew from their words.

Soon after the bishop's death, extracts from two or more of his letters were published by the reverend gentleman to whom they were addressed, which may be found in the February number of *The Church Eclectic* for 1880. One of these letters refers to this interview and search; they were written hastily, not for publication, and contain an emphasized prohibition of any public use of them, but they clearly repudiate that estimate of the doctrine of the real presence which logically leads to reservation for eucharistical adoration. He would not be led to any inference drawn by human logic applied to God's reserved teaching. He believed in, but would not pry into, God's mystery. His views with regard to the holy eucharist are shown in letters written to a professor in one of our colleges who had asked him to criticise an essay in which the doctrine of the real presence was repudiated (see page 154 of this volume).

To one who had written to him on the subject of the divine service he had recommended Freeman, and on the return of the book with strictures on the author's theory with regard to the holy eucharist, he wrote:

BALTIMORE, January 26, 1870.

My Dear B.:

Your comments on Freeman are just the kind of thing of which I stand in need. [He had thoughts of publishing the work in a cheap form for American students.] In so far as Freeman attempts to define, describe, or otherwise settle the doctrine of the manner in which our Lord fulfils his promise in the sacraments, I eschew his or any man's teaching as strongly as you can, heart and lip. It is only as against other attempts to do that thing that I value his. I regard the main importance of his work as lying in its disposal of the whole broad subject of Christian worship—nay, of all worship of the one true living God, from Adam down to me—in proving that it is one great design, and carried out under divine direction (from first to last by intimation rather than by prescription) on one great really unchanged plan.

There are great faults in the execution of the work; but, notwithstanding, it goes farther toward the establishment of the thesis which I have just enunciated than any other book with which it has been my fortune to meet, and in doing so effects more also in maintenance of the primitive Catholicity of our American provisions for divine worship than whole volumes written directly with that aim.

Ever lovingly yours,

W. R. W.

At an earlier date—immediately after its issue in 1867—he had sent to this correspondent the charge of the Bishop of Salisbury, which at that time excited comment, commending it, yet saying, "though he philosophizes here and there more than I think desirable or right."

They who are supposed to hold views respecting the holy eucharist not to be distinguished from those of Roman Catholics are charged also with priestly assumption in respect to remission of sins. The bishop's estimate of the power of the keys was long ago given by Bishop Andrewes. He neither went to confession nor did others go to him "in the tribunal." But yet all by which the practice of confession is maintained he accepted; that is, the power to absolve and the need sometimes to use that power. His views on the subject were Anglican, not Roman. Denying that priestly absolution after auricular confession is the exclusive cure for post baptismal sins, he believed in the benefit of priestly probing of the conscience, and that declaration of remission of sins in God's name has a blessed meaning. He would have turned away no sinner needing and asking for priestly assurance of God's forgiveness, for he had met such a demand, and had absolved from sins confessed to him in private, not simply admitting the penitent to the holy sacrament and sending him to the priest at the altar for absolution. Yet all teaching in his diocese on this matter, or perhaps it should be said all reports to him of such teaching, was not acceptable to him. *Ex*

cathedra * he complained of " over-strained statements of
the doctrine of the Church concerning the relief of burdened consciences so as to distort it into inculcation of the
mediæval sacrament of auricular confession, penance, and
private absolution."

Rightful resistance to "what he had learned to know as
mediæval accommodation of primitive truth" betrayed the
bishop into an act of injustice to the most learned of his
presbyters, one who had filled Dr. Whittingham's own chair
at the Seminary.

Dr. Mahan, rector of the parish church of Baltimore, had
been nominated, without his consent, to the chair of Sys-
tematic Divinity. When this nomination was to be acted
on, June, 1869, the bishop, relying on what he supposed he
had learned from Dr. Mahan personally, opposed his election on the ground of a too near approach to Roman errors,
especially with regard to confession and direction.†

Notwithstanding the opposition of so influential a person
the clerical and lay trustees gave a four-fifths vote in favor

---

* In the same letter of admonition the bishop expressed his disapproval of
"attempts at imitation of the Romish minor orders by putting young lay persons in the chancel and assigning them, or allowing them in, practices not prescribed nor provided for in the rubrics."

† Some, who must have been surprised to see the Bishop of Maryland doing
their work, wrote to thank him for his faithful protection of the Seminary
against such as fail to make broad the line that separates us from Rome.
Dr. Mahan was as thoroughly loyal to the American Church as was Bishop
Whittingham. He was also as accurate in his knowledge of primitive teaching
and of mediæval and later departures from it. But, from whatever cause, he
did not estimate as the bishop did all that is Roman and not Anglican; nor did
he fear the tendencies of the Catholic revival. One night, passing the cathedral in Baltimore, where there was at the time some continued service, he said
to a friend, "Our wicked old step-mother has a great many beautiful things
which I wish we could have." And after his return from Europe in 1869, when
this friend asked, "Did you find any Romanizing in the Church of England?"
he said, "Yes!" To the further question, "Conscious or unconscious?" he
answered, "Some, I doubt not, are consciously going Romeward, and wishing
to take the Church with them; more are unconsciously in the same way. But
what of that? There is never any great work done among the people without
extravagances. Better a far greater amount of what we must regret than
deadness. There is life in the Church and abundant sign of it everywhere."

of the doctor. But the bishops, claiming what they had never claimed before, the right of a vote by orders, defeated the election by a vote of four to two, and the Board adjourned to meet in October.

Dr. Mahan was in Europe when he heard of the injurious charges brought against him by his bishop, and, deeply grieved, returned to meet them. It required only an interview and explanation to efface all the false impressions made upon the mind of the bishop, and when the trustees met he withdrew all that he had advanced at the former meeting, acknowledged the wrong he had done, offered no exculpation of his error, and declared that consciousness of how treacherous his memory was in his then feeble condition ought to have prevented his positive assertions.

No friend of the bishop could have heard his words without sorrowing sympathy with him in his self-abasement, and admiration for the honesty and courage which enabled him to thus undo a wrong so far as retraction at his own cost could.

After this Dr. Mahan not in the manner of one defending himself, but as if for their sakes disabusing the minds of friends, gave a clear exposition of his views. Having, he said, made himself thoroughly acquainted with Anglican and Roman teaching, and to a sufficient degree with that of Eastern Churches, he repudiated all doctrine not wholly in accord with that of the Church which had given him orders; and in especial as to "direction"—using the term in the sense meant when it was imputed to him, a priestly guidance which takes the place of conscience—his soul abhorred it. All this explanation and dissertation, wholly out of order, was permitted by the bishop presiding because of the unusual circumstances and evident great interest. Dr. Mahan was promptly elected by a large majority, the bishops, who again voted separately, giving in his favor fifteen ballots out of sixteen. The chair was declined ; but on being re-elected to it a year later the doctor was induced to accept it by the urgency of friends, and more by the hope that the duties of the professorship being to him lighter than those of the parish he was so unwilling to give up, his strength might suffice for the accomplishment of literary work which he had begun or which he contemplated. Before the beginning of the session at the Seminary, and while he was yet parish priest, this strong man in our Church was called from all service on earth.

Dr. Mahan's noble nature did not permit him to share the resentment against Bishop Whittingham which some of his friends felt and some have since expressed. He continued to cherish the admiration he had always entertained even when contending against him, and not long before his death expressed the strongest confidence in the justice and generosity of the bishop, who, he hoped, would always be his bishop.

The incident here related is a marked instance of what was, perhaps, most to be regretted in the character of Bishop Whittingham. That quickness of feeling which contributed to the making him so capable of moving other men had a tendency to an impetuosity which, like to a quality that did not characterize him, "o'erleaps itself." But when there came a consciousness of having transgressed, nothing could be more beautiful than his promptness to acknowledge error and as far as possible rectify it. He would contend earnestly, not always advisedly, as others judged. Yet there was in that earnestness nothing that made it hard to him to humble himself—no pride or self-seeking.

As sometimes the bishop reached a conclusion too rapidly and thus excited resentment if that conclusion led to rebuke, so his estimate of certain offences being very grave, there was in his manner that which made him to be reckoned sometimes hard and harsh. His language in censure was vehement and his bearing severe when condemning evident but unacknowledged faults; but this covered up an exceeding degree of tenderness. To show how winning this tenderness was when evinced, it is enough to copy the testimony of one who had felt it.

Anent our dear old master and friend, I have nothing to add excepting that where I have sometimes thought him wrong in his conclusions and judgments, I now think he was mainly right. Remember this judgment upon himself that one of his presbyters is willing to give.

And in another letter:

There were several "occasions" when he had "occasion" to write to me very sharply, and especially about personal matters—personal to me. I have no doubt you will find such in his letter-book. I think I have told you that our master was a rightful father dealing with a bad boy. At any rate I shall never forget the grand old man's loving tenderness. I recall one interview with him. When he had rightly rebuked me, I knelt down, as I went away, and begged his blessing. I was just at the door of his library. His eyes filled with tears and his voice trembled. He gave me that blessing and took me up with the great comforting words, "O my dear, dear brother!"

As a sturdy churchman the bishop not only, as has been seen, in sentiment held to the discarded petition of the litany, "from the tyranny of the Bishop of Rome, and from all his detestable enormities, good Lord deliver us," but in no way would he sanction departure from the Church. He would have nothing to do with societies composed of "all evangelical brethren," on the principle involved in the unconscious testimony of a once leader of the "Evangelical" party, "Thou shalt not plow with an ox and an ass together." Nor would he in any way imply that the outward constitution of the Church is a matter of little importance.

His opinion respecting the honesty of mixed societies, and his regard for those who claim to act in Christ's name but follow not with us, are shown by letters in this volume. The Rev. Leonard W. Bacon, to whom one of these letters was addressed, was a warm personal friend despite the re-

cognition of the exclusiveness of the High churchman.
He himself occupied a most liberal position. He had had
charge of a body of congregationalists in Baltimore. At the
time the bishop wrote to him he was acting as minister
to an English congregation at Coburg, so far as preaching
and reading service for them; and he desired to accede to
whatever might be necessary to enable him to administer to
them more fully, if only his so submitting to episcopal ordinances would not hinder his rendering like services, as heretofore, to all non-episcopal Christians. He would not belie
his past life. It need not be said that the correspondence
served only to strengthen the bonds of friendly regard.

If there were those who thought the bishop violated
charity through opinions which made him exclusive, no one
could say that he did so through neglect of the precept,
"Give to him that asketh thee." He did not wait to be
asked. His hand was open as day. It is a matter of surprise how, with his means, he managed to give so much.
How much no man could know while he lived. It required
the intrusiveness of a biographer to be able to guess at the
proportion of his income that went to supply other wants
than those of himself and his family. Poor students and
poor clergy were chiefly benefited by his liberality, but all
who needed or pretended to need seemed to lay claim to
share it. That he was often imposed on when he confided
is a matter of course, for his readiness to confide was a
matter of amusement in his family. But it was not necessary that he should confide in order to give. He took to
himself literally the injunction of Tobit, "Never turn thy
face from any poor man."

Among his letters is one of a multitude which in itself
and with his comment is touching. A young man describes
himself as having come to Baltimore, hoping to be an en-
gineer or a clerk; failing in this he had sought any work
that would give him bread, and had found none; and now
hunger made him ask of the bishop. This was on a Satur-

day. A dollar was given him with a note saying, "Come and see me Monday." But before Monday despair had driven the poor fellow to suicide.

On one occasion at least the bishop's benevolence was amusing. Late one night he heard some one engaged in forcing a door in the back part of his house, which is reached by a private alley having but one outlet. Without hesitation and without calling for any aid he went out from the front door, entered the alley, closed the door behind him, and thus had the robber without means of escape excepting over him. A struggle followed, but he proved to be the stronger and dragged the burglar into the house. Here, after a lecture, he was about to give the conveyancer* an opportunity to try his luck elsewhere, when the fellow complained that in the fight his hat had been demolished, and he had the impudence to ask for another. The bishop ordered one to be given him; but the family for once refused to obey their head, and through their lack of charity the poor thief was turned out with the chance of catching cold. Other stories of like fearlessness belong to the family lore.

When telling of the visit to Chester in 1853 an instance was given of courage of another character. Some time later a similar incident occurred which may find its record here.

The bishop was crossing the bay, going to the Eastern Shore on a visitation, and was unaccompanied. The steamboat was crowded. Among the passengers was a gay party of men such as any one familiar with Southern boats will have no difficulty in picturing, unrestrained in act or word and bent on having a good time. There was also on board a Bible agent and temperance lecturer. During the passage this honest man in his zeal approached the party of pleasure-hunters and lectured them on a theme

---

* *Convectare juvat prædas et vivere rapto.*—*Æneidos,* vii.
"Convey, the wise it call."

which, perhaps, some of his hearers might have been the
better for heeding. One of the party attacked—as was
afterward learned an able and well-known Washington
editor—took up the cudgels and gave back as good as
they had received. Having discussed temperance and the
Bible arguments adduced by the lecturer, with a view to
tease the assailant (for he was not in truth an unbeliever),
the champion of freedom went further and seemed to
impugn the Bible as an inspired book. "It is a good
book doubtless. My mother taught me a good many good
things out of it; but there are other good books of which it
can be also said that they are inspired." As an instance of
such the works of Shakespeare were adduced, and from
them passages of high moral teaching and of beauty were
quoted. The lecturer, taken off his ordinary routine, was si-
lenced; and his opponent was about to conclude in triumph,
when a tall, gaunt figure, but little noticed before, moved
from the outer circle and stepped quickly into the ring
which had been formed around the disputants. The new-
comer made a bow, dropped his hat, and apologized for intrusion by stating his great interest in the matter under discussion, more particularly that which had been last treated.
He had been pleased, he said, with hearing passages quoted
from an author with whom he had been familiar in earlier
life, and in praise of whom too much could not be said;
whose pages abound in passages of beauty inculcating virtue.
To what he had heard he would venture to add others. For
these writings the gift of inspiration has been claimed. He
would not deny the claim if "inspiration" be used in a sense
which is true, one admitting that every good gift and every
perfect gift is from above and cometh down from the Father
of lights. But the term inspiration as applied to God's
Word is used in a special sense. If it be supposed that
Shakespeare would have allowed the term in this sense to
be applied to his writings—if it be supposed that he did not
recognize the Word of God as from God in a sense which is

true of no production of man—then there is shown a lack of knowledge of Shakespeare and of his writings.

Here he quoted passages showing a familiarity on the part of the poet with Holy Scripture, and others evincing his acceptance of Christian teaching; and then, briefly declaring why God's Word is given to man, and the momentous interests which depend on a right use of what is given by inspiration of God, the bishop made his bow, picked up his hat from the deck, and went back to his book. But he was no longer left to himself. The inquiry went round, Who is this? But no one knew. The lecturer earnestly thanked his unexpected supporter. A gentleman went to him, and introducing himself as Dr. Gibson asked if this could be Bishop Whittingham?

This story was current in Baltimore soon after the occurrence. Through a desire to know its accuracy it was repeated to the bishop as here told. He admitted its truth, and added: "So long as the good man was blundering through with his temperance cause I merely listened, for it was neither my Master's cause nor mine. But when God's Word was attacked the case was changed. I felt that I should be recreant to my Master did I not at least attempt to uphold His truth, and, asking His guidance, I spoke, I suppose in effect what you have heard."

Since this relation was penned the same story—the same in all material points—has been heard from Bishop Pinkney, whose informant was the genial proprietor of *The Congressional Globe*, the person whose jesting was so unexpectedly and seriously answered. To his account of his adventure Mr. Rives added: "I have heard not a few lecturers on Shakespeare, but never a man who seemed more thoroughly master of his theme. I have heard all our prominent men in public life—at the bar, on the stump, in Congress, and I assure you I never heard a man more eloquent than Bishop Whittingham was in that speech delivered on the spur of the moment. I was thrilled."

It was on such occasions as this that the power of the bishop as a speaker was most felt—when his heart was hot within him and he spake with his tongue because the fire kindled. No conception of how the glow of that kindled fire spread can be formed by one who only reads what he wrote. Perhaps the words may be the same, but if so the effect produced is no more the same than the admiration with which we look upon a painted storm is like the awe produced by Nature in her wrathful mood. As he became excited by his theme and perhaps forgot his manuscript the man seemed to change, and his rapid but clear utterance, his intonations, his flashing eye, his forcible gestures, carried away those who, with the least sympathy, saw and listened.

Bishop Pinkney often found pleasure in telling of the effect produced by his predecessor's discourses. Speaking of the volume entitled " Fifteen Sermons by Bishop Whittingham," he expressed a regret that it had been published, because it does injustice to the preacher. " I have heard," he said, " the greater number of these sermons, that is, I have heard the bishop preach on these subjects, and from these same texts, but the sermons are not the same. Not only has the fire gone out, but the form is not the same. One could see that as he kindled he no longer used his manuscript. In fact, his most effective speeches were made when he had no paper before him."

A visitor in Baltimore was taken to St. Paul's Church to hear the bishop. When the preacher came forward from the back part of the chancel, where he had not been seen, the stranger said to his friend : " You have brought me to see the ugliest man in Maryland." After a while he whispered : " I was mistaken ; he is not so bad looking." And again, after a while, he gave vent to his feelings : " He is the handsomest man I ever saw."

In his ever-varied confirmation addresses the bishop was peculiarly happy. Many letters show how his words were long after remembered by those who had received the bless-

ing from his hands. The custom of always giving instruction and exhortation on these occasions was continued when
he was no longer able to preach often. The rector of St.
Luke's in Baltimore tells with emotion of what occurred at
one of his last visitations in that congregation. The bishop
was very feeble, uncertain whether he should be able to
keep his appointment, and having reached the church, uncertain whether he could perform his office, but he would
not hear of the proposal to postpone the service. The candidates were called up.   Under the circumstances an address
was not looked for ; when, moved perhaps by something in
the constitution of the class, which was composed of young
and old, white and black—perhaps by the thought, " It is
the last time," the bishop broke forth in an impassioned
appeal to God's children to live worthy of their high vocation and of the aids offered by the loving mercy of their
Father. He had spoken some time in a manner never to
be forgotten by his hearers, when suddenly he placed his
hand to his head, and said : " Rankin, I can do no more ! "
and was led back to his chair tottering. At a signal from the
rector the choir began an anthem, and prevented the disturbance which would have followed a perception of what
had happened. When it ended the bishop resumed his interrupted duty, and passed from one to another of his children bestowing the gift, but with such evident weakness
that the thought was suggested, " He wishes to die blessing."
To have thus died would have been a fitting end to a life of
loving labor.

As the bishop was moving as a speaker and instructive
by his reverence in act and tones of voice in worship, so his
bearing when a listener in church may have been exemplary
to some ; to some it certainly was provoking. All through
the longest or dullest sermon he was motionless as a painted
listener. No one not trained as a Quaker ever was so still.
Perhaps this Quaker "quiet" was the result of early drill.
In other ways he showed the training of his boyhood and

babyhood. By nature he was bright, jocose even; but restraint upon himself as a Christian and reverence for one in holy orders had been instilled with the dew of his morning, and by not many, nor often, were seen the flashes of his nature in merriment. "After the most straitest sect of our religion" he lived in early life, and there remained the influence of early habit of thought. The first day of the week was to him the Lord's day, but there was a Sabbath tinge upon it that was gradually brightened only after he came to Maryland.*

Many Christians consider attendance at an oratorio to be a devotional act, an aid to the religious life. The bishop judged differently. In 1831, after being present at an oratorio given by the New York Sacred Music Society, he wrote in his diary:

The music was certainly very fine : a large orchestra admirably conducted, vocal performers well trained . . . solo singers of acknowledged excellence, but—and that but destroys all—it was anything but sacred. I have resolved never again to go to one of these sacred concerts. . . . They leave a decidedly injurious effect upon the audience—*a*, in creating delusion as to supposed religious sensibilities, in reality nothing more than animal excitement; *b*, by blunting their sense of the sacredness of God's name and worship; *c*, by creating associations of the most injurious character, linking the most sublime passages of Holy Writ, the most fervent expressions of intercourse with God, or of the emotions of a soul filled with penitential anguish or holy ardor, with the scenes and performers on such occasions.

---

* Of course it is not meant that Judaic notions of the Sabbath were ever entertained. At the Seminary he taught that the primæval institution was made a burden to the Jews because of their sins. But. as written in Exod. xx., the fourth commandment is of moral obligation. After he was bishop, when told of certain Quakers who were doing farm work on Sunday. he remarked : "If a man be so sunk in the scale of being that manual labor is the highest service he can render to the Lord, let him so labor on the Lord's day." He earnestly opposed every public measure for Germanizing the American Sunday. Never rode in a street car on Sunday, and after the company determined to run trains seven days in the week, he declined the free ticket he had until that time thankfully accepted.

They are hurtful to the performers, accustoming them to a dissociation of the expressions of religious feeling from the thing itself, hardening them against all good impressions, emboldening them to place the holy realities of the Gospel upon a level with the unholy delights of worldly amusement.

Such was the impression produced on him in early manhood by an oratorio. It was never effaced. Toward the close of life he expressed the same views with a wider scope, and confessed that at times he was ready to reject all influences of art upon religion. Perhaps the minds of all men of sober thought are crossed at times by a like shade of doubt as to whether what strikes the senses be a real aid to the spirit. Not a few of the men who in this country have been most complained of as Ritualists have expressed an entire indifference, so far as they are personally concerned, to what they yet think seemly and profitable to the generality.

Let us not apply to our bishop a name given to the earnest and spiritual by those who mind earthly things, and also by those who too much mind things of less importance in religious matters. Let us call him ascetic. Such was his temperament. Endeavoring to be temperate in all things, he was, in things merely pleasurable abstemious, always keeping under his body, but without any display of effort. It was only when overcome that he gave any sign of weakness; and pain, which was his lot the greater part of his life, he endured in silence, never intruding complaint upon others.

As he thus strove to bring his lower nature into subjection, so it was his ceaseless endeavor to raise his better being into conformity with the standard he had set before him. He gave himself continually to prayer, to the study of God's Word, to self-communing, to the ordering his life as in the sight of God, to the effort to glorify Him in the little things of life as well as in the greater. It may be thought that there was in him a morbid sensitiveness consequent upon a constant trying himself by a perfect law and bewailing his shortcomings, his failure to fulfil his promises to God. In this he was like to one whom he much admired, Lancelot Andrewes, whose *Preces*, filled with expressions of loving confidence, was yet left by him blistered by his tears. A Paul, who knew himself to be the chief of sinners, could at the same time glory in the crown of righteousness. This is better. But if Whittingham in his deep humility too often deprived himself of the comfort of his faith, how many there are who heal the hurt of their soul lightly. Our bishop was very humble. A phrase frequently used by him was, "I desire to be but as dust beneath my Saviour's feet;" and it was by lowliness of mind alone that he was at times brought to full assurance of hope. To Bishop Kerfoot he said: "Yesterday was my birthday. I lay in bed and thought upon the seventy-three years of my life. I searched and proved them all singly. As a long scroll they were unrolled before me. One after another since my dawn of life I looked upon. Sin, sin, sin! was written upon them all. But after awhile Jesus my Saviour came. He rolled it all up and nailed it to his cross."

Through a sense of utter unworthiness, which too often in his life had caused despondent pain, he was enabled to turn severest bodily pain into a reason for rejoicing.

When first permitted to see him after the exceedingly sharp attack, under which it seemed as though he must die, he said to me, "God's mercy has sustained me. I have not had one pang too many. God has helped me to feel his love, to bless him for every pain as for a token that he had not forsaken me. WHOM HE LOVETH HE CHASTENETH!" He said this with a face beaming with rapture.

CHAPTER XI.

LAST DAYS.

1878–1879.

WHEN Bishop Whittingham attended the Council in New York in 1878, he taxed his remaining strength severely. As on other like occasions, it responded to the call, but for the last time. The part he took in the discussions during five days in August, and the length of the sessions were exhausting. One night, after a session of twelve and a half hours, he arrived in Orange at an hour when no carriage could be had, and reached home after midnight, worn out by the fatigue of a long walk added to those of the day, and yet the next morning he was in his place in the House.

September and October were spent in Orange, where, among the people over whom he had been ordained priest, but of whom there remained not many, save those whom he had baptized or taught as children, he for the last time committed to another the charge he had borne. On November 7th he admitted to the priesthood a deacon of his diocese, the Rev. William Richmond, who was transferred the next day to the Diocese of New Jersey, and became an assistant in the bishop's first parish.

The bishop bore the fatigue of the long service so well that he ventured to precede his family and return to Baltimore in the company of his intimate friend and well-trusted presbyter, Dr. Lewis, who was in Orange as the presenter of Mr. Richmond. A letter from his faithful daughter Margaret, written without a thought of its being so used, will be here more acceptable to the reader than any other narrative.

. . . "And of those two years of waiting and suffering! It seems like recalling a vivid dream.

"In the winter of 1877–78 he did some duty, saw visitors, and would read to himself; but I did almost all his writing, for even signing his name was an effort; his whole left side was always cold and numb after the seizure of the winter before. He brightened up toward summer, so that mamma and I left him to come on here and open the house. He followed us with only a colored boy as a companion.

"Sometimes in that summer he was very bright; he went to church, and, I think, up to my brother's.* But he depended on me more and more to read to him; and it grew to be a custom then that I should read some light book in the evening to interest mamma and the children; he used to enjoy their interest in it, discussing novels and travels and ghost stories alike. During this summer he took up Coptic again, for occupation's sake, and even in 1879 would study it when able to hold a book. He has left several books of notes made during these two summers. We remained late that fall, and father ordained Mr. Richmond here, his last official act. The long service told on his strength, so that he repeated part of the ordination service, and afterward begged pardon of the clergy for an act which proceeded, he said, from his infirmity, not from a desire to alter the service in any way. He was so elated afterward at finding that his strength served him for such a service, that he insisted on doing his own packing and going home the next day after with Dr. Lewis. He reached home but to go to bed, and to be so ill in the night that mamma and I were telegraphed for. We had remained to close the house here, but we followed at once. For weeks father never left his bed. At Christ-

---

* The mention of such a fact will show how strength came to him in the discharge of imperative duty. It was at this time that he attended the council in New York.

mas, I remember, he was still there. I had to go out and buy for him his Christmas gifts for the whole household, which he did up and labelled, on the bed, himself. Then it was that Dr. Smith was called in by Dr. Donaldson [for a surgical operation] and we got Jones as his nurse. . . . I read incessantly all day long, and till 10 or 11 o'clock at night. When the mail came in I would read his letters, and write answers from his dictation. He was wonderfully patient here; for he would dictate so much faster than I could write that he would have to repeat; and that always confused him more or less. Every letter must be attended to and filed away, and the official journal written up, before we began reading. Then there were always so many interruptions from visitors whom I would see, and report their business and his replies; so that his was not like an ordinary sick-room. There was little mental resting. . . . Looking back now, I see how wrong we were in not insisting on his taking mental rest. Instead of which, we were always encouraging him to do more. Think of it! Up to two or three days before he left us, I read his letters, got his replies, and wrote out the journal; when he was so weary of it all, that when I sometimes told him that the post had brought no letters, he would say, Thank God! He never wanted us to know how he was suffering. I have watched the veins swelling in his forehead, his hands clasp so tightly that the finger-nails would become purple, and he the while unconscious that I had stopped reading till the paroxysm would be past.

"He would then say, 'I lost that last sentence; please repeat it;' exactly as if he had fallen asleep. And he was so scrupulous not to give trouble! To make his sick-room pleasant for the children, when allowed to enter it to bid him good-morning or good-night, he always had fruit or something nice for them. To this day Johnny, when he speaks of grandpapa, will repeat the formula, 'Mr. Jones, a fig for Johnny, please.'

"On Sundays I always read the service, lessons, Keble's Christian Year, and his favorite hymns, Miss Havergal's collection.

"So that winter wore on; and he strengthened sufficiently to be brought here."

Did a clergyman find admission to his room during the period thus told of, the bishop asked the benefit of his office, at least a priestly blessing. On one such occasion he was asked if he was then suffering. His answer was given with a smile: "I am a twofold man; one side of me is dead, and the other is one pain." Visitors could be excluded; but from the sick-room, as has been said, the care for the churches was not shut out. In especial the bishop, during this winter, was much troubled by having to deal with a city missionary who, although his commission had been withdrawn, still did not cease to minister. Also there was trouble through the renewal of accusations againt the Mt. Calvary clergy, in consequence of a Mission held for them by Cowley fathers. Against the teaching of these evangelists a protest signed by clergymen of the city and neighborhood was addressed to the public. Complaints, probably, were also laid before the Standing Committee. If not, they acted on their own knowledge; for the printed extracts from the bishop's official journal show that on the first of April "sundry resolutions relative to practices at late Missions * held in the diocese" were received by him from the secretary of the committee.

The bishop regretted the excitement that attended these revival services, and, as reported to him, he could not sanction the "practices" of the fathers nor their doctrine respecting remission of sins. He therefore expressed his disapproval to his own clergy, and inhibited the evangelists, and thus abated what was complained of. He would do no more.

---

* A Mission had been held also in St. Paul's Church by members of the order of S. J. E.

The Standing Committee seem to have desired something more. With this view they, or one acting in their name, approached the bishop with an intimation that it would be well, in his feeble condition, to entrust his jurisdiction to his assistant. It is possible that more was understood than was intended; whatever the intention of the committee, this proposal deeply wounded their suffering diocesan. He frequently referred to what he looked upon as an insult, and as often declared, "I shall die Bishop of Maryland;" therefore the plate on his coffin bears, with his name, the inscription "Bishop of Maryland."

The transmission to the Convention of a copy of his official journal for the year 1878–79 was his answer to the suggestion that he could not bear the burden of an office which he would not commit to another.*

In 1878 the bishop presided at the opening of the Convention, and made an address that was afterward written out. In 1879 he sent his last address and report from his room of sickness and pain. It begins:

Through a year of more than usual debility and suffering the official work of your bishop has been almost exclusively limited to endeavors to oversee and regulate the observance of the law of the Church in the prosecution of its work in this portion of the field. As my only available mode of reporting to you the nature and extent of the work thus done, I have placed in the hands of your secretary a transcript of the official journal kept in obedience to the

---

* A member of the Standing Committee, much honored and loved by the bishop, having seen in manuscript this statement, namely, that the bishop had been requested to commit his authority into the hands of his assistant, wrote across it: "This should be modified. Such action, if taken by the Standing Committee, was only for the dear bishop's relief, as he afterward learned, much to his satisfaction." And again: "The bishop did not regard this as an insult, except under the first and erroneous impression." Respect is due to these remarks, but they do not make it impossible to believe the report, current at the time, that the committee had desired of the bishop the temporary or partial surrender of his jurisdiction, with a view to the prosecution of the offensive clergy. What is said with regard to the bishop's impressions is simply true. Courtesy must have led him so to speak to his ever-faithful and trusted friend, Dr. Leeds, that his abiding resentment was not perceived.

canons. If you endure the tediousness of its public reading you will learn the occupation of from five to fifteen hours a day of your executive officer during the conventional year just expired, and the multiplicity of interests concerned in the exact dischargs of the duties so fulfilled.

He was enabled to report for a year of extraordinary suffering the work of from five to fifteen hours a day!

His last communication to his diocese, excepting his blessing, was his "sense of joy and comfort in the quiet, steady, unwearied work of our noble band of laymen commissioned as lay readers."

Not long after the adjournment of Convention, through the kind provision of friends in Baltimore he was taken in a special car to within a short distance of the Homestead, his New Jersey home. And here we take up again Miss Whittingham's narrative.

"How great was his delight at seeing the country again! How he feasted on the green things of the earth! He was almost a boy again; and for a day or two it seemed as if new life had been given him. But he soon fell back to the old state, loathing food, shunning talk, and only craving the rest that he knew would come at the end. . . . I have wandered on with my pen just as memory brought the scenes before me; but I am quite conscious that I have not given, nor ever can give, any clear report of those months and months of suffering, working, and waiting, any more than I can repeat the continual prayers that he uttered aloud when he was unconscious of speaking."

Although needing the attendance of a nurse, the bishop, during this last summer, was not even confined to his room. Nor must the expression depicting his weary craving for rest be taken to imply a ceasing to take interest in the things he had always cared for. The ready disturbance of his brain made it necessary that he should be the greater part of his time alone; but his brain could not be unoccupied, and he continued to "gather instruction." More than ever he confined himself to the Holy Scriptures, and especially to the Greek Testament. The near approach of death was not marked until the end of life was very near.

About a fortnight before his departure I visited him, and, having spent the night at the Homestead, in the morning received a request to come to him in the parlor. To my eyes he was not so feeble as when I had last seen him, and I had no thought that I then saw him for the last time alive. We conversed as on other occasions. He spoke of a book of travels which gives a vivid picture of manners in South America. By what he said I was reminded of "Catholic Communion," a so-called "Oxford tract of 1871," but in reality a Roman catch for Puseyites, published in Baltimore when he was first bishop. I asked if he could tell me whether the author, a Jesuit, who had written as an Anglican, did become, as I have heard, what he had pretended to be? The bishop tried for a moment to recall a matter long before examined, but unable to do so, he referred to the fly-leaf of a book in the Episcopal library, and then said: "My head is becoming disturbed. You must now leave me. But before you go, do for me your priestly duty." The better was blessed of the less. And thus ended the friendship of forty years, unbroken for an instant so far as loving confidence is a bond.

On the evening of October 16, 1879, his elder son, Dr. Edward Whittingham, said to the bishop, "Father, you are better; and I do not see why you should not expect to live. I have had a patient older than you, with all your symptoms, live a long while." The father raised his joined hands devoutly and said, "May God, of his great mercy, save me from such a life!" When the doctor was afterward asked of what his father had died at last, he answered, "He died in answer to his prayer."

During the night of the 16th, or early in the morning of the next day, the faithful nurse Jones awakened Mrs. Whittingham and her daughter Margaret, telling them that alarming symptoms had shown themselves. Palliatives were administered, but it was soon seen that all help was vain. Members of the family in the neighborhood, and a clergyman, were sent for, but before any one of them could reach the house he had ceased to breathe. As the end drew near his wife exclaimed, "Your father is dying!" He heard her, smiled, fixed his eyes on her, stretched himself out to his full length, and, as the day was breaking, passed away. There was thus no commendatory prayer save that of the daughter. But his whole life had been an offering up of himself to the Lord, who now called him to eternal rest.

In full confidence that he was so called, and looking for the blessed first resurrection of the dead, he was laid, four days later, beside the remains of his father and mother in Orange cemetery. The burial was of the simplest character, in accordance with his wishes.

The one addition to the service for the burial of the dead was very impressive. The volume of voice of many men reciting, as earnest hopeful believers, the Nicene Creed gave to the service a more than usual note of triumph. To and from S. Mark's Church he was borne on a bier by men, attended by the Standing Committee of Maryland as pallbearers, and was followed by a long train of robed bishops and surpliced clergy from his own and other dioceses, some of whom had come from far, and by very many other sorrowing friends. The body was committed to the ground by the bishop on whom was now placed the burden from which the long-tried servant of God was delivered.

Over the sacred deposit has been raised an enduring monument of granite—a tomb of old English form, bearing a polished cross its full length and width, and resting on a calvary. On the grades is the inscription :

WILLIAM ROLLINSON WHITTINGHAM,

Fourth Bishop of Maryland,

IN THE FORTIETH YEAR OF HIS EPISCOPATE.

Born December 2, 1805. *Entered into rest October* 17, 1879.

I have fought the good fight, I have kept the Faith.
When I shall awake after Thy likeness I shall be satisfied.

When certifying his Convention in 1872 that God had been pleased to release from their earthly toils three of the more aged of the clergy, Bishop Whittingham said:

"When a man known by a long course of unremitting labor in an exemplary life receives his Lord's permission to enter into rest, however the Church on earth may grieve to lose his cherished companionship in work, she cannot grudge him the blessedness proclaimed as theirs who die in the Lord."

After a brief episcopate full of labors, Bishop Pinckney, who performed the last rite over the body of his bishop, has been also called to enter into rest. He died while on a visitation, suddenly, on July 5th. This memoir had then been given to the printer.

LETTERS.

THE letter that closes this memoir was the last written by Bishop Whittingham. After July 25th he made notes in his books, and he signed his name to papers dictated by him, but he did no more than this with pen or pencil. This last letter is given, as was the first written by the precocious child, not merely because it was the last, but for reasons which the reader may perceive. It shows a glimpse of the inner man disclosed by one who felt that he was in the presence of the Searcher of hearts—by one who found comfort only when he could look away from himself. He could not bear that any one should suppose that he ever forgot that God's mercy in Christ was his only trust.

The letter to which it was an answer is without date also, but is marked received July 23d, answered July 25th. It was from the senior bishop, the venerable Bishop of Kentucky, B. B. Smith, who about a year ago celebrated the fiftieth anniversary of his consecration, and who still awaits God's summons. He wrote:

MY DEAR AGED BROTHER:

I often think of you by day and still more frequently in my night watches.

I recall the scene in Grace Church Chapel when you assured me you had already reached that elevated point "having a desire to depart and to be with Christ which is far better." Up that blessed height I am still toiling, "faint yet pursuing."

Four of us are very near the confines: ourselves, and our brethren of Northern New Jersey and Mississippi.

All these I join in the prayer, "May none of us outlive our reason or outlive our usefulness," closing with this petition, "So soon as our discipline is accomplished and our work is done, may we be gently summoned to enter upon that rest which remaineth for the people of God."   B. B. S.

Through the kindness of Mrs. Lincoln Phelps, of Baltimore, a much-esteemed common friend of the two bishops, is presented a vivid picture of the scene in Grace Church Chapel referred to in the foregoing letter.

While the body of the Bishop of Maryland waited burial, Bishop Smith wrote:

NEW YORK, Sunday, October 19, 1879.

MRS. LINCOLN PHELPS—

My dear very aged friend: The event (sad I cannot call it, but rather to be thankful for) which has been so long looked for has come upon us—the death of your honored and beloved diocesan. . . .

Whilst daily together for some time pending the trial of poor Bishop McCoskry we had time to exchange the thoughts uppermost with us both—the near approach of the end of earth to us.

Said I, "I have got as far as this: 'In this tabernacle we groan, being burdened; not for that we would be unclothed but clothed upon, that mortality might be swallowed up of life.'" His reply was, "I have got further than that!"

"At times," I said, "I feel as I once did when speaking with Bishop McIlvaine, 'Waiting for—and hastening unto—the coming of our Lord Jesus Christ'—hastening to meet him!" To which the dear bishop replied: "I have got further than that!"

"Ah!" I replied, "I am praying and struggling to get one step higher—'having a desire to depart,' but I have so many dependent upon me—not yet!"

"Not so held back, I can say and do say," was his reply, "I have that desire."

I told Bishop Odenheimer of this long afterward; hearing of which he wrote me recently from Orange warning me from attaching an enthusiastic meaning to it. . . .

my very de

earnestly, .
of your two
now and he
But, u
you have do
in our com
to depart. .
any full as
my right t.
of the blessed
as appertain
I merely po
my heart th
br.it Entertai

my very dear friend and brother

   I thank you, most
earnestly, for the great Kindness
of your loving private notes; both
now and heretofore.

  But, my dear brother in Christ,
you have overestimated my Expression
in our conversation about readiness
to depart. I meant no profession of
any full assurance on my part of
my right to take up the expression
of the blessed confidence of St Paul
as appertaining to my own Experience.
I merely poured out of the fulness of
my heart the hope that I could not
but Entertain, that even to such an one

as we it might be allowed to share the
trust in our loving LORD which makes
all else as nothing in the prospect of
being called to be with Him

By day and by night my thoughts
have dwelt on your loneliness in
the remnant of this life, and on the
increased zest with which it must
tend to make you look forward
to the blessed release of receiving
the call to be "Ever with the LORD"
Your loving
friend and brother
WRWhittingham

Rev Dr Smith

INDEX.

www.ingramcontent.com/pod-product-compliance
Lightning Source LLC
Chambersburg PA
CBHW032141110726
47902CB00003B/650